LIFE'S TURNED UPSIDE DOWN
BOOK 3 in the SHOW ME SERIES
Published by Anne Stone

Copyright ©2017 Judith A Seligstein Living Trust
978-0-9970691-7-4

Editing & Proofread: Mosaic Editing

Printed in the USA.

Cover Design and Interior Format

Life's TURNED UPSIDE DOWN

The Showme Series

BOOK 3

Anne Stone

To my grandmother, Gega. I hope you're celebrating today. And as always, to you Dad. I wouldn't be on this journey without your encouragement.

Prologue

"ASHTON, GET AWAY FROM MATTHEW! Leave him alone," Gabriella yelled.

Whenever Angelina and Alejandro Alvarez held a party at their home, there was always some type of excitement—once again, the attendees weren't disappointed.

Right before the party celebrating Angelina and Alejandro's daughter Angel's christening began, Ashton Holder found himself apologizing to Matthew Alvarez, the adopted son of Angelina and Alejandro, who'd recently had a kidney transplant. Ashton was Matthew's pediatrician and had accidently caused him to distrust the very doctors that had saved his life. Alejandro and Ashton had had a meeting to discuss Matthew's fear that Ashton had caused. As a result of their meeting, Ashton agreed to speak with Matthew at the christening and put his issues to rest.

"Matthew, I'm sorry I upset you at your last appointment. I need you to understand that I didn't know about your Dad's past. I misspoke. Can you forgive me?" Ashton waited for his reply as Matthew kicked a rock on the sidewalk.

With a toothless grin, Matthew smiled up at him. "Yeah, I forgive you. I know my Dad is just trying to protect me—that's all."

"He certainly is, and I know how much he loves you, your Mom and baby sister."

A huge smile broke out on his face. "He does, and I'm lucky they adopted me. I love them so much, but I still miss my real parents." He stopped speaking and then changed the subject. "Do you like baseball?"

"I do."

"Do you follow the Rivermen?" Ashton nodded. "We should go to a game sometime."

Gabriella, Alejandro's sister, happened to dislike Ashton with a passion. Her dislike was quickly on display as she interrupted their conversation and verbally started to attack him while he was apologizing to Matthew. Ashton just ignored her tantrum and finished his conversation with Matthew. While talking, they discovered they both enjoyed baseball and were making plans to attend a game when Alec joined them.

Alec had witnessed his sister's verbal assault and approached Ashton. He couldn't actually hear what she'd said to him, just heard her raised voice and then saw her hurrying off in a huff. *That's my sister*, Alec thought. *There's never a dull moment when she's around.*

"What was that all about?" Alec asked as he approached Ashton.

"I haven't the faintest idea. One minute I'm putting all of my issues aside with Matthew and the next Gabriella is yelling at me to stay away from him. All I can say is, women!"

Alec laughed as he and Ashton joined everyone on

the patio. He knew Gabriella disliked Ashton with a passion. He didn't fully understand why, just that she did. The afternoon proceeded, and just when it was time to cut the cake celebrating Angel's christening, Alec grabbed Kelly's hand and moved towards the cake table where he announced their engagement. Both families were thrilled with the news.

Alec had just finished receiving his congratulations when he glanced up and noticed Gabriella and Ashton going at it again. Commenting to Alejandro, "Hey, what's up with them? That's the second time today I've seen her yelling at him."

"I don't know, but you never know. Love may just be in the air." Alejandro patted Alec on the back and moved towards his wife.

∽

Alejandro and Angelina had just finished cleaning up after all of their guests had left. Angel had gone down for a nap, tired from the excitement from the day, and Matthew had elected to go home with Gabriella. They had a special bond, and Matthew often stayed overnight at his aunt's house watching movies. Now that baseball season was well underway, they often watched a Rivermen's baseball game, cheering on their hometown team.

"I'd say this house is blessed with another successful engagement announcement," Angelina said to Alejandro. "First ours, and now Alec and Kelly's. I do have to say I was a little concerned with Gabriella. I was worried she was going to cause a problem with Ashton. She sure has it in for him, doesn't she?"

"That she does," replied Alejandro. "She did have a

few altercations with him, but thankfully they didn't escalate to where our guests were aware of it." Alejandro grabbed Angelina's hand and led her into the house. "I do have to say that I was right when I predicted Alec's future at our wedding." He chuckled when Angelina looked up at him. "I have to wonder if love is in the air with Ashton and Gabriella."

"You've got to be kidding me. I can't believe you just said that," responded Angelina. "She'd rather see him swim up river with alligators chasing him then ever think of him in that manner."

"Sweetheart, I don't know. If I was a betting man, I'd definitely have to wonder if love is a possibility."

"Okay, let's place that bet. I don't think they'll ever see eye-to-eye."

"And I think we'll be hearing wedding bells within a year."

"Okay then, let's write this down." Angelina headed into the kitchen to retrieve her planner. Flipping one year out, she wrote, *Ashton and Gabriella – wedding announcement.* "Our bet is written down. One year from today, July 17th, we'll see who the winner is."

"And what are we betting?" He asked.

"I don't know. We'll have to think that one through, but first I think they have to agree to just be in the same room without fighting. I don't see that happening."

"We'll just have to wait and see," Alejandro laughed as he reached out to shake his wife's hand. "A bet is a bet, no reneging on it. And it *is* written in stone—or rather, in your planner."

Angelina gave her husband the look that he'd gotten used to over the years. She raised her eyebrow whenever she doubted her husband. "Never. Never will these two ever begin to get along, let alone fall in love."

Alejandro pulled his wife into his arms. It was the end of a long day, but so many good things were the result of it. Angel had been baptized, Alec and Kelly were engaged, and a bet had been made on the future of Ashton Holder and Gabriella Alvarez. Time would tell who would be the winner of their bet. He wasn't worried. After all, he did predict Alec's future.

Chapter One

A SHTON WAS JUST FINISHING UP with his dictations for the day when he heard a knock on his office door. He looked up and was surprised to see Matthew Alvarez staring back at him from the doorway. "Matthew," Ashton said as he stood and approached the eight-year old. "Come on in. Are you here to visit your uncles?"

"Yeah, I spent the night at Aunt Gabriella's and she needed to drop something off for Uncle Alec. We watched the Rivermen's game last night. I can't believe the walk-off homer Gomez hit to end the game."

"That was a surprise," he said as he watched the excitement on Matthew's face. "So, what else are you up to?" Matthew walked into Ashton's office and looked around. "Does your aunt know that you're in here?"

"Nah, she left me with Nurse Sadie. I just decided I wanted to say hi and ask you a question."

"Shoot, what's your question?" Ashton asked as he leaned against the corner of his desk, folding his arms across this chest. He watched Matthew as he walked further into his office. He remembered when not long ago Matthew didn't like him, wanted nothing to do with him. Thankfully, Matthew had forgiven him and they were on better terms.

"Do you know what you're doing this Saturday?" Matthew asked.

Ashton thought for a minute and shook his head. "Nothing, why?"

"You know there's a Rivermen's game Saturday afternoon."

Ashton nodded his head.

"Well, my dad's in charge of the Transplant Awareness game. You know, where anyone who's had an organ transplant comes to the game?"

"Uh huh," he said, smiling at Matthew. The University and Hospital Transplant Centers in the St. Louis area recognized the recipients, donors, physicians, and staff who were living proof of the positive outcomes from these transplants. These efforts were celebrated yearly.

"I was wondering if you would come with us. You know, since you like baseball, too. And the best part is we get to go out onto the field before the game. My dad's doing something down there. I'm not sure what he has to do, I just know that I get to go on the field. The same field the Rivermen play on... Can you believe that? I get to walk on the grass field. I can't wait."

He laughed as Matthew became more and more animated as he spoke about the game. "I'd love to go. Have you cleared it with your parents?"

"Yeah," Matthew said. "My dad said to call him if you didn't believe me. Oh, and to find out everything about the day. There's just so much that we get to do—a tour of the stadium, the clubhouse... I even get to meet some of the players! Can you believe that?"

He shook his head and chuckled at Matthew's excitement. The more Matthew talked, the more excited he became. "How about this? I'll give your dad a call, and if everything checks out, not that I don't believe you, I'll go."

Jumping up and down, Matthew smiled up at him.

"Now, don't you think you should find your aunt? I'm sure she's looking for you."

"Yeah, okay. Thanks, Dr. Holder. I can't wait for the game. I'm glad you can come." Matthew quickly turned around, and as he ran from his office, waved. "Bye," Matthew called over his shoulder as he ran down the hallway.

He couldn't believe that Matthew had asked him to attend the baseball game. This was a special day for him to be included and meant a lot to him, considering where they'd come from just a few short weeks earlier.

Ashton recalled exactly why he hadn't been in Matthew and Alejandro's good graces. Before Angelina and Alejandro had adopted him, Alejandro had been his doctor while he waited for his kidney transplant. On a rain slick highway, Matthew's parents had been killed. At that time, Angelina didn't think she'd be able to have children, so she and Alejandro had adopted him.

After Matthew's kidney transplant, Ashton had become his pediatrician when Alejandro's father had retired. Alejandro, being Matthew's father and previous doctor, wanted to ensure Ashton ran a specific series of tests when he visited him for a check-up. Ashton hadn't appreciated Alejandro questioning him and called his actions into question with Angelina while Matthew had been in the examining room.

Not only had he questioned Alejandro's orders, he also questioned his overprotectiveness. At the time, he didn't know all of the circumstances around Alejandro's loss of his first wife and son in a flash flood. That one incident had shaped Alejandro into the man he was today. Life was about taking care of his family—plain and simple.

When Ashton discovered this, he knew he'd made a serious mistake; thus, he sought out Alejandro to apologize for his behavior. During the meeting, Ashton agreed to apologize to Matthew, fully understanding the seriousness of his actions.

From that moment on, until Ashton apologized at Angel's christening, Matthew had a low opinion of doctors excluding his grandfather, uncles, and his own father.

Ashton felt lighter, like a weight he'd been carrying on his shoulders had been lifted. He didn't realize he'd had that weight until now. Ashton felt like he'd made amends and was on the road to being fully accepted by the Alvarez family.

He finished up his dictations and decided to phone Alejandro. The phone had barely rung when Alejandro answered.

"Alejandro?"

"I take it Matthew spoke with you?" Alejandro asked.

"He did. Are you sure about this? I don't want to cause any problems."

"It was Matthew's idea, Ashton. He's the one who wants you there. Let's put our past issues aside—I've forgiven you as has Angelina, and more importantly, so has Matthew. He's excited about the day and wants you to join us. So, how about it?"

Ashton smiled. He'd come a long way and was thankful that everything was behind them. "Sure, I'll go."

"Okay then," said Alejandro. "Why don't you meet us at gate four? Say noon? I have the tickets and our passes to get us onto the field. Matthew is really excited about this."

"I know he is. In fact, I thought I was talking to Alec for a few moments listening to him, the way he just rambled on and on."

Alejandro chuckled. Alec was known to ramble, especially when he was nervous or excited about something.

"I'm looking forward to it."

"See you Saturday," Alejandro said just as he was ending the call.

Ashton was excited about attending the game. He'd seen fliers in the hospital about the Transplant Awareness game and had thought about attending. He didn't know why he hadn't pursued it—it must have slipped his mind.

Ashton completed his dictations for the day and gathered his briefcase. As he walked out of the office, he decided to run by the grocery store and pick up something to grill.

~

Gabriella quickly dropped off the information she had for Alec and took Matthew home. Angelina greeted them in the living room when they returned. "Would you like to stay for dinner?" Angelina asked.

"Nah, I'm going to head on home. I have a few

things I'm working on for my classroom and would like to try and finish them up, if I can. I can't believe how fast summer has gone by and that school's just around the corner. So much has happened this summer, and I still can't believe my brother's engaged to your sister. I feel like that came out of nowhere."

"Yes and no," said Angelina. "I'm just happy for both of them. Hey, did Matthew ask you about Saturday?"

"I don't know what you're talking about."

"Alejandro's heading up the Transplant Awareness game for the Rivermen. Matthew gets to go down on the field and take a tour of the stadium." Waving her hand back and forth in front of herself, she added, "I can't think of everything they get to do, just that he's over the top excited. How about joining us? You haven't been to a game all year. And it's for a good cause."

She didn't even have to think about it. "Sure, I'll go. But I'll need to meet you there—I have choir practice at eleven o'clock."

"That's fine. I'll drop your ticket off Friday afternoon so you can meet us." Angelina pulled Gabriella into a hug. "Thanks again for letting Matthew spend the night. He loves spending time with you. I don't know what he'll do when he returns to school. He won't be able to call you on a whim and invite himself for a sleepover."

Gabriella chuckled, "That's for sure, but he knows just the right thing to say to make me cave. I love it when he comes over. He sure livens up the house." Gabriella pulled away and started out the door. "Thanks again for the invite. I look forward to the game."

Gabriella jumped into her car. She saw the note she'd left on the dash reminding her to stop by Schulers, the local grocery store. It was getting to be rush hour and she absolutely hated shopping that time of day since she always seemed to run into someone she knew. Today, she just wanted to breeze in and out of the store as she didn't feel like socializing.

She had a lot left on her project for school, and she felt like she'd been working on it all summer. She'd designed some new games for her classroom, and she'd just completed one that focused on reading. She was still finishing up the math games, and she'd be happy if she had it all completed by the end of the week. She was going to reward her efforts by letting herself attend the baseball game.

Ashton pulled into the parking lot of Schulers. Just as he put his car in park, his cell phone rang. He answered the call, and while he talked to the hospital, he watched the shoppers entering and exiting the store. Out of the corner of his eye, he caught the flash of long, flowing brown hair. The woman slightly turned and he saw her profile. *No, it can't be*, he thought to himself as he listened to the nurse speaking to him. *Is that her? I can't believe my luck. I definitely don't need to have a run-in with her at the grocery store.* Ashton continued to watch as the woman grabbed a shopping cart and entered the store. It took a few minutes for him to end his conversation. As he approached the doors to the store, he blew out the breath he'd been holding. He convinced himself it hadn't been Gabriella. His eyes were playing tricks on him.

As fate would have it, Gabriella ran into one of her

neighbors as she entered the store. Mrs. Alma was struggling with pulling her cart out from amongst the other carts. She didn't mind seeing Mrs. Alma. She just hoped she didn't run into one of her past students as those conversations always seemed to drag on. Tonight, she had too much to do and she hoped Mrs. Alma was the only person she saw.

"Here, let me get that for you."

"Oh, Gabriella dear, thank you. You know, I don't know why this happens to me every time. I can never get my cart unstuck from the one in front of it."

"I know what you mean. I think it has to do with the child safety buckles. They get all wrapped up and stuck in the grooves of the carts. I just don't understand why they don't latch them together before they line the carts up to bring them in. It would be so much easier on everyone."

At that moment, Mrs. Alma caught sight of her husband and headed in his direction. "Thanks again, Gabriella. I'll see you when you take your nightly walk. I so enjoy our conversations."

"I do, too," Gabriella said as Mrs. Alma joined her husband in the produce section.

Gabriella stopped by customer service to pick-up a store ad. She knew she needed something that was on sale, but just couldn't remember what it was.

She grabbed the ad and started scanning it as she wheeled her cart towards produce. She wasn't paying attention to her surroundings, and the next thing she knew, she heard, "Will you watch where you're going?"

Gabriella knew that voice. Whose was it? She sheepishly raised her eyes and opened her mouth to apologize before seeing those blue eyes and that scruff that she was familiar with. She shut her mouth abruptly. *What is he doing here? What is he doing in my grocery store? Better yet, what is he doing in my neighborhood?* she thought to herself. She narrowed her eyes and looked at him—rather, looked *up* at him. He was at least six foot five, much taller than her average height of five foot eight. She'd never really noticed how blue his eyes were. It must be the lighting, she thought. He looked tired. His blond hair was standing on end, like he'd recently been running his fingers through it. Taking a deep breath she said, "What are you doing here?"

"What does it look like? Shopping. I need to eat just like you do."

Gabriella looked away from him. She really didn't want to have this conversation. So much for her quick in and out. "I can see that." She looked down at her ad, deciding that civility was the best way to get out of this conversation as quickly as possible. "Sorry about running into you—I wasn't paying attention. I was trying to figure out what I forgot that I needed."

Ashton was visibly uncomfortable—he knew she didn't like him. "Well, I'll let you get to your shopping." He turned and walked away from Gabriella, and she relaxed.

She found everything that she'd been looking for on her list. As she approached the checkout lanes, she realized she'd forgotten the boneless chicken breasts she needed to make her enchiladas. She spun her cart around and headed towards the meat aisle. As she neared the refrigerated section that contained the chicken, she became distracted by something falling over in her cart. She absentmindedly reached for the chicken with her left hand as she reached into her cart with the other. She jumped as the hand reaching for chicken grabbed what seemed to be someone else's hand.

Startled, she looked up. "Oh, it's you again."

He looked back at her, his mouth thinning in recognition. "Yes, it's me. And these are my chicken breasts," he said as he pulled the package out from under her grasp. "I was here first."

Gabriella pursed her lips, shook her head, and walked away from him. She'd had enough of Ashton Holder for the night. Instead of chicken enchiladas, she quickly decided on a salad instead—she had all of the makings in her cart anyway. She'd make the enchiladas another day when she didn't have to deal with Ashton.

Ashton placed the chicken in his cart and watched Gabriella storm away. He had been there first and he wasn't going to give in to her. She was spoiled, and from what he could see, she always got her way. Well, that wasn't how it would be with him. He'd seen enough of Gabriella Alvarez for the day.

He decided to check out the freezer section of the store. Maybe a sweet treat would put him in a better mood, and by delaying, hopefully he wouldn't have to face her again.

He used the self-check lane as he normally did. Just as he exited the store, he saw the same flash of brown hair go flying past in her car. *Yes, Gabriella Alvarez, you are certainly a thorn in my side,* Ashton thought as he made his way to his own car. He didn't understand why Gabriella disliked him so. He'd made amends with both Matthew and Alejandro. He tried to stay as far away from her as he could since she always found a way to create a scene, and he'd had enough of that for the time being.

Chapter Two

GABRIELLA CHECKED HER PURSE TO make sure she had her ticket to the game. The day before, while Gabriella had been out running errands, Angelina had dropped off her ticket leaving it under the doormat at her front door. Angelina had texted her that she was sorry she'd missed her, told her where she'd left the ticket, and that she couldn't wait to see her at the game. Angelina had ended the text with, "Don't forget to wear your red."

She had just completed choir practice and quickly ran by her house to exchange her pantsuit for shorts and her Rivermen t-shirt. July in St. Louis was generally unbearable with the summer heat and humidity. Just walking to your car you could find yourself overheating. It was going to be a warm day at the ballpark and she definitely didn't want to be overdressed.

Just as she headed out the door, her eye caught her battery-operated mister and fan. "I can't forget this," she said to herself. She also grabbed a huge package of peanuts that she purchased the last time she'd been at Schulers.

She threw her hair up into a ponytail and then slid it through the back of a Rivermen's baseball cap. All set to go, she grabbed her purse and tote bag and headed out the door.

❦

Alejandro could barely control Matthew's excitement as they headed to gate four where they were set to meet up with Ashton. They'd left Angel at home with a babysitter since it was expected to be a warm day. Alejandro could hardly keep up with Matthew as he dragged them to the gate. Angelina pulled out her cell phone to take a picture of father and son. She caught a photo just as Alejandro looked over his shoulder at her. The smile on his and Matthew's face told the story—of a happy little boy who'd overcome the death of his parents and a kidney transplant. Thankfully, his transplant had been successful without complications. Today, he was more than prepared to celebrate the day with other transplant recipients and donors.

As they approached the gate, Matthew turned to Alejandro, anxiously looking around, and said, "Where is he? He's not here."

"He'll be here, Matthew." Alejandro chuckled as he added, "After all, we're a little early." He glanced at his watch. "I told him we'd meet him at noon, and we're fifteen minutes early. Knowing Dr. Holder, I'm sure he'll be here right on time."

"Did I just hear my name?" At that moment, Ashton strolled up and Matthew ran to his side.

"You came."

"I said I would." Reaching out his hand, he shook Alejandro's and waved at Angelina.

Angelina approached him and placed a kiss on his cheek. "Thanks for coming. I know it's going to make Matthew's day on top of everything else. He's talked non-stop about this game for weeks now."

Matthew reached up and clasped Ashton's hand. Ashton looked down at their joined hands and smiled. "So, what's on the agenda? I gather they open the gates at noon."

"Yep," Matthew said pulling on Ashton's hand. "Come on, I want to be the first in line." Matthew yanked on his hand and they headed to the front of the line.

Angelina stood watching them make their way to the front. "I think Matthew's found a new friend," she said as Alejandro reached for his wife's hand. They followed behind, listening as Matthew continued to spout what their plans were for the day.

Matthew not only made his way onto the field during the pregame ceremonies honoring the Transplant Awareness programs at the University and Children's Hospitals, but he also was lucky enough to get Alberto Gomez's autograph, along with those of several other players. Matthew pulled Ashton along while Alejandro and Angelina laughed watching their son have the time of his life. They made their way to their seats after buying out the concessions stand. Not only did they purchase hot dogs, sodas, and nachos, they also bought cotton candy, popcorn, and licorice ropes. Angelina kept staring at the bag of peanuts with the Rivermen logo on the front. She passed on them because she knew Gabriella would bring them.

Alejandro had secured five tickets—their entire row. Alejandro sat on the end of the row with Angelina next to him, then Matthew and Ashton with an open seat next to him. They stood for the National Anthem, and while they waited for the game to begin, Ashton and Matthew filled in the player names on the score card. Ashton liked to keep track of the game and purchased the score card on his way into the stadium.

Just as the first pitch was thrown, Gabriella made her appearance. She tapped her brother on the shoulder. He stood and gave her a quick hug, welcoming her to the game.

"Where have you been?" asked Angelina. "I've been dying for peanuts."

"You could have bought a bag," Gabriella laughed.

"Yeah, but why would I when I knew you'd bring them?"

She kissed Angelina on the cheek, and just as she neared Matthew, she noticed Ashton sitting next to her nephew.

She stopped. "What are you doing here?" she asked him. She turned to Angelina, exasperated. "I didn't know he was coming."

"Now, now, Gabriella," Angelina said. "Just sit down and pass the peanuts."

Ashton stood so she could pass. He wasn't going to give up his seat next to Matthew—he was going to show Matthew how to keep score. As she passed in front of him, she pushed her bag into his chest. He hadn't been paying attention and she practically knocked him off his feet.

"Geesh Gab-ri-ella, what do you have in that bag? You could have knocked me out."

Gabriella gave him a look that could kill. She hated the way he said her name. She sat down in her seat. As she tried to get situated, she elbowed him in the ribs.

"Hey, there. What is the matter with you? You just

got me in the ribs."

She glared at him and rummaged through her bag, searching for her peanuts. She flipped her head to the side and her ponytail whipped across Ashton's face.

"Would you please settle? Before I know it, you're going to knock me out of my seat."

"Ah ha," Gabriella said as she pulled the humongous bag of peanuts from her bag. She continued searching her bag until she pulled out a plastic bag for Angelina's share. She worked at trying to open the bag of peanuts when the bag suddenly flew open, her elbow hitting Ashton in the nose and peanuts flying out all over them. Ashton grabbed his nose and reached for the bag of peanuts at the same time.

"If I didn't know better, I'd think you were trying to take me out."

She glared at Ashton. "Maybe I was," she said, then thought for a minute. *Maybe I should just get out of here... No, this is Matthew's day, and I can't do that to him. I just wish I wasn't sitting next to Ashton...*

"Gab-ri-ella, do you plan on eating this gigantic bag of peanuts all by yourself?"

She looked at him. "What do you think I was just doing?"

"Well, I can't say for sure. It seems like you were trying to injure me with your ponytail, the elbow to the nose and to my ribs..."

"How could my ponytail hurt you?"

"Well, you did slap me in the face with it."

She just shook her head and reached for her bag of peanuts. It was practically a tug of war with him over the bag when it split open the rest of the way. Exasperated, she got on the ground and started picking up the peanuts that had landed everywhere. He started to help her, but she slapped his hand aside.

"I've got this. You just mind your own business and go back to your game." Gabriella swept the peanuts into the plastic bag that she'd been searching for.

"Hey, what's going on down there," called Angelina. "I'd like some peanuts."

"Well, what do you think I'm doing?" Gabriella called back. "Ashton made me spill them all over the place."

"I did not," he called back. "You're the one that couldn't open the bag correctly."

Angelina listened as he gave Gabriella hell. She leaned over and whispered to Alejandro, "I don't think this was such a good idea."

He looked at her and she pointed in their direction. Alejandro just shook his head. "I don't care what you say, we still have the bet, and I'm going to win it." Alejandro leaned in for a kiss and turned back to the game.

After what seemed like an eternity, Gabriella had retrieved all of the peanuts from the ground. She leaned up in front of Ashton and called for Angelina's attention. Ashton wasn't going to give her a chance at hitting him again, so he grabbed the bag from her hand and passed it along to Angelina.

She shook her head at him. "I can't believe you just grabbed Angelina's peanuts from me."

"Gab-ri-ella, just be quiet and watch the game."

Just then, Alberto Gomez hit a single to left. Everyone started screaming in the stands. Ashton reached over and showed Matthew how to score the single.

The next thing Ashton was aware of was a cracking noise. He looked over at her and she was shelling her peanuts. He watched her as she split the shell, discarded the skin from around the peanut, and popped the nut into her mouth. Before he knew it, his shoes were covered in peanut shells. "Would you please keep your peanut shells on your side? These are new tennis shoes, and I don't need you ruining them."

Gabriella rolled her eyes. Shelling peanuts was half the fun of attending a game. Apparently, he wasn't much of a fan of peanuts.

The game was progressing rather slowly. As they sat there, the temperatures rose and the sun came out from behind the clouds. Gabriella was roasting and started to fan herself. Ashton looked at her out of the corner of his eye. He was waiting for her to jab him in the ribs when he heard her call out, "Oh, I forgot about my fan."

Gabriella leaned over and started rifling through her bag. Ashton leaned back, fearing she would clobber him in the face with her elbow again. Next thing he knew, he heard a buzzing sound. He looked over and she had a battery operated fan. *You've got to be kidding me,* he thought.

He looked away and the next thing he knew, he was getting wet. He looked up at the now cloudless sky, and he felt it again. He turned to her. Not only did she have a battery operated fan, but it was also a spritzer. She was cooling herself by triggering a spray of water from the bottle that blew in front of the fan.

"I've seen it all."

"Huh?" she said, not looking at him.

"I can't believe you. This is not a spa. We're at a baseball game. You're supposed to be hot. It's July in St. Louis. If you didn't think you could handle the heat, you shouldn't have come."

He saw a spark of anger in her eyes, and she turned,

pointing the fan directly in front of him and pulled the trigger. A spray of water filtered in front of him. It was a nice, refreshing feeling, but he wasn't going to admit that to her. "Stop it, will you?"

Gabriella continued to spray the water in Ashton's face. He'd finally had enough and grabbed the bottle from her hand, turned off the fan, and somehow stuffed it into his pants pocket. Gabriella sighed and took a loud, deep breath. She couldn't believe he grabbed her fan. She started to reach for it, but it was in his pocket. She didn't want to create a scene, so she refrained from trying to get her fan back. She'd just wait until the end of the game.

"Hey, what's going on?" asked Matthew.

"Your aunt is being childish, that's what's going on."

Matthew smiled at Gabriella and went back to recording the latest strikeout on the score card.

After the incident with the fan, the game flew by and the next thing they knew the Rivermen were catching the last out in the ninth inning, winning 3-0.

She grabbed her bag and stood, waiting for Ashton to move down the row. It seemed like it took him forever to exit. When she got to the end of the row, Angelina was waiting for her. Alejandro, Matthew, and Ashton had already started down the stairs to exit the stadium. "What was going on down there with you and Ashton? It didn't look like you were having a very good time."

"I had a miserable time. Never, ever ask me to attend a baseball game again if he's going to be here."

"I'm sorry you didn't have a good time. Maybe next game will be better."

"Yeah, only if he isn't present."

Gabriella and Angelina made their way out of the

stadium. They said their goodbyes as Gabriella was parked in the opposite direction of the garage they were in.

Gabriella started walking and noticed Ashton walking by her side. "What do you want?"

"Well, being the gentleman that I am, I thought I would escort you to your car."

"Gentleman, ha!" Gabriella said. "If you were a gentleman, you wouldn't have acted the way you did earlier."

"I don't know what you're talking about."

She just looked at him and continued walking. She made her way to her car and surprisingly, she and Ashton were parked in the same parking lot. He opened her car door for her. Leaning in, he said, "See you soon, Gab-ri-ella. Safe travels."

She scrunched her face when she heard his use of her name. "I told you I hate it when you say my name that way. It's Gabriella, not Gab-ri-ella." She grabbed her door and slammed it in his face.

He stepped away from her car as she put it into reverse and started backing out of her parking space. She stuck out her tongue at him as she drove away.

Ashton had no clue why she disliked him so much. If it was because of how he'd first treated Matthew... well they were all past that. Matthew loved him. Alejandro and Angelina seemed to think he was okay. He shook his head and made his way to his car, muttering under his breath—she's definitely not worth it.

All in all, he'd had a good day. That is, if he left Gabriella out of the equation. He unlocked his car and got in, realizing as he sat down that he still had her fan stuffed into his pocket. Pulling it out, he spun it around in his hand. *This is a pretty neat little gadget. I guess I'll have to return it to her,* he thought as he put his car in drive and headed for home.

Chapter Three

MONDAY MORNING STARTED OFF AT the clinic with their normal staff meeting. Alec, Joe, and Ashton, along with the nurses and office personnel, had a standing meeting at seven thirty in the morning. Since office hours didn't begin until nine, they had plenty of time to review the schedule for the week—patient scheduling, vacation staffing, and any other additional information that affected the practice.

Right at the end of the meeting, Alec reminded Ashton that he was their liaison for Career Day that was scheduled at St. Margaret's school. Alejandro had originally participated when Mary Flynn, the principal of St. Margaret's, had debuted the event a few years earlier. Alec and Joe had taken their turn, and now it was Ashton's turn to represent the clinic. Every year the day had grown and changed. The first few years, Mary coordinated all of the planning, but this year she'd decided to take a different approach. She had asked for a volunteer from the group of professionals while she was choosing a teacher representative to help organize the day. She thought they'd have better ideas on how to change up the day.

Unfortunately, he'd had no say in the matter since Alec had volunteered him for the job. "Oh, before I forget, I need to leave right after my morning appointments on Friday. Mary scheduled a meeting for the afternoon to discuss Career Day. Since school is getting ready to start, she wanted to get this under her belt before she got too busy with her teacher meetings."

"That works out just fine," Joe replied. "I know we've been using Friday afternoons to get caught up with our dictations and such. In fact, I think we should continue with this schedule—Friday afternoons off through the fall, taking only emergency patients. Maybe we should think about making it permanent."

The change in schedule had actually been Alec's idea. He'd started it when he used to travel back and forth to Knoxville, Tennessee when he and Kelly had first started dating. They realized that everyone in the practice benefitted by the shortened day and had decided to give it a try. With a half-day on Fridays, the staff could get caught up on the week and prepare for the following week. Everyone seemed to like the new schedule. In fact, the office personnel seemed more productive as they rotated staff off for the half-day. Everyone was a winner—doctors, nurses, and the remainder of the office personnel.

As everyone disbursed from the meeting, Alec and Joe sat around with Ashton discussing how their weekends played out. Alec told his brother that he and Kelly had set a date for their wedding—January 14th.

"January? Did you just say January?" asked Joe.

"Yep, sure did. Kelly wants to get married as soon as we can, and January's it."

"But the weather..."

"We're going to take our chances. It's what she wants, and I love her too much to say no. It'll be okay, maybe just a little cold."

"A little cold? What about snow?"

"Like I said, we're going to take our chances. Actually, I think it will work out just fine. Anyway, not too many people get married in January. Changing subjects—Hey Ashton, how was the Transplant Awareness game? Did Matthew have a good time?"

"You're asking me if he had a good time?" Ashton asked, incredulous.

Both men nodded.

"Of course he had a great time. I've never seen a kid as excited as he was to go down onto the field." Pausing, Ashton added, "He even got Alberto Gomez's autograph."

"Really? I didn't think he gave out too many autographs."

"Well, he did. But how could anyone pass up Matthew? He's the cutest, most polite child I know. And he's also a transplant survivor. He was grinning from ear-to-ear and no one could pass up that sheer happiness. In fact, Alberto was extremely kind. Maybe he just gets a bad rap. I was impressed with him—that's all I can say."

"What made the day even better was a Rivermen's win," said Joe.

"You could say that!" Ashton huffed.

"Why do you sound so disgusted?" asked Joe. "I thought you had a good time."

Pursing his lips and shaking his head, Ashton said, "I did, except when I had to deal with your sister's antics."

"Angelina's?" asked Joe, confused.

"Hey, is Angelina our sister?" asked Alec, smirking. "I

bet he's referring to Gabriella."

Pointing to Alec, Ashton said, "Right on. She's a piece of work. Her seat was next to mine, so as I stood to let her pass, she practically pushed me down with that monstrosity of a bag she brought. Then she elbowed me in the ribs and nose, smacked me across the face with that damn ponytail of hers, and then cracked peanut shells and threw the shells and skins all over my brand new tennis shoes. I was ready to kill her."

"It sounds like you were." Ashton nodded, "I didn't realize she was going. I don't get the elbowing, though. Why would she do that?"

"Well, let me tell you. She went to retrieve her bag of peanuts out of that bag of hers and got me. Then, when she tried to open the biggest bag of peanuts I've ever seen, the bag popped open, her elbow got me directly in the nose, and she spilled the peanuts all over the place." Sighing, Ashton stood and started towards the door. "And to top it all off, she has this fan that sprays—"

"Water," both Alec and Joe said in unison.

He raised his eyebrows. "You guys are familiar?"

Joe laughed as he pointed to Alec, "We've both been on the receiving end of it."

"At least it was a warm day," Alec said as Ashton made his way out the door.

As he was about to walk out into the hall, he abruptly turned around. "Hey, I was wondering if either of you were interested in joining a co-ed softball team? St. Margaret's is starting a fall league, and since I live in the parish, I thought I would join. I think the games are on Friday evenings, under the lights. It's a short season. I think it runs until mid-October."

"I'm going to pass," said Alec. "Kelly doesn't like softball, and I won't play without her."

"I played in a summer league, so I think I'm done for the year," said Joe.

"Okay, then. I just thought I'd ask. Gentlemen," Ashton said as he saluted them and walked from the room leaving Joe and Alec in the conference room.

Alec turned to Joe with a huge smile on his face.

"What?" asked Joe.

"Oh boy is he in for it. I think Gabriella is on that same team. She said something to me the other day that St. Margaret's was having a team and she was planning on joining it."

Both men laughed uproariously as they departed the conference room for their offices. Nurse Sadie passed them in the hallway. "Are you two okay?"

"We are, but I think Ashton isn't."

"Huh?" said Sadie.

"Never mind," Joe said. The men chuckled as they made their way to their offices. They could only imagine what was in store for Ashton when he saw Gabriella on the team.

Gabriella stopped by Angelina's before heading into St. Margaret's to prepare her classroom for the year.

"Hey, I just got the photos back from Angel's baptism. Let me show you." Angelina handed Gabriella the packet of pictures.

Gabriella felt her face harden when she came across a photo of Ashton and Matthew. She shook her head, grumbled, and moved on to the next picture.

"What was that for?" asked Angelina.

"It was nothing."

Angelina didn't believe her. She grabbed the pack of photos from Gabriella and pulled the bottom one from the stack.

"What is up with you two? I've been meaning to ask you why you went after him at Angel's christening and then again Saturday at the baseball game."

Gabriella didn't say a word. She just looked at her friend and reached for the photos while Angelina continued to question her.

"I just don't get it. Alejandro, Matthew, and I have forgiven him for the way he treated them. It's water under the bridge. Whatever it is, just let it go—life's too short." Angelina handed her back the stack of photos.

Gabriella just couldn't understand why they'd forgiven Ashton so quickly. No one should ever have had to experience what her brother did. She was proud of him with the way he moved on after his wife and son's deaths. She knew Alejandro still grappled with the memories something of which she was sure Ashton knew nothing about.

She ignored Angelina's prodding, quickly changing the subject, "Oh, I forgot to tell you. I've signed up for St. Margaret's co-ed softball team."

"I didn't know they had a league this late in the year."

"They had so many people that played during the summer that wanted to continue into early fall, so they spoke with the neighboring parishes that are in the summer league. They garnered enough interest so they decided to try it this year. It's going to be a short season—just until the middle of October."

"Sounds like fun."

"I hope so. I've wanted to play on a team for a while

now. I just hope I don't make a fool of myself."

"I wouldn't worry about that. From what I remember, you're a pretty good player."

"Yeah, but that was in college. It's been a few years since I last played."

"Just have fun—that's what it's all about."

"True… I'd better let you get back to whatever you were doing."

"Cleaning?"

"If that's what you were doing before I interrupted you," Gabriella laughed. "I'm headed in to school to start working on my classroom. Mary also called and asked to meet with me. I have no idea what about." Gabriella stood and headed towards the door. "I'll talk to you later."

Angelina caught up with her friend at the door. "Love you, Gabriella," Angelina said as she pulled her friend into a hug.

"I love you, too."

Gabriella waved back to Angelina as she walked to her car. As she drove off, she tooted a goodbye to Angelina, who'd been standing in the doorway. She felt tired and decided to stop at Mochas & Coffee before heading into school. She hadn't slept well the night before as she'd replayed Saturday's game over and over again in her mind. Maybe she'd been too hard on Ashton. He did seem to be trying… but she still couldn't get over how he'd treated her brother and nephew.

Gabriella recalled when Matthew had seen Ashton for his check-up. According to Angelina, he'd torn into her regarding Alejandro's interference. Alejandro had requested a series of tests that Ashton hadn't planned on running. Alejandro wasn't Matthew's doctor—he was his father. Ashton thought he was overstepping his bounds.

Then, Ashton accused Alejandro of being overly protective when Matthew had said he was always asking him how he was. Ashton had taken his concern the wrong way—not knowing about Alejandro's loss and that he always put family first knowing how quickly they could be taken away in a heartbeat, or in Alejandro's case, a raging flash flood. Alejandro didn't want to see any of them sick or injured. He couldn't fathom the consequence as he still grieved for Tammy and Michael years after their deaths.

Ashton had no idea what Alejandro had been through with losing his wife and son in that flash flood. Gabriella was just happy that Alejandro seemed to weather the storm this year and hadn't seemed too affected by the grief that he still seemed to carry. Ashton also didn't understand the relationship Alejandro developed with his patients. He had no business butting in and making assumptions. Alejandro was a one-of-a-kind doctor, and she just didn't like that Ashton inferred otherwise.

She went through the drive-thru at Mochas & Coffee where she ordered a regular iced coffee and a cinnamon streusel danish. She couldn't wait to put her straw into her drink and take that first sip. *Ahh,* she thought. *That's sure good.* She made up her mind as she drove the last few blocks to school that she'd do her best and try and get along with Ashton. If nothing else happened for him to change her opinion, at least, in her own mind, she'd known she tried. Gabriella reflected about all Angelina had to say about forgiving Ashton. Maybe she was being bullheaded in her refusal to forgive him. Maybe she should give him a second chance to right himself in her eyes. She wasn't sure she understood her rational for disliking him any longer.

Mary just happened to be standing at the front door when Gabriella walked into school. Mary warmly greeted her.

"I can't believe summer's almost over," Gabriella said as she followed Mary into her office. Gabriella placed her purse and the bag with her danish on the ground. She held her coffee.

Mary sat behind her desk as Gabriella got situated in the chair across from her. "It just seems like yesterday that I was being dunked by Matthew at the church picnic. He couldn't wait for me to get into that dunking booth."

"Yeah, he's pretty funny. I just love that we end the year with the picnic. It's a great way to celebrate the end to the school year." Gabriella took a sip of her drink. "Have you talked to Angelina lately?"

"Not since right before Angel's baptism. I was sorry I couldn't make it, but I was out of town on vacation."

"Well, I guess you haven't heard the good news then. Alec and Kelly are engaged."

"Are they now? Well that's a surprise, isn't it? I thought she lived in Memphis."

"Knoxville, but now she's moved back to St. Louis. They surprised us at the party following Angel's baptism. I was shocked to say the least. I knew they were close, especially after what Kelly had gone through at her job, but I had no idea they were that close. I'm really happy for them. I never thought in a million years Alec would give up his bachelor status and get married. But I guess when you find the right woman, your whole life can turn itself upside down. And I guess Kelly did that for Alec. I am so happy for my brother. I've never seen him happier."

"Well, please send him my congratulations. I don't know Kelly but if she's anything like Angelina, she's got to be one hell of a woman."

Mary then got down to the reason for the meeting. "Gabriella, I wanted to speak with you about Career Day. This year I'd like to mix it up a little. I'd like to have a teacher representative and a representative from our volunteer professionals plan the day."

Gabriella nodded.

"I'd like you to be the teacher representative. You'll work with me along with someone from the group of professionals to plan the events. I think this may breathe new life into the day."

"I thought it went well last year."

"It did, but after listening to some of the feedback I received from both parents and students, I thought we'd do it differently. I'm glad I decided to do a survey. It seems like we should have fewer individual classes and focus more on some major careers and then add a few other options. The students seemed overwhelmed with choices. We'll see how it goes. My time is going to be limited as I prepare for our self-study. There's more planning that goes into that than I ever imagined. Who would think that it takes a year of constant planning to have a few people come in, evaluate our programs over a week's time, and tell us how we are performing as a school? I know how well we're doing, especially with the way the students' test scores have continually increased over the years. Unfortunately, we have to have an independent group of people come in and tell us the same thing. Busy work is what I say. I can't believe some of the things we have to get together for this evaluation. It's ridiculous, but it's something we have to do to stay accredited. Enough of my complaining do you have any questions?"

"I appreciate you selecting me for this. Just let me know when you want to get started and what you want me to do."

"Well, I'd like to meet this Friday afternoon, if that fits into your schedule."

"I have nothing planned other than working in my classroom. Do you have a time yet?"

"How about one o'clock? It's early enough in the day that you should still be able to get out of here and enjoy the late afternoon."

"Sounds good to me." She flung her purse over her shoulder, stood, and reached for her coffee and bag containing her danish. "If you don't need anything else, I'm going to head down to my classroom."

She thanked Mary and headed off to begin preparing her classroom for another school year. She hadn't thought to ask if Mary had chosen a partner for her to work with. She'd ask her when she headed out for the day if she were still in her office.

Gabriella lost track of time. Her stomach started to rumble when she looked at the clock. She couldn't believe that it was almost three. She decided she'd done enough for the day and elected to head on home. Her iced coffee had helped, but she was still a little tired.

Since it was only Monday, she decided she needed to plan out the remainder of her week. She grabbed her planner to write down her goals. First off, she decided not to return to school until Friday when her meeting was scheduled. She'd gather enough projects to keep herself busy at home.

Wednesday, Gabriella decided she'd run by children's hospital, so she could set-up her tutoring schedule of the long-term patients. Some of these children were recovering from burns, some had suffered broken bones and were in traction, and others were cancer patients going through extended rounds of chemotherapy.

Gabriella loved volunteering—she felt like she was giving back. Her father had originally gotten her involved when she first graduated from college and she'd been doing it for about ten years now. Some week's she didn't have any children to plan for and other weeks she had several children to work with. No matter what, the children and families were always so grateful for the support.

Gabriella packed up her things and locked up her classroom for the day. She took enough projects with her that she could finish at home. She could sit in front of the television, watch the baseball game, and trim the laminated letters and flyers for her classroom.

After looking at her week, Gabriella decided she'd work in her classroom before her Friday afternoon meeting. Her goal was to have her classroom completely arranged by Friday afternoon as she wanted to take a few days off before Mary's teacher meetings started up the following week.

When Gabriella left for the day, Mary's office was dark. She guessed she'd have to wait until Friday to see who she'd be working with.

Chapter Four

WEDNESDAY AFTERNOON GABRIELLA MET WITH Margot Chambers, coordinator of the volunteer tutors at the children's hospital. She had worked with Margot since she began working with the children ten years ago.

"So are you ready for another school year?"

"I am. I always love the beginning of the school year. Everyone is fresh and excited to be back—full of new ideas." Pausing, Gabriella added, "It just feels good to get on a schedule again. Don't get me wrong, I'm going to miss my summer vacation."

"I get it," said Margot. "What about your schedule for the year? Should I put you down for three days a week, if needed?"

"About that… My boss asked me to help out with planning the school's annual Career Day. I'm not sure how much time that will take out of my schedule. I hope not too much since I love working with the children here at the hospital. Are you comfortable assigning me three days and if I have to cut it back…"

"It's not a problem, Gabriella. We'll take whatever

hours you can give us."

"Thanks, I appreciate it. Career Day is scheduled for some time in January, so when it's over I can definitely do three days a week."

Margot and Gabriella chatted for a few minutes more when Margot said, "Is it true? Is your brother Alec engaged?"

Smiling, Gabriella said, "Indeed he is. The confirmed bachelor has finally fallen for a beautiful woman. He's marrying my best friend and sister-in-law's sister, Kelly Samuels."

"Really now? I hadn't heard that—just that he was getting married. I've known Alec a long time and never thought he'd get married."

"I know. Alejandro keeps telling everyone that their course was set at his wedding."

"How's that?"

"Well, Kelly caught the bouquet and Alec the garter. Alejandro believes their fate was sealed that day." Margot laughed as Gabriella relayed the wedding story. "All I know is I am thrilled for the two of them. They make the perfect couple."

Gabriella had barely finished her sentence when Margot's phone began to ring. Gabriella excused herself and waved as she left Margot's office.

Margot's office was on the second floor, right around the corner from the wing that the various pediatricians kept their on-site offices. She knew Alec and Joe each had an office because they often overnighted on their office couch when one of their patients was hospitalized. Alejandro's offices were located on the opposite side of the hospital where transplant services was located.

Gabriella started down the hallway when she heard

her phone beep. She retrieved it from her purse and read the message. Her mother had texted and had invited her to dinner. She had just started to turn the corner when she ran smack into something that felt like a brick wall. It startled her so much that she dropped her purse and her cell phone flew into the air. She lurched for her phone before it could hit the ground.

"Will you watch where you're going?" the voice said. Her eyes followed the arm of a white lab coat to the face of the man that she didn't have the time of day for. "Gabriella, what the hell are you doing? You know better than to walk and text, especially when you're coming around a corner."

"Give me my phone," Gabriella hissed at him.

"Now Gab-ri-ella, didn't I just save you a few hundred dollars by catching your phone before it fell to the tiled floor, more than likely cracking the screen and rendering it useless?"

"You did."

"Now Gab-ri-ella, what do you have to say?"

"What I have to say is quit saying my name that way. I hate it! Now, please hand me back my phone."

"And what else?" he asked.

"What else? What else would there be to say to you?"

Ashton stood grinning from ear to ear. She threw her hand on her hip and said, "Okay, I give up."

"Come on, you're smarter than that. What do normal people say when someone saves their cell phone from being ruined?"

She narrowed her eyes. "Okay. Thank you. Thank you for saving me from having to buy a new phone. Thank you for catching it before it hit the floor."

"And?"

"And what? What else could I need to say to you? Ashton, you get on my last nerve—"

"How about," Ashton raised his right hand and said, "Repeat after me."

"Huh?"

"Do as I say. 'I promise.'"

She couldn't believe her ears. She gave him a look that could kill.

"Gabriella. 'I promise.'"

"Okay, then… I promise."

"Ah, first you need to raise that right hand of yours and repeat after me."

Gabriella growled at him and shook her head. "Are you going to hold my phone hostage until I say whatever it is you want me to say?"

Smiling at her, he leaned up against the wall with her phone in hand. "Again."

She raised her hand.

"And…"

"I promise."

"'To not text and walk the halls of the hospital at the same time.'"

"You've got to be kidding me. You want me to say that?"

He pulled his lips in, grinned, and nodded. "Indeed I do."

"Well then," she snapped at him. "I promise to not text."

"And?"

"And for God's sake, not walk the halls at the same time."

"Again."

"For crying out loud, give me my damn phone."

He raised it over his head. Given his nine inch height difference and his long arms, there was no way she could jump high enough to grab her phone from his hand. So she gave in. "I promise to not text and walk the halls of the hospital at the same time."

Lowering his arm, he said, "Was that so hard to do?"

She huffed at him, grabbed her cell from his hand, bent over to retrieve her purse from the floor, and ran for the stairway. She had had enough of his games for the day. She hoped she wouldn't have to lay eyes on him for a good long while. He got on her last nerve.

Gabriella reached the doorway to the stairs and shoved it open. She turned as she started towards the stairs, and when she heard a roaring laughter, she closed the door behind her.

Ashton leaned against the wall as he watched Gabriella escape his wrath. He had really gotten to her. He had no idea what he'd done for her to be so annoyed with him. No matter what he did, she disapproved of him. He decided to just take it in stride and hope that eventually she'd come around.

Gabriella slowed her pace as she made her way down the stairs with her phone clutched in her hand. As she exited the stairway, she texted her mother that she would see her at dinner. She hadn't seen her parents in a few days and always enjoyed her mother's cooking.

It was just her luck that she happened to run into Alejandro as she was heading out the front doors of the hospital.

"Hey, sis. Where you headed off to?" Alejandro said as he pulled her into a hug.

"Actually, I just got a text from Mom and she invited me to dinner, so I'm headed over there."

"That sounds like fun. What brings you into the hospital?"

"I came by to see Margot to set up my schedule for tutoring."

"That's good. Maybe with you starting back, I'll see you a little more often."

"Don't you see me enough as it is?"

"Never. I still feel like I'm making up for all of the lost time when I lived out of state."

He gave her a quick peck on the cheek and headed off to answer a page. Gabriella lost sight of her brother as he headed towards his office. Just as she turned around, she caught sight of Ashton as he walked out the front doors of the hospital. She was thankful that Alejandro had delayed her exit as she didn't have the strength to deal with him again today.

She took her time making her way to her car. She elected to go straight to her parents' house where she'd help her mother prepare dinner. Twenty minutes later, she was walking into her mother's kitchen. Maria had already begun preparing the meat sauce for lasagna. She poured herself an iced tea and sat down at the table as her mother worked on the sauce. "Hi, there honey. I tried calling you before I texted you."

"I was meeting with Margot at the hospital trying to set up my tutoring schedule." Gabriella sat at the table, playing with the silverware.

"That's exciting. I know how much you love working with the children at the hospital."

"Yeah, I do." Gabriella sighed.

"What's wrong? You seem a little distracted."

"Oh nothing. I just ran into Ashton when I was

looking at your text."

"And that's a problem?"

"For me it is. Mom, I just don't understand it, but he just gets under my skin."

"Have you tried to talk to him about it?"

"No, I haven't. In fact, I literally ran right into him today when I was reading your text. I almost dropped my phone. He caught it but then taunted me. He made me raise my right hand and repeat after him that 'I will not text and walk in the hospital' before he would return it to me. He thought it was hilarious, but I certainly didn't."

"Sweetheart, it sounds to me like he's just playing around with you. He's just egging you on. If you play along too, maybe you can work things out."

Gabriella rearranged the silverware absentmindedly.

"Maybe its Ashton's way of saying he likes you."

She looked at her mother, wide-eyed. "I think not! He dislikes me as much as I dislike him."

"Are you sure about that?"

She looked back down at the table setting.

"You know sometimes that's the way men let you know that they like you. They keep you on edge, ready to fight…"

"Who's ready to fight?" John asked as he joined his wife and daughter in the kitchen.

"Oh Dad, it's nothing. Just me and Ashton going at it again."

"I don't understand what it is between you two. Can't you forgive him and move on? Alejandro certainly has."

"I know that, Dad. I just don't know."

Her father reached out and squeezed her shoulder. "Honey, he's changed a lot over this last year. In fact, he's a completely different doctor from the one I first ran into. He had the worst—and I mean the worst—bedside manner until I took him under my wing. That's why I asked him to join the practice when I retired. I saw that he was receptive to change. And I for one can attest to the fact that he's a changed man."

Since she hadn't given him the time of day, she didn't know if he'd changed or not. She'd decided to give him a chance just a few days ago and she truly didn't understand why he'd upset her earlier when, after all, he *had* saved her phone. She realized she needed to just settle down in his presence and give him a chance.

Gabriella and her parents caught up on things while the lasagna was cooking. She told them about Mary choosing her to work on coordinating Career Day. "I meet with Mary Friday afternoon. I'm not sure how much time it will take up out of my week—I just hope that I can continue to work three days a week at the hospital."

At that moment, Joe walked through the door.

"I didn't know you were coming to dinner, too," she said to her brother.

"I never pass down a home cooked meal. Do I, Mom?"

"Never. In fact, you drop by even when I don't ask you."

They all enjoyed Maria's dinner. Gabriella and Joe cleaned up the kitchen and then Gabriella decided to head home. She still had the letters she needed to trim for her bulletin board. She wanted to finish that up so she could move on to a few other things that she needed to have completed before returning to her classroom on Friday.

"Mom, I'm going to head on out. I have a few things

I'd like to finish up for my classroom."

"Okay, honey," Maria said as she hugged her daughter goodbye.

"Come here, you," Joe said as he also hugged his sister goodbye. "You need to stop by the clinic sometime so we can chat. Friday afternoon's work great since we only see patients in the morning."

"Ugh, I'll think about it."

"What's that for?"

"Nothing." Gabriella grabbed her purse and made her way to the door.

"Gabriella, you need to think about what I said." Maria raised an eyebrow at her daughter.

Gabriella just looked at her mother.

"Gabriella."

"Okay, Mom, I will."

With that, she opened the door. Turning back, she waved goodbye to her mother and brother.

"What was that all about? And what should she think about?" Joe asked.

"Ah, you know. Ashton. She just doesn't get along with him."

"Yeah, I know."

"I think he's just pulling her leg. I think he might be interested in Gabriella and likes keeping her on edge."

"You could have something there."

Joe and Maria made their way into the family room where John was watching a Rivermen's game. Maria thought back over her conversation with Gabriella. She knew her daughter could be pig-headed. John had shared with Maria some of Ashton's background—maybe he needed to share a little bit more with his daughter about Ashton's life in boarding school. Then, maybe she'd come around.

Chapter Five

ASHTON WAS RUNNING BEHIND. HE needed to be out of clinic by noon so he could grab something to eat on his way over to St. Margaret's for his meeting with Mary. His first patient threw him behind and he'd been playing catch-up all day.

He'd just finished with his last patient when Alec caught him heading out the door. "Shouldn't you have left like a half-hour ago?"

"Yeah, but it couldn't be helped. I phoned Mary to let her know I was running late. So much for lunch."

Ashton hurried out the door, deciding he'd eat after his meeting.

Gabriella arrived at school at nine o'clock. She immediately dove into getting the desks in order, arranging the text books on the tables, and just as she started to work on her bulletin board, she noticed the time. If she wanted to order lunch from Pedals Diner she needed to call her order in right away.

She phoned the diner, ordering a patty melt, fries,

and a strawberry milkshake. She decided this would be her last hurrah before heading back to school and the beginning of her annual school diet. She always found it easier dieting when she worked. She made her lunch ahead of time and wasn't tempted during the day to snack. She wasn't overweight but felt it easier watching what she ate while in school.

She stopped for lunch at noon, thinking she'd have plenty of time to eat before her one o'clock meeting with Mary. So much for the best laid plans. She got stuck in traffic on her way to pick up her lunch. She barely made it back to school by one. She hurried to her classroom, threw her purse into her desk drawer, and laid her lunch on top of her desk. *So much for a hot lunch,* she thought. She'd just have to warm it up after her meeting. Grabbing her planner, she hurried to Mary's office forgetting her milkshake on her desk.

Gabriella arrived right on time. She knocked on Mary's door and entered. Mary was the only one in the office—the secretaries had already left for the weekend. "Are you ready for our meeting?"

"I am," she said as she grabbed her seat in front of Mary's desk.

"So how's your classroom coming along?"

"I'm getting there. I have a few things left to hang up on my bulletin board. Depending on how long our meeting runs, I might come back tomorrow and finish up."

"You have all of next week," Mary chuckled.

"I know, but I'd like to spend some time with Angelina and the kids before we start back up with faculty meetings."

"That sounds like fun. I so miss her teaching here, but I understand that she wants to be a mom first.

Maybe someday she'll teach again.'"

"I hope so. And when she does decide to go back to work, I hope she returns to St. Margaret's."

"I'm in agreement with that."

Gabriella heard someone clearing their throat. She turned in her seat and glanced at the door. Her eyes widened and her mouth fell open. Ashton stepped into the room and walked over to a chair.

"What are you doing here?" she said, jumping up. She closed her eyes, thinking she was seeing things, but when she opened them again he was still standing there.

"Ah Gabriella, Ashton is here to be a part of our team for Career Day. You are both going to organize the day."

Gabriella looked back at Mary. She opened her mouth, but found she couldn't speak. She clamped her mouth shut and slowly returned to her seat. It wasn't Mary's fault that she had issues with Ashton. As she sat down, she started forming a plan. She'd make him step down. He didn't belong here. He had a horrible personality, so how did he think he had it in him to organize a day that benefitted the kids? Her mind was reeling with how she was going to make him quit.

"Have a seat," Mary said to Ashton. Ashton looked at Gabriella out of the corner of his eye as he took the seat beside her. He could tell she was fuming just by her posture. He was sure she wished she could take him out with her elbow again, or better yet, deck him.

Mary pretty much spoke the entire meeting. She had not only gone over the results of her survey, but also set a calendar of due dates for important tasks. The whole while Ashton sat there he was starving. The longer Mary talked the more hungry he became. Finally, at three o'clock, she decided to schedule another meeting. "Do Friday afternoon's work for you?" she asked, addressing him.

"Right now they do."

Looking at Gabriella, Mary said, "I'll get someone to cover your classes, so plan on meeting Friday afternoons beginning next week."

"Next week? We have our faculty meeting."

"That's right," Mary said. "I'm off on my weeks. Let's plan on meeting in two weeks, and I'll take you both out to lunch."

"You don't have to do that, Mary," Ashton said.

"I want to."

Gabriella stood to leave.

"Ashton, can you stay for a minute?" Mary asked. "I'd like to speak with you."

Nodding, Ashton stood as Gabriella said her goodbyes and left the room. Ashton couldn't believe what fate had dealt him. Of all the people he could be paired with, Mary had chosen Gabriella.

He could only imagine the look on his face when he first laid eyes on Gabriella. In fact, he did his best to contain his shock, but knew he hadn't done an especially good job at it.

He wasn't happy about organizing Career Day, but after discovering Gabriella's part, he was even more dissatisfied.

He looked forward to giving his presentation, but not working beside her.

He watched as Gabriella hurried down the hallway away from him. When Mary could see that she'd cleared the office and was heading back to her classroom, she closed the door.

Mary returned to her seat. "I hope this won't be

an issue for you. Gabriella seemed upset when she realized you were going to help out. I don't want to cause a problem. When Alejandro suggested that you'd be the perfect candidate for the job, I spoke with Alec since he'd already signed you up for the day. He seconded it and was in full agreement when I called him. Neither one of them seemed like it would be a problem."

"Don't worry about it. I'll talk to Gabriella. We'll put whatever differences we have aside to organize this day. In fact, I'm excited to help out. It should be fun."

Gabriella practically ran down the hallway to her classroom. She'd known that Mary had consulted with Alejandro regarding Career Day, but *Ashton*? When she was done here, she was going to have a little chat with her brother.

By the time she made her way to her classroom, she'd lost her appetite. Her milkshake was completely thawed anyway. She took one sip and decided to take it home and put it in her freezer—maybe she could salvage it. She took one look at the sandwich sitting on her desk and thought about throwing it in the trash. She would just take it home and warm it up for lunch the following day.

Gabriella gathered all of the letters for her bulletin board, pulled out her ladder, and positioned it by the far wall. She set the letters on the top rung and climbed the ladder. She'd just gotten started stapling the letters to the border when she heard a noise from the hallway. Surprised, she turned quickly and her foot got caught on the ladder's side. She lost her balance, arms pinwheeling, and started to fall backwards. She knew she was going to hit the ground hard when she felt herself fall securely into a set of strong arms.

She sat there, breathing hard, and flung her hair out of her eyes, whipping it across her savior's face. When her face was clear of her hair, she realized who'd saved her.

"Put me down. Put me down this instant."

Ashton set her down and looked her squarely in the eyes. He hadn't noticed the lighter flecks of brown that surrounded her deep, dark brown eyes. Her eyes were sparkling with anger.

"What the hell are you doing? You almost made me hurt myself."

"No, actually I saved you from falling."

"You're the reason why I almost fell. Scaring me to death like that."

"How did I scare you? All I did was stop at the doorway to your classroom. I didn't even say a word."

"Well, you made a noise and it scared me."

"Let's get real here, Gabriella." Pausing to get ahold of his temper, he continued. "Just what is your problem? Why do you dislike me so much? Mary was concerned about us working together, but I put her concerns to rest. I told her all was well with us. So you better get your act together and decide to put aside whatever issues you have with me because I'm not going anywhere. I'm here for the long haul. And I'm sure you don't want your boss questioning her decision for selecting you to take on this responsibility."

Ashton caught a glimpse of her uneaten sandwich. Since he was starved and had missed lunch, he decided he wanted to piss her off even more, so he grabbed her sandwich, unfurled the paper that surrounded it, and took a huge bite.

Gabriella looked on in utter shock.

"That's a good patty melt, albeit a little cold and could use a warming." He then reached for her milkshake, taking a long swig from the straw. "Ah, strawberry, my favorite. It needs refreezing." He set her sandwich and milkshake back on the desk, turned, and walked out the door. He liked upsetting her. In time, he'd have her eating out of his hand. He just knew it.

Gabriella watched Ashton leave her classroom. She couldn't believe what he'd just done. *What an ass*, she thought. She'd had enough for the day. She grabbed her lunch, threw it back into the paper sack that it came in, and grabbed her milkshake and purse. She locked her classroom and headed out the door, throwing her lunch away in the kitchen before exiting the building. She didn't have to think twice as to where her next stop was. She jumped into her car and headed in the direction of her brother's house.

Ashton meanwhile was headed back to the office. He had a few things to say to Alec. *What has he gotten me into?* Ashton thought as he drove back to the clinic. *That sister of his is a hothead, that's for sure. I don't know what I'm going to do with her.*

A half hour later, Gabriella pulled up at her brother's house and rang the doorbell. Angelina answered the door and Gabriella rushed through the doorway yelling, "Where is he? Just where is he?"

"Where is who?" Angelina asked as she followed Gabriella into Alejandro's office.

"I know he's here. Where is he hiding?"

"Gabriella, Alejandro's in surgery right now. He's been there since mid-morning."

Gabriella threw herself down on the couch and covered her face with her hands. She drew her hands through her hair, looked at her friend, and said, "How could he do this to me?"

"How could who do what?"

"Angelina, stop playing dumb here. You know who and what I'm talking about."

"I have no idea why you're so upset. All I know is that you came in here yelling like a banshee. I'm just glad Angel's not here, or I'd be dealing with a crying baby, too."

She looked at her friend. "You don't know?"

"No, I don't. You're my best friend—you know I don't keep secrets from you, so spill. What's got you so upset?"

"My brother."

"Alejandro?"

"Who else do you think I'm referring to?"

"Well, it could be Joe or Alec."

"Well, I'm mad at them, too. How could they do this to me? How could they?"

"Gabriella, you have to calm down and start from the beginning. We can't keep asking each other questions or we'll get nowhere." Angelina sat down beside Gabriella and reached for her hands. She looked her friend directly in the eye and saw tears starting to form. Gabriella never cried so whatever had upset her had really gotten to her.

"Angelina, I've never been so mad at my brother as I am right now. He's betrayed me."

"What has he done?"

Gabriella stood and looked out the window towards the backyard. She walked around the room.

"Gabriella, please don't start pacing. Your brothers do it and it drives me crazy."

"I know. It drives me crazy, too." That little back and forth seemed to settle Gabriella down enough that she returned to her seat. "Angelina, I had my meeting with Mary about Career Day."

"And, how did it go?"

"That's the problem. It was awful."

"Awful? How could it be awful? I thought you were looking forward to it."

"I was until *he* showed up."

"He? Who's he? Just spit it out."

"Ashton, that's who."

"Oh," was Angelina's response.

"Oh is right. How could he?"

"Gabriella, what did Alejandro supposedly do?"

"Recommend Ashton to Mary."

"Okay, but I'm sure Alejandro didn't know that she'd chosen you to work with him."

"Really now, I bet he did know. It's his way of making me get over my dislike of him. Angelina, I'm trying. I really am, but every time I see him, I forget the promise I made to myself and just become unglued. Sometimes when I'm going at him, I can't believe some of the things that come out of my mouth. But today, today was the last straw. I'm furious."

"You can't blame Ashton because I'm sure he was just as surprised as you were."

"You know, I think he was. He even came down to my classroom to talk to me about it and then, me being me, I almost fell off my ladder. He caught me, and then I tore his head off. Angelina what's wrong with me? I feel like every time I'm near him, he's turning my life upside down. I'm a mess."

Before Angelina could say a word, her husband walked in. She took one look at him and knew that he was in for it. Thankfully, Gabriella had calmed down and he didn't have to face nearly the wrath that Angelina had faced just a short while before he came home.

Dejectedly, she looked up at her brother. "How could you," is all she said.

On that note, Angelina stood, leaving her husband and his sister to speak in private.

"How could you?" she whispered. Alejandro knew she was more than upset with him and he knew the reason. Alec had phoned him to warn him that their sister was on the war path. Ashton had returned to the clinic asking why Alejandro had volunteered him for the job. Alec didn't know that Ashton would be working with Gabriella—he just agreed to give Ashton the time to work on the project. He had not only heard an earful from Alec, he was also preparing himself to hear what his sister had for him.

"I'm sorry, Gabriella. I didn't know you'd get this upset. I thought you'd work well together. Maybe put your differences aside—

She looked up at her brother. She wanted to believe him. She was tired... tired of fighting this battle with Ashton. "You know, you're right," she said, surprising not only herself, but her brother as well. "I'll give it a go. I want to do this for Mary and for the children." She leaned over and kissed her brother on the cheek, stood, and walked out the door.

His sister had done an about face. He wasn't sure what had just happened before his eyes.

Angelina walked in, pointing her finger at her husband. "Gabriella just left. What did you say to her?"

"Just that I wanted her to put her differences aside."

"That's all?"

"Uh huh."

"I know why you did this, husband of mine."

He smiled at his wife.

"I do, and it's not going to work. You are not going to win this bet by playing this little game underhanded."

"I don't know what you're talking about."

"Sure you don't," she said as she neared Alejandro. "I know the real reason you made this suggestion to Mary. It's all about the bet. Well, I hope your sister forgives you when this all comes out. And I for one won't be there to support you."

Alejandro shook his head as he watched his wife stroll from the room. Originally, he'd spoken to Mary shortly after the last Career Day half a year ago. Not only had he suggested a team approach to the planning, he'd also suggested Ashton for the job. Ashton had received a bad rap right after joining his brothers' practice after his father's retirement. He wanted him to overcome the differences that had overshadowed him at first. Ashton was a good doctor and an even better person for overcoming what had happened to him when he was a child. His parents had sent him away to boarding school, pretty much forgetting that he'd ever existed. He'd overcome that sense of loss and had turned into a fine doctor. Then, after Alejandro had placed his bet with Angelina, he realized that Ashton had already been asked to partake in the project. He never said anything to Angelina or even Alec. He was just going to sit back and see what happened. From the looks of things, he was going to win that bet.

Chapter Six

GABRIELLA GOT HOME FROM ANGELINA'S with enough time to eat a snack before leaving for her first co-ed softball practice. It was an experimental season being their first fall league—only four games. The actual games were scheduled to begin the following week. They were allowed one practice to get to know the players, set up who would play what position, and just practice.

She'd lost her appetite after Ashton had taken a bite from her sandwich and a drink from her strawberry milkshake. What a wasted lunch. She elected to take a quick shower, washing away all thoughts of her meeting earlier in the day. She was going to move on and try and forget it. She dressed in shorts and a t-shirt, as it was another warm and humid August night.

Gabriella cut up an apple and had a slice of cheese. It would be enough to hold her over until she could have dinner. The team was scheduled to go to Oxfords Bar & Grille for dinner and drinks after their practice. The bar was owned by Brant "Ox" Oxford. He was a member of St. Margaret's parish and also a member of the team. He'd already informed everyone that he would set aside his back room for the team to meet after each game. She was looking forward to it because she loved the greasy bar food that he served. Oxfords Bar and Grille was a mainstay in the community. He often donated goods and services to the school whenever they had a scheduled event, like the annual trivia contest that was held during the cold winter months.

Gabriella polished off her apple and cheese, grabbed her ball glove and baseball cap, and headed out the door. She was looking forward to playing softball again. She'd played in college and was named player of the year in their conference. When she started teaching, she played a few summers but then stopped for some reason that she couldn't even remember. She'd wanted to get back in the game for a while now, and when this fall league started up, she decided to take the bull by the horns and signed up.

Ashton left the clinic after his discussion with Alec. He'd informed him of his sister's behavior. "Alec, I'm going to do my best representing the clinic. I'm not going to let Gabriella taint my name or the clinic's. If she can't get past whatever it is that bothers her about me, it's her problem not mine. I'm sure she's going to come to you with some angle that I wronged her—"

"Ashton, don't worry about it. I know what my sister's like. I saw how she reacted to you at Angel's baptism when you were making amends with Matthew. Whatever's gotten under her skin, she'll get over it in time. If she doesn't settle down soon, I'll talk to her."

"That's all I can ask for. I know we've had our skirmishes. When I saw her in Mary's office, I decided to put our past issues aside. I want to make this Career Day a successful event for everyone. I'm trying, really I am. I went to her classroom right after my meeting with Mary, so we could have an honest discussion about her feelings, and she fell off a ladder."

"What? She fell off a ladder? Is she alright?"

"She fell off the ladder right into my arms and then she blamed her misstep on me. Anyway she's fine. When she started yelling at me that it was my fault, well... I kind of egged her on by taking a bite from her uneaten sandwich. I really wasn't thinking at the time, except that she was making me so angry."

Alec roared with laughter. "You did not eat her lunch."

"I did. Rather, just took a bite. But if looks could kill..."

"You've got to quit goading her. I know you're just playing around with her now, but Gabriella can be a tough cookie to break and goading isn't the way to do it."

Ashton chuckled sheepishly. "I know that. I'll get her to see me for the man I am now and not the one she first met. Between you, Joe, and your father, I've learned a lot since I've joined this practice. Now she has to be the one to see it, too."

He stood and made his way to the door. "I've got to get going. We have our first softball practice tonight and I don't want to be late. Have a good weekend."

"You too, Ashton," Alec said as he walked out of his office. *Oh boy does he have his hands full. He has no idea what he's walking into,* Alec thought. Both he and Gabriella were on the same team. If they wanted their team to be successful, then they had to get along as teammates. Maybe this softball thing would be the best thing for both of them.

❧

Ashton rushed home and exchanged his suit for a pair of shorts and a sleeveless shirt. He was looking forward to practice so he could work off his pent-up frustration from earlier in the day. He grabbed a water bottle from the cabinet, filled it with tap water, and reached for his glove and shoes. He sat down at the table, took a swig from his water bottle, and put on his tennis shoes. He'd only lived in the neighborhood for a few months and had just recently joined the parish, living right down the street from the church and school. He'd been to mass a handful of times, coming in right at the beginning and often leaving early because of a page he'd received. He'd met Father Xavier, the pastor, when he joined the parish. He was middle-aged and seemed like he was quite involved with the various activities that were held through the church and school.

Fr. Xavier took time to get to know Ashton. He told him he was a pediatrician and that he worked for the Alvarez practice. Fr. Xavier spoke of Angelina and Alejandro and how much he enjoyed spending time with them at the various events. He made Ashton promise that he would attend Trivia Night in February since it was a huge fundraiser for the parish. He mentioned that Alejandro's table had won the previous year.

Ashton elected to walk to softball practice. He wanted the extra exercise since he'd been missing his runs of late. He enjoyed jogging but for some reason hadn't found the time lately because of his schedule. He'd planned to also attend the after-practice get together at Oxfords, just down the street from church. He liked the neighborhood he lived in as everything was within walking distance of his home.

He headed out earlier than he needed and arrived at the practice field fifteen minutes early. Brant Oxford was just getting out of his car. Ashton knew of him from visiting his bar.

He greeted Ashton, "Hi, I'm Brant Oxford. My friends call me Ox."

Ashton shook his hand. "Hi, Ox. I'm Ashton Holder."

"Nice to meet you Ashton. Are you new to the parish?"

"I am. I recently registered, and Fr. Xavier told me about the team so I signed right up."

"Glad to have you. From what I understand there's going to be sixteen of us on the team and Fr. Xavier is our manager. He loves to be involved in almost everything that goes on here at the church. He loves baseball and is a riot to listen to as he coaches. He's been our manager for as long as I can remember."

"That's great that he can be so involved in all of the activities."

Ox nodded. "Hey, here come some more members of the team. Everyone played on the team this summer except you and—"

A woman walked up to them. "Hey, Ox. How goes it?"

Ox turned to Liz Young, the owner of the floral shop in town. Ashton had met her when he purchased a bouquet of flowers that he'd taken to Angel's christening.

Ashton started walking towards the baseball diamond. There he was joined by several other members of the team that had appeared from the building that housed their equipment.

He was introduced to Ox's wife Joy, as well as Harold Busse, the branch manager of Louis Bank. While Ashton was learning the other names of the members of the team, Clifford Wise appeared and patted Ashton on the back.

"I didn't know you were joining the team." Clifford was a pharmacist at the hospital. Ashton often saw him in the cafeteria.

Ashton was good with names but so many new ones were being thrust upon him that he knew it would take him awhile to learn them all. He was introduced to Jack Olds who owned Olds Furniture store. He was Jane's fiancé. He recognized Perry Graham as he was the manager of one of the healthcare providers the clinic worked with. Jane Gold introduced herself as the first grade teacher at St. Margaret's. This was her first year teaching there.

Oscar Yunt and Gerry Matthews worked for a car dealership. Oscar was a salesman and Gerry a mechanic. Sharon Sorentino, a hair stylist, and Tamron Graham, a party planner, arrived at the same time. Fr. Xavier arrived with Christy Escondido and Abe Perry. They were married and both attorneys.

"I think we're missing one person. Why don't we start warming up, and maybe they'll arrive in the next few minutes." Ox grabbed his glove and jogged onto the field.

Everyone started to pair off to play catch. Christy paired with Abe, Jack and Liz paired up. Ox paired with his wife, while Harold and Clifford paired up.

Ashton, being new, knew no one. Perry had called him over to join him and Jane when he noticed someone walking over from the parking lot. Ashton started laughing.

⌇

Gabriella had been scanning the players and then she heard the laughter and looked to her right. There stood her nemesis. If she didn't see him with her own eyes, she wouldn't have believed what fate had in store for her. He was like a bad penny and always seemed to turn up in her hemisphere. She looked at him and had to laugh herself. It was just her lucky day. Who would have believed the odds of them being on the same team? If she didn't know better, the gods were shining down on her, telling her to make it right. She'd have to get along with him if she wanted to be a team player, and she did.

She walked over to Ashton. "Just my lucky day," she said to him. "Who'd have thought you'd play softball on this team? I didn't know you even lived in the parish."

"It's fairly recent. I certainly thought you knew I lived in the neighborhood after meeting in Schulers."

"I didn't think about it." She decided to try and start over. She reached her hand out to Ashton and introduced herself as though they'd never met before. "Hi, I'm Gabriella Alvarez."

He raised an eyebrow at her. "I know who you are."

"And you are?"

"Gab-ri-ella, what are you doing?"

She gave him the evil eye. He knew she didn't like how he said her name.

"I'm introducing myself. I thought maybe we could start over, forget what's happened in the past and start anew."

Ashton grinned at her. Maybe she was going to come around.

"Well, then. It's nice to meet you, Gabriella. My name is Ashton Holder."

"Nice to meet you, Ashton," she said as she pointed towards the field. "Would you like to play catch?"

He nodded and ran towards the field. He tossed a ball to her as she joined him on the grass. He had no idea what she was up to, but he decided to play along. He could only hope that she'd make an effort to get along.

The two hour practice flew by. Gabriella had the time of her life out on the field. Ox called everyone to the infield and called an end to practice. "I hope everyone can come down to the bar for a drink and some food so we can get to know everyone a little better."

All of the players told Ox they'd see him in a few minutes. Everyone headed to their cars while Ashton and Gabriella hung back. "Are you going to Oxfords?" asked Ashton.

"I am. I've been dreaming of a greasy burger all day. In fact, I distinctly remember almost having one not too long ago…"

"Sorry about that. You know I did it just to get back at you. In fact, you didn't miss anything. It wasn't that good."

"Well, it was cold," she laughed as she walked in the direction of her car. He started for the sidewalk. "Aren't you coming with us?"

"I am, but I'm on foot."

"I'll take you. Come on and ride with me."

Ashton couldn't believe the woman standing in front of him. He wondered what had happened with the Gabriella he knew from just earlier in the day. This Gabriella was much more likeable than the one he'd seen only hours before. He hoped she didn't have a personality switch again because he kind of liked the Gabriella that was standing beside him.

Chapter Seven

IT TOOK LESS THAN FIVE minutes for Gabriella to drive them to Oxfords. It was extremely crowded for nine o'clock on a Friday night. *More than usual.* Gabriella had to park in one of the free lots down the street from the bar.

She parked the car and turned to reach into the back seat to retrieve her purse. She grabbed it and turned back to open her car door only to discover that Ashton had already opened her door and had reached out his hand to help her from the car. She was surprised by his gentlemanly action and grabbed ahold of his hand. She was so caught up looking into his blue eyes that she tripped getting out of the car. His other arm reached out and grabbed her, stopping her from face-planting in the parking lot. She wondered where this kindness had come from. *He must realize I'm trying to get along. I guess I did the right thing in starting over by reintroducing myself. Maybe we can get along—after all he's not that bad. In fact, I kind of like him myself.*

"Are you okay?"

Gabriella was a little embarrassed. "I'm fine. I do

that all the time. I guess I just don't lift my feet high enough, and I get them caught. You think I'd know better by now—it's not like I just bought this car."

He laughed.

"Don't laugh at me. I could have gotten injured."

"Yes, you could have. But at least I was here to catch you."

She stepped away from the car and he closed the door. He placed his hand on her lower back and led her towards the bar. "Boy, this place is crowded." Ashton said as they neared the bar.

"Yeah, it's a Friday night. I think the Rivermen are on the west coast for the weekend, too. It's a late-night game. I guess that's why it's packed."

As they walked into Oxfords, Ox pointed for them to head to the back room. Apparently they were the last to arrive. Everyone was seated around a large rectangular table. Ashton and Gabriella grabbed the last two chairs near the door.

As they sat down, Ox handed them their menus. "Tonight, drinks are on the house," Ox said as he made his way around the room.

Ashton looked at her and noticed a sense of calm about her. She seemed relaxed, unlike earlier during their meeting with Mary where she'd sat ramrod straight in her chair.

Everyone was talking and it seemed loud in the room to Ashton. He leaned over and whispered in her ear, "So what's new?"

"What do you mean?"

"You seem different, relaxed. Earlier today I thought you were going to bite my head off."

She looked him directly in his eyes and said, "I had a revelation."

"A revelation?"

"Yep, but we shouldn't discuss it now. Just be thankful that I may be seeing you through a different set of eyes."

Ashton pulled back. He grinned at her and said a little louder than necessary, "Thanks for giving me a second chance."

Liz who was sitting right next to Gabriella perked up. "So are you two dating?"

They both looked at her, shocked. In unison, they replied, "No." They looked at one another and started laughing.

"No, we're not dating," Gabriella said, turning back to Jane. "We're just friends."

As Gabriella said that, she turned back to Ashton and smiled at him. He felt like they'd turned a corner in the last eight hours. She'd gone from hating him to declaring their friendship. He wasn't sure what she'd had to drink in the short time that he'd last seen her, but he was thankful just the same.

While they waited for their food, Ashton turned back to Gabriella. "So you're new to the team, too?"

"I am. I've wanted to get back into the game for some time now, and when I saw the fall league, I thought I'd join."

"And you've clearly played before."

"Not for a few years now."

"You looked pretty good out there."

"Thanks. As I said, it's been a while."

Liz asked Gabriella a question and drew her attention away from him.

Clifford walked over to Ashton and started talking shop. "I haven't seen you at the hospital lately."

"Joe's been on call, and I haven't needed to go in

for the last couple of weeks. I've been lucky, but I'm sure that's going to change with the flu season almost upon us."

"I'm sure it will. I can't believe it's almost September. Before you know it, the end of the year will be here."

"Time certainly flies by, doesn't it?" Ashton said as their food was delivered. Clifford returned to his seat and Ashton focused his attention back on Gabriella. She'd ordered another patty melt and fries, replacing what she'd missed at lunch. In exchange of her milkshake, she drank white wine.

"I see you finally got your burger and fries," he said sheepishly. "I want to apologize again for taking a bite of your sandwich today. I shouldn't have done that. In my defense, I was starving."

"Well, so was I. I was late getting back to school from picking up my lunch, so I had to leave it or I would have been late to our meeting. And then, I lost my app—Well, it doesn't matter. I ended up throwing my lunch away. So this makes up for it, right?"

Just as Gabriella took a bite of her sandwich Ashton put his arm around the back of her chair and leaned towards her. Some of the cheese gushed out as she took a bite, landing on her chin. His eyes were immediately drawn to her chin and the cheese. "Do you forgive me for eating your lunch?" he asked. What he wanted to do was wipe the cheese from her chin. Instead, he pointed to her chin. "I think your burger lost a little cheese."

"I guess it did," she wiped her chin.

"You missed a little," pointing to the side of her lip.

"Thanks."

Ashton watched her as she enjoyed her burger. He

was surprised that she ate with such gusto.

"Hungry?"

"Mmm hmm."

Ashton was then distracted by the waiter and pulled away. What was he thinking? He was thankful that the waiter interrupted his thoughts as he knew he had no business letting his mind drift down that direction.

Ashton had ordered a reuben. He took a bite and continued watching Gabriella.

"Is there something wrong? Do I have food on my face again," she asked as she took a sip of her wine.

"No, no food. In fact, you look beautiful."

She looked at him, her eyes narrowing. Clearly she thought that he had some angle going. He shrugged and went back to his sandwich.

By the time they finished their food, it was almost eleven thirty. Ashton caught Gabriella turning away from the table, yawning. He leaned in again, which had become a comfortable gesture for him, and asked if she wanted to leave.

"No, why do you ask?"

"Because for the last half-hour you've been trying to hide the fact that you can't keep your eyes open and keep yawning."

She looked surprised. "I thought I was being pretty creative with that."

"Well, you didn't get it passed me. Let's say our goodbyes and head on out."

They located Ox sitting at the opposite end of the table. "Thanks again for the drinks tonight. That was really kind of you," Gabriella said.

"It's not a problem. It's the least I could do for my teammates. I guess we'll see you both next Friday? Our first game… I have a feeling we're going to win."

Ox started laughing. "I always have that feeling and more times than I can count we end up losing."

Everyone at the table laughed in agreement.

"Well, maybe our luck is about to change," Ashton said as he shook Ox's hand and waved goodbye to everyone.

He guided her towards the parking lot where she left her car. She unlocked the door and he opened it for her. "Are you alright driving this late at night?"

"I am, but don't you want a lift home?"

"Nah, I think I'm going to walk back. I need to work off that reuben," he said as she got in the car.

She started to close her door but then reached across the front seat and grabbed his baseball glove. "Here, you can't forget this."

"Oh, thanks. I almost did."

She handed him his glove and smiled up at him.

"Gabriella, I had a nice time tonight. I wish it would have been a little quieter, so we could have had an actual conversation, but we'll save that for next time."

She looked a bit perplexed, but nodded.

He steeled himself and asked, "Would you like to go out sometime? I mean, I do owe you a patty melt, fries, and a strawberry milkshake. I can take you to Pedals... isn't that where your lunch came from?"

She laughed, "Yes, it is, but you don't owe me any-thing."

He wasn't sure if she was turning down his date or just the offer of a burger. "You don't want to go out with me?"

She raised her eyebrows and smiled a little, "I didn't realize you were asking me out on a date."

He nodded, suddenly nervous. "Well, I think that's what I was asking? If you don't want to go out with me, that's fine. I understand. After all, we just started being able to speak to one another amicably." He realized he was rambling and felt his face getting red. He should just end the conversation now. "Well, on that note, you drive safely."

He moved away from her car door and started to shut it. She stopped it with her hand. "Hold on. Are you going to let me respond?" She said, fully smiling now.

"Well, you just said that I didn't owe you anything."

"Ashton, let's start this conversation over. It seems like we have to do this an awful lot. Okay, ask me again."

"Ask you what?"

She rolled her eyebrows in exasperation, still smiling.

He laughed, "Okay, okay, I'll re-ask you... Would you like to go out with me sometime?"

She pretended to think about it. He laughed, but was still feeling pretty nervous about her response, clenching and unclenching his hands.

"Hmm, should I or shouldn't I?" she said.

"Would you quit playing around with me?" he laughed nervously. "Will you or won't you? If you don't want to go out with me, it's no big deal. I just thought I'd ask. Maybe we can find a common ground and actually start getting along—"

"Yes," she whispered.

Ashton froze. "Did you say yes?"

"Yes. I said yes."

"Well, okay then." He couldn't control the huge smile on his face. He turned and started down the sidewalk, then rushed back to her car. "I did hear you right, right? You said yes?"

Gabriella laughed, nodded, and then started her car.

He was still in shock as she pulled away from the parking lot and only realized as he watched her drive way that he'd forgotten to get her phone number. He slapped his forehead. *How will I get her phone number? I can't just come out and ask Alec or Joe for it... I know. I'll ask Alejandro,* he thought as he jumped onto the sidewalk and started jogging home. *Yes, that's what I'll do. I'll phone Alejandro first thing tomorrow.*

Chapter Eight

SATURDAY MORNING CAME AROUND BRIGHT and early for Gabriella. She hadn't slept too well. She got home late from Ox's and had a hard time falling asleep. She wanted to blame it on her glass of wine, but knew better than that. She attributed her lack of sleep to Ashton.

Ashton took her completely by surprise when he'd asked her on a date. She knew he'd been anxious as he asked her the all-important question while she'd stood there nervous as all could be.

Gabriella hadn't really dated much since her heart had been broken by her one-time love. She didn't want to put herself out there, but for some reason Ashton was different.

Gabriella knew she'd been different with him. More like a first class bitch. By agreeing to go out with him, she believed she'd put her anger aside. She'd really give this date, whenever it was, a try. If her brothers and father liked him, why shouldn't she?

She knew she couldn't lounge in bed trying to make up for her lost sleep. She had to get up and get going as she had way too much to do. She decided since she hadn't completed setting up her classroom the day before, she'd head into school. She was determined to put the finishing touches on her room today so she could spend her last remaining days of summer vacation doing whatever she wanted. She'd already arranged to spend part of the week with Angelina and the kids. They'd planned a 'staycation.' They were going to Grants Farm and the St. Louis Zoo. They'd already planned two days of getting up early so the kids could enjoy as much of each attraction before it got too warm. More than likely they'd be home by early afternoon each day.

She didn't feel like making coffee, so she dressed in shorts and a sleeveless shirt before heading off to Mochas & Coffee. On her drive over, she decided to get a cinnamon streusel coffeecake muffin, along with her usual coffee. The drive thru lane was backed up, so she decided to head inside to get faster service. Gabriella parked and reached for her purse down on the floor of her car. As she turned to sit back up, she noticed the torso of a man standing next to her car. She slid her purse underneath her seat, not sure if she was about to be robbed, when the man bent over and looked her squarely in the eye.

Gabriella threw her hand up to her chest and yelled, "You scared me to death," as she reached for the door handle. She opened her door and started to get out. "I can't believe you just snuck up on me like that. You could have given me a heart attack."

A smooth voice replied, "I doubt that."

She got out of her car and started to close her door. "Aren't you forgetting something?"

"Yes, I am," she said. "See, Ashton, you've startled me

so I don't know whether I'm coming or going," she said, reaching down to pick up her purse.

"Well, good morning to you too, sunshine. I thought we had worked past this," pointing back and forth between them, "I thought you'd had a revelation of sorts…"

"I did," she said raising her finger to her temple. "Or I thought I had," she said, teasing him. He looked awfully warm for this early in the morning. She noticed the fine sheen of moisture on his brow. His hair stood on end as though he'd just finished running his hand through it. He was dressed in a white t-shirt that was peppered with perspiration. As her eyes drifted downward, she noticed his running shoes. She closed her car door and said, "What brings you here on this fine Saturday morning?"

"I just finished up my jog, and thought I'd pick up something on my way back home. They have the best coffeecake muffin…"

"I know," she smiled. "That's what I came for as well."

"Shall we?" he asked gesturing towards the entrance.

"I was getting mine to-go. The drive thru lane was too long for me."

"So where're you off to?"

"Back to my classroom to finish up."

"Would you like some help?"

"Really? You want to help me?"

"Why not? I've got nothing planned today that I can't put on hold for a few hours."

"Well, okay then… I'll take you up on your offer, but only if I can buy your breakfast."

"Breakfast? This is just a snack," he said as he grinned at her. She looked at his eyes and his handsome grin and wondered how she'd missed his cuteness before. She gathered it was because she was always furious with him.

"A snack?"

"Yep, a snack. I've already eaten my real breakfast."

"And what was that?" Pausing, she said, "Never mind. I don't need to know. I just can't believe you eat two breakfasts."

"Not every day, just some."

She shook her head at him as the counterperson asked for her order. Gabriella ordered two cinnamon streusel coffeecake muffins and a large café mocha for herself. She turned to him and asked what he wanted to drink. He pointed at her, meaning he wanted the same thing.

"So, are we in tune or what?"

"Huh?" She asked as they waited for their food. "What do you mean?"

"Well, we like the same muffin, the same coffee drink, and we also like strawberry milkshakes. I wonder if that means anything."

"I'm not sure what you're implying."

"Just think about it is all I ask," and with that their coffees and muffins arrived. He reached for his coffee. "How about I meet you at school in say ten minutes?"

"You live that close?"

"I do."

"I could drive us."

"Thanks, but I need my car because I have to go to the hardware store after I help you out. Ten minutes?"

"See you there. And I'll take the muffins with me."

He smiled, saluted her, and headed off in what she presumed was the direction of his home. She still had no idea where he actually lived. She was taken aback with his presence and desire to help her. It appeared like fate was playing a part here. It seemed like every corner she turned Ashton was there. Schulers, softball, and now Mochas & Coffee. Each time she interacted with him she felt more at ease. Maybe they were getting somewhere with their friendship.

True to his word, he met her ten minutes later in the parking lot of the school. She was standing beside her car, waiting for him, as he drove up. He parked his car and exited with his coffee in hand. It looked like he'd taken a quick shower because he'd changed clothes. "Do you need any help with anything?"

"Nope. I think I've got the most important thing," she said pointing to the bag that contained their muffins. He followed her to the door as she unlocked and opened it for him. He held the door for her, and after they entered, she turned and relocked the door. He followed her to her classroom.

It was just after seven thirty, and for some reason, she felt like she'd already run a mile for the day. She unlocked her classroom and propped open the door. Flipping on the lights, she headed to her desk where she put down her purse and bag of muffins. She looked over at him and took a swallow of her coffee, burning her throat in the process. She started to cough.

"Wow, that was hotter than I expected."

"Are you alright?"

"Yeah. I just didn't expect my coffee to be so hot. Normally, it's not that hot." She turned for the bag containing the muffins. She pulled out a handful of napkins from her desk drawer and spread two out on her desk. She reached into the bag, pulling a muffin out for herself then passed the bag to Ashton.

Slowly, she pulled the paper liner from her muffin.

She picked up her muffin and started picking off small pieces dropping them into her mouth.

He watched her as she meticulously tore away at her muffin. "Do you always do that?"

"What?"

"Eat your muffin in layers? You're definitely not like most of us," he said as he took a large bite of his.

"Well, I'm not a caveman, that's for sure," she said, raising her eyes to him.

He smiled at her as he chewed his muffin. "So what's on the agenda? What do you need help with first?"

She tore another piece off her muffin and popped it into her mouth. She took a swig from her coffee and wiped her hands with a napkin. She strolled over to the ladder, as she hadn't completed hanging her letters for her boarder. She started to climb the ladder when Ashton hurried to her side. "Hey, let me do that. You did almost fall yesterday."

Gabriella pushed him aside and started up the ladder. "As I recall, I almost fell because you startled me—it seems to be a habit of yours. Now, just stand there and make sure I don't fall, and I'll have this done in no time."

Ashton stood with one hand on her leg, supporting her, and the other holding his cup of coffee. At first she wasn't sure about him holding on to her, but she realized it was better than ending up on the floor in the middle of the classroom.

She looked down at him. "Really, now? You think you're going to catch me if I fall? I think you're more interested in your cup of coffee."

"I wouldn't say that," he said. He set his coffee down on a nearby desk and returned, putting both of his hands on her waist. "Is this better?"

Her breath hitched, and she cleared her throat to cover it. "Better."

She turned back to her boarder, grabbed her stapler and a letter, and started to align the letter, but his hands were extremely distracting and she missed stapling the letters multiple times. She shook her head, trying to focus, and reached for another letter. She reached up to staple it when she felt his fingertips moving about her waist. She stopped and looked down at him. "Ashton, please stop that." He shrugged his shoulders and looked sheepish.

She went to staple the letter in place when she realized what he was doing. He was ramping up to see if she was ticklish! "What the hell are you doing? Do you want me to fall?"

And with that, he went full force. She started laughing and couldn't stop. She tried to remain upright on the ladder, but her laughter took her over the edge, and next thing she knew, she was sprawled in his arms.

"Put me down. Please put me down."

Ashton complied. "Is something wrong?" he asked, raising his eyebrows in innocence.

"Something wrong. Something wrong?" and with that she launched herself at him. She went for his waist, trying to tickle him. He, in fact, was more ticklish than she was. And the next thing she knew they'd fallen to the floor in a fit of laughter. She pulled away from him as he pleaded, "Stop it, please stop."

Catching her breath she said. "You can't do this here. It's a school. We're in my classroom."

"Gabriella, will you please just chill out? I just wanted to see you laugh and have a little fun. I didn't mean any harm by it." Ashton stood and reached out his hand to her. She grabbed it, and he helped her up from the floor.

"I need to get this done today, not next week," she said, attempting to be stern. She couldn't keep the smile from her lips, though. "So, if you want to help me, I'll take your help, but I don't have time for fun and games. Got it?"

"I do. I just couldn't help myself. I'm sorry. It won't happen again," he said, chagrined.

Pointing her finger at him she said, "It better not or you're banished from my classroom. Understand?"

"Yep, sure do. So, let's stop talking about it, and let's get back at it."

She scampered up the ladder and quickly finished stapling the letters to her border. She couldn't believe she just participated in a tickling match with Ashton right in the middle of her classroom. It seemed as though each minute they spent together she learned something new about him. He seemed like a kid at heart and she liked what she was seeing.

After completing the border, he helped her put all of the books on the desks. As far as she was concerned, she was pretty much finished with the heavy stuff. She had a few small things that needed finishing up, but she could do that before or after the faculty meetings. She thought she had at most an hour left of work tops to put the finishing touches on her classroom.

Ashton looked around Gabriella's room. "I like it. You put a lot of thought into it," he said as he walked around her room. "How long have you been teaching?"

"This is my eleventh year, all at St. Margaret's. I love it, and I love Mary. She's a phenomenal principal."

"From what I've seen, she seems like she's pretty hands-on. She seems a little disappointed that she's had to turn the Career Day planning over to us."

"She is, but she's so busy planning for our accreditation review that she doesn't want to slight the planning for Career Day. It means so much to her. I think she's worried about our site visit, but she doesn't have anything to worry about. We'll pass with flying colors..." She turned, "I think I'm about done for the day." Gabriella gathered the stapler and the extra paper and returned it to her closet. She went to close up the ladder when Ashton hurried over to grab it from her.

"Where do you want this?"

She led him to her closet where she showed him where she stored the ladder.

"Are you finished?"

"No, I still have a little work left, but I'll finish up next week while I'm here for faculty meetings."

She grabbed her coffee cup and finished up the last bit.

"So what are your plans for the day?" asked Ashton.

"I have a few errands to run, and then I may go for a hike."

"Where do you hike?"

"I like going to Pieres Trail Park. It's not too far from here. I like hiking it because it has an abandoned railroad track that I like walking along. It also has some large hills that definitely get your heart pounding. I love it when I get to the top because the trails overlook the Meramec River. It's just beautiful up there."

"I've never heard of that park before."

"It's not as popular as it used to be. Not too many people hike it any longer. A lot of people like to go to Cliff Cave Park or Greensfelder Park. At Cliff Cave you hike amongst the limestone formations, while at Greensfelder you mostly hike on forested trails. I like going to Pieres because I can get there in minutes whereas, if I go to Cliff Cave or Greensfelder, it takes me a half-hour or longer. I think the views are breathtaking at all of the parks, I just prefer one that's more convenient with as busy as I am."

"Well, maybe sometime I'll have to hike this Pieres Park. In fact, maybe you can show me the ropes."

She looked at him and smiled. She wasn't exactly sure what was going on between them. They'd gone from adversaries to what? He appeared to have put her mistreatment of him aside because he seemed like he wanted to spend an awful lot of time with her. And he *did* ask her out on a date. She thought for a second and realized that she wanted that, too. She was definitely seeing a different side to him and she really liked it. Changing the subject she said, "So, whatchya buying at the hardware store?"

"Some lumber and stain."

"Are you planning on building something?"

"What do you think I'm going to do with lumber and stain? Sit on it?" he said, grinning at her.

"Well…"

"I'm building a pergola for my backyard."

"That sounds hot and tiring, especially on a day like today."

"And hiking doesn't?"

"Just carrying the lumber sounds so intense. On a hot, humid day like today, I get hot just thinking about it."

"I'd have to say the same about hiking out in the woods. But you have to add bugs to your day. Ticks, mosquitos, spiders…"

"Okay, I get your point. Both of our plans sound hot and tiring just thinking about them." She reached for her purse and keys. She was satisfied with the way she was leaving her classroom. Ashton followed her out with coffee cup in hand.

"I think I'm going to run back by the coffee shop and get another muffin. That was sure good today."

"Another muffin? Your third breakfast for the day."

"Well, I need my energy for purchasing my lumber, you know."

She laughed as she locked up her classroom. He followed her down the hallway and watched as she unlocked the door so they could exit the building. "Thanks for letting me tag along," he said as she re-locked the doors to the school.

"No, thank you. I appreciate your help. You saved me at least two or three hours of additional work. I owe you."

They walked the remainder of the way to their cars in silence. She unlocked her car and Ashton reached to open the door for her. She slid into the driver's seat and looked up at him. "Thanks again for the help."

"Not a problem. I enjoyed it."

She screwed up her mouth at him and said, "Really?"

"Really, I did. I had no idea so much went into planning a classroom for the beginning of the year. I have a lot more respect for teachers with just the little help I gave you." Ashton finished the last of the coffee dregs. "Off to the hardware store."

"And not Coffees and Mocha?"

"No, I was just kidding," he said as he started walking towards his own car. "I'm past breakfast—it's almost time for lunch." Laughing he said, "Don't get overheated climbing those limestone formations."

"Oh, I won't," she called over to him. "And don't you get overheated carrying all of that lumber."

"Wouldn't think of it," he called. Gabriella headed out of the parking lot. She waved as she passed him. She'd noticed him watching her as she pulled onto the street. She'd been surprised when she ran into him at the coffee shop, but was glad that she did.

When she reflected on how their relationship was transforming, she just didn't understand why she'd treated him so badly. She was concerned that she'd fall back into the trap and turn on him again, and then she realized each moment they spent together surprised her. He was more of a gentleman than she thought. Surprisingly, he had a funny sense of humor. *Maybe he's not all that bad.* She was glad she decided to put the past behind her. He might turn into a really good friend. She was proud of herself that she decided to move on.

Chapter Nine

G ABRIELLA LEFT SCHOOL AND HEADED over
to her parents' house. She hadn't seen her mother
for a few days, and she decided she needed a little
Mom time. She stopped by Laketown Bakery on her
way over—her mother loved their gooey butter cof-
feecakes, and for some reason she was craving another
sweet for the day. Not only did Gabriella purchase
the coffee cake, she also added a couple of danish nut
horns for her Sunday morning breakfast, along with
a couple of glazed pretzel donuts that, when warmed,
melted in your mouth. She had a definite sweet tooth
for the day. She had to put an end to her treats when
she returned to school.

She walked into the kitchen unannounced. Maria
was cutting up vegetables for a stew that she was preparing for dinner. She went directly to her mother
and kissed her cheek. Her hands were full with the
coffeecake, or she would have pulled her mother into
a hug, too. She held up the coffeecake.

"Is that what I think it is?" asked Maria.

"It is," Gabriella said as she went to the cupboard to

gather their plates and silverware for their treat. "Oh, Mom, this looks really good today."

Maria wiped her hands on a towel and reached for two glasses. She went to the refrigerator and pulled out a gallon of milk. She poured the cold milk into glasses and returned the milk to the refrigerator. Maria grabbed the glasses and sat down across the table from her daughter.

Gabriella could feel her mom watching her as she methodically cut the cake and set the slices on their plates. She ran her finger across the back of the knife licking the gooey filling from her finger. "Umm, umm," she said as she swallowed the luscious sampling. "Wow, is that good," Gabriella said as she pushed her mother's cake towards her.

Maria took a bite of her cake and agreed with her daughter's comment. Her mom was still watching her as she played with her fork, running it through the slice of cake, forming lines through the powdered sugar.

"So how did you spend your day so far?" Maria asked, her eyebrows raised.

Gabriella told her about going into school and working in her classroom.

"I'm almost done. I have a few things left that I'll finish up next week."

"So, what else is going on, Gabriella? What aren't you telling me?"

Gabriella looked up at her mother and then looked back down at her slice of cake. She should have known her mom would see through her attempts at normalcy. She stabbed her fork into her cake and broke off a piece. She raised the fork to her mouth, looked at her cake, and then set the fork back down onto her plate. "I don't know what's wrong with me." She looked at her mother then retrieved her fork again. She played with her cake, and then ate the bite that was sitting on her fork. She chewed her cake and reached for her milk. Taking a sip, she sat her fork back on her plate and looked at her mom. "Mom, I keep beating myself up about this…"

Maria reached her hand across the table and took hold of her daughter's hand. "Honey, what are you talking about?"

"I don't understand why I've been so mean to Ashton." Pausing, "I keep trying to get along with him, and then out of the blue I fall back on my ways and treat him horribly." Gabriella told her mother about the previous day. "And then you'll never guess who's on my softball team."

"Ashton?"

"How did you know?" Pausing, Gabriella asked, "Did Alejandro tell you?"

"No, it was Joe."

"Joe? Huh." Gabriella took another bite of her cake. "Yeah, I went to practice last night and he was there. I did my best to get along with him, and then we went to Oxfords after practice with the rest of the team." She took a drink from her glass. "I even enjoyed myself with him. In fact, I ran into him this morning at Mochas & Coffee and he volunteered to help me in my classroom."

"He did, did he? Did you let him?"

"I did. Mom, I'm really trying but deep down, I think I'm still really angry at him. I got along with him this morning, but I just…" Pausing, she thought for a moment and added, "And you'll never believe this. To top it off, I agreed to go on a date with him. I have no idea why I said yes when I have these feelings.

When he asked me, he seemed really nervous, unsure how I would react.

"I don't know what happened. One minute I was remembering my anger for him and the next minute I found myself saying yes. I'm really confused. Mom, I don't want to get hurt again. I've protected my heart for so long—I can't go there again, Mom. I just can't."

"I know you've been shy about getting into relationships. Honey, why don't you try and talk to him about it? Tell him why you feel the way you do."

"I did tell him I had a revelation of sorts and was trying, but then I…"

"Sweetheart, give it time. You didn't develop this sense of animosity toward him overnight, and it's definitely not going to go away overnight. As long as you know deep down that you're trying to overcome this, then I don't understand." Maria took a bite of her coffee cake. "Gabriella, you've never been shy about addressing your feelings about a subject. Maybe after your next game you'll have a better handle on what's really troubling you. And then you can talk to him about it. It's better to be open and honest with your feelings, especially since you're trying to get along with him. Ashton's not a bad guy. From what your father's told me, he had a rough childhood, and I know he can be a little rough around the edges. But from what Alec and Joe have told me, he's come a long way since first joining the practice. I believe he learned a lesson with what happened with Matthew. You need to give him a chance. You should share with him what's going on with you so you can move forward and try and develop a friendship."

"Friendship?"

"Well, I don't know what you call it today, but you

should try and get along because he's not going anywhere, and he will be around the family more and
more since he's a member of the practice." Gabriella
knew what her mother was saying was true. They ran
the practice as though each member was a part of the
family all the way up from the receptionist, nurses, and
doctors. It was a family in all sense of the word.

"I know, Mom, and I hear what you're saying."
Gabriella finished off her cake, drank the last of her
milk and carried her plate and glass to the sink where
she rinsed them and put them into the dishwasher.

Gabriella thanked her mother for the talk and headed
off to the grocery store. She went to Schulers and
picked up a few groceries for the week. By the time
she returned home from visiting her mother and running her errands for the day, it was almost five o'clock.

She quickly put her groceries away. It was still
quite warm, and since she hadn't gone on her hike
like she'd planned, she decided to take a walk around
the neighborhood. She changed her clothes filled her
water bottle with ice and cold water, grabbed her tennis shoes, phone and earbuds and headed out the door.

She often walked her neighborhood in the afternoon after school ended for the day. She did her best
walking most of the year, except during the frigid
winter months and the ungodly heat of the summer.
She hadn't been as vigilant with her walks this summer
with the heat and humidity. With the events of the
past couple of days, she needed to work off some of
her anxiety, so she locked her house, put in her earbuds
and started down her front walk. She barely got to
the corner when she was stopped by one of her prior
students.

"Hi, Ms. Alvarez. How's your summer?" Micah said

from a bike.

"Hey there, Micah. My summer's been great so far. How's yours been?"

"We went on vacation to Colorado, but other than that I just played baseball. I can't believe we go back to school in two weeks. Summer went by fast."

"It certainly did," Gabriella added as she could tell Micah was in a hurry to get somewhere. "Well, I'll let you go. I'll see you in a couple of weeks. Enjoy your last bit of summer."

"I will," Micah called over his shoulder as he continued riding his bike down the sidewalk. Seeing her students and their families was one of the things she enjoyed most about living in the neighborhood. Sometimes when she was rushed, or after having a bad day, she didn't like it as much, but in general, she loved the family atmosphere that surrounded her.

Gabriella continued on further down the street. She was listening to some classical music when she approached Mrs. Alma's house. She was at the edge of her driveway watering her flower beds. Gabriella stopped and removed her earbuds from her ears. "Mrs. Alma, how are you this evening?"

"I'm hot. Look at my flowers, dear. They're having such a hard time in this heat. I water them every night…"

"They look beautiful," Gabriella commented. "I was listening to the weather on the way home from my parents' house, and I think we're supposed to have storms tonight. Maybe it will cool down a little."

"I hope so. We've sure had a spell with this heat. Now, dear, you take it easy on your walk and don't overdo it."

"Thanks for your concern, Mrs. Alma. I don't plan

on walking too much further—just around the block, and then I'm in for the night."

"That's good, dear. I'll let you go so you can get home and into the air conditioning."

Gabriella said her goodbyes and continued down the sidewalk. She got to the corner right past Mrs. Alma's. Instead of following her normal route, she turned right and walked towards the church. *Something different,* she thought. She headed down the sidewalk, listening to her music, when something caught her attention. She looked to her left across the street, and right on the corner, less than a block from St. Margaret's, was Ashton's home. *No wonder he made it home, took a shower, and met me back at school so quickly,* she thought. He was in his side yard doing what he said—building a pergola.

Gabriella looked before crossing the street and walked to the other side of the road. He was standing on a ladder, hammering away. His back was to her, and he had no idea he had an audience. She stood there watching him—shirtless and in gym shorts. She could tell he'd been at this for a while as sweat glistened on his back and shoulders. She watched him, taken in by his broad muscular back. She couldn't take her eyes off of him as he held a board and hammered a nail. Not ever had she witnessed such toned muscles. She also took in his waist and lean hips. Never in her wildest dreams did she believe Ashton was so physically fit.

He'd just stopped hammering and was reaching for another piece of wood. As he raised it to set it on top of the frame he'd built, it caught the edge of the ladder with a force greater than he realized. His weight wasn't squarely in the middle of the ladder, and the ladder started to sway. Gabriella yelled at him just as the ladder toppled over with him. He jumped off the ladder before it finished falling and rolled as he hit the ground.

Gabriella ran to his side, calling his name. He was more than surprised to see her.

"Gabriella, where did you come from?" he asked as he sat up, his blue eyes piercing hers.

"What the hell were you doing?"

"Exactly what I said I was going to do. I'm building my pergola."

"Yeah, I can see that. Why don't you have someone helping you? You could have killed yourself."

"Like you could care," he said. "Wait, I didn't mean that. I'm sorry." Ashton started to stand, but quickly sat back down, clutching his knee. "I don't think I would have killed myself. I'm fine. Really I am," he said as he rubbed his knee.

"Yeah, sure you are—that's why you're checking out your knee." She kneeled down beside him. "Do you want me to call an ambulance?"

He made an exasperated noise, "For Pete's sake, no. I'm fine."

"What about Alec or Joe or Alejandro? You should get checked out."

"Gabriella, I'm fine. Really, I am. Let me just sit here for a minute, and then I think I'll call it quits for the day."

"See, you are hurt."

Ashton lay back on the ground, closing his eyes. Gabriella reached over and brushed his hair out of his eyes. She noticed a towel sitting next to the house and reached for it. Wiping the sweat from his brow, he opened his eyes.

"Now what are you doing?"

"I was wiping your brow."

"Right, but why? I told you I'm fine."

"You looked hot." She thought that was a good answer.

"Hot? Of course I'm hot. It's like ninety-five degrees out here." He sat up and started to stand. He paused as he put weight on his leg, but fully stood. "See, I'm fine," he said as he reached for his tools.

"What can I do to help you?"

He looked at her and shook his head.

"Ashton, please let me help you. No matter what you say, I know you're hurting."

"Just grab my hammer and that box of nails, and I'll get everything else."

Gabriella grabbed the items. "At least this box didn't break open—we'd have nails all over the place."

He smiled at her. "Yeah, and I'd probably end up with a flat tire on my lawn mower, too." He shook his head. "Yes, we were lucky with that. I don't know why I closed the box when I pulled that last nail out. I guess it was premonition." He closed the ladder and set it against the house along with the wood that he'd cut earlier and had stacked in a neat pile. He picked up the ladder and motioned for her to follow him. She grabbed her water bottle that she'd thrown on the ground when she'd run to him and followed him.

Ashton led her to a shed that sat towards the back of his yard. It looked like a pint-sized house and even had a little front porch with Adirondack chairs lined up in front of the doorway. Very quaint, she thought. He stored the ladder and supplies that she carried inside the shed and closed the door. He motioned her towards the chairs.

Pointing towards the shed as she sat down, she said,

"This is so cute, did you build it?"

Ashton eased down into his chair. He was trying to hide how much his knee was bothering him, but she wasn't buying it.

"Nah, it was here when I bought the house. I think the previous owners used it as a play house for their children. It was never finished on the inside, so I decided, what better way to use it than to store my tools and stuff? It works for me."

She watched him closely. Ashton rested his head on the back of the chair and closed his eyes. She knew he was in pain, but knew better than to mention it. "Have you eaten yet?" she asked.

"No, I was going to grab something when I finished up for the night."

"How about I go get us something to eat and you go in and get cleaned up?"

He turned his head and squinted at her.

"What are you in the mood for?"

"Gabriella, why don't you just go on home? I'm fine. I don't need a nurse."

She ignored him, which was a huge step for her. In the past, she would have taken his head off. "We both need to eat. Come on, let me do this. After all, you did help me out just this morning, so why can't I return the favor and help you?"

"Gab-ri-ella," he said looking her directly in the eyes.

For some reason the way he said her name didn't bother her as it had in the past. "Ashton, please let me. I want to do this. Quit arguing with me and say yes."

He mulled it over for a few seconds and said one word, "Yes."

Clapping her hands, she jumped from her chair. "Do you want anything special? Or should I just surprise you?"

"Do whatever you want—it seems like I can't stop you."

"No, you can't," she said as she stepped from the porch. "Do you need help getting inside?"

He gave her that look that let her know she'd gone a little too far. "Well, okay, then." She started to walk away. "Give me a half-hour, and I'll be back."

Ashton sat in his chair, contemplating what he should do. His knee was killing him, but he also knew he'd better get cleaned up before Gabriella came back or she'd have him in the emergency room.

Ashton slowly raised himself from his chair. Testing his knee, he stepped down off the porch. He took his time and made his way to the back door of his house. He glanced at his watch. Five minutes had already elapsed since she left. And one thing he knew about Gabriella, she was always on time. That left him twenty-five minutes to shower and change.

As he stood, he realized how lucky he was Gabriella had appeared out of nowhere when he'd tumbled off the ladder. He was lucky he hadn't hit his head or done more damage than he did. When he'd seen her approach, he saw the immediate look of concern on her face. She hadn't freaked out but stayed calm as he assessed his injuries. He gathered that was a learned behavior after having grown up with a doctor in the house.

He moved as quickly as he could. When he walked into the kitchen, and started to move about the house, he glanced around as he made his way towards his bedroom. *The house doesn't look too bad for a bachelor,* he thought. She'd just have to get past the few plates that were in the sink and the medical journals that were lying on the couch. Otherwise, the house was fairly presentable.

Chapter Ten

GABRIELLA RUSHED HOME. SHE RAN in the back door and took out her phone. She knew Joe was home as Alec and Kelly had gone out of town for the day. She dialed Joe's cell and hurried into her bedroom. As she listened to the phone ring, she grabbed a pair of slacks and a blouse. She decided to change in the event Joe suggested she take Ashton to the hospital.

Joe answered on the fourth ring. "How's my favorite sister?"

"Favorite? You mean only," she said as she buttoned up her blouse.

Joe chuckled. He always answered the same way—it was a standing joke between them. "So what are you up to this fine Saturday evening?"

"Joe, I need your help."

Joe's tone of voice changed, "Gabriella, are you okay? What's wrong?"

"It's not me, Joe. It's Ashton."

"Ashton?" he asked. "What's wrong with him?"

Gabriella told him her story about taking a walk and discovering his house, and then him falling off the ladder. "Joe, I really think he hurt himself. He had a hard time standing, and he grimaced when he went to sit down. I think I should take him to the emergency room."

"Where are you now?"

"At home, changing. I told him I was going to get us something to eat, but instead I ran home to change my clothes and call you."

"Gabriella, I'm in the car right now. I'm about fifteen minutes from your house. You finish changing, and I'll pick you up."

"Thanks, Joe."

"It's not a problem."

"Joe?"

"Yeah?"

"He's going to be really mad at me, just so you know."

"I know," is all Joe said, then Gabriella heard a dial tone.

True to his word, Joe pulled up in front of her house fifteen minutes later. She was waiting for him on the front steps. She jumped in his car and closed the door. He looked at her and shook his head. "What's up with you being at Ashton's house? I didn't think you even liked him."

"I told you, I was taking a walk. I had no idea where he lived, just that he lived in the neighborhood." She looked out the window as Joe drove around the corner towards Ashton's house. He pulled into Ashton's driveway and turned off his motor.

"How are you going to explain my presence and your change of clothes?"

"I'm not. It really doesn't matter. Come on, let's get going so you can examine him." She flung open the door and jumped from the car.

Gabriella rang the bell once, and she was getting ready to ring it a second time when Ashton appeared at the door. She turned back to glance at Joe and Ashton frowned when he noticed him. Shaking his head, he held open the screen door for Gabriella. "Gabriella, now what have you gone and done?" he asked as she and Joe stepped into the foyer. Ashton closed the door behind them.

Ashton raised his arm, motioning them towards the kitchen. His kitchen was huge and filled with stainless steel appliances. She raised her eyebrows as she took it in. A Viking cooktop with six-burners, a built-in grill, and a set of double ovens were built into the wall. An island sat in the middle of the room near the appliances. A bookshelf was cut into the outside of the island where he did have actual cookbooks lined up along with various other knick-knacks. At one corner of the island, a wine cooler had been installed that contained several bottles of wine. His single-serve coffee maker sat near the sink, along with a toaster and knife block. Except for a few dishes that she saw laying in the sink, his kitchen was neat and well-organized.

Ashton rested up against the island as he watched Gabriella taking in his kitchen.

"Wow, this is really nice. Do you use it?"

She grimaced at her implication.

"Of course I do. What do you think it's just a show piece?" He shook his head. "And here I thought we were getting along."

"We are," she huffed. "I just asked a question."

Turning towards Joe, he said, "And to what do I owe the honor of your presence?"

Joe shook his head as he looked back and forth between Gabriella and Ashton. "My sister tells me you had a little accident."

Ashton nodded and moved towards the table where he pulled out a chair. Joe watched him as he carefully sat down. "It looks like you're a little banged up."

"As I told your sister," Ashton said, glaring at Gabriella, "I am fine."

"It doesn't look that way to me," Joe said as he sat down next to Ashton. "I see that you're favoring your right—"

"Joe, I am fine. I just banged my knee up. It's a little stiff, but I'm fine. Okay?" Turning towards Gabriella, he said, "Where's my dinner you promised? Or is Joe dinner?" he said, laughing dryly.

"Dinner? I'm definitely not your dinner," Joe added.

She turned away from Ashton and her brother and looked out at Ashton's backyard. It was well-manicured. The grass was precisely cut, and she was surprised to see flowerbeds. She'd missed them earlier, too concerned about Ashton. She went off into her own world and didn't hear Ashton talking to her.

"Gab-ri-ella?"

Joe started laughing loudly. She heard his voice but just wasn't listening to what he was saying. "Are you tuning me out or what?" Speaking to Joe he said, "You'd think we were married." Joe looked at his sister and started laughing hysterically. Joe's laughter caught her attention.

Gabriella snapped out her reverie. "What'd I miss?"

Ashton pursed his lips, and shook his head as Joe said, "Nothing... Now what about dinner? Let's order in pizza from Pizzas, Pie & More. They deliver." He pulled out his phone and located the number. "Anything special?"

"Anything works for me," Ashton said.

"I know what my sister likes." Joe placed an order for a large, deep-dish pizza topped with hamburger, as well as a large, thin-crust, meat-lovers pizza. Turning to Ashton, he said, "Do you have anything to drink?"

Ashton started to stand, but Joe put out his hand to stop him. "Just tell me, I'll get it."

"What are you in the mood for? Beer, soda, wine?"

"A beer sounds terrific right about now."

Ashton pointed towards the mini-refrigerator underneath the countertop of the minibar. Joe strode to the refrigerator and looked over at her. She looked away, apparently not wanting anything to drink. She was in her own world—unsure where that was. She was worried about him not believing a word he said.

Joe returned to the table and pointed to Ashton's knee. "Let me take a look at that while we wait for our pizza." Joe squatted down in front of Ashton. It wasn't swollen, and he felt around. "I don't feel anything, and it isn't swollen. If you're still having problems in a few days, I'd say you should have an MRI. Otherwise, I think it's just bruised."

"That's my diagnosis, too. When I went down, I fell more onto my left side than anything—that's why I don't think I did anything. I'll watch it, but as I said, I don't think it's anything."

Gabriella walked over to the table and sat down. "Hey, I think I'll have a beer."

"Where have you been?"

"I guess I wasn't paying attention."

Ashton pointed in the direction of the mini-refrigerator. She started to rise when Joe hopped up and got one for her.

"You want one, too?" he asked Ashton.

"Nah, I don't think so. I'll just take a cola."

He grabbed Ashton a soda and Gabriella a beer. Handing off the drinks, he said, "This is a nice house. How long have you lived here?"

"It's been about four months."

"I remember when you bought it earlier this year." Joe walked over to the window and looked out across the backyard. "I didn't realize you had such a large yard."

"That's one of the things that attracted me to this house. I love the corner lot as it is larger than most of the properties along here. From what I could tell when I purchased it this winter, it looked like the previous owners maintained the yard, and that's important to me. I love all of the mature trees, and I was pleasantly surprised with the landscaping. I knew I wanted to build a pergola and a patio area for entertaining, outside of what's already here. I guess I'm going to have to put that on the back burner for another week or so. I'd hoped to have it built this weekend so I could stain it on my day off this week. I'd like to have it complete before fall kicks in."

"What are your plans beside the pergola?"

"I'm putting in a stone patio with a fire pit and in-ground lighting. It's coming right off the exterior entrance to my lower level. This winter, I plan on tearing apart the lower level, putting in a full bar and media room."

"Are you doing this all by yourself or are you contracting it out?"

"I hope to be able to do most of it myself. The plumbing and electrical I will definitely contract out. I've hung drywall before, so that's not an issue. We'll see how it goes, but I hope to have it done by the Superbowl—nothing like watching the Superbowl on a big screen TV."

No sooner had Ashton finished talking then the doorbell rang with their pizza delivery. Gabriella answered the door. "This smells delicious," she said as she put the pizzas down on the kitchen table. She'd already scouted out where the plates were, so she pulled them from the cabinet. The napkins were already sitting neatly on the table in a napkin holder.

Joe opened the box of deep-dish pizza and passed it over to Gabriella. He then flipped open the lid on the thin-crust pizza and grabbed a piece. "This is hot," Joe said as he took his first bite.

She stared down at her pizza. She didn't know what to think. They'd enjoyed their morning—and now this. She thought back to her earlier conversation with her mother. She just needed to let go and see where things went. The past was just that—the past. Ashton was different, not like—

She couldn't let her emotions travel back there. She'd come so far in the last several years. She'd regained her self-confidence and would just see where she and Ashton went from here. All she knew was that his fall really scared her. Thankfully, he seemed okay—just a little bruised up.

"Something wrong with your pizza?" Ashton asked as he took a huge bite of his. Sauce squished out over the crust, running down his hand. He licked it off and waited for her response. She slowly looked up at him, handing him a napkin to help clean up his mess. "I'll eat in a minute. Where's your powder room?"

"You mean bathroom?"

"Whatever. Just where is it?" Ashton pointed towards a closed door off the kitchen. She took off for the bathroom.

By the time she made her way to the bathroom, her hands were shaking uncontrollably. She didn't know why, they just were. All of her emotions came crashing down on her and she needed a minute to get herself under control. She thought a few moments alone would help her gather her herself. Ashton was fine and that's what mattered.

Leaning over towards Joe, Ashton whispered, "I don't get your sister. One minute she's friendly, and the next minute she's acting like I have the plague. I can't win with her."

"I think she's just worried about you. Gabriella gets this way when she's scared or troubled about something. She gets quiet, and when she does communicate, no one wants to be around her."

"Huh."

"She called me thinking she needed to take you to the emergency room. She'll settle down. Just give her some time."

"You know we didn't see eye-to-eye, and then yesterday she told me she had a revelation of sorts and was trying. I actually believed her last night and even today when I helped her in her classroom."

"Did you just say you helped her? Today?"

Ashton took a bite of his pizza and nodded.

"Well then, she must have had that revelation because normally she won't let anyone help her except Angelina. She's really particular with her room. You should feel honored."

"Well, then I do," he said. Looking up, he saw the bathroom door open and Gabriella reappear.

She sat down at the table and reached for a slice of her pizza. "Where can I find your utensils?" she asked. Gabriella liked to eat her pizza with a fork since deep-dish pizza was practically impossible to hold and she was able to eat more slowly and not devour her slice in one or two bites.

While they ate their dinner, Joe and Ashton discussed several different topics while she sat in her own world. She pretended to listen to their conversation, but her mind was going from point A to Z: from earlier that morning through that evening and his fall. She couldn't stop. She closed her eyes momentarily, gathered her thoughts, and then began eating. She finished her pizza and rinsed her plate and utensils off, placing them into the dishwasher. She returned to the table and closed the box that contained her pizza. She watched Joe and Ashton chow down on theirs.

"Wow, I'm stuffed," Joe said as he watched Ashton chase his remaining bite with the last of his cola.

"I am, too." Upon hearing that, Gabriella moved the remaining pieces of their pizza placing them into her pizza box. She closed the box again and strode over to the refrigerator and placed it in it.

Joe looked at his watch. "I hate to eat and run, but I'd better get going. I need to run by the hospital and see a patient before it gets too late. Gabriella, do you want me to run you home?"

Smiling at her brother, she said, "No, I think I'll walk home. Thanks, though."

"Are you sure?"

"Yeah. I'm good."

Ashton eased himself from the chair and walked Joe out. Gabriella finished tidying up the kitchen and waited for Ashton to return.

"I guess I'd better head on home." She said as Ashton reached for her hand.

"Come sit with me."

"Like I said, I'd better get home."

"What's your hurry? Is someone waiting for you?"

"Well, no." She didn't trust herself right now. Her emotions were running at an all-time high and she didn't want to do or say anything that would upset the progress she'd made in the last two days.

"Then, what's the problem? I just want to spend some uninterrupted time with you. Is that a lot to ask?"

"No, it's not."

Ashton grabbed her hand and pulled her into his family room. He led her over to the couch where he sat down and pulled her down next to him. She eased away from him slightly, putting more room between them on the couch.

"Do I smell or something?"

"Ah, no."

"Then, why did you move to the other end of the couch. You're in a different country all the way down there. It's not like I'm going to bite you."

"I know. I just like to settle into the corner." She drew her legs under her and leaned back into the curve of the couch. She closed her eyes and took a deep breath.

"Are you sure you're feeling alright? You don't seem like yourself."

She slowly opened her eyes. "I'm fine."

"Then why did you get so quiet when dinner came? And then you acted like you didn't want to eat. Out with it. What's up?"

"Nothing, really," she said as she clenched and

unclenched her fists.

He slid down the sofa and sat next to her, grabbing her clenched hands. "Gab-ri-ella, please tell me what's troubling you. And don't say nothing is, because something is."

Swallowing loudly, she hung her head.

He moved a hand to her chin and eased her head up so she would look him directly in the eyes. "Gab-ri-ella?"

Barely above a whisper, she said, "I told you. I don't—"

"I know what you told me, but tell me what's troubling you."

Taking a deep breath, she looked him directly in the eyes and said, "I thought you were really hurt. When I saw you start to fall, and then the ladder falling on you…"

"Hey, there," he said caressing her cheek. "I'm okay. I didn't get hurt." Glancing down towards his knee, he added, "I admit I was lucky. It could have been worse, but hey—I'm fine. No broken bones, no blood…" When he pulled back to study her more closely, she tugged her hand from his and wrapped her arms around herself. He could tell she was closing down. He didn't know what to say, so he asked her if she wanted to watch some television.

"No, in fact it's getting late, and I need to head on home."

"How about I drive you?"

"Ashton, I'm right around the corner. I'll be fine," she said as she stood. He scooted to the edge of the sofa and rose. She started down the hallway towards the front door and he followed her. She pulled open the door and turned back to him. "I'm glad you're okay. Take care of that knee," she said as she opened the screen door. Turning back before she stepped down to the sidewalk, she added, "I guess I'll see you around." And with that, Gabriella headed down the street towards her house.

She was hard to figure out. When he reviewed the last two days in his mind, he wondered what he really just wanted from Gabriella. Yes, he'd asked her out on a date, but what did he want—need from her? Friendship or something more? That was a question he would grapple with.

One minute she was warm and the next minute she was colder than cold. He watched her until she turned the corner. He hoped she wasn't regressing back to that cold, unfriendly person that she was before softball practice the night before. He closed the door on the night and headed back to his family room where he turned on the Rivermen game and watched them win another blow-out of a game.

Chapter Eleven

ONDAY, GABRIELLA WAS STILL TROUBLED
by Ashton's fall on Saturday evening. Sunday,
she'd spent the entire day cleaning and working in the
yard. It had been another warm and humid day, so
she worked outside in the yard early and then spent
the afternoon cleaning and doing laundry. While she
weeded and watered her flower beds, her mind drifted
back to Friday evening. She'd been surprised to say
the least when she drove up to the softball fields discovering Ashton was on her team.

She was even more surprised with his kindness at
Oxfords. He was friendly and really seemed like he
wanted to get to know her. When he asked her to go
out on a date, it practically floored her. Never did she
ever think he would ask her out, especially with the
way she treated him. She'd been cruel and that was
putting it mildly.

She knew she should have checked in on him yesterday, but she just couldn't get her arms around what was
happening between the two of them. Yes, she accepted
his offer to go on a date, but the two times she'd been

in his presence since, he never brought it up again. Did she imagine it? She knew she hadn't. Maybe he was having second thoughts and decided to let the offer pass.

Monday morning, she drove to Angelina's. They were going to the St. Louis Zoo for the day, but she wasn't sure how long they'd last since it was supposed to be another sweltering day. She pulled into Angelina's driveway right at eight o'clock. She was just getting ready to exit her car when she heard her name.

"Gabriella, are you ready for another scorcher? The zoo's going to be mighty hot," Alejandro said as she exited her car.

She met her brother on the driveway. She was carrying her ginormous bag that she'd taken to the Rivermen game.

"I see you have that infamous bag that you practically knocked Ashton out with."

She glared at her brother.

"Do you also have your fan and peanuts, too?"

"Will you stop with the sarcasm? Yes, I do, except this time I don't have peanuts—I have healthy snacks like carrots, celery sticks, and granola bars."

"Well, good for you." Alejandro was just about ready to climb into his car when he shouted out, "Hey, I heard about Ashton's accident. Is he alright?"

"I guess so. He was when I left there Saturday evening."

"You didn't go check on him yesterday?"

"No. Why should I? He said he was just fine. No injuries."

"Gabriella?"

"Alejandro, stop. Just stop. No, I didn't go check on him. I had plans, and he didn't fit into them."

"Like what? Cleaning?"

Her brother knew her too well. He knew exactly how she spent her weekend, especially during the summer months.

"I'm just giving you a hard time. You're not his keeper. I'm sure Joe and Alec will give him the once over. Stubborn, is all I can say. He should have gone and had it checked out."

"That's what I said, but what can you do with a grown man? He knows what's best for himself, right?" She said, chuckling as she made her way to the kitchen door. "I'll see you later."

"Have a good time and don't get too much sun."

"We won't," she called back as he started down the driveway.

Angelina met Gabriella at the kitchen door. Before Angelina could question her, she stormed through the open door with her hand held high, palm facing away from her, "Don't you start on me, too."

Angelina looked startled. Closing the kitchen door behind her, she raised her eyebrows in question.

"You look like you have no idea what I'm talking about."

"I don't."

"Huh. You mean Joe didn't call... Alejandro just stopped me in the driveway. He knew."

"Knew what? I'm clueless here." Gabriella spun around and looked at her best friend. "You don't know, do you?" Shaking her head, she looked at Gabriella.

Gabriella dropped her purse on the table and her tote bag on the floor next to her chair and sat down. "Ashton. It's about Ashton."

"Did something happen to him?"

"You could say so." Closing her eyes, Gabriella ran

her hands through her hair and placed her hands across her eyes. Sighing, she told her story. "I was taking my walk on Saturday. I ran into Mrs. Alma as she was watering her flowers. It was warm but not too warm, so after I left her, I decided to take a different route than my usual one. As I started down the street, I came across Ashton's house. I had no idea that he lived so close to me." Gabriella leaned back in her chair. "I crossed the street thinking I'd say hi since he was working in his side yard. He was on a ladder, hammering some wood." She stopped and thought for a second. "If I didn't see it myself, never in my wildest dreams would I think of Ashton as a carpenter or a builder, but he's building a pergola. I almost didn't believe him when he told me Saturday morning—"

Angelina put her hand up to stop her. "Hey, wait a minute. Back up here. You saw him Saturday morning?" Angelina stood and walked over to the coffee pot. She grabbed two mugs from the counter and poured both of them cups of coffee and returned to the table. "I think you've left out an important part of your day. Start over with... let's say Friday night. How was softball practice?"

"You know about that?"

"Well, that's one thing I do know about. You're both on the same team."

Gabriella poured half-n-half into her cup and stirred her coffee. She watched as the cream mixed with the coffee, turning it to a caramel color— just like she liked. "It seems everyone knew about us being on the same team except the two of us. Anyway, we made it through practice unscathed. We went to Oxfords with the rest of the team after practice, and I have to say I had a nice time with him." She took a sip of her coffee while Angelina sat waiting for her friend to continue her story. Since she was questioning whether or not they were going on a date, she decided not to mention it.

"Saturday morning, I got up early. After my little ordeal with Ashton at school on Friday, I still needed to finish up my classroom. I went to Mochas & Coffee where I ran into him. He volunteered to help me in my classroom, so I took him up on it since I needed the help."

"I didn't think you liked anyone helping you in your classroom."

"I don't really unless it's you, but he asked if he could help, and I decided to take him up on his offer." She took another sip of her coffee. She added another drop or two of half-n-half and swirled. "Now about Saturday night. I saw Ashton on a ladder. As I approached, he was lifting a piece of lumber. It clipped his ladder and knocked him over. I stood there helpless in the street watching him fall. All I could do was yell his name."

"Was he alright?"

"Well, he said he was fine, but he was having problems with his knee. Stubborn as he is, he wouldn't let me take him to the emergency room. So, after I got him inside, I told him I'd go get us dinner. Instead, I hurried home and phoned Joe who came to the rescue. He checked him over and thought it was just a bruise."

"Well, I wonder when Alejandro found out. He didn't say a thing to me." Angelina narrowed her eyes a bit.

"That's weird that he didn't say anything," Gabriella said.

"Yeah it is…" Angelina trailed off. She shook her head and said, "Did Alejandro say anything else?"

"Only to have fun and stay out of the sun—like we could do that at the zoo."

"Well, on that note, we'd better get the kids up if we plan on getting there when the zoo opens."

It didn't take much effort on either of their parts to get the children up. Angelina took care of getting Angel dressed, and when Gabriella went to get Matthew up she found him already dressed and putting on his shoes.

"Ready?"

"I am. I can't wait to go to the zoo. It seems like its been forever." Matthew could be melodramatic at times and today was one of them.

They got to the zoo fifteen minutes before the gates opened. They were lucky to find one of the free parking spaces right outside the entrance.

By the time Angelina secured Angel in her stroller, the gates had opened. The St. Louis Zoo was a free zoo except for the Children's Zoo that was attached. They also had a program called Zoo Parents. Anyone could adopt an animal and the donation went towards the animal's care. Alejandro had surprised Matthew and adopted a sea lion in his name. When they'd first visited the zoo after deciding to adopt Matthew, he'd called them 'Mom and Dad' for the first time in front of the sea lion exhibit. Both Angelina and Alejandro thought it a momentous time in their lives and decided to always remember it. And what better way than adopting the animal that brought their family full circle? Gabriella thought it was precious.

They made their way to the Children's Zoo when Matthew asked to push Angel's stroller. He was a proud brother and wanted to show off his sister.

"Be careful with her," Angelina called out as Matthew sped ahead. They walked around visiting the various animal exhibits when Matthew stopped at the outdoor play area. "Can we play?"

"Sure. Just watch your sister." Matthew unstrapped Angel from her stroller and picked her up, placing her gently on the ground.

"Come on Angel, let's go." Ever careful of his sister, Matthew carried her to the animal rockers where he helped her onto a turtle. "Hold on, Angel," Matthew called as he gently pushed her. She laughed in glee as she rocked back and forth.

"He's so good with her," Gabriella said, watching her niece and nephew.

"He is."

They sat watching the kids.

"Mom, can we go visit the sea lions next?"

"Of course we can," Angelina called back and turned to Gabriella, "We never miss the sea lions."

"I know you don't. I remember the day you had that break through with him. When he called you Mom and Alejandro Dad for the first time. I didn't think I'd stop crying after you told me."

"Yeah, that was a special day." They sat a while longer when Angelina asked, "So, tell me the truth—what's really going on between you and Ashton?"

Gabriella had been waiting for that question since she first arrived at Angelina's that morning. They were the best of friends and neither of them held back when something was on their minds. But this was hard. She started chewing on her lower lip.

"Gabriella?"

"I don't know for sure."

"What do you mean?"

"Well, I don't even know." She thought for a second and decided to tell her about Ashton asking her out. "He asked me out."

"You mean on a date?"

"Umm…" That was an excellent question.

"Either he did or he didn't."

"Well, I think he did." Gabriella went on to explain that even though they'd been together twice since he'd asked for the date, he hadn't mentioned it again.

"Well, how do you feel about it?"

"That's the problem. I'm not sure."

"What do you mean?"

"I want to go out with him, but I'm scared. Scared that I'll ruin it. Angelina, even though I've tried really hard, I just can't get over how he treated Alejandro and Matthew. And I'm afraid…"

"Afraid because you don't want to experience what happened before?"

"Yeah. My break-up really affected me. I haven't dated much because I don't want to get hurt like that again. It about killed me."

"I know it did, but from where I'm sitting, if you don't at least give it a try you'll always wonder if he was the one that got away." She thought for a second. "I almost let that happen with Alejandro. He kept Tammy and Michael from me, and that almost ruined our relationship. If I hadn't been caught in that mini-flash flood, I don't think we'd have found our way back to one another. Gabriella, you need to let go of the past if you want a future. Trust in him and in time you'll learn to put the past behind you. We've forgiven him, and I think it's time you did, too."

"Mom, can we go?"

Angelina reached for Gabriella's hand. Squeezing it gently, she called back to Matthew, "Put your sister back in the stroller, okay?"

"Okay," Matthew exuberantly shouted.

Angelina smiled at her friend. Gabriella smiled back.

Angelina squeezed Gabriella's hand one last time before saying, "Let's go visit the sea lions."

Nodding at her friend, Gabriella leaned over and kissed her cheek. "Thank you, Angelina. I don't know what I'd do without you in my life."

"Right back at you, friend."

Matthew strolled up with Angel. They headed off to the sea lions exhibit, then called it a day. The temperatures were spiking and Angel was ready for a nap. As they drove home, Gabriella contemplated what she really wanted from Ashton.

Ashton walked into the office and was immediately greeted by both Alec and Joe. "So, how's the knee?" asked Alec. "I heard you took a little fall."

"You could say that," Ashton said as he made his way towards his office with both brothers in pursuit. He placed his briefcase on his desk and turned to sit down and was surprised to see they were still with him. "Is there a meeting I missed? I'm not late, am I?"

"No, you're not," said Joe. "We have plenty of time before our staff meeting. We just wanted to make sure you were alright."

Ashton leaned against his desk and ran his hand across his jaw. Smirking at the two of them, he thought for a second then said, "Yeah, I'm fine. I've got one hell of a bruise, and it's a little sore, but I think I'll survive." He chuckled and added, "Thanks for the concern. That's more than I received from you sister."

"I thought she stayed after I left Saturday evening."

"She did, and she seemed pretty upset after I fell. With the way she acted, I certainly thought she'd check in yesterday, but she didn't. I haven't seen or heard from her since she left in a hurry shortly after your departure. When I think I've figured her out, she reverts back to her—"

"We know what you mean," said Joe. "As I told you last Saturday, she gets that way when she gets scared. Let it go and see what happens."

Ashton nodded and moved towards his chair. "Gentlemen, I hate to be rude, but I have a couple of things I need to do before our staff meeting."

Joe and Alec said their goodbyes and headed for their respective offices. As they walked towards their offices, Alec commented on Ashton's knee, "He seems like he's doing alright."

"Yeah, he's stubborn just like us and didn't want to own up to the fact that he was hurting at the time. His limp was pretty pronounced Saturday, but I didn't notice anything out of the ordinary when he walked in today."

"I'd say he's fine," Alec said, looking at his watch. "Fifteen minutes until our meeting starts. I'm going to go get a cup of coffee. I'll see you in the conference room."

Alec headed off to the coffee bar while Joe went to his office. He was glad that Ashton was okay. He was lucky that he didn't hit his head or break a limb when he fell from the ladder.

Before Gabriella knew it, the week was over. She and Angelina had gone to the zoo and Grant's Farm. She didn't know how they made it past noon each day due to the sweltering heat. She spent Thursday and Friday at St. Margaret's in faculty meetings. Gabriella stayed late both days finishing up the last of the preparations in her classroom. School began the following Monday.

Gabriella left school at five o'clock. She figured she had plenty of time to shower and change before heading off to their first softball game. She hadn't spoken with Ashton all week and wasn't sure how he was doing since his fall. She'd been afraid to seek him out. Her emotions had been all over the place during the week. She'd even dreamed of him falling off the ladder, only her dreams didn't end as positively as reality.

Gabriella had just finished her shower and had thrown her jersey on when she heard the doorbell ring. She wasn't expecting anyone and held off answering it until it rang a second time. She threw her wet hair up into a ponytail and made her way to the door. She peeked out the living room window and was surprised to see Ashton at her door.

Gabriella threw open the door just as the he started down the walkway. "Ashton," she called out. He slowly turned around and retraced his steps.

"I didn't think you were home."

"I was just finishing up getting dressed. Come on in." Gabriella stepped away from the doorway and watched him as he walked up the stairs into her house. He looked like he'd just come from the clinic as he was dressed in dark blue pants and a white long sleeved shirt. The top buttons of his shirt were open and she noticed that he wore a t-shirt underneath his dress shirt.

"I thought I'd stop by on my way home."

She looked at him, still unsure why he stopped by.

"I'm not going to play this evening. My knee's still a little tender, and I don't want to aggravate it. I'll be in playing form next week for sure."

Gabriella led him to her kitchen where she grabbed her water bottle and filled it with water. "See, I was right. You should have gone to the ER."

Shaking his head, he reached for her arm. "Gab-ri-ella, I am fine. I'm just taking it easy."

"Whatever," she said as she pulled away from him and reached for her duffle bag. "I've got to finish getting ready, so you've gotta go."

"Stop it. Will you at least listen to what I have to say?" He went to her side and reached for her hand, stopping her as she zipped her bag closed. "I did go see my doctor. I'm fine. Just a bruise, like I thought. The real reason why I'm not playing is I've been up since yesterday and I'm tired and don't want to chance it."

She looked at him, not quite understanding what he was saying.

"I was at the hospital all night with a sick child and then had clinic today. I plan on being at the game, cheering you on. I just don't think it's in my best interest to play. That's all."

Gabriella tightened her lips. She was still shocked by his presence and was trying to wrap her head around what he'd just said to her. She couldn't look at him. He placed his hand on her shoulder and leaned down, trying to get her attention. He stared at her until she looked him directly in the eyes.

"What?" she barked at him.

"Come on and get your things. I'll take you to the

game."

She wanted to be mad at him, but she couldn't. She was the one that hadn't checked in on him after his fall. She knew how tired he must be after an overnight at the hospital. Even if he didn't have a bad knee, he was smart not playing. She didn't know what to say, so she finished gathering her things, grabbed her ball cap, and headed towards the door. Ashton followed her out the door and watched as she turned to lock the door.

"Are we good?" he asked as he led her to his car.

She stopped halfway down the walkway, turned towards him, and nodded, "Yeah, we're good" she said and then added, "at least for now."

He chuckled as he opened her car door. Sitting down, she slid her bag under her legs and looked up at him as he closed her door. He was shaking his head as he turned away from her.

Chapter Twelve

IN WHAT SEEMED LIKE THE blink of an eye, the first week of school passed and Gabriella again found herself getting ready for the Friday night softball game. Surprisingly, they had won their first game. Ox had been so excited that he'd sprung for everyone's drinks again.

Gabriella was tired from her first week, getting back in the swing with a new class. It always took her a few weeks to settle in getting to know her students. Almost immediately, she knew this class was going to be a challenge. They were extremely talkative, and she had more than her fair share of special needs children. Several of her students left her classroom during the day to receive classes more designed to fit their needs. She hoped that she had the strength to get through the school year. This was going to be the most challenging class she'd taught in her ten years of teaching.

She sat down on the couch to put her tennis shoes on and decided to close her eyes for just a minute. The next thing she knew, she heard a pounding on her front door. She couldn't understand why her visitor hadn't used the doorbell—it was in perfectly good working order. As she jumped from the couch, she stumbled over her shoes and almost fell on her face. She caught her balance and made her way to the door. In a huff, she threw open the door and was almost met with the fist of her visitor as he went to knock on the door again.   Gabriella stumbled backward and this time she landed on the floor.

She caught her breath just as Ashton made his way to her side. "What the hell are you doing?" she said as she came face to face with him.

He crouched down in front of her and brushed her hair behind her ear, "Are you okay? I was worried when you didn't answer."

"Worried, huh?" she said as she pulled away from his hand. "Let me repeat my question—what are you doing here?" She looked him over. He was dressed in shorts and his softball jersey. She assumed he was going to play.

"I came to pick you up before the game. When you didn't answer the doorbell, I knocked. That's when you decided to finally answer."

Gabriella shook her head and made an effort to stand. Her stockinged foot slid across the hardwood and she ended back up on the floor. He stood and held out his hand. She looked at it.

"Take it, will you?"

She reached for his hand and he pulled her to her feet. "Now, tell me what's up with you."

She retraced her steps to the family room where her tennis shoes were just where she'd left them, beside the couch. She sat down and reached for her shoes.

Ashton watched as she struggled to get them on. "Having problems?"

She looked up at him and rolled her eyes. "To answer your question, I guess I dozed off." She brushed her hand across her forehead and leaned back against the couch.

"You look like you've been through the ringer. What's up?"

"First week of school. It's always like this as I get back into the swing of things, except this year I'm afraid every week is going to be this exhausting. I'm afraid this is going to be the class from—"

He didn't let her finish her statement. He grabbed her hand and pulled her from the couch. "Come on, let's go. We're going to be late. You'll feel better once you start moving around." He stopped abruptly and she ran right into him. "Before I know it, you'll be in rare form, attacking me as always." He grabbed her duffle bag as they neared the door. He waited while she locked the door and then reached for her hand. Surprisingly, she wrapped her hand in his and followed him to his car. It was a comfortable feeling holding his hand after a long week.

Within minutes, they were at the park. Of course, they were late. As soon as they made their way to the dugout, Jane Gold approached Gabriella. "Hey, you okay? I wasn't sure you'd show up after what happened today."

Gabriella's week ended with two students getting into an argument on the playground. One of her student's hauled off and punched the other in the face. She spent the rest of her day dealing with the aftermath. She hoped that this was an isolated incident as everyone got to know one another, but she wasn't sure. The student who led the attack was new to St. Margaret's. His parents were going through a divorce and he wasn't adjusting well to his new living arrangements and being forced away from his friends.

When she met with Jake and his parents, she could feel the tension all around the room. She liked him and prayed that he'd soon adjust to his new surroundings. He was living with his father and wondered if that was the problem. Maybe he needed his mom a little more as he got the feel of his new school and learned how to make new friends.

Ashton stopped and turned back when he heard Jane speaking with Gabriella. He wondered what her comment was all about but acted like he hadn't heard her.

The game started and she just didn't seem herself. He knew she was a much better player than how she was playing.

She seemed disgusted with herself and asked to be pulled from the line-up. "Hey, Ox... I need to sit out the rest of the game. I'm going to make us lose and—"

"Don't worry about it, Gabby. I understand."

She had no energy left in her body and threw herself down onto the bench. Ashton watched her from the field as the opposing team was at bat. Something must have really upset her.

Their team had won again and were ready to celebrate a second win at Oxfords.

Ox approached Gabby. "You coming?"

"Not tonight, Ox. I'm really beat. I'll see you next week." She grabbed her stuff and started to head off the field.

Ashton caught up with her. "Hey, wait up. Did you forget that I drove?"

Turning slightly, she slowed her pace and said, "Nah, I just wanted to get a head start. Ashton, can you run me home first before going to Oxfords? I need to go home and go to bed."

He nodded and watched her as she got into the car. She seemed stiff as she folded herself into the car. "Are you sure it's not more than being tired? Gabby, you look like you can hardly move."

"I'll be fine. I just need a good night's sleep."

Ashton drove her home and walked her to her door.

"Thanks for the ride." She unlocked her door and turned back to him. "Have a good time with the gang."

"I don't think I'm going to go. It won't be the same without you."

"I'm not so sure about that. See you next week." And with that, Gabriella closed the door behind her. Ashton was also tired and elected to go home instead of joining the rest of his teammates. He wondered what had upset her. He knew the beginning of the school year was trying, adjusting to a new schedule and leaning the personalities of her new students, but whatever was bothering her seemed so much more. He decided to see how she was the following week and then he'd try and talk to her.

Gabriella's second week of the school year was much better than her first. Jake seemed to be making friends and adjusting to his new school. Monday morning, Jake came in with three letters. One for her, Mary, and Isiah, the child he punched. They were apology letters that were written from the heart. Jake told her what he did Friday was not him. He was having a difficult time with all of the changes that had been forced upon him in such a short amount of time. He asked if he could hug her. He wanted to have a do-over and show her that he wasn't who he appeared to be.

Jake told her he had to make the best of the situation. He missed his old friends, but he also realized that he had to make new ones, and that was what he was going to do. By the end of the week, Jake had not only started making friends, but he also reached out to Isiah. She smiled knowing they'd become friends.

Gabriella got home early enough to shower and change, and waited for Ashton on her front steps. They hadn't spoken all week but she just knew he'd be stopping by to pick her up. She had been surprised both times when he'd stopped by before the game. Instead of being reactive to his appearance, she decided to be proactive and anxiously waited for him.

She sat there on her steps until she realized that she would be late to the game if she didn't leave. She hurried to her car and made it to the game just in time.

As she pulled into the parking lot, Ashton's car was nowhere to be seen. She wondered where he was. She warmed up with Jane. She was distracted and, on two occasions, missed the ball Jane had tossed to her.

"What's up, Gabriella? I threw it right to you."

"Sorry, I guess my mind was elsewhere." The game started and still no Ashton. She was worried about him. With the little she knew about him, he would have called or at least stopped by. Something was wrong, she just knew it.

After the third inning, she approached Ox. "Hey Ox, where's Ashton?"

"I don't know. I got a message from him late this afternoon and all he said was he wouldn't be here tonight."

"Huh," Gabriella said as she headed to the lead off circle. She was surprised by her performance with as

distracted as she was. She got a hit in every at bat
and made the game winning play with two outs and
the bases loaded. A line drive had been hit directly in
front of her face. Initially, she didn't think she'd get
her glove up fast enough. She threw her glove in front
of her face and caught the ball. The force behind the
line drive caused her glove to smack her in the face.
"Ump," she groaned. She was thankful she was able to
catch the ball—otherwise she'd have ended up with a
broken nose. Overall, she was pleased with her night.
She more than made up for her poor performance
from the week before. She just wished he'd been there
to see it.

She followed everyone to Oxfords. She sat next to
Clifford and did her best to keep a smile on her face,
but it didn't last. She was concerned about Ashton.
Why hadn't he told her he wasn't coming? And why
was she so bothered by his lack of communication? It's
not as though they were dating or anything.

"Hey, where's your boyfriend?"

"Boyfriend?"

"Yeah, Ashton."

"He's not my boyfriend." Playing with the straw in
her drink she added, "And to answer your question, I
have no idea. I haven't spoken to him since last week."
She wondered where he was, but she wasn't his keeper.
She barely knew him and she was still unsure about
him in general. She was trying to get along with him
and she would continue to. If he wanted her to know
where he was, he'd tell her.

Ashton found himself sitting in the living room of

the Castillo's. Javier Castillo was his Little Brother. His
mother Jacinta had phoned him just as he was getting
ready to leave for the day. As soon as he answered,
Jacinta was crying with worry over her son. "Ashton,
I can't find Javier. He hasn't come home from his
friend's house." He instructed her to phone the police
while he grabbed his things and headed out the door,
only remembering to phone Ox that he wouldn't be
at the game.

By the time he arrived at the Castillo's, the police had
located Javier. Ashton sat down and listened to Javier
explain his disappearance. "Ashton, I missed you. I
wanted you to see my new helicopter, so I decided to
walk to your house."

"Javier, do you think that was wise? First of all,
you've never been to my house, and secondly I live
like ten miles from here."

"I know you live in Kirkwood."

"That's right, but—"

Javier didn't want to listen to his scolding. He knew
he was wrong. "I'm tired, Mom. Can I go lie down
now?"

Jacinta turned to her son. "Yes, you may, Javier, but I
think you owe—"

Before his mother could say another word, he added,
"I'm sorry, Mom. I'm sorry I worried you. I just
wanted to show Ashton."

"I know, son, but next time please tell me before you
go and act, okay?"

Frowning, Javier knew he'd done wrong. "I understand Mom. I'm sorry that you had to come all the
way over here, Ashton. I think I learned my lesson."

Javier stood and hugged both his mother and Ashton. He was a good child who terribly missed a father

figure. His father had been killed two years earlier on Christmas Eve and he was still having a hard time adjusting to life without his father. "Ashton, he misses his father so much. I don't know what I am going to do."

"I'll tell you what we're going to do. I will check on him every day, and when my schedule permits, we'll go out and do what every child and their father does. We'll go to the park, we'll play soccer. I'll do whatever it takes to make him miss his father less. Jacinta, he's a good boy. A six-year-old doesn't know right from wrong. In his mind, he wanted to see me and he was doing everything in his power to show me that helicopter. We're just lucky that he got thirsty, went into that convenience store, and encountered that police officer. He's fine. Now, why don't you go tuck him in to bed?"

"Thank you, Ashton. He's so lucky to have you as a Big Brother. I'll be in touch," Jacinta said as she walked out of the room. He watched her until she entered Javier's bedroom, then he got up and left the house.

Ashton got into his car and started driving. His mind drifted through the various stages of his childhood. He hadn't lost his father when he was young, but it felt like he had. Ashton's father had been a resort owner in Branson, Missouri. His father, Ian, was from old money. He had rarely seen his father, as his life was the resort. He'd worked eighteen-hour days, often missing holidays, birthdays, and special occasions. His father had never put him first in his life. It had always been work, work, work.

His mother, Jana, blamed her troubled marriage on Ashton. She'd always tell him that she wished he'd never come along because her marriage with his father had been wonderful until she'd become pregnant with him.

Ashton as a little boy heard his mother's gripes anytime she wanted something and his father wouldn't comply. On top of his relationship with his parents, he'd been a rather sick child when he was young. He'd had asthma and was constantly in the hospital because his mother had neglected the warning signs. On several occasions, his nannies were the ones who had called the ambulance and went with him to the hospital. His mother ignored him except when she had to parade him around their wealthy friends during special occasions at the resort. Otherwise, Ashton was far from either of his parents' minds.

He rarely thought of his childhood. He presumed his encounter with Javier brought out the memories he'd so carefully buried away. He had so few happy ones, he only remembered the painful times when he thought of his youth, and he carried those around daily.

When Ashton hit grade school, his mother had had enough of him and his asthma attacks and sent him away to boarding school. He'd only seen his parents during Christmas break. Otherwise, he stayed at school, even during the summer. He hated his mother for her treatment of him. She was the one with the cruel and hurtful comments that still remained with him today. He'd disliked his father as well because he ignored him, but he'd never spoken meanly to Ashton. Because he had never been there to speak with him. What he had were parents in name only.

Ashton's father died five years ago and his mother still lived in Branson in their mansion on the hill that overlooked the town. He rarely spoke to her, let alone saw her. When he thought about it, he hadn't seen his mother since his father's funeral, and even then he'd left as soon as the casket was lowered into the ground. He'd never looked back.

He carried around the pain of his childhood on his shoulders every day. And that's why he decided to be a Big Brother. He was matched up with Javier and he wanted to be there for him whenever he needed him. He'd never turn his back on Javier. Never. And that's why he couldn't have made it to the softball game that day. Javier needed him and he wasn't going to let him down.

He didn't know how, but he'd somehow made it home. He'd been driving in a fog of emotions since leaving the Castillo home. As he pulled up to his house, he thought about heading over to Oxfords, but then decided against it. He pulled into his garage and turned off the motor. He sat there for a few moments before he exited the car and walked into his house.

Ashton headed straight for the bar, pouring himself a stiff drink. He downed his bourbon and poured a second glass. He made his way to the family room where he sat down on the couch and rehashed his evening. He couldn't replace Javier's father, but he could be his mentor and role model and point Javier in the right direction.

In all honesty, he didn't know how he'd become the doctor he was today. He thanked John for taking him under his wing and helping him straighten himself out. When they'd first met, Ashton had had the worst bedside manner around. But through John's tutelage, along with that of Alec and Joe, he was turning into a man that he was starting to become proud of. He'd had a rough start at first, and he'd come a long way since he first joined the practice. He'd learned a lot when he'd been dragged into Alec's office and told he needed to toe the line or jump off the train. His experience with Alejandro and Matthew taught him a lesson he'd never forget. He was a better man and a better doctor by that experience. He'd be even better with Javier in his life.

Chapter Thirteen

A NGELINA HAD JOINED ALEJANDRO ON one of his business trips, and Gabriella was watching the kids. Originally, Angelina was going to drop the kids off at her mom's house since Gabriella's last softball game was that evening, and then Gabriella was going to pick them up afterwards. But Maria told Gabriella to have fun and go out with everyone after the game—the kids could stay with her for the night as she needed her grandma time. Gabriella didn't want to take advantage of her mom, but Angelina warned her that Maria would probably try and keep the kids overnight. Angelina was fine with that as Maria doted on her grandchildren. In the end, Gabriella agreed and told her mom she would pick them up bright and early Saturday morning.

Gabriella had learned her lesson the previous week and decided to drive herself to the game. When she pulled up, she saw Ashton's car, and Ashton warming up with Perry. He and Perry were discussing something about healthcare. As soon as Ashton saw her, he stopped playing catch with Perry and headed in her direction.

"Gab–ri–ella," he called across the field.

She narrowed her eyes at him—she absolutely hated it when he said her name that way.

"Gab–ri–ella, wait up," he called as she headed in the opposite direction. He jogged to her side and grabbed ahold of her arm, stopping her mid-stride. "What's wrong? Didn't you hear me call your name?"

She stared him down.

"Hey, I'm sorry about that. I know you don't like it when I string out your name, but after all you were halfway across the parking lot, and I had to get your attention."

"That you did," she stated as she broke loose of his hold and headed for the dugout.

"Hey, wait up," he called to her, but she was hurrying away from him. She was upset with him as she hadn't seen or spoken with him in what seemed like weeks. What about their so-called date? That had yet to materialize.

The game began, and before they knew it, it was the bottom of the seventh inning and they were behind by three runs. St. Margaret's was the last to bat. Ox led off the inning with a double to right field. He advanced to third base when the right fielder bobbled the ball. Next up was Oscar. He was heckled by the crowd, shouting comments about him being a car salesman. He struck out and turned to the crowd and bowed. He received quite a few laughs as he walked off the field.

Christy was the next up to bat. Everyone knew she was an attorney so she wasn't bothered by noise from the opposing team. She singled to right field and Ox scored. They were losing 3-1 with one out. Liz, the florist, followed Christy. She broke under the pressure and struck out.

Now, there were two outs and they were losing by two runs with Christy on base. Ashton could tie the score and possibly throw it into extra innings. He was at bat and had a count of three balls and two strikes. One more strike and the game and season would be over. He stepped out of the batter's box and caught Gabriella's eye. Amazingly, she smiled at him after having ignored him most of the game. He hoped that she'd gotten over whatever had irked her. He stepped back in and waited for the pitch. The pitcher wound up and threw the ball. Ashton couldn't move quickly enough and was struck in the hip with the ball. He at least kept their hopes alive and walked to first base.

Next up was Gabriella. She'd definitely had an off night, striking out at all three of her plate appearances. She walked to the batter's box and cocked the bat on her shoulder. She waited for the pitch and watched as it crossed the plate. "Strike one," yelled the umpire.

"She's going to strike out, you know she will," yelled someone from the opposing team's dugout. Gabriella stepped out of the batter's box and glared towards their dugout.

Ashton knew by the look on her face that she wasn't happy with the comments that were being thrown her way. She stepped back in and watched as the next pitch was delivered. She swung and missed.

"Strike two," yelled the umpire. St. Margaret's was down to one strike.

Gabriella stepped out again and looked towards Ashton who was standing on first base. He pointed at her and smiled. She took another practice swing and stepped back into the batter's box. She waited and waited until the pitch was delivered. She watched the ball as it left the pitcher's hand and headed her way. She waited and then swung. The ball loudly cracked off the aluminum bat and flew into center field, well over the center fielder's head.

Christy flew around third base and easily made it home. The center fielder was still running to the ball when Ashton flew across home plate. Gabriella chugged her way around the bases. Just as she rounded third base the ball was leaving the outfield. She was going for broke. She ran as fast as she could, and just as she got within a few feet of home plate, she dropped down and started her slide. The catcher was standing at home plate, blocking the plate. Gabriella and the ball made it there at the same time. She plowed into the catcher, causing the catcher to flat out miss the ball. She had scored the winning run.

Ashton started jumping and turned to congratulate Gabriella, but she was lying on the ground, not moving. He immediately rushed to her side. Not only had the catcher got banged up in the collision, but so had Gabriella. Ashton kneeled on the ground, calmly saying, "Gabriella, Gabriella, are you okay?"

Slowly she opened her eyes. A smile broke across her face.

"We won?"

"We did. Are you injured?"

Gabriella tried to stand up, applying pressure to her hands. That's when she yelped in pain and sat back down.

"What is it?" Ashton whispered. "Is it your ankle, your leg? What hurts?"

She pulled her right hand towards her and tried moving it about. "I think I may have jammed my wrist. I'm having problems moving my hand."

"Here, let me take a look."

The rest of the team was joyously celebrating their win that they were oblivious to what was happening at home plate. After a few moments, Ox finally approached them. Ashton had his arms around her and was helping her stand.

"Gabby, are you hurt?"

"I'm okay," she said as she glanced up at Ashton. "Just give me a minute." Ox turned and went to shake hands with the other team while Ashton helped her from the field.

"Here, sit down," Ashton said as he led her to the dugout. "I want to look at your hand."

She sat down and watched as he gingerly moved her wrist about. Thankfully, she didn't seem to be in too much pain. Then he touched her hand and she pulled back. "Let me look at your hand a little more closely." He reached again for her hand and studied it. "Try and move your fingers." He watched as she moved each finger individually. "Does that hurt?"

"Not so much anymore. I just jammed it in my collision with the catcher. I'm sure it will be alright." Pulling her hand back she added, "Let's go celebrate."

"Not so fast, missy," he said. "I think you should have an x-ray. I'm taking you to the ER."

"Nope, not going. I'm going with everyone else to Ox's and having myself a cold beer."

"Gabriella, I really think you should have this looked at."

"Hmm," she said. "Seems like we've been down this road before. I'm sure my hand's fine. Now are you coming or not?"

Ashton smirked as he recalled the same conversation

she'd had with him when he fell off the ladder. He decided not to make a big deal of it—he'd watch over her at the celebration and then decide what she should do.

All of the players and their wives or significant others met at Ox's shortly after the game, including Fr. Xavier. He'd missed a good part of the entire season because he'd been traveling throughout Europe with a group from St. Margaret's. They'd been gone for three weeks and everyone was thankful that he was able to celebrate their victory. "The season was sure a quick one," Fr. Xavier commented.

"It was experimental since we've never had a fall season. Since this year went so well, I hope to encourage additional parishes to join us. I'm hoping to have a six or eight game season next year," Ox said as he served them their drinks.

While everyone was deciding on what they were going to order, Ashton put his arm around her shoulder and leaned in close, whispering in her ear, "Be honest with me, how is your hand?"

She kept staring ahead and decided she didn't want to answer him. She didn't want him to know how badly it hurt. He pulled her against his side and leaned in so he could look into her eyes. "Come on, now Gabby. Be honest with me. How is your hand?"

"Fine," was her quick response. With her one word answer, he knew she had to be in pain or else she would have jabbered on and on to get him to stop. He didn't want to make a scene, so he elected to end their one-sided conversation for the moment. He stood and headed over to chat with Abe.

She could hear them talking, referencing some kind of attorney lingo and decided to just sit there quietly until their food was served. She watched Ashton move about the room. When he finished speaking with Abe, he moved on to Gerry. She heard him ask when the best time would be to drop his car off for an oil change. Next he spoke with Joy, Ox's wife, about planning a party in the next couple of weeks to celebrate their winning season.

Before she knew it, Ashton was back at her side chomping into the greasy cheeseburger that he'd ordered. She watched him drag one french fry and then another through some honey mustard sauce. She shook her head, watching him savor the combined flavors. She couldn't understand his choice in sauces. *Honey and mustard, ew.*

Gabriella looked at him out of the corner of her eye as he took a bite of his burger. She felt his eyes on her as she moved in to grab her sandwich, only to pull back her right hand. She knew by the look on his face that he wanted to drop everything and take her to the ER.

In time, she figured out a way to eat her sandwich. Several of her teammates inquired about her hand as they were leaving. She just smiled and said she was just fine.

She wanted to out-sit him and was waiting for him to leave before leaving herself. Then, he put his arm around her shoulders again and said, "You finished?"

She nodded.

"Let's say our goodbyes and go."

She was tired and in pain. She was thankful that she'd agreed to leave the kids at her parents' house for the evening. She'd go home and have a good night's sleep and get them in the morning.

It took them another half hour before they left the

bar. She'd run into several families from her neighborhood. She'd introduced Ashton, but never went into
what their relationship was all about. She still wasn't
sure what they were, especially since he hadn't brought
up their date since their first night at Oxfords.

Ashton reached for her hand as they neared the
door, but she pulled away. He shook his head, realizing Gabriella wanted nothing to do with him, yet
again. He hoped they'd moved on and were beginning to forge a friendship, but now he wondered. He'd
noticed a significant change in her at the outset of the
night. She seemed reserved. *Now what did I do?* He
wondered. Then he realized that they hadn't spoken in
two weeks since he'd missed the game the week before
when he was dealing with Javier's situation. Maybe
that's what it was about. In the end, he decided he
wasn't going to push her. Either she had an injured
hand or she didn't. He was going to let her deal with
it in her own way.

The next morning, Gabriella jumped up out of bed,
forgetting about her hand. She reached for her hair-
brush and her game-winning slide came rushing back
on her. Her hand still ached. She knew she'd been
stubborn and should have listened to Ashton the night
before. She decided she'd let her dad look at it and
then would decide if she needed an x-ray or not.

She arrived at her parents' right at eight o'clock. She
walked in the back door and discovered her mother
trying to get an eleven-month-old Angel to eat her
cereal. Angel wanted nothing to do with her food and
even pushed her bowl off the highchair. Luckily, she

was able to get there right before the bowl crashed to the ground, splattering her cereal all over the floor.

"She doesn't want to eat. That's not like her," Maria said as she handed Angel her bottle. Her niece even pushed that away. "I guess she misses her mom," Maria said as she went to pour Gabriella a cup of coffee.

"I'm sure that's all it is," Gabriella said. "Hey, is Dad here?"

"No, he left early this morning. He's playing a round of golf, and then this afternoon we're leaving for the lake."

"Oh, I forgot about that." Her parents' decision to take a mini-vacation at the lake was the real reason why Gabriella was watching the kids. "I'm sorry I missed him," she added as she glanced at her hand. *So much for his opinion*, she thought to herself.

She watched her niece. She looked alright, but she kept tugging on her ear. Gabriella got caught up in conversation with her mother and lost track of time. In the midst of their chat, Matthew appeared and wanted to leave. He had just gotten a new set of Legos and wanted to go home and put them together. Something about a pirate ship is all Gabriella could get out of him.

Gabriella packed up the kids and headed to Alejandro's. She was staying at their house until they returned from their trip sometime late Monday afternoon. St. Margaret's was closed on Monday because of staff meetings, so Gabriella had the day off.

As soon as she unlocked the door, Angel started screaming. She had no idea why she was crying and decided she may be hungry since she hadn't eaten a bite at Maria's. For hours Gabriella tried everything that she could think of to settle her niece, but nothing worked. When she finally looked at the time, it was almost five o'clock, and she knew her parents had already left for the lake, so she couldn't have her dad look at Angel. She wondered if Angel had an ear infection with the way she kept tugging on her ear. Angel had drifted off for maybe ten minutes when she started screaming again. When she picked her up, she was quite warm to the touch. She located Angelina's thermometer and discovered that she was running a temperature. Not sure what to do, she started to phone her brothers, but she knew Joe and Alec were both unavailable for the day. Alec and Kelly had gone down to Knoxville to start packing her condo for sale while Joe was playing in a tennis tournament. Her last resort was to contact Ashton. She hated bothering him since he was the only doctor available in the practice for the day, but she really had no other options. He was one of her pediatricians, so she picked up the phone and dialed him. He didn't answer, so she left him a message. She hoped he'd get back to her soon. If not, her next step would be to call the exchange and then she'd be placed in contact with him for sure.

It took him an hour or so before he returned her call. "I'm on my way back from the hospital, so I should be at your house in say ten minutes."

"Ashton, I'm not at my house. I'm at Alejandro's."

"Okay, then add another ten minutes or so to that."

Gabriella watched for him out the front window and opened the door before he could ring the bell. She greeted him with an upset Angel in her arms. "Hey there, now… What's this I hear that you're not feeling well?" He reached for Angel as he entered the house. She led him to the nursery where he lay her down to examine her. He took her temperature and looked in her ears. "Just as I thought—an ear infection."

Gabriella had no idea what he did, but Angel went to sleep almost immediately after he examined her.

"I guess she wanted to let me know what was troubling her," he said as they quietly closed the door to her room.

Ashton stopped by Matthew's room on the way from visiting Angel. "Hey there, buddy. How goes it?"

"Great. How come you're here?"

"I was checking on your little sister."

"Oh," was all Matthew said as he went back to putting his pirate ship together.

He followed Gabriella to the kitchen where she put on the kettle for tea. He sat down and watched her put water in the kettle. "Do you care for tea or hot chocolate?

"Whatever's easiest for you—tea's fine with me."

"Good," is the only comment she made as she gathered the tea leaves and pot to brew it. Ashton watched as she moved about the kitchen. The more he was around her, the more he liked Gabriella. Yes, she'd been a thorn in his side, but as he'd gotten to know her in the last few weeks, he realized that she was becoming important to him. He'd witnessed a loving, caring aunt as she'd taken care of Angel—something that actually really surprised him. He'd seen how she'd interacted with Matthew, but there was a special quality she had about herself. Her look, her smile. He didn't understand where these feelings were coming from. He'd experienced little to no love as he grew up but somehow he recognized it—saw it in her gestures.

In speaking with Jane at the softball game, he discovered why Gabriella had been so upset after their second game. He learned about Jake and the fight, and it only brought back his own memories. Different, but also similar to Jake's. He was learning just how special she truly was, and she was getting to him slowly but surely.

The water boiled, and as she poured it into the tea pot to steep, she turned the timer on. She grabbed two cups and the specialized sugar that Angelina used in her tea. She didn't know if Ashton liked sugar in his tea, but she knew that she certainly did. She dropped a teaspoon of sugar into her cup and passed it towards him as she waited on the timer to signal the tea had steeped long enough. "Sugar?" she asked as she stood to remove the tea leaves from the pot when the timer rang.

"Certainly," he said as he spooned sugar into his cup. "The right sugar definitely brings out the flavor of the tea."

"Do you know a lot about tea?"

Pausing, he looked down into his tea cup and then said, "When I was growing up, my babysitter often used sugar in her tea." He didn't want to let on that he was actually talking about his nannies. That would make him sound like he was from a certain class of people. Nannies were for the rich, while babysitters were used by average people. The Alvarezes knew very little about his childhood, and he wanted to keep it that way. John knew a little more than Alec and Joe, but even John didn't know that Ashton had come from the wealth that he had. He liked to keep his family history under wraps.

Gabriella poured the perfectly steeped tea into the cups, returned the pot to the stove, and settled across from Ashton at the kitchen table. She sipped her tea and then reached for a cookie from the plate that she'd set down earlier on the table. Taking a bite from her cookie, she picked at the crumbs on the table, never looking at Ashton. He, too, sipped his tea and complimented her on the fine cup that she'd prepared.

She said suddenly, "You were good with her."

He looked at her quizzically, "What are you talking about?"

"You surprised me with how good you were with Angel. From what I'd heard about you, Ashton, you had awful bedside manner."

He reached for a cookie from the plate. "Mmm, sugar, my favorite," he commented as he took a bite. Thinking momentarily, he said, "I owe my bedside manner to your father. Yes, I know I had a reputation for not being the kindest doctor, but one day your father saw me in action, pulled me aside, and gave me a talking to. John's worked with me and has taught me how to approach a situation. He's the reason why I replaced him when he retired. He saw something in me that I hadn't seen in myself. I've learned from not only your dad, but also from Alec and Joe, and I hope to keep growing and someday have the reputation that your father has." He stopped for a second and added, "I know I messed up with your brother and Matthew when I first arrived, but we've cleared things up, and from what I can tell, we're getting along just fine."

"Well, I think my dad rubbed off on you, and for me to notice it, it must be pretty noticeable. After all, I wasn't your biggest fan."

"Indeed, you weren't." Ashton's phone rang at that moment. It was another parent worried about a sick child. He took the call and then indicated he had to leave.

"Call me if you have any more problems. Tell Angelina

that Nurse Sadie will phone her to set up a follow-up appointment." Ashton didn't know why, but he leaned forward and kissed her cheek. "Get some rest," he said as he stood from the table.

Just as he got to the door, he reached for her right hand. He'd forgotten to ask about it when he first arrived because she practically threw Angel into his arms. "I don't want you to think I forgot, but how's the hand?"

"It's a little sore, but I'm getting by."

"If you continue to have problems…"

"I know. I'll go to the doctor."

"Good," he said as he walked through the door. She watched him as he got into his car and drove away. She didn't understand what was going on between them, but she felt as though they were on the path to friendship and maybe something more. Time would tell, but it wasn't something that she was going to proactively seek. She'd let it take its course, especially since they hadn't discussed the promised date. If he asked her out, and truly meant it followed by actually setting a day and time, she decided she'd let him stew. Of course, she'd say yes, but she wanted him to know just because he'd finally gotten around to arranging a time didn't mean that she'd automatically be available. But in all honestly, she wasn't going to let those thoughts cross her mind. She couldn't be consumed by what ifs. Time moved on and so would she until she needed to make that all important decision. With that, Matthew called for her—he wanted to try and float his pirate ship in the tub. She didn't know what she was in for, but hoped that it didn't sink.

Chapter Fourteen

IT WAS MID-OCTOBER AND GABRIELLA had launched a new agricultural science program for her class. She was working with several farmers so the students could experience what it took to bring their food to the table. She teamed up with cattle producers, corn and soybean farmers, and an apple orchard and general produce farmer.

Since the apple harvest was in full swing and nearing its end, she took her class to the Lapinsky Orchard. Even though many of these children visited the orchard when they were younger to pick apples, this time they were learning about the maintenance of the orchard during the off-season, the process for pressing apples into cider, and the organization behind running the various picking processes during harvest. Surprisingly, Gabriella learned a great deal herself while they toured the operations.

They were just getting ready to board the bus to return to school when she noticed a class of kindergartners, maybe first graders, getting ready to hop on the farm wagon to be taken into the orchard to pick apples. Each child had a bag that they could fill as a part of their day at the orchard. A voice speaking sweetly to a child caught her attention. She spun around to take in the scene when the man became all too familiar to her. Was that Ashton? No, it couldn't be. He was working and definitely didn't have a child. Or did he?

Her thoughts went back and forth, unsure if it was truly Ashton with a small child when, just as she boarded the bus, she looked back. Just as he hopped onto the wagon with the boy, he turned. He raised his head to listen to someone and she confirmed what she thought she'd seen. Yes, indeed Ashton was at the orchard with a child in tow.

Gabriella was taken aback by her discovery. Never once had he divulged that he had a child. Had he been married? In fact, she was a little hurt by the scene she'd just witnessed. Did he think he couldn't share his child with her or with his partners? Did Joe or Alec know about this child? She didn't know if she should say anything or not. He was on personal time. He certainly didn't have to share all of his personal life with her. If he wanted to keep his child under wraps, so be it.

When Javier had asked him to go on his field trip to the apple orchard, he was almost speechless. They had developed a good rapport since he'd become his Big Brother six months earlier, but this was even better than expected. Jacinta couldn't get off work, so Ashton jumped at the chance to visit the orchard. He loved watching the kids running through the orchard, picking more apples with blemishes than good ones. He was going to make sure that Javier's apples were good and weren't filled with worms or bad spots.

As he hopped on the wagon to be taken to the apple trees, he noticed a woman board a school bus of older children, and she looked oddly familiar from behind. Before he could get a good look at her, Javier had called his name and reached for his hand, taking his attention away from the woman. Javier had gathered quite a few apples, all of them in fine shape. Ashton examined them and they appeared to be free of bad spots and worms.

Ashton turned to one of the owners of the Lapinsky Orchard that rode with them on the wagon. He started up a conversation and then he remembered the busload of older students. "When we got on the wagon, I noticed a group of older students boarding a bus. Were they here to pick apples?"

Sharon Lapinsky grabbed an apple as it started to roll off the wagon. One of the children's bags had toppled over when they hit a small pot hole in the road. She returned the apple to the child and then turned to Ashton. "No, they weren't here to pick apples. My husband has partnered with a few schools in the area and is introducing agricultural sciences into the classroom. He, along with several farmers that specialize in different fields, is introducing the various aspects of farming to include animal science and crop management so the children can understand more about farming in general. We're hoping to maybe teach these children a little about our business. Most of the time the kids come and pick apples and leave—they don't understand about how we care for the orchard outside of harvest. On the tour, they also get to see up close how the apples are pressed into apple cider. We're really excited about this new endeavor. This is the first year, and we're hopeful that it continues."

"That's interesting. How did you get involved in this?"

"Several teachers from the area schools got together and decided to weave this into their curriculum, then they sought us out. I think it's a fabulous idea to make the students more aware of agriculture in general."

He was just about ready to question her further when she started yelling at some of the students to sit down. By the time they were under control, the ride was over and he'd lost sight of Sharon.

He helped Javier off the wagon and they headed to the play yard where they played several games before boarding the bus to return to his school. Ashton had never visited an apple orchard before and he had an absolute blast helping Javier and his friends pick apples. He even purchased a bag of apples and apple cider to take into the office the following day. Life was good, especially with Javier in it. He was making up for a lot of things that he missed as a child.

He couldn't wait until his next adventure with Javier—his Cub Scout Troop was going to the pumpkin patch that weekend for their monthly Pack meeting. They were going to pick out a pumpkin, more than likely get lost in the corn maze, and have roasted marshmallows over a fire. He felt like he was a child again, experiencing the childhood he'd never had.

∽

Gabriella didn't think any more about seeing Ashton at the orchard. When she'd thought about it on the bus ride back to school, she'd decided that the man she'd seen couldn't be Ashton. It was Tuesday, and from what she remembered, Ashton's day off was Thursday. She realized she'd been mistaken and recalled the adage that everyone had a twin somewhere.

She finished out her work week and decided to drop by Angelina's Friday afternoon after school. Matthew greeted her at the door filled with excitement. He pulled on her hand and dragged her into the kitchen where Angelina was starting to prepare dinner. "That smells really good," Gabriella said as she made her way to the stove. Angelina was preparing a pot roast.

"Are you inferring something?"

Chuckling, she said, "Why would you say that?" It was well known that Angelina wasn't necessarily the best cook in the world. She had a few dishes that were stellar and then others…

"I am a good cook," Angelina insisted. "Ask you brother."

"Whatever you say," she added as she turned away from her friend and sat down at the table. Matthew ran up to her side and started jumping up and down. Gabriella had no clue as to why her nephew was acting so excited.

"Gabriella?"

"Yes, Matthew."

"I have a question for you."

"I gathered that," she said as she gestured for him to sit down beside her. "What's up?"

"Well, my Cub Scout Pack is going to the pumpkin patch on Sunday. We get to go through a corn maze, pick a pumpkin, shoot a corn cob through a cannon…" Stopping briefly, like he was thinking, he turned to Angelina, "Mom, what else is there?"

"Let's see… A play yard, farm animals, a jumping pillow, a corn maze."

"I already said that."

"I think there's a hay ride and I believe a fort."

"Wow, Matthew that sounds like fun," Gabriella said.

"I think it will be, and I want you to go."

"You want me to go?"

"I do. Dad can't go and Mom will have to watch Angel, so can you come? Please, pretty please?" Matthew jumped up off his chair and got really close to her face.

"Matthew, settle down," Angelina said, "or your aunt will definitely say no."

"Okay, Mom. I hear you." He sat down and looked at Gabriella with puppy dog eyes. She couldn't help but start laughing at him. He sat there quietly waiting for her reply.

"You really want me to go?"

He nodded his head so quickly, Gabriella was glad it was attached or else it would've flown off. She was over the moon excited that he would ask her to go with them. "Sure, I'll go. What time do I need to be here?"

"Mom, what time—"

"Matthew, I am standing *right* here. I heard your aunt. You go on and play, and Gabriella and I will work it out."

"Okay. Thanks, Mom. Thanks, Aunt Gabriella," and with that he skipped out of the room.

"You don't have to go, Gabriella."

"Of course, I do. I want to. I'm thrilled that he asked me. I haven't been to Olson's since I was a little kid. I can't wait to get lost in the corn maze," Gabriella said and rolled her eyes. Angelina laughed. "No seriously,

I am looking forward to it. And you'll be there, too."

Angelina walked over to the stove to check on her pot roast. "Do you want to stay for dinner? After all, you did think my pot roast looked good."

"Thanks for the offer, but I'm headed over to Ox's for a post-season party. I still can't believe we won all of our games. The last one was touch and go, but we pulled it off."

"I keep meaning to ask you, how's the hand?

"How did you know about it? I didn't tell anyone."

Angelina pursed her lips and turned back to the stove.

"Out with it."

"Who else? My husband. He heard about it through Joe, who was told by—"

"Ashton! I'm going to kill him."

"Gabriella, just forget about it. He was concerned and mentioned it to Joe, and then Joe asked Alejandro. Forget about how I know. I'm just glad that it's better. It is, right?"

"Yeah, it is. I was going to have Dad look at it, but I missed seeing him and then... It doesn't matter. It's okay, that's all you need to know."

"Okay, then," Angelina said, and at that moment, the phone rang.

Gabriella couldn't tell who it was, so she waved goodbye to Angelina and walked out the door. They'd figure out what time she needed to meet them for their trip to Olson's Pumpkin Patch later.

Chapter Fifteen

SUNDAY ARRIVED WITH A COLD chill in the air. Gabriella dressed warmly in jeans, a turtleneck, and a heavy sweater. On top of that, she threw on a down jacket. They weren't supposed to meet Matthew's Cub Scouts until two in the afternoon. The Pack meeting would last an hour or so, and with the days getting shorter, Angelina had decided to arrive at the farm around noon so they could choose their pumpkins, play in the play yard, take a wagon ride, and lastly tour the corn maze. Angelina didn't want Matthew to be disappointed, and she hoped they could get everything in before the sun set.

When Gabriella arrived at Angelina's, she was greeted at the door with a pouty-faced Matthew. "What's the problem, Matthew? You don't look too happy."

"I'm not," he replied as he closed the door behind her. "Angel's got a cough and a runny nose, and Mom doesn't want her out in the cold."

"Well, that's okay. It'll be just you and me then."

His pouty-faced turned into a bright smile. "Really? You'll still go?"

"Why wouldn't I? Let's check in with your mom and see what her plans are, and then we can pack up and go." He ran from the room towards Angel's nursery. She chuckled as she watched him put the brakes on right outside his sister's room, sliding past in his socks on the hardwood floor. He screeched to a stop and almost fell flat on his face. Laughing, he got up and slowed his pace as he entered Angel's room.

"What's going on out there?" Angelina asked when Matthew finally made his way into the room. Gabriella followed in a fit of giggles.

"You okay, Matthew? I thought you were going to go head-first into the wall when you put the brakes on and skid past the door."

"I'm good," he said turning to his mother. "Mom, I know you can't go since Angel's sick, but Gabriella said she'd still take me."

Angelina looked at her friend. "Are you sure?"

"Yep. I've been looking forward to this adventure since Matthew asked. We'll have a good time, won't we?"

Matthew nodded vigorously.

"Now, go get your shoes on and wear your boots— they'll be warmer," Angelina said as she picked up Angel. "Sorry about today. Angel just woke up from her nap and she has—"

"I know, Matthew told me. Don't worry about it. We haven't gone out together for quite some time. We'll be fine. I just want to make sure he dresses warmly enough because it's chilly out there." Looking down at herself, she added, "I hope I'm not overdressed, but I'm in layers so I can take off something if I need to. I hate this time of year. One minute it's hot, and the next cold. Prime time for everyone to get sick." Gabriella left Angelina in the room with Angel and sought out Matthew.

"You need to dress warmly," she called out as she made her way to the kitchen. Matthew found Gabriella patiently waiting for him. He'd followed his mother's instructions having put on the heavy hiking boots that he wore for Scouts. He had a heavy fleece and down jacket. "I don't want to get sick like Angel."

Gabriella yelled goodbye to Angelina as they headed out the door. She knew Matthew would talk non-stop on their ride. And true to form, he did.

They arrived just as Olson's was opening their gates. She knew it would be extremely crowded today since it was the second to last weekend before Halloween. Matthew decided that he wanted to take a wagon ride first and then choose his pumpkin. They jumped on one of the first rides and toured the farm before getting dropped off in the pumpkin patch. Matthew spent at least fifteen minutes trying to decide between two pumpkins when Gabriella finally told the person helping them that they'd take both. Matthew looked up at Gabriella. "Really? Both?" he asked.

"My treat," she said as they watched the pumpkins being loaded onto the wagon. Olson's had been around for as long as she could remember. When she was a little girl, Olson's just offered hay rides and pumpkin picking, therefore, one could get in and out in under an hour. They'd spent a long time deciding on their pumpkins and she was worried they wouldn't get to see everything before their meeting. The farm had expanded so over the years and she wanted to see all of the new additions before the farm closed.

They ended up getting through the entire farm except for the maze when the Pack meeting began. She was completely surprised with how many Cub Scout Packs held their Pack meetings on the farm. She was glad that Matthew knew his Pack as Olson's had a map indicating where each Pack's respective bonfire had been set up. Matthew's group was towards the back of the farm. She promised him they'd go through the maze after the meeting as long as they had enough time before the farm closed for the day.

Matthew enjoyed his meeting, and roasting a marshmallow for his s'more over the fire was almost the highlight of his day. She watched as the warmed chocolate oozed out from underneath the roasted marshmallow down his chin. She laughed as she watched him try and grab the marshmallow and stop it from also oozing out when he took his next bite. By the time Matthew had finished eating his s'more, he was covered in chocolate and gooey marshmallow. She wet a napkin and started to clean up his face when Matthew stopped her and said, "I can do it."

"Okay, then. You clean up your face." She walked away wondering just when her nephew had grown up, not needing her assistance.

Ashton was running late when he got to Javier's to pick him up for the pumpkin patch. He'd lost track of time while he was working on his pergola. He was moving a lot slower than he expected since his hands weren't working as agilely in the cold weather. He wanted to finish building the pergola before winter and he hoped for a warm day so he could stain it as well. He wasn't sure that would happen before winter, but he could hope for one.

Javier was excitedly waiting for him. Ashton barely had a chance to say hello to Jacinta when Javier was pulling him down the sidewalk to his car. Within minutes of his arrival, he buckled him into his car seat and they took off for Olson's Pumpkin Patch.

Jacinta reminded Ashton that the Pack meeting began promptly at two-thirty. Javier was really only interested in picking out a pumpkin and going through the corn maze. "I can play at the playground anytime I want to."

"But it's different stuff…"

"I know, but I don't care if we have time for that or not. I want to pick a pumpkin and get lost in the corn maze."

"Really, get lost?"

"Yeah. It'll be fun."

"Whatever you say."

They arrived with enough time for Javier to choose his pumpkin and for them to take it to the car. They were a couple of minutes late to the meeting but everyone was just standing around talking when they sat down on their hay bale. Ashton noticed that, as they sat there, the temperatures dropped dramatically. He leaned over and asked Javier if he was cold, but he shook his head as he listened to one of the dens perform a skit. Javier laughed at the antics and Ashton chuckled and shook his head at the absurdity of it. All of the kids seemed to enjoy it, though, and that's all that mattered.

Javier wasn't a fan of s'mores, so they said their goodbyes to everyone and made their way to the corn maze. It was almost four and the farm closed at five. He hoped they could get through the maze in an hour.

～

Gabriella and Matthew made it to the corn maze. The sun was heading for the horizon and she looked at her watch. They had just about an hour to make it through the maze before Olson's closed. "Come on, Aunt Gabriella."

"I'm coming." She got to the entrance of the maze. "Which way do you want to go?"

"Let's go left."

"Well, okay then. Let's do it."

She had a hard time keeping up with him as he sped off through the maze ahead of her. She got to a turn in the maze and lost sight of Matthew. She started worrying that she was going to lose him. She got turned around and went one way, and then she saw his Cub Scout shirt and called his name. He looked over his shoulder and waited while she caught up to him. "I thought I'd lost you," she said breathlessly.

"Why are you breathing so hard, Aunt Gabriella?"

"I was trying to find you. I was kind of worried."

"Like I'd get lost in here," he smirked.

"Let's stay together, okay?"

Matthew nodded but sped off again in front of her. When Gabriella really thought about it, she knew he couldn't get lost, so she let him run ahead. She continued walking through the maze and heard a voice that seemed familiar to her. She really knew no one in his Pack, so she guessed it was just her imagination.

～

Ashton was right handed, so he gravitated to the right

as they entered the maze. He and Javier took their time walking through the maze. Javier was amazed with how they designed it in the first place. Ashton had spoken with the worker that greeted them when they first entered the maze. He learned that Olson's designed the theme for the maze and turned it over to a company that loaded their design into a specialized computer program that used GPS technology to cut the corn field. The field was cut in a matter of hours, but the time spent designing it took several weeks. The maze they were walking through was designed after an American Bald Eagle and covered more than fifteen acres of corn.

As they walked, Ashton kept hearing a certain voice. He'd heard it when they first entered the maze, but hadn't thought anything of it. As Javier and he wound their way through the maze, he kept hearing a woman's voice calling out the name Matthew. He knew there were no Matthews in Javier's Pack and thought the boy must have been from a different one.

As Gabriella and Matthew wound deeper into the maze, she stopped and looked at the map. "I think we're lost," she said as Matthew kept walking ahead of her.

"No, we're not."

"I think we need to raise our flag and let someone know we're lost. Matthew, it's getting late and the sun's starting to set."

"Let's go a little longer, and if we don't find our way out, we can raise our flag."

They continued on through the maze and Gabriella stopped to tie her shoe. She could tell Matthew was getting tired as he stood next to her with his head held low.

"Aunt Gabriella, I think you're right. We are lost."

"Lost? Did I hear you say you're lost?"

She heard the voice that was so familiar to her. She looked up. Standing before her and Matthew was Ashton with his son. She was speechless. She didn't know what to say. Ashton hadn't told them about his son and now she was standing—no, squatting—tying her shoe as he held out his hand to help her from the ground.

"Oh, hi Ashton… Fancy meeting you here."

"Ashton," Matthew called out. "Is this Javier?"

Javier? Who is Javier?

"Matthew, it certainly is. I'm glad we ran into you and you two could finally meet."

Matthew knew about this Javier and she didn't. What was going on here? Did her brothers know about him, too? She didn't think so…

She stood there, shocked that her nephew knew about his son and she didn't. She didn't know what to say. Her wheels were spinning and she could only imagine the look on her face. She noticed his grin as he watched her closely. She knew he was getting a kick out of her expressions as she watched Javier and Matthew talking about their day at the pumpkin patch.

She didn't know what to say to him. Should she ask him about his son? Ask him why he kept him from her and her family? The questions kept spinning in her head. She opened her mouth to ask a question, but stopped. Ashton wasn't paying attention to her.

Gabriella decided that Javier must look like his mother because she couldn't find one thing about his appearance that linked him to Ashton. He had dark hair while Ashton's was blond. Ashton had blue eyes and Javier's were brown. She kept looking back and forth between father and son. She decided maybe his nose might look like his father's, but then again maybe not. Ashton finished talking to the boys and turned back to Gabriella.

"I'm surprised to see you and Matthew. Where are Angelina and Alejandro?"

"Alejandro's on call and actually in surgery, and Angel came down with a runny nose right before we left so Angelina decided to keep her in. She didn't want her out in this cold."

"Huh. I can understand why she stayed at home."

She didn't know what to say, so she looked around the maze and said, "It's getting close to closing, and I think we need to find our way out of here."

"Oh, it's not too difficult. We're almost to the front."

"Really? I was sure we were lost."

"Maybe you were, but we weren't." He said, laughing as he egged the kids to move forward towards the front of the maze. Less than five minutes later, they were walking across the parking lot. The boys had run ahead to get their photograph taken in front of a massive pumpkin.

"Be careful," she yelled. "I swear, he's full of energy today. I'm glad I was able to bring him. I didn't want him disappointed since he was looking forward to this day for weeks."

"Kind of like the Transplant Awareness baseball game?"

She stopped and brushed her hair from her face. "Yeah, kind of like that."

They made their way to the boys and took their photograph. Matthew and Javier were trying to set up a playdate when Ashton stepped in.

"Javier, we'll have to check with your mom, okay? Maybe the next time we get together Matthew can join us."

She blurted without thinking, "Can't you make that decision? After all, you are his father."

He raised his eyebrows at her. "I am not his father."

"But… I saw the two of you the other day at Lapinsky's Apple Orchard. You were there with him to go apple picking."

"So that *was* you."

"What are you talking about?"

"I saw you, too, when you were boarding your bus. I wasn't sure that it was you, but before I could say anything, you were gone. Then I forgot all about it."

"Well if you were at Lapinsky's and are now here at Olson's, just what is your role in Javier's life?"

"I'm his Big Brother."

"No way. Really? I didn't know you had a younger brother. In fact, I thought you were an only child."

He gave an exasperated huff, but before he could say anything, she had turned away. "Hey, boys! Stop crawling all over the pumpkin," yelled Gabriella as Ashton reached for her hand and led her to a hay bale where he sat down beside her.

"I don't understand, Ashton. You never told us about him. Why hide that?"

She had only just started with her questions when Ashton leaned in suddenly and kissed her. Her eyes got as big as saucers but she didn't move. She was stunned into silence. She was completely taken off guard. She didn't know what to think about his kiss. It came out of left field and took her totally by surprise.

"What was that for?"

"To get you to shut up for just one minute so I could explain."

She tried to stand but Ashton grabbed her hand and

pulled her back down beside him. "Gabriella, Javier is my Little Brother, and I am his Big Brother. We're brothers through the Big Brother Big Sister Program." He rubbed his thumb against her palm as he explained Javier's situation. Sadness overcame her as she listened to Ashton tell the story of Javier's father being killed on Christmas Eve almost two years ago. "His mother knew almost immediately that he needed a male influence and reached out to the program. We were matched up fairly quickly. He's a great kid."

"Gabriella, can we go home now? I'm getting cold and hungry," Matthew called.

"Sure Matthew," she called back as she stood to leave. "Sorry about the misunderstanding."

"Don't worry about it. I expected it from you."

She pursed her lips, shook her head in dismay, and turned around, heading to her car. She and Matthew had already put the pumpkins in the trunk before their meeting, so they were ready to go. "See you later, Ashton," Matthew called back. "Javier, call me, okay?"

"Sure thing, Matthew," Javier yelled at the top of his lungs.

She looked in the rear view mirror as she drove off down the dusty dirt road towards the highway. What she realized was he didn't understand why she hadn't trusted him. He could have told her all about Javier, and she knew they had a long way to go in the trust department.

Halloween came that Friday. Gabriella's school had a dress-up day and the children paraded around the block that circled the school grounds. Parents and neighbors dressed in their warm coats and sat in lawn chairs as the children walked around the neighborhood in their costumes. The teachers decided to dress as characters from the various Disney movies, and Gabriella chose to dress as Cinderella. Jane dressed as one of her step-sisters, and Mica, the second grade teacher, dressed as the remaining step-sister. Mary dressed as her step-mother.

Gabriella had a beautiful dress that she modified from one of the weddings she'd been in over the years. It was blue and three-quarter's length. She found a crinoline slip which puffed out her dress. She wore red shoes that resembled glass slippers and looked exactly like Cinderella. She was absolutely stunning. She took her costume off for the class party—she didn't want it to get dirty because she was heading over to the hospital to tutor one of the patients and then participate in a Halloween party for those children that could attend.

She cleaned up her classroom and packed up her car with everything that she thought she may need over the weekend. She had several papers that she wanted to grade and she didn't want to have to return to school to get anything that she may have forgotten. Once she left for the day, she didn't plan to return until Monday morning. Often, she worked in her classroom on Saturdays, but not this weekend. She wanted to enjoy it before things got hectic with the upcoming holidays.

She exchanged her party clothes for her dress and headed off to the hospital. Ever since she'd been a little girl, she went to the hospital on this magical day and celebrated it with those children that were ill. She loved helping to brighten their day.

She quickly completed her tutoring session as Elliot, her student, was too excited for their party. She left

Elliot with his parents, and then visited with Margot until it was time for her to leave for the day. Margot often stayed for the party but this year her son was old enough to go trick-or-treating, so she decided to go home and take him out.

Since the party wasn't until six-thirty, she ran by both Alec and Joe's on-site offices. She was quite surprised when she was not only greeted by Joe, but also Alec and Kelly. All of them were dressed in costume and ready for the party. Joe dressed like he always did, as a tennis player in shorts and his tennis shirt. He completed his outfit with sweat bands on his head and wrists. Alec and Kelly were dressed as Batman and Batgirl. They were the superheroes of the night.

"Is everyone ready to have some fun?" Gabriella asked.

"Wow, look at you, Gabriella. Are you dressed as Cinderella?"

"I am, and I even have my glass slippers," Gabriella said as she pointed to the red slipper in her hand. She had found a pair of red shoes and added sparkly rhinestones to give it the added flashiness needed for her part. She loved how they turned out.

"Now all you need is your Prince," Alec said with a snicker.

"You stop it over there, Mr. Superhero. You've got your girl."

"That I do," Alec said as he reached for Kelly and pulled her into his arms. "I have my Batgirl," he chuckled as he kissed her. Turning back to Gabriella, Alec said, "Why are you here so early? Were you tutoring Elliot?"

"I was, but he was so excited and couldn't concentrate, so I just ended our session early. I ran by and spoke with Margot for a few minutes, but she left to take her son out. She wanted to get an early start and get back as he's so young. She hoped he made it past the end of the block. And that's only three houses."

"Well, it's hard on the wee ones. I think he's only two, maybe three," Joe chimed in.

"She told me he's three, but after a long day at day-care he's usually wiped out by six o'clock." Gabriella looked at her watch and it was almost six thirty. "Hey, have you guys eaten yet? If not, maybe we can get a bite to eat at the diner after the party. Gus told me he's having a costume party at nine or so. Prizes, too."

"I'm starving right now," Kelly said as she nibbled on her finger. "I'll be there for sure."

They decided to head over to the conference room where the party was being held. When they entered, many of the kids were already dressed in their costumes playing various games that had been arranged. Some of the children were able to walk while others were in wheelchairs, pushed by their parents or a nurse. All of the children were excited to see Dr. Alec and Dr. Joe. Several asked where Dr. Ashton was, when they looked up and there was Ashton dressed in his finest as a handsome prince.

Ashton put on his best bedside manner as he greeted the children. Gabriella stood in awe as she watched him interact with the kids. If she hadn't seen it herself, she would have never believed how carefree he was. He acted like a kid himself.

Ashton worked the room, talking to the parents, nurses, and children. He had just finished listening to a joke one of his patients told when he raised his eyes and caught hold of her own. She was taken by surprise. He was dressed in a black tuxedo. He actually looked like a prince in his formal attire. Who would have thought they'd dressed as Cinderella and the Prince? Most people probably believed it was pre-planned but they knew it hadn't been. Fate must have played a role as he walked up and reached for the glass slipper that he found sitting on the floor next to the chair she'd been sitting in.

"I believe I have found the glass slipper that belongs to my lady. May I try it on?" The children gathered around as they watched Ashton try the glass slipper on his Cinderella. He knew it would fit but he kept the children on the edge of their seats as he tried slipping the shoe onto her foot. He pretended it didn't fit, acting like her foot was way too big for the shoe. "I don't believe it fits." She had scrunched her toes up inside the toe, preventing it from going on easily, adding to the drama.

Ashton made grunting sounds as he tried fitting the shoe. The children started cheering him on and then, he glanced up into her eyes and that was the sign for her to relax her foot. "Shall I try again?" he asked the children.

"Yes," they called out in unison.

"Okay, here we go. If you are my Cinderella, this shoe will fit. One...Two...Three," and with that Ashton acted like he was using all of his strength to ease the shoe onto her foot. And then, miraculously, it slid easily onto her foot. "It fits," he called out. All of the children started cheering. He stood, looked his Cinderella directly in the eyes, and kissed her sweet lips. Cheers rang out. She was stunned. He actually seemed like he was enjoying himself. She'd never quite seen him this relaxed. He'd smiled at her and chuckled as the children cheered his accomplishment.

He was acting almost like a child himself, and then when he kissed her—she couldn't believe it.

They got caught up in the moment. After the kiss, she smiled sweetly into his eyes and said, "I guess I've found my Prince Charming after all." She wanted to replay their scene with the children, but she also wanted to see where the kiss led.

"Indeed you have," he said as he looked out amongst the children. By the expressions on each of their faces, he would have never known how ill some of them were. They enjoyed the little play-acting that he and Gabriella had put on.

Shortly after their skit, the nurses called out that it was time for the children to return to their rooms for the night. She stood and watched him wish each of the children a Happy Hollows Night. She was glad that she'd witnessed his true bedside manner. She had a new appreciation for him. He would surely win the title for best bedside manner, she was sure of it.

"Did you two plan this little scene out in advance?" Alec asked as Ashton joined them at the snack table. He grabbed the last cookie and looked at her.

"No, we didn't. I always dress as a prince. I have for years. That way all of the kids can dream of a time when their dreams will come true, just like Cinderella's. They hope that whatever ails them can go away for just that one minute so they can believe in a happily ever after."

"I have to say you two played that scene out well for not having planned it in advance," Kelly mused. "Now, I'm starving. Let's go to the diner and grab us something to eat. And maybe one of us will win Gus's costume contest," Kelly said as she grabbed Alec's arm and headed towards the door.

She waited for Ashton. "I hope you can join us. Coming?"

He took a bite of his cookie and nodded. She smiled to herself as they followed everyone out of the hospital.

Chapter Sixteen

GABRIELLA COULDN'T BELIEVE HOW CROWDED the diner was when she arrived. Gus had advertised his costume contest and the diner was practically full. She was thankful that she'd called ahead asking Gus to set aside his large booth for her. She had taught his daughter when she first started teaching at St. Margaret's. She had a special relationship with Gus and his family and he always thought to include her in his family gatherings. "Are you dressed up?" He asked when she had phoned in her reservation. Pedals didn't take reservations, but he did for Gabriella.

"I am, and I have a few others that I think may steal your show."

"Huh," Gus said and thought for a moment. "Who all's coming?"

"Just the regular crowd," She said as she'd stopped at a stop sign. She looked over at the car beside her and was thrown a kiss. She started laughing.

"What's so funny?"

"Oh, Gus, I was just thrown a kiss from the cutest guy in the car next to me."

"Gabby, how many times have I told you not to flirt and drive?"

"Too many. And I wasn't flirting, I was talking to you. I guess he just liked my costume."

"Well, in that case, I can't wait to see it. Hey, Gabby, I've got to let you go. I've got a large crowd walking across the parking lot. I'll see you shortly."

She chuckled to herself as she ended the call and threw her phone into her purse. From the huge smile on the passerby, she guessed she must look pretty good in her costume. Maybe Cinderella would nab her Prince. Her thoughts drifted to Ashton and his kiss. Maybe she had already .

Gabriella thought she was the first one of their group to show up at Pedals, but she wasn't. Kelly and Alec had already been shown to their table. Joe was just walking in the door when she pulled into the parking lot. He waited and held the door for her, bowing as she walked through the door. Gus stood at the entry and was greeted by Joe, "Now, may I introduce you to Cinderella?"

"Well now I can see why you were thrown that kiss."

Joe raised his eyebrows at her.

"It's nothing," Gabriella said as she leaned over and kissed Gus on the cheek.

"Gabby, you look gorgeous. I think you'll steal the show."

"Hey, what about me and my costume," Joe said.

Rolling his eyes, Gus said, "You call that a costume? You wear that getup all year long."

"It's easy," Joe replied as he sat down at the booth. He slid in and let Gabriella sit on the outside, making it easier for her to get in and out in her dress.

"So, where's your prince charming? I guess we'll

find someone for you amongst this crowd."

"I'd say you will," Ashton said from beside the booth. "I believe I've found my lady." She slid from the booth and watched as Ashton bowed to her. In a fit of giggles, she covered her mouth. "What are you doing?"

Ashton looked at her and he too broke out into laughter. "I don't know. I'm just playing my part."

She leaned in and kissed his cheek. "You've saved me from my ugly step-sisters. You are my Prince Charming," she said as she batted her eyes at him.

Gus started laughing heartily. "I'll leave Cinderella to her prince. Now, changing the subject, can I get you all something to drink?"

All of them placed their drink orders, then Ashton helped Gabriella slide back into the booth and sat opposite her. She felt giddy. She'd never acted like this. Yes, she enjoyed having a good time, but this evening—she was having a blast. She thought for a moment and looked at him. He had a huge smile on his face and really seemed to be happy, too. She liked seeing this side of him and hoped to see more.

"I think all of the kids really enjoyed the party," he said as he reached for his glass of water. He took a sip and watched her over the rim of his glass. She smiled at him.

"They really did," Kelly said as she leaned over to Alec and kissed his cheek. "I don't know how I missed this all these years. The children had a ball, and for a time, were able to forget about their illnesses. I loved seeing all of their smiles. I really had a good time." Alec smiled at his fiancée.

Promptly at nine, Gus began his costume parade throughout the diner. Each table was given a ballot where the table collaboratively voted on the best dressed male and female, best dressed overall, creepiest costume, and the list went on. It seemed like the whole neighborhood turned out for this adult-only contest.

Each table took their turns to parade around the restaurant. Alec and Kelly went first from their table in their Batman and Batgirl superhero costumes. When they returned, it was Joe's turn. He wasn't sure he wanted to participate, but Gus egged him on. "What kind of costume do you call that?" Joe heard from one table. Another told him he should have stayed home, or better yet, gone to the gym and played a game of tennis. Joe took it all in good stride. "I guess I'd better find a different costume for next year."

"I just think you need to find an actual costume," snickered Gabriella. "If you think that's a costume, think again."

It was Ashton and Gabriella's turn. He stood, bowed to her, and reached for her hand. He helped her from the booth and led her throughout the restaurant. In several cases, he dropped to his knees and acted like he was trying on her glass slipper. In the end, when they returned to their table, he bowed again and then leaned in and gave her a kiss on the lips. "My lady, I believe our meal awaits us." Both Kelly and Alec watched the display before them. They were surprised to see Gabriella and Ashton openly sharing their kisses. Was it for show, or was something else playing out before them?

Joe laughed, "Ashton, don't you think you've carried this a little far?"

He turned to them, pursed his lips, shook his head, and sat down. "Can't a guy have a little fun?"

"If that's what you call fun," Joe said as he picked up

his sandwich and took a bite. Chewing he added, "I'm just glad to see you two getting along, and Gabriella's not yelling at you."

Ashton shifted his eyes to Gabriella. Shyly, she looked up at him. He smirked at her. "Yep, for once that's true." They had been getting along much better since they'd both been injured in their separate accidents, albeit Joe hadn't been around them enough to see the change in her.

As they enjoyed their meal, the conversation switched to Thanksgiving. It was Maria's turn to host Thanksgiving for the Alvarez and Samuels's clan. For the last several years, they'd taken turns hosting. Christmas was a different affair altogether. Lately, Jackie, Angelina's mother, hosted a get together right after Midnight Mass while Maria started a tradition the year Alejandro moved back to St. Louis and had an open house. They'd made a few changes along the way to accommodate Alejandro and Angelina having children, but for the most part it was all about family. Time spent with family was important to all of them.

"Ashton would you like to join us for Thanksgiving?" Alec asked as he reached for his glass of iced tea. He was on call for the evening and couldn't have alcohol like the others. Gabriella was astounded by his invitation and hoped her look of surprise didn't show on her face.

"That's really kind of you, but I hate to intrude on your family time."

"We consider you a part of the family, so why wouldn't we include you?"

Gabriella looked down at her salad, pretending not to pay attention.

"I'll have to think about it. Can I get back to you?"

"Sure. I've extended the invitation. It's up to you whether you want to join in."

"I appreciate it, I really do. It's just that I may—"

Alec's phone rang at the moment. "Well, that's the hospital, and I have to go in." He turned to Kelly, "Sorry, to ruin our night, sweetheart. I wanted to see if we'd win the costume contest."

"In that getup?" Joe murmured.

"At least we're dressed better than you in your tennis outfit."

Ashton moved out of the booth and let Alec out.

"Joe, can you take Kelly home for me?"

"I'll do it," Gabriella said as she reached for her fork, stabbing it into her lettuce. "We need to discuss Christmas."

"Christmas?" Alec asked as he started to move away from the table.

"Yeah, we do have a niece and nephew now, so planning their gifts is a must," she quipped.

Alec shook his head and headed out the door. "I'll call you if it's not too late."

Gabriella smiled at her soon-to-be-sister-in-law. "You're good for him, you know."

"I do. He's changed a lot since we've been together. He's not as focused on his career as he used to be."

"It's true, Kelly," Joe said. "Alec lived for his job. He was always at the hospital or the clinic. He never went out or had fun. Since you've been together, it's like a breath of fresh air being around him. He even cracks a joke now and then. It's good to have the old Alec back. The one I grew up with."

Joe had barely finished his comment when Gus started talking loudly through the diner. He was announcing the contest winners. As they listened, they realized Gus had added a few more categories where he chose the winners. "And the winners for best hero costume goes to Alec Alvarez and Kelly Samuels." He turned to their table, "Where's Batman, Batgirl?"

Kelly laughed as she got out of the booth to retrieve their award. "He went to save the day?"

"Without Batgirl," someone called from across the diner.

"Yep, unfortunately this Batgirl couldn't help him save the day. He had to do it himself." Everyone laughed as Gus handed her a bottle of wine.

Next, he called out best-dressed couple. "And the winners are Ashton Holder and Gabriella Alvarez, our Cinderella and Prince Charming."

Ashton stood and bowed before Gabriella and presented her his hand. She grabbed ahold of it as she slid from the booth. He escorted her to the front of the diner where Gus presented them with a gift card to the local winery. "A romantic dinner for two," he said as he reached in and kissed Gabriella's cheek. "If I didn't know better, you two make a beautiful couple. It's a shame that I know the truth." The crowd erupted in laughter as Gabriella eyed Gus. "Well, you're really not a couple…"

Ashton stepped in. "Well, we just might be," he teased as he grabbed her and kissed her lips. She again was taken aback by the kiss and went with it. The crowd cheered them on as they kissed. The kiss had gone on a little longer than expected when she pulled away. Her lips were quivering when Ashton looked at her. She'd felt something in that kiss that she hadn't felt before and she was sure he had, too.

Gus interrupted them when he started to declare the final winner of the evening. Ashton reached for her hand as they stood there waiting for Gus' final announcement. He squeezed her hand and smiled at her. Leaning over, he whispered, "We'll talk later." She nodded her head as they listened to Gus's final winner. She wondered what he meant by his comment but decided not to dwell on it. Their conversation would happen soon enough.

"And the winner for worst dressed is…" Before Gus could call out his name, the crowd started to chant, "Joe, Joe, Joe…" Gus spun around to the crowd, "How did you all know?" Everyone started laughing. "Joe Alvarez, come on up," he yelled in true Bob Barker fashion. He handed him a gift card to Johnson's Vault. Johnson's was the premiere place in St. Louis to get party supplies and costumes. "Next year I expect you to come in a full-blown costume. No tennis gear. Got it?" Pointing at Joe, he added, "That was such a lame costume. You might as well have not dressed up and come as yourself." Everyone howled.

Scowling at Gus, Joe said "Okay, I got your point."

Everyone returned to their seats and finished up their drinks. "Ready to go?" Kelly asked Gabriella. "I need to get up early tomorrow. I promised Angelina I'd stop by and help her with a few things."

"Okay, let's go then." Gabriella stood and glanced at Ashton as he also stood and let Kelly out of the booth.

"How about another round?" Joe said to Ashton as he was just about to follow Kelly and Gabriella out to the car.

"Sure," Ashton said as he watched Gabriella and Kelly leave. Alec had paid their bill on his way out of the diner when he headed off to the hospital.

Ashton sat down and reached for his glass of wine. He still had a mouthful left which he swallowed all at once.

"What's up with you two?" Joe asked as he motioned for Gus to refill their drinks. He wasn't expecting that question from Joe and started choking on his wine.

"You okay over there?"

"Yeah. You just surprised me, that's all." Ashton got himself under control. "Your guess is as good as mine. One minute she's friendly and the next she's…" He paused. "I haven't a clue what's going on between us. Every time I make plans to talk, something comes up. I just go with the flow and try not to set her off." Ashton waited while Gus poured their drinks, then went on. "I think she had a good time playing up the Cinderella thing, but I can't tell for sure. Your sister is a hard nut to crack. Maybe, in time, I'll begin to understand what makes her tick."

"Well if you ever figure that out, let me know… All kidding aside, Gabriella has a good heart. When she loves someone, she goes all out. I think she's just taking her time getting to know you. After all, you didn't get off on the right foot with the whole Alejandro and Matthew thing. I'm going to tell you something that you can't repeat." Ashton edged closer to Joe "Gabriella hasn't dated seriously in quite a few years. She's dated, but nothing that's lasted more than a few casual outings. The last time she did was right after college. I thought my mom was ready to pull out her wedding dress, that's how serious it was. And then… then they weren't. I'm not sure what happened, but what I do know is Gabby was hurt. It took her a long time to get over him, and I'm not fully convinced that she's gotten over him. He was her first love and whatever he did hurt her to the core. I think that's why she's being so reserved with you. One minute she's accepting and the next minute she's being what I like to refer to as her witch-self. Give her time. Take it slow, and I'm convinced she'll turn around."

"I don't know, Joe. It seems like we go one step forward and three steps back. I almost think it's a game she's playing."

"My sister isn't like that. She definitely doesn't play games. After watching her tonight and how she acted with your little skit, I think she's starting to see a different side to you. Watching her after you planted that kiss on her, I saw her eyes. I know she felt something just as I know you did, too. Just take it one day at a time."

Joe then turned their conversation onto Alec's upcoming January wedding. "I still can't believe they want to get married in the dead of winter. But it's their wedding, and he'll do anything Kelly wants. I think she's crazy, but that's what love's all about, right?"

"If you say so."

Ashton and Joe finished their drinks and decided to leave Pedals.

"Thanks, Gus," Ashton called out.

"Anytime, Prince Charming. Hey, where'd your Cinderella go?"

"She had to be home by midnight. Isn't that when her coach turns back into a pumpkin?" The men all laughed. "Well, I'd better know the story if I'm playing one of the main characters," Ashton called over his shoulder to Joe as they walked out of Pedals.

"Keep on reading the fairy tales. Maybe, one day, the tale will turn into reality." Ashton shook Joe's hand and headed to his car. He had listened intently to Joe as he shared the story about Gabriella's former boyfriend. Maybe she was gun-shy... Afraid of being hurt again.

He decided he wasn't going to get too caught up with her life. If she had any interest in him, he was going to let her approach him. In the coming weeks, they would see one another quite a bit as they prepared for Career Day—they were scheduled to meet weekly.

Ashton would see enough of Gabriella in the next couple of months to determine if he was getting anywhere with her. He'd let it run its course and let Gabriella choose if she wanted to be with him outside of school and the various family activities that he was sure he'd be invited to over the holidays.

Chapter Seventeen

A S IT TURNED OUT, MARY had lost track of the dates and forgot that she had a staff meeting scheduled on the first Friday of the month, so Ashton didn't see Gabriella again until almost mid-November.

He'd had an easy day at the clinic as they'd maintained the hours they'd started during the summer. Friday half-days seemed to work out well and everyone had the chance to recharge at the end of the week. He arrived at school early and was greeted by Mary at the front doors to the school. She looked a little gloomy and blamed it on the frigid temperatures they were experiencing. "Did you notice that it started snowing? It's really coming down out there, and the roads are starting to get a little slick."

"Yeah, the kids are bouncing off the walls excited with the first snowfall of the year. I'm glad it's Friday so we won't lose a day of school. I just hope everyone makes it home okay. At least this is a neighborhood school, so most people live within a mile or so of school."

"I imagine that's the best part of going to school so

close to home. I didn't have the luxury of snow days in boarding school. The only time classes were cancelled was when the power went out and that happened occasionally when we had ice storms. Otherwise, the only break we had was at the holidays and at summer, and I only came home at winter break when the campus totally shut down. Since summer school was offered, I stayed and took classes then, too."

"You never came home?"

He shook his head no.

"Didn't you miss your parents, family?"

"I didn't know any better. I had friends and what I considered family at school. In fact, many of my friends from boarding school are my closest friends today." Before he could say anymore, he heard someone approach in a fit of sneezes and coughs. He turned towards the door and was greeted with a red-nosed Gabriella.

"Sorry if I'm late. I couldn't stop coughing and had to dig around in my purse for a cough drop." Ashton took one look at her and could tell she was miserable.

"What happened to you? When did you start feeling bad?" asked Mary. "I just saw you and you seemed fine."

"This cold or whatever it is has been coming on for days. It hit me right after break this morning, and I haven't stopped sneezing or coughing since."

"Why don't you go home? It's near the end of the day, and I can find someone to cover your classroom for dismissal."

"No, I'll be alright," she said as she started sneezing uncontrollably. Her eyes were glassy and her nose ran like a faucet. Between blowing her nose and coughing, Ashton decided she should be home in bed.

"Gab–ri–ella, why don't I take you home?" She looked up at him and frowned. He knew she hated how he said her name, but he drew her name out only to get her attention. He was pretty much done teasing her with how he said her name. "Gabby, listen to Mary. Let me take you home before you get any worse."

"No, you stay here and hold your meeting. Mary can fill me in later." Pausing, she looked down at her hand that was filled with tissues. "I think I'll take you up on your offer. I'm going to pack up my stuff and go home." Looking out at the snow falling heavily, she groaned. "I didn't realize it was snowing so hard. I've got to clean off my car, too. Thanks again Mary. I appreciate it. I'll see you Monday."

"Only if you're feeling better."

"Yeah, okay," Gabriella said as she turned and slowly walked down the hallway.

Ashton threw on his coat. "I'll be right back. I'm going to clean off her car for her."

Ashton had just finished clearing the snow from her car when he heard Gabriella coming down the side-walk, sneezing all the way. He opened her car door, reached for her bag when another coughing fit hit her as she slid into the seat. "Are you sure you just got sick a few hours ago?" He bent down beside her and removed his glove. Reaching in, he placed his hand on her forehead. "I think you've got a fever."

"Yeah, I know I do," she said softly. "I just want to go home and crawl into bed for the night. I'm sure I'll feel better in the morning."

He cupped her jaw, forcing her to look him in the eyes. "Leave your back door unlocked, and I'll come by in a couple of hours and check on you."

"That's not necessary."

"Don't argue with me," he said as he stood. "I'm coming by and if you don't leave the door open, I'll jimmy the lock. Shall I bring a new lock with me?"

She shook her head and started her engine. He knew she'd do as he asked.

"Take it slow and be careful. The roads are slick, and I definitely don't want to have to dig you out of a ditch."

"I'm just driving down the street. I don't think that'll happen."

"You never know. Isn't that how Alec and Kelly got together in the first place? He found her car off the road and had to dig her out."

"Yeah, but there was also a deer involved, and I don't think I'll be running into a deer in the middle of town." She put her car into gear and drove off.

He was quite concerned with her so-called cold. If it came on that quick, he wondered how long she'd really been sick.

He hurried back into school to meet with Mary.

"How do the roads look?"

"In the short time I was in here, I bet an inch of snow has fallen and it doesn't look like it's going to let up for some time." In the end, Mary decided to postpone their meeting. She hated to not include Gabriella and she could also tell that Ashton wasn't concentrating on a thing she said.

"Ashton, let's hold off on this meeting. I hate that you drove out here in this weather, but I'd rather Gabriella be here, too. And I'll be honest with you, my mind is elsewhere."

"So is mine," he admitted. "I'm a little concerned about Gabriella. I know she says she just got sick..."

"I agree with you. Now that I think back, she has

been coughing off and on for the last couple of days. The only reason I remember is because I was observing her classroom just yesterday and she had to stop a few times and take a sip of water."

"When it comes down to it, she's bullheaded just like her brothers. I'm going to run by the store and get her some soup and then check on her. Don't worry, Mary. I'll take care of her."

"I know you will," Mary said as he put his coat back on and headed out the door.

Ashton went to Schulers and picked up some chicken soup from the deli, then grabbed a carton of fresh squeezed orange juice and some ice cream. His reasoning: ice cream makes everyone feel better. By the time he ran home, changed and cleaned his driveway from the snow that had fallen, it was almost five o'clock. He briskly walked over to Gabriella's and tried her door. She'd listened to his instructions and had left the door unlocked. The house was dark except for a light she'd left lit over the sink and one that was on in the foyer. He found his way to her bedroom and discovered she was sound asleep. He knew she had a fever as the covers were thrown aside. He approached her and again tested her forehead for a fever. She was burning up. He was wondering if she'd taken anything for her fever when he noticed a bottle of aspirin by her bedside, along with a tall glass of water. He assumed she'd taken the aspirin before falling asleep. He covered her once again and headed off to her garage where he grabbed her snow shovel and began shoveling her long driveway and sidewalk.

By the time he finished shoveling, it was well past

six-thirty. He was cold and tired. He located her coffee and made himself a cup while he warmed himself by the fire he'd started when he first arrived. He took his shoes off and stretched out on her couch. Before he knew it, he'd drifted off to sleep.

Ashton woke to her experiencing another coughing fit, except this time she couldn't seem to stop. He jumped to his feet, which scared her enough that she stopped coughing. Throwing her hand across her chest she blurted out, "You scared me to death!"

"Sorry about that. I drifted off to sleep and woke when I heard you coughing. I came running to make sure you were alright, forgetting that you didn't know I was here. I apologize for that. Now, let's take your temperature. Where's your thermometer?"

She pointed towards her bathroom. "It's in the top drawer."

He retrieved her thermometer and handed it to her. He grabbed her water glass, refilling it with cold water. When he returned, he placed out his hand for her to hand over the thermometer so he could read it. Shaking his head, he sat down beside her on the bed. "You've got quite a high fever. It's 103."

"I know I do. Who would think with a fever that I'd be as cold as I am, but I'm freezing."

"Scoot over," he said as he stood and lifted the blankets. He slid into bed beside her and pulled her into his arms. "Maybe my body heat will help."

She looked at him funny. "I have a fever, Ashton. I don't think your body heat will help. In fact, I'm going to make you sick."

"Let me worry about that," he said as he rubbed her back.

Within minutes, she was fast asleep again. As he lay

in her bed with her wrapped in his arms, his mind drifted back to the conversation he'd had with Joe in Pedals Diner about her lost love. He didn't know why they'd broken up, but what Ashton did know was he didn't want her to feel alone.

She was too independent and she needed someone to look after her and be there for her in times like this when she was ill. His thoughts had been all over the place lately. Should he or shouldn't he? Should he take that chance, follow through and ask her on the date he'd promised months ago, or shouldn't he? After seeing her in this state, he made-up his mind—he should. He decided to take on that role himself. He wanted to be the one to make sure she was well. He wanted to be the one to put a smile on her face. And he wanted to be the one to share and make memories with her. Yes, he'd take that chance and see where it led them.

Somewhere along the way, she had gotten under his skin. He didn't know where or when… When she felt better, they'd have that talk that had been looming out there. He decided he wanted to go on this journey with her. He didn't know where it would lead, but he was going to be there, guiding them down whatever path lay ahead for them.

Chapter Eighteen

A SHTON HAD STAYED WITH GABRIELLA until the next morning when her fever broke and she seemed like she was on the road to recovery. He re-shoveled her driveway and sidewalk, clearing the snow that had fallen overnight before returning home. She thanked him for watching over her and assured him she'd take it easy the remainder of the weekend. She couldn't believe he had spent the night with her. He took care of her. He was concerned about her well-being and she liked that. She didn't know how she'd make it up to him.

She graded papers and felt well enough to start getting her Christmas decorations out. Since Thanksgiving was the following week, she wanted to have her house decorated so she could enjoy watching her tree during her evenings grading papers. She loved watching her tree, listening to Christmas carols, and just soaking in the season. Christmas was her favorite holiday and nothing was going to prevent her from enjoying it.

By the time she dragged her tree up from the basement, she was exhausted and decided to hold off on decorating until the following week. She still had some lingering effects from her cold and decided to just hunker down on her couch and watch TV. She drifted off to sleep and was awakened with the ringing of her doorbell. Slowly she rose from the couch and made her way to the foyer when her doorbell rang again.

It was Sunday afternoon and she wasn't expecting anyone. She slowly opened the door and was greeted by Ashton. He was holding a grocery bag in one hand and a movie in the other and barreled through the doorway. She was exasperated as she watched him head towards her kitchen. "I don't recall inviting you in," she called out as she followed him to the back of the house.

"You didn't," he called over his shoulder as he unpacked the grocery bag, adding its contents to her refrigerator. "I've got a roasted chicken, some vegetables, and a salad here… Oh, I've also got the first of the Christmas cookies from Schulers."

She watched as he made himself at home, grabbing a coffee cup and envelope of hot cocoa that she had sitting on the counter. He filled her tea pot and set it on the stove to warm. Turning back from the stove, he had a huge smile on his face. "What? What's wrong? Are you still feeling ill?"

"What's wrong is I don't like the fact that you barged in here with what I presume is dinner, and that you've taken the last of my favorite flavor of hot cocoa. I gather you intend to stay awhile, too."

"Well, I did bring a holiday movie. You do like them, don't you?"

She hesitated. "I do," she said. "But why? Why are

you doing this? I don't understand why you're being so nice to me. You took care of me Friday night, shoveled my driveway... I just don't understand," she said, shaking her head.

He walked to her side and reached for her hands. Squeezing them gently, he leaned down and looked her directly in the eyes. "I was worried about you. I thought you'd be lonely this weekend, and since I wasn't doing anything special, I decided to spend it with you. Do I need a reason to visit a friend who's been ill?"

She looked away from him, not wanting him to know how much his gesture really affected her. She'd never had anyone outside of her family or true friends check on her when she was sick. She started to pull away, but he drew her near. "Gabriella, I just want you to know—" and then her phone rang. He released her hand and she walked across the kitchen to answer her phone.

Ashton tried not to listen to her conversation. He heard Angelina's name and decided to check on the tea pot. The water was boiling, and instead of making the cup of cocoa for himself, he poured the water for her, stirred the cup, and set it on the kitchen table. He searched her cabinets and located another brand of hot chocolate and made it for himself. By the time he completed stirring the chocolate in his cup, she'd finished her conversation and joined him at the table.

She grabbed her cup and wrapped her hands around it, warming her hands. "Is it cold in here?"

"I'm okay. Maybe you're still sick?"

"No, I'm fine now—just a little cough now and then. Right after my fever broke, my nose cleared up, too. I'll just warm my hands and enjoy my cup of deliciousness." She took a sip of her drink and closed her eyes in ecstasy. "I love this hot cocoa. One of my student's gave it to me last year for Christmas. I haven't been able to find it in the stores. I guess I'll have to look a little harder."

He watched her as she savored her drink. She had a look of pure joy on her face as she swallowed the warm liquid. He wished he could put that look on her face as well.

He stood and reached for her hand. "Come on, grab your drink and let's watch this movie. I heard it's a holiday classic. I wouldn't know, but I'm willing to give it a try."

She grabbed her cup while he grabbed his, along with the cookies and movie. She followed him into the family room and settled herself onto the couch, placing her drink on the coffee table in front of her. She watched him as he put the movie into the DVD player and pressed play. He walked to the couch, sitting down beside her.

"What?" he asked as he took a sip of his drink.

"I don't get it. You've never seen this movie before, yet you rented it."

"I did, for you. Alec and I were talking earlier today, and I was telling him about your cold."

"What did you do that for?"

"We were talking about a patient, and I told him it sounded like you—how quickly you got sick."

"Oh."

"Then he told me The Bells of St. Mary's was one of your favorite holiday movies. I don't know why, but he did. So, I decided to rent it and come by and check on you… That's okay, isn't it?"

"I guess," she said as she reached for her drink. "I'm

just surprised, that's all." Taking a sip of her hot cocoa, she added, "Thank you for checking on me. That was kind of you."

"Not a problem. I would do that for any neighbor who isn't feeling well."

"But I'm not your neighbor."

"Close enough," he said as he reached for a cookie and became engrossed in the movie. As the movie played, she'd catch a glimpse of him out of the corner of her eye. He really seemed to enjoy the movie. At one point, he threw his arm around her shoulders and drew her close. Even though this was her favorite movie, she couldn't concentrate on the storyline. Her thoughts kept drifting to the man sitting next to her.

She didn't understand him at all. Why did he come by? Why did he take the time and rent her all-time favorite holiday classic? She closed her eyes momentarily and snuggled into his side. She enjoyed being with him, she really did. She just didn't understand him or his motives.

The movie ended and she sat up, pulling away from him. He jumped up and turned off the DVD player and television when he noticed her Christmas decorations sitting in the corner. "Where'd all that come from?"

"Oh, I pulled it out earlier today. Since I'm feeling better, I thought I'd have the energy to start decorating. Not the case—I'm still a little tuckered out, and I think I'll work on it this week. We have a half day on Tuesday and then the rest of the week we're off for Thanksgiving. When I'm not helping my mom with the dinner preparations, I'll fit it in somewhere." She turned back to him, "You're coming for dinner, right?"

"I..."

"Ashton, you have to. My mom's expecting you. She doesn't take no for an answer, and Alec did invite you weeks ago. What's the problem? If you're wavering because you're not family, don't. You are family. Anyone who works for the practice is family. If you haven't figured that out by now, you're not the smart, intelligent man that I thought you were."

"I normally just spend the day alone."

"Why would you do that? Don't you have a big Thanksgiving blow-out with turkey and all of the fixings?"

"I have turkey, but it's not a big family affair."

"Really? Don't you see your family?" She knew his mom was still alive, but knew little about her or any of his other family.

"I haven't seen my family in a long time. I don't remember the last Thanksgiving we spent together."

"You mean… Ever?"

"I wasn't ever home for Thanksgiving."

She stared at him. "Where were you? On a tropical island, on a ski slope in the middle of nowhere? What were your traditions for Thanksgiving?"

"I have no traditions. I pretty much stayed in my room and did homework, and then had a meal. Nothing special."

"You mean your mom made you do school work while you were on holiday?"

"I wasn't really on a holiday."

"I'm still not following you."

He stood and grabbed their mugs and started towards the kitchen. She jumped up and followed him. He went to the sink and started washing the mugs, staring out across her backyard. It was barren of her beautiful flowers that filled it during the warm summer months.

Everything was brown that laid atop the snow. No leaves were on the trees, just a lonely cold looking environment.

When he thought back to being in school, he just remembered being cold inside most of the time. He had no family to speak of except for the handful of friends that were in the same boat as he was. He'd made friends with them, but outside of that, he felt nothing. And that's why he believed he'd had such a rough demeanor around that hospital. It took her father to turn the cold, unfeeling doctor into one that focused on his patients, making sure they were taken care of and loved. That was definitely not a feeling he'd had growing up. His parents had ignored him, never calling or visiting him while in school. He was on his own from the time he was seven. He'd made his own enjoyment and that often included reading and studying. He didn't really know how to make friends outside of those he lived twenty-four/seven with in boarding school. He had been cold-hearted until that one day that changed his life—the day that he met John Alvarez and his whole life changed. He felt like he'd gained the father he'd never had. The coldness that enveloped him slowly began to fade as John took him under his tutelage and turned him into the doctor and man that he'd slowly become over the last several years.

Ashton was slowly beginning to feel like he was part of a family. Joe and Alec had welcomed him into the practice with open arms. Although they'd hit a few rough patches along the way, Ashton felt like he was a part of something. He was a part of a loving family that saw the good in him. He was thankful for that cold winter day that he'd met John. He didn't know if

John knew that he felt that way, but he did. Someday he'd fully divulge to John how he'd changed his life forever.

He did his best to change the subject of Thanksgiving, and he was actually successful when he suggested they warm up the chicken and start dinner. While she gathered the dishes to warm the chicken and vegetables in the oven, Ashton returned to her family room and started pulling out the decorations. He took out what he could tell was a handmade ornament that, he assumed, was from one of her students. Ornament after ornament he could tell came from someone important to her.

Gabriella stood in the doorway, watching him. A somber looking expression crossed his face. He fingered each ornament, looking as though he'd never experienced this in his lifetime. After his comment about Thanksgiving, she wondered if he'd celebrated Christmas, and if he did, did he even decorate a tree?

She walked over and placed her hand on his shoulder. "Ashton, I'd rather wait to do this. I'm really not feeling up to it... I normally play carols and dance around the room as I decorate, and I don't have the energy. I'll do it later in the week."

"Can I help?" he asked softly. She wasn't sure she'd heard him correctly. He stood and looked her in the eyes, "I'd like to help, if you'll let me." He walked away from her and looked out the window. "I don't really remember ever decorating a tree. I'd like to help you and maybe hear the stories behind some of these ornaments."

She was shocked. She wondered about his childhood, but more importantly, she wondered about his
parents, about who raised him. Sadness overcame her.
"Sure, I'd like that. I'd love to tell you about all of the
wonderful people that have touched my life."

Gabriella was thrilled that she only had a day and
a half of school before Thanksgiving break. She still
wasn't feeling totally herself, and when the bell rang
signaling the end of school on Tuesday, she was overjoyed. She still had her lingering cough though, and
if she didn't know better, she thought she might be
running a low-grade fever again.

She went home directly after school and threw on
her lounge pants and a sweatshirt. She phoned her
mother, begging off helping her make pies for Thanksgiving. "Mom, I'm just beat. I can't seem to get over
this cold. I hope I'll feel better so I can help you
tomorrow." Knowing how her mother would react
she added, "Why don't you call Angelina. She'd be
more than glad to help."

All she heard was dead air on the phone. "Mom, are
you still there?"

"I am... And you know how your sister-in-law is. I
think she could burn boiling water."

"Now Mom, Angelina's not that bad. In fact, she's
improved since marrying Alejandro."

"I'm just kidding. She has turned into a pretty
decent cook. I just don't want to bother her."

"I'm not buying that one, Mom."

"Well, I don't," Maria said, chuckling into the phone.
"I hope you feel better, dear. Don't worry about
tomorrow. I'll be fine if you can't make it. I did it

alone all those years ago."

"I know, I just enjoy helping you."

"I know you do. Now, lie down and get some rest. Oh, by the way, I haven't spoken with Alec in a few days. Do you know if Ashton's coming?"

"I don't know, Mom. I really don't know."

She hung up the phone with her mom and replayed her conversation with Ashton from Sunday regarding Thanksgiving. He must have had a lonely childhood... It must explain the way he once acted with Matthew: reserved and distant. She remembered how he'd treated Matthew and Angelina at one of Matthew's office visits. He'd been cold and unfeeling about Alejandro and his treatment of Matthew. In time, he'd grown and had apologized for his ways. From the little he'd told her about his childhood—or rather, non-childhood— it seemed to have turned him into the man he'd been when she'd first met him. But then her father got ahold of him and helped mold him into the man he was today. She liked what she saw and hoped he continued to grow.

As per the last few days since getting sick, she fell asleep on her couch. She felt a draft and slowly began to wake. As she opened her eyes, she saw a shadow on the floor in front of her. She knew she wasn't seeing things and became scared. Slowly she raised her eyes and saw the legs of a man standing before her. She screamed and tried to rise into a sitting position. A hand flew out, causing her to pause mid-rise.

"Gabby, it's me," Ashton called out. She raised her eyes and saw him standing before her.

Throwing her hand up to her heart, she said, "You scared the living daylights out of me! Again! How the hell did you get in here? And why didn't you knock?"

"I did knock. I rang the doorbell, knocked on the window… I did everything I could to wake you, then decided to check your back door. And you know what I found?"

She rolled her eyes.

"An unlocked door. Don't you know better? You need to keep your doors locked."

"And what, pay for a new lock?"

He chuckled.

"I was so tired when I came home, I just wanted to lie down. I guess I forgot to flip the lock."

"Indeed you did. Now, what's this about still not feeling well?"

"I was just tired after a long week."

"Long week? It's Tuesday."

"Well, it was long for me… Now, why are you here? What do you want?"

"Did you forget? I thought we were going to decorate your tree tonight. I even brought pizza from Pizzas, Pies and More."

She sat up on the couch and pulled her hair back from her face. "I forgot. I'm sorry."

He reached out a hand and felt her forehead. "You're a little warm, but not too bad. Do you have a fever?"

"I think I had one earlier. I'm just really tired and a little hungry, too." She put her legs of the floor and started to stand. Losing her balance, she fell back to the couch. "Oops, I lost my balance."

"You could say that. Luckily the couch was behind you. Are you dizzy?"

She stood there for a few seconds, moving her head from side to side. "I feel a little pressure in my ears. I guess it's sniffing from my cold. Let me stand here for a second… Okay, I'm better." She led him towards the kitchen where she moved to the cabinet to pull out plates and glasses for their pizza.

"You sit down. I'll do that," he ordered her as he grabbed her elbow and led her to the table.

"I'm fine."

"Just do as I say, okay? I'll feel better about it."

She scrunched her face and dropped down onto her chair. Gabriella watched Ashton move about her kitchen. He seemed to know where everything was. It was almost as if he lived here. She shook her head at the thought. She enjoyed seeing him move about her kitchen so freely and hoped that it wouldn't be the last time she felt this way.

He grabbed the plates, glasses for the iced tea he'd purchased, and napkins. She set a place in front of her while she watched him. He placed the pizza on the table and lifted the lid. "Hamburger and mushroom, deep dish. One of your favorites, right?"

"How did you know... Joe?"

He nodded as he reached for a slice of the deep dish pie. The cheese oozed out as he placed the piece on her plate. "How could I forget our first pizza together? Joe was the one to order it." He set her plate in front of her. "For my lady," he said in his princely voice, smiling at her.

"Thanks," she said, taking a bite of her pizza. "Oh my," she said around chewing. "This tastes wonderful. I think this is the first thing I've been able to taste since last week."

"It is good. In fact, this is the first time I've had a deep dish from Pizzas, Pies and More. I normally eat the thin crust pizza." He took another bite. "So, tell me about your week."

"It seemed like it would never end."

"You were only in school a day and a half," he laughed.

"I know. I just didn't feel well. But I do feel a lot better since I came home and took my nap. Maybe I'll be able to help Mom tomorrow with Thanksgiving preparations." Taking a sip of her tea, she continued, "Speaking of Thanksgiving, are you coming over? My mom asked me earlier, and I didn't know what to tell her. So, are you? Are you coming for dinner?"

He picked at his pizza, avoiding her gaze. He pulled a mushroom from amongst the cheese and sauce and popped it into his mouth. She watched him as he tried to avoid her question. "You know, I really don't care whether you come or not, but I think you owe my mother an answer. It's not like another mouth will impact how much she cooks, but it would be nice if she knew to set a place setting for you."

"I haven't decided yet."

"Haven't decided? Today's Tuesday. You really only have tomorrow to let her know."

"And Thursday, too."

"That's kind of rude of you to wait until you appear at the door to let her know."

"It's just that…"

"Do what you want, Ashton," Gabriella said tersely. "That's all I have to say." She started to stand, and Ashton placed his hand over hers.

"I'm sorry, Gabriella. I'm just not good at this."

"Good at what? Accepting an invitation to dinner?"

"No, at family time."

She paused and looked at him. He really meant what he said. He didn't do families. "Well, you came to Angel's christening."

"I had an ulterior motive. I had to apologize to

Matthew."

"That's not why you came, and you know it. You came because you were asked, and you wanted to be a part of your new family. I get it, Ashton. I get that you didn't have a good life growing up, but don't make my mother be the bad person here. She wants you to feel a part of our family. In fact, you *are* a part of our family. Working at the clinic is being part of one big family. She wants to include you, so why are you withdrawing? Embrace it and start over. Be a part of our family, one that you can call your own. Latch on to it. Thrive, grow. We want you there. Or be a part of Javier's family, if not ours. But do something, and quit feeling sorry for yourself. You'll never grow as a man or a doctor if you can't embrace friends and family. That's what life's about, at least that's what I believe. I don't know what I'd do without my friends and family. They make me whole. Maybe if you started to feel this way, your attitude toward life and others would be different."

"Gabriella..." He stood and carried his plate to the sink. She watched as he rinsed it off and added it to the dishwasher. He braced his hands along the sink and leaned over slightly. Standing upright, he turned around and leaned against the cabinets for support. "Okay, I'll do it."

"Do it? Don't think it's something that you have to do. Come because you want to, not because you feel like you have to. We don't want you there if you are going to be in a bad mood. Thursday is Thanksgiving. We are to be thankful for so many things. In fact, Thanksgiving was once a day that greatly affected our family, and not for the good." She cleared her throat. "Angelina was in the hospital with peritonitis after having donated a portion of her liver to Colleen. It was a scary time for everyone, especially Angelina and Alejandro. They made it through that holiday, not on the best of terms. But then, things changed. Our family looks at Thanksgiving now as a blessing. We are thankful for so much. So, if you plan on coming just to come, putting a damper on the day, forget it. I don't want you there."

"I'll call your mother."

"Do what you want. Now, I think I'm tired and would like to go to bed. So, please leave."

She didn't understand him. One minute he was caring for her, and the next he seemed like he was walking away. He was afraid of something and she couldn't put her finger on it. And right now, she didn't even want to.

He grabbed his coat and made his way to the door. "I hope you feel better."

"Thanks," she said gruffly. Gabriella watched him as he stepped onto the porch. She saw him look back as though he wanted to say something, but he continued down the sidewalk. Her mind was reeling. She was confused and also sad. Confused about where her feelings were headed and sad for Ashton. She couldn't imagine a life without her family. They meant the world to her. She only hoped he listened to her and would decide to join their family celebrating a day of thanks.

Chapter Nineteen

THANKSGIVING MORNING DAWNED AND
GABRIELLA was still feeling poorly. She phoned
her mother, apologizing that she just didn't have the
energy to come over early and help her with the
preparations.

"Don't worry, honey. Kelly volunteered. She and
Alec came by last night and helped me with the stuff-
ing and cranberries. You take it easy, and we'll see you
later."

"Thanks, Mom." When she hung up the phone,
she realized her mother didn't say whether Ashton
had RSVP'd or not. Right now, she didn't have the
energy to deal with whether or not he was coming.
She assumed that he wasn't.

Gabriella laid down and fell asleep. She woke when
she heard her phone ringing off the hook. She tried
to ignore it. Whoever was calling her refused to leave
a message. When it started ringing for the fourth time,
she hauled herself off the couch and made it to the
phone before it hit the answering machine. Breathlessly, she answered, "Hello?"

"Where have you been? And why are you out of breath. I've been trying to reach you for the last fifteen minutes."

"I've been here all along, Ashton. What do you want?"

"Well, I am standing on your front porch, so could you let me in?"

"You're where?"

"Don't ask questions, just let me in."

She made her way to the door, and true to his word, Ashton was standing at her door. She opened the door and glared at him. He ignored her stare and asked, "Are you feeling okay? Your mom said you still weren't feeling well."

"When did you speak with her?"

"Last night and again this morning."

"Oh," was all she said as she headed off towards her family room. She bent over and grabbed the throw that she'd covered herself with. She started to fold it when he grabbed it out of her hands.

"You didn't answer me. Are you still ill?"

"I'm fine as far as you're concerned. Why are you here?"

"I offered to drive you."

"I guess I've missed something. Why did you offer to drive me and where are you driving me?"

"To your parents'."

Gabriella sat down on the couch. Huffing, she said, "Who put you up to this? My mother?"

"No, it was my idea. Come on, Gabby. I know you're not feeling well. Let me do this. Let me do this for you."

She took another deep breath and stood. "I need to get dressed. It will only take me a few minutes. Make yourself at home—it's not like you haven't done that already."

Ashton watched her as she slowly made her way to her bedroom. The witch-like Gabriella was back. Joe was right when he referred to her in that manner, especially when she didn't get her way and was unprepared. He recalled leaving her house Tuesday evening. He remembered turning back and looking at her. He knew she was upset with him, but what could he do? What could he say? He was who he was—damaged to the core. His parents had done quite a number on him. Yes, John had helped him, but he thought he'd never be able to let people into his heart. He didn't do family and never would. And now, today here he stood in her house preparing to go to a Thanksgiving celebration with her family. Just a few days ago, he never would have seen that coming. She was really starting to get under his skin—making him see the importance of family.

Gabriella reappeared. He really didn't know what she'd changed. Maybe she'd pulled her hair back… She definitely hadn't put any make-up on. Not that it mattered to him, but he knew she wasn't feeling better and wondered if, in fact, she should be attending the festivities. He didn't comment because he didn't want to get into it with her again.

They drove in silence to her parents' home. He parked his car next to Alec's in the driveway and came around to her side of the car and opened her door for her. He held his hand out, wanting to help her from the car. Surprisingly, she allowed him to help her. She grabbed onto his hand and held it as they walked to the door. He squeezed her hand just as she started to open the door. "Thanks. Thanks for coming with me."

"Like I had a choice." She released her hand from his and walked through the door. Her father greeted her with a peck on her cheek. "Hi, Dad," she said as she started to take off her coat. Ashton helped her with it and hung it on the coat tree beside the door.

"Ashton, I'm so glad you could join us. Maria is thrilled."

"I appreciate the invitation, sir."

Maria came bustling into the room. "Honey, how are you feeling?"

"Better, Mom."

"Are you sure?"

"Yep," she said trying to convince both her mother and herself. Ashton stood beside her, placing his hand on her back. She glanced over her shoulder at him and started to move. He walked alongside her, ensuring she was okay. She sat down in the family room. He sat next to her and reached for her hand. "Are you sure you're okay?"

"I said I was, and I am."

"Okay, then," he said as he stood and left her side.

Kelly joined Gabriella and kept her company. Before she knew it, the house was overflowing with people. Angelina and Alejandro arrived with Matthew and Angel. Alec appeared after having made an emergency run to the grocery store for half-n-half. Maria had used the last of it on her famous potatoes and had forgotten to pick up a spare. Almost everyone used it in their coffee and she wanted to make sure she had it on hand in case someone wanted coffee with their pumpkin pie.

Gabriella had zoned out when she realized Kelly's brother and sister had joined her. Wyatt wanted to watch a game on the television while Colleen was texting one of her friends on her phone. John and Ben, Angelina's father, were having an in-depth conversation about one of the football teams. Her mind was spinning when she felt someone sit down beside her on the couch. Ashton leaned over handing her a glass of iced tea. "Your mom said to give this to you.

"Thanks," was all she said. She sipped her tea and tried to listen as her father and Ben discussed the football game that would be held later in the day. Ashton had placed his arm on the back of the couch. He seemed like he was relaxed, enjoying his time. He chimed in occasionally on her father's discussion and then his cell phone rang. He seemed familiar with the ringtone and ignored it at first, but when it rang a second time he pulled it out of his pocket and stood, leaving the room. She couldn't make out who he was speaking with, just that he wasn't happy with whoever was on the other end. She heard him end the call and then he returned to her side. She didn't inquire who was on the other end of the conversation—it was his business.

Just as they were ready to sit down to eat, Ashton's phone rang again. It was the same ringtone as earlier. He stood again and left the room, except this time she heard how he answered the phone. "What do you want now?" he said gruffly. And then, he changed his tone. "Alistair, what? What happened? How is she?"

Who is he speaking with and who was this Alistair?

"Yes, I understand." Gabriella watched as Ashton started to pace back and forth. "Yes, when I spoke with her earlier, she didn't make sense... I should have picked up on something. No, no. It's not your fault. I'll be there tonight...Yes, I'll call you when I get to the hospital. Yes, and I'll be staying at the house. You can prepare my room. Yes, yes, I understand. Don't worry. I'll call and let you know what the doctors say."

Gabriella had entered the room just as he was completing his call. "Is everything alright?" she said as she approached him and placed her hand on his forearm. He glanced from her hand to her face before he pulled away. She could tell something was seriously wrong as his demeanor had changed in the few moments that had elapsed since taking the call. "Ashton, what's wrong. Is there something I can do?"

"No, you can't do anything. I need to go," he said as he started looking around the room, looking for something. "My coat, I need my coat."

"What's happened? Ashton, tell me so I can help." She didn't think he'd be receptive to her and especially with the way she'd treated him lately. She wanted him to know she was there wanting to help. Help as only a family member would.

"There's nothing you can do. It's my mother. I believe she may have suffered a stroke."

"Your mother? Where is she? I'll go with you to the hospital."

"No, you can't. She lives out of town." Ashton was becoming agitated. She knew a little about his lack of relationship with his parents, but also knew that in times like these history faded as you dealt with the situation that was right before your eyes. He was reaching out to his mother in her time of need, and she wanted to be by his side, supporting him, knowing that he'd have someone to fall back on.

"I'll go. Please let me."

"No, Gabriella. I don't need you. Please, I need to leave right now." Ashton made his way to the dining room where everyone had gathered to start their meal. "I'm sorry, Maria and John, but I need to leave. It's my mother. I think she's had a stroke."

John stood and Maria came to Ashton's side. She reached for his hand. "What can we do, Ashton?"

"Nothing. I just need to get on the road. It's going to take me about four hours… I hope she can hold on until I get there."

"Where does she live?"

"Branson. I'm from Branson…" He paused, looking momentarily lost. "I apologize for putting a crux in your dinner, Maria. I appreciate the invitation."

"Ashton, we're glad you came. You need to get to your mother. Please stay in touch. Let us know how she fairs."

"I will. And thank you for your concern."

Gabriella had reappeared with his coat in hand. She walked him to the door.

"Thank you, Gabriella. I hope you feel better."

"Ashton, please don't concern yourself with me. You need to focus on your mother's health, not mine."

"But I do," he said as he leaned down and kissed her forehead.

"Keep in touch, please."

"I will. I promise." And with that, Ashton passed through the doorway into the night.

From the little he had spoken of his mother, she hadn't thought that he was in touch with her at all. Apparently she'd been wrong since his mother was his first call. Ashton needed family and she certainly hoped that he became cognizant of that after spending a little time with hers.

Ashton didn't know how he did it, but he made his way to Branson in less than four hours. The wind must've been at his back, he thought as he walked through the doors of Branson's Memorial Hospital. He approached the information desk. "My name is Ashton Holder, and my mother Jana was rushed in here a few hours ago."

The volunteer took her time looking up his mother's information. She was an older woman with grey hair that was wound into a french twist. She reminded him of his mother when he'd last seen her five years earlier at his father's funeral. But this woman was kind and seemed gentle, whereas his mother was neither of those things. He realized he needed to get those thoughts out of his head. His mother's life was in the balance, and he needed to be in a more positive frame of mind.

The kind lady told him she'd been moved to the intensive care unit located on the fifth floor. Ashton thanked her and headed for the elevator.

Ashton heard a beep on his phone and pulled up the incoming text. "Did you arrive safely? How's your mom?" Gabriella. Her text didn't surprise him in the least. Ashton knew he'd be hearing from her and had actually expected her call while he was on the road. He knew she was concerned about both him and his mother Knowing Gabriella as he did, that was just a part of who she was. She wanted to be supportive and be there for him if he needed it. He'd answer her later. He decided to turn off his phone as he entered the elevator and headed towards the fifth floor. He wasn't sure what would greet him when he crossed into the Intensive Care Unit. He hoped for the best, after all she was his mother.

ـے

Joe had had enough of her worrying and brought her home after Thanksgiving dinner. Gabriella was beside herself. Ashton hadn't phoned or texted her back. When she tried calling him, his phone went directly to voicemail. Early Friday morning, she was staring at her phone, waiting impatiently for it to ring, when her doorbell rang instead.

"Come on, pack a bag and let's go."

"Go where?" she asked as she watched Joe enter her house. He had left late the night before after spending some time with her. He'd done everything in his power to get her mind off of Ashton, but it hadn't worked.

"Just do it." Joe said as he walked towards her bedroom. She grabbed an overnight bag and threw in some clothes. "That's good. We won't be gone long. I need to be back by Sunday afternoon. I'm going to cover for him." And with that, Joe walked out of her bedroom towards the front door. *Cover for whom?* she thought and then she realized. He was doing this for Ashton.

At a little after one on Friday afternoon, they walked through the doors of Branson's Memorial Hospital. They sought out the information desk and discovered that Jana Holder was in the fifth floor ICU. Just as they were ready to hop on the elevator, Joe's cell rang. "I've got to take this call. You go on ahead, and I'll meet you." She nodded at her brother and watched the elevator doors close, leaving him on the first floor.

Her stomach rolled as the elevator climbed to the fifth floor. She wasn't sure how Ashton would greet her. She was thankful that her brother elected to drive her all the way to Branson. She'd been worried about Ashton and his mother. And Joe had picked up on her concern.

The doors whooshed open and she departed the elevator. Her stomach took another spin. Nerves, she thought—she didn't know how he would take to her presence. She placed her hand on her stomach as she began to walk down the hallway towards the ICU.

As she neared the closed double doors that signified the entrance to the ICU, she came upon a waiting room that sat right outside the unit. As she turned to enter the room, she discovered the room had one occupant. He sat facing the wall of windows with his back to the entrance. He sat in a chair, his head bent over. She couldn't tell if he was sleeping or just resting his eyes. His legs were stretched out in front of him, crossed at the ankles and his hands were clasped in his lap.

She approached him and was unsure how to let him know she was there. She reached down and placed her right hand on his shoulder. She didn't speak a word. It was as though he knew it was her—he reached up for her hand and squeezed it, interlocking his fingers with hers. She squatted down and threw her left arm around his shoulder, hugging him. She stayed in this position for about a minute when she sat down beside him. He reached for her hand and held on.

"How is she?"

"She's in critical but stable condition. She suffered

a stroke."

"Ashton, I'm so sorry."

They sat with their hands enmeshed. Then Joe appeared and sat down across from them.

A few minutes passed when Joe finally spoke. "Ashton, you look a mess. Why don't you and Gabby go get something to eat? Take a break. Do something. I'll sit here, and if there's a change in her condition, I'll text you."

"Come on, you need to eat something. I bet you haven't eaten a single thing," she said as she started to stand.

"No, I haven't had anything since breakfast yesterday. I could use a coffee."

"You know you need more than that. Take your time," Joe said.

Ashton stood and reached for Joe's hand. "Thanks, man. I appreciate it. I appreciate you coming all the way down here, especially when you've never met my mom and know absolutely nothing about her."

"That's what family's for," she chimed in, standing and stretching her hand towards his. He latched onto it and squeezed it tightly. "You're a part of our family, whether you want to believe it or not."

He nodded. "We won't be long," he said as she led him from the room.

"Take as long as you need," Joe called out as they headed down the hallway.

Gabriella pressed the down button on the elevator. When she and Joe had arrived, she'd noticed the hospital had a restaurant of sorts near the lobby and thought they'd have a little more privacy if they ate there. They entered the elevator and were the only ones in it. After pressing the button for the first floor, she looked up into his eyes. He looked so forlorn that she wrapped her arms around his waist and hugged him. He put his arms around her and dropped his head on top of hers. They stood in one another's arms until she heard the elevator ding signaling they'd reached their destination.

She grabbed his hand and led him from the elevator, down the hall towards the restaurant. They'd just missed the lunch rush and there were still a few diners eating in the small establishment. The hostess led them to their table and took their drink orders. They both ordered iced teas. He reached his hand across the table grabbing ahold of her fingers. "Thanks for coming. It really means a lot to me."

"Well, when you didn't answer my texts, I was worried. Joe saw my concern last night and decided to drop everything to bring me down here. We have to leave tomorrow since I have school on Monday and he plans on covering for you."

He sipped his iced tea and said, "I appreciate any amount of time that you stay. You don't know what it means to me that you came all this way to be with me."

"As I said, you're family. I—rather, we—didn't want you being alone. Alec couldn't come since he's covering the practice. And don't forget my dad can also jump in and help out, too. You need to focus on your mom. Alec and Joe will make sure everything's covered."

"I know." He grabbed his iced tea and started to take another sip. He pulled his hand away from hers and began staring off into space. She didn't say a word. She wanted him to express what was on his mind, what he was feeling.

"I haven't seen her since my dad's funeral five years ago. I rarely spoke with her, and that's why I was taken aback when she called me yesterday out of the blue. I should have known something was wrong, but I just didn't want to deal with her. I was enjoying myself and didn't want her putting a damper on my day. She was rambling on and on about nothing. In fact, when I think about it, her speech was somewhat slurred, but I thought maybe she'd been drinking." He took another drink of his tea. "I should have been more aware, focused on what she was and wasn't saying."

She reached for his hand. "Ashton, you can't blame yourself. You just can't."

"I realize that now. When I heard Alistair's voice, I knew something was wrong."

"Alistair?"

"My mother's butler. He's worked for the family since I was a baby."

She was surprised. A butler? What kind of life did Ashton lead?

"Alistair calls me about once a week and fills me in on what's happening at the house and the resort."

Resort? She just let him speak. She'd find out what he meant by resort at another time.

"Alistair is more than aware of my relationship with my mother. But he also knows that somewhere deep down she cares about me. And I have to say, I care about her, too. She is my mother. I just can't be in her presence."

The waitress interrupted their conversation and took their order. She ordered a garden salad while Ashton ordered a club sandwich. The waitress brought a basket of rolls to the table and Ashton grabbed one. He pulled the roll apart and took a small bite. He stared at his roll and then proceeded with his story. "Alistair was with her when she collapsed. He was just getting ready to call me and instead dialed 911. He was so upset. He blames himself for not recognizing the change in her. He'd been busy preparing for Thanksgiving dinner and hadn't paid much attention to her and her mannerisms. When he recognized the slurring of her speech, that's when she collapsed... I'll call Alistair and have him prepare two more bedrooms. No, maybe I'll have you check into the resort... I don't know. It's a holiday, so they're probably booked."

Ashton pulled out his cell phone and pressed a number. He cleared his throat and started speaking, "Alistair, she's holding her own. Would it be too much trouble to prepare two bedrooms for the evening in addition to mine? What? No, I have a couple of friends that came down from St. Louis to sit with me... They have to be back tomorrow, so it's only for the night. Yes, I am spending the night there tonight. If anything changes, the hospital can phone me..."

She hated sitting here, listening to his one-sided conversation. And then it was over. He set his phone on the table. She hated to inconvenience this Alistair. Maybe they should stay at a hotel.

"Alistair's going to freshen up a room for each of you. In fact, he's looking forward to visitors. He said it would help put his mind at ease."

"Oh, that's good." She didn't want to press him, but she gathered that his mother must have a rather large home if Alistair could freshen up not only his own room, but two additional rooms for her and Joe. She was glad that she'd come to sit with him, if only for the day. This visit would definitely give her a glimpse into the life Ashton Holder once lived.

The waitress brought their lunch. They pretty much ate in silence. The waitress had left the bill when she delivered their food, so when they finished Ashton threw down a twenty dollar bill. He rose and reached for her hand. "Ready?"

"If you are." She grabbed ahold of his hand.

Instead of heading towards the elevators, he led them out the lobby doors and down the sidewalk towards a sculpture garden that was tucked into an alcove next to the hospital. The temperatures in Branson for late November were rather mild. The trees were barren with a few scattered leaves blowing about the garden as he led her to a bench. They sat down and he put his arm around her shoulders drawing her close to his side.

"I didn't notice this when we came in. How did you know it was here?"

He seemed a little reluctant to answer, but she saw resolve in his eyes. "I knew about it because my father established the gardens in honor of my grandparents."

She was shocked.

"My grandfather helped start up this hospital. He was a pediatrician, too. When he died, my grandmother came up with the idea to start the sculpture garden. Sadly, she died before it was completed and never saw all of these beautiful sculptures honoring children, families…" Ashton stopped and took a deep breath. "I haven't been here in a long, long time."

As they sat there, the wind picked up and the few leaves that remained on the ground started blowing around in circles at the base of the sculpture across from them. It depicted a mother, father, and small child. The parents were holding hands and were looking down at their small child that was holding a bouquet of flowers.

"That sculpture held some meaning to my father. I don't know what since it definitely didn't depict my childhood. Maybe it reminded him of growing up. Who knows?" He stood and reached for her hand. "Come on, I'll show you around and then I think it's time we go back and see how she's doing."

They took their time taking in the remaining sculptures and returned to the ICU. Joe had drifted off to sleep while waiting for them to return. In fact, they startled him when they returned, causing him to almost fall out of his seat.

"You okay?"

"Yeah, I just dozed off for a minute. I checked with the nurse about twenty minutes ago and she's still holding her own."

She sat down in a chair that overlooked the sculpture gardens. She stared out the window, replaying their earlier conversation. Not only was his grandfather a pediatrician, but he'd also built the hospital that she now sat in. She had learned a great deal about Ashton during their lunch.

The longer she sat there, the more tired she became. They sat in the waiting room until six when she started yawning. She was tired from their drive and her damn cold that she just couldn't seem to shake. She wasn't feeling a hundred percent, that's for sure. The next thing that she was aware of was his hand holding hers and their walking down the hallway towards what she didn't know. Soon she'd get a further glimpse into his life as a child—entering the childhood home that held only a few happy memories for him.

Chapter Twenty

JOE AND GABRIELLA LEFT BRANSON at six o'clock Sunday evening, staying a day longer than they'd originally planned. Joe estimated they'd get back around ten o'clock. Ashton walked them to the lobby. He reached out to shake Joe's hand, but instead Joe pulled him into a hug. "Don't worry about the practice. Stay as long as you need to."

"Thanks, I appreciate it. Just go easy on John for me."

Joe chuckled—Ashton was referring to the times that their father had substituted for Alec while he was visiting Kelly in Knoxville before she'd moved back to St. Louis.

Ashton turned towards Gabriella and pulled her into a tight embrace. He held on to her longer than needed, and as he pulled away, brushed a kiss on her forehead. "You take it easy. Get rest and try to stay well."

"I'm fine. It's you and your mother we're concerned with. Stay in touch. No call is too late." And with that, they walked out of Branson's Memorial Hospital. Ashton watched them as they made their way to the parking lot. He stood, looking out the windows for some time before he turned and headed back to the ICU.

~

"He looks really exhausted, doesn't he?" Joe asked Gabriella as they merged onto the highway headed for home.

"Yeah, he does. I don't think I've seen him look so tired in all the time I've known him. Outside of not getting any sleep, I'm sure the stress from worry is taking its toll, along with their lack of a relationship."

"I would have to agree. Maybe something good comes out of this and they'll find their way back to a mother-son relationship."

"I hope so, Joe. I know he really has difficulties accepting a family. He had a hard time accepting Mom's invitation to Thanksgiving. I guess when you have grown up with little attention from your parents, you have a distrust in family. I don't know about you, but did you know he came from money?" She recalled following Ashton back to his home.

They had wound their way through the Ozark Mountains until they came upon a gated driveway. Ashton had slowed his car as he approached the drive. She'd watched him as he engaged the opener to the lighted gates, waiting for them to open so they could pass through and head up the long winding driveway.

She'd been speechless as they passed through the gates. The entrance spoke of sheer wealth. As they wound their way along the lighted roadway towards the house, her eyes had about popped out of her head.

They'd driven through a stand of trees and the brightly-lit mansion had loomed before her and Joe. Joe had looked at Gabriella and they'd both said, "Wow!" in unison as Ashton slowed the car to a stop. "Look at that house," she'd whispered, hardly able to speak.

She hadn't known what she should say to Ashton. She didn't want to overplay his apparent wealth, so she hadn't said a word. They exited his car, meeting Ashton at the bottom of the stairs. He'd escorted them into the house, never once addressing his obvious wealth.

"No, in fact I was totally surprised when he brought up the fact that his mother had a butler," Joe said as he drove. "And then when we pulled into their gated driveway and drove up, what like a mile-long driveway?"

"It was long, that's all I can say."

"And when we pulled up at the portico, I was amazed at the view. It overlooked the entire town of Branson."

"I know. You could see for miles."

"Maybe Dad knew of his wealth. I don't know, but Gabriella, his dad owned the largest resort in Branson. Can you imagine?"

"No, I can't. And to think, he currently lives a pretty simple life. He definitely doesn't flaunt his wealth."

"No, he doesn't."

"I wonder what happened, and why he doesn't get along with his mom. In fact, I wonder if he and his dad got along."

"Who knows? I'm sure Ashton will tell us when he wants us to know."

About twenty miles outside St. Louis, Gabriella dozed off.

❦

His mother had improved and her doctors hoped to move her to a regular room the following day. If all went well, she'd be moved to a rehabilitation facility at the end of the week.

The stroke had affected her speech and she had some weakness on the right side of her body. The doctors believed that with therapy she would fully recover. Ashton was going to make sure she settled into the rehab center, and then he was returning to St. Louis. He'd follow her progress through the doctors at the facility and then Alistair would continue daily updates when his mother returned home.

Jana improved more quickly than the doctors first thought, and they released her to the rehabilitation center earlier than expected. Ashton made sure she was comfortable and then headed back home to St. Louis. He spent more time in Branson than he wanted to and left Friday morning after visiting with his mother one last time. She was still having difficulties with her speech, but each day she'd shown improvement. The last thing she said to Ashton before he left her was, "I love you, son."

He hadn't been able to return the same words, and in fact, had a hard time even kissing her on the cheek when he'd said goodbye. He didn't know if he'd ever be able to say those three words to his mother again. He cared for her, sure, but he wasn't sure if he'd ever be able to tell her he loved her.

He hadn't spoken to Gabriella since she left the previous Sunday. He texted Alec and let him know that he was returning to St. Louis and would be able to fill in for him that weekend. Alec replied, saying not to worry, that they'd see him bright and early Monday morning. He was lucky to have partners like Alec and

Joe. They were businessmen, yes, but were also family men, too. Family was an important part of their lives and a huge piece to their practice, and he guessed he needed to learn how to be more accepting of it. He also needed to learn how to embrace being a member of the Alvarez family because he *was* a member of the family. They'd accepted him from the get-go, but he needed to learn how to show them how much each of them truly meant to him.

He pulled into town at four o'clock. He quickly changed his clothes and then ran to Schulers. He wanted to do something special for Gabriella, so he picked up some steaks, potatoes for baking, makings for a salad, and cheesecake for dessert. He didn't think she'd decorated her tree yet, or at least he hoped she hadn't because he wanted to help her. He didn't recall decorating a tree and wanted to do it this year—with her. He wanted to start doing things that families did, making memories of his own, and he hoped she'd let him start making those memories with her.

By the time he reached her house, it was a little after five. He knew she got home around five on Fridays from school. She liked to stay a little later, tidy up her classroom, and set out the materials she needed for Monday.

∽

Gabriella had just walked through the door when she heard a knock at her kitchen door. Most everyone came to her front door, so she was a little concerned who would be at her back door. She flipped on the outside light and was pleasantly surprised when she saw Ashton standing there with several grocery bags at his feet. She flipped the lock and opened the door. "What are you doing here? How's your mom?"

"Let me in before you inundate me with questions, okay?"

She chuckled and stepped aside as he reached down for his bags and walked through her door. She didn't know what she should do. Should she hug him, kiss him on the cheek... she just didn't know. He put her questions aside as he pulled her into his arms and soundly kissed her on the lips. She definitely didn't expect that. The kiss took her by surprise, and once she calmed herself, realized that she enjoyed it—almost expected it.

"Oh my," she said as he released her and went directly to the counter and began pulling food out of the bags. "What do you have there?"

"Let's see. I have steaks, potatoes, makings for a salad, and..."

"And what? Is that cheesecake I see peeking out the side of that bag?"

"I believe it is," he said as he threw open her refrigerator and placed the steaks, salad makings, and cheesecake inside. He closed the door, spun around, and grabbed her hand.

"What now?" she asked as he pulled her towards the family room where he'd last seen the Christmas decorations. Her decorations were still sitting stacked in the corner of the room. He pulled her behind him as he approached the pile of boxes that had grown since he was last at her home.

"More?" he inquired as he pointed to the stacked boxes.

She wasn't sure what he was asking. Since she hadn't felt well, she hadn't finished pulling all of her decorations out when he'd come at Thanksgiving.

"Of course there're more decorations. This is Christmas."

"Last time I was here, you only had that stack," he said, pointing to the tree and some of the lights. "Now, there's this huge stack, and what's this?" he said, pointing to some of her wooden, lighted displays.

"I just finished pulling everything out. At least, I think I have everything. Those are my ornaments, candles, table linens…"

"No, that," he said, pointing to her reindeer display that was covered with plastic trash bags.

"Oh, those are my lighted reindeer that I put up in the front yard. They're animated. Their heads move up and down. And that's my lighted display that I put on the front porch. It's a snowman welcoming everyone to the house."

"Wow," he said as he lifted the lid on one of the boxes that contained her ornaments. He pulled out one of her antique glass ornaments, unwrapping it. The glitter on the ornament sparkled under the light. He carefully looked at it, setting it back into the box. "These are beautiful." He lifted the lid on another box, then swiftly turned around and reached for her hands. He pulled her closer into his body. She wasn't sure what he was doing—this was so unlike the Ashton she knew. Sure, they'd kissed a few times, but she thought he'd mainly done it to just shut her up. She didn't believe he meant anything by them, but this time… he seemed different. More serious.

"Will you do me a favor?"

"If I can," she replied as she closely watched his face. At first he had a faraway look in his eyes, then it changed to one of sadness, and then, it slowly brightened.

He cupped the side of her face as he spoke. "Will you let me help you decorate your tree, your house? As I told you the other week, I don't think I've ever decorated at Christmas. At least, I don't remember a time... I've never done it before, I'm sure of it." His thumb caressed her lips as he continued, "I want to hear about all of the ornaments, the stories behind the children—everything." He pulled away and turned his back to her, waiting for her response.

Gabriella reached for his hand, drawing him back into her space. She, in turn, cupped his cheek. "Ashton, of course you can help me. In fact, I welcome it. It's quite the job unpacking all of this," she said as she pointed to all of the boxes. "When do you want to start?"

"Now."

"Now? I just got home from school. Do you mind if I relax a bit before we start this endeavor?" She pulled him towards the couch and sat down. "I don't want you to bail on me. This house doesn't turn into wonderland in a matter of minutes... This is going to take time. Hours, maybe even days."

"I don't care. I want to do it. I have all weekend to help you. I thought about this the entire way home from Branson, hoping that you hadn't decorated yet. For some reason, I want to enjoy the season. Since I don't have a family of my own, I normally work letting those with kids spend time with their families. But this year is different. I want to experience what it's like to be in a real family."

She wasn't sure what brought these intense feelings for family to Ashton. Maybe it was his mother's stroke? Maybe being included in their Thanksgiving?

She didn't know. What she did know was she liked the changes she was seeing in him. She was starting to see the thawing of his heart, his emotions. She hoped it would continue because she believed in him and knew he had the love inside him. It just needed a little encouragement to get out.

"Why don't you get started on dinner while I change into something more comfortable? I'll put on the holiday carols. We can enjoy a relaxing dinner and then jump into transforming my house into a winter wonderland of sorts." She started to rise from the couch when he pulled her back down. She fell into his lap and she smiled. "Ashton, what's this all about?"

He took her face into his hands and looked her directly in the eyes. She noticed his blue eyes were sparkling. They'd taken on a hue she'd never seen before. Normally, his eyes were dark, gloomy. Yet today, she saw life in them. He seemed happier than she'd ever seen him. Maybe his mom's illness would have a lasting effect on him.

She started to get a tad bit nervous with the way he was looking at her. Nervously she licked her lips as she watched him closely. He leaned in and brushed a soft kiss against her lips and instead of ending the kiss as quickly as he'd started, this time he lingered. She felt his touch as he moved his hand from her face to her neck to her arm. This was definitely a different Ashton. More gentle, caring. She wondered if he'd made amends with his mother and was now seeing the light. But then, as quickly as it had started, he stopped and pulled away. He helped her stand and pushed her into the direction of her bedroom. "Time's a-wasting. Get yourself changed, and I'll start on dinner. The faster we eat, the sooner we can start decorating." Ashton rubbed his hands together and headed off towards the kitchen. She watched him for a second, then walked to her room.

She quickly exchanged her skirt and sweater for yoga pants and a sweatshirt. If she was going to decorate, she wanted to be comfortable. She pulled her hair back into a ponytail, took one last look in the mirror before applying a bit of lip gloss, and returned to the kitchen. She opened her bedroom door, and as she started down the hallway, noticed Ashton had returned to the family room and had begun sorting through the boxes of decorations.

She was an organization freak. All of the boxes were neatly labeled so it was easy to sort the decorations when it came time to put them away and set them out. She stood in the doorway, watching him as he placed a box here and there. He looked like a kid in a candy store, a huge smile on his face as he read each label. He came across the box that held the ornaments she'd received from her students over the years. She knew the box had intrigued him from his last visit. She watched as he carried the box to the couch, sitting down. Carefully, he opened the lid and looked inside. Gabriella had stored each ornament in its own bag. There was a class photograph of the child along with a quick description of the ornament and a note about the child and their family. It was a way that she could always reminisce about her student as she added the ornament to the tree and a way that she could safely file it away for the next year.

She watched as he carefully pulled a snowflake ornament out of its storage. It was hand crafted, she believed, crocheted somehow with a glittery yarn that sparkled as the light hit it. Ashton held it up to the light, inspecting it. After a moment, he wrapped it and placed it back for safe keeping. He then reached in and pulled out another, but this time it was an ornament made out of dough that had been shaped into a snowman, painted, and labeled with the year and her name. She watched as he held it in his hand. A smile crossed his lips as he ran his finger across her name. She wondered what he was thinking.

She walked to the couch and sat down beside him. He set the ornament down, not looking at her. She knew he must be having some sort of problem relating to everything. In all of her mishmash of decorations, there was a sense of history, family, and love. She could only imagine what thoughts were crossing his mind. She picked up the snowman and ran her finger across the back of the ornament where the name of the child that had given it to her was written. She didn't need to look at her notes because she remembered everything about this ornament and all of the other ornaments that were contained in the box. She'd received this one her first year of teaching, and it held a special place in her heart.

"I received this snowman my first year of teaching. Aemelie was such a sweet girl and had a unique spelling of her name. I never quite understood it, but she was a joy. I get a Christmas card from her every year. She got married over the summer. I wish I could have attended her wedding, but Angel was christened on the same day." She smiled at him as she wrapped the ornament, placing it back in the box and then pulled another ornament from the box.

"Jack Bugle gave me this ornament." She unwrapped it and held it out to Ashton.

"A bugle for a bugle?"

"Yeah, it was a joke with us. He actually learned to play the bugle and attended West Point."

"And I guess he played the bugle every day for Reveille."

"I'm not sure about every day, but I know he was a member of the West Point Band." She set the ornament down and pondered for a moment. "I lost track of him when he graduated and was deployed. I hope that he's okay." She got nostalgic and little teary eyed. Ashton reached for her hand. They were a part of her family for a year as she helped to shape their lives. And they were still a part of her heart all these years later.

He squeezed her hand. "Enough of this for the time being. Let's fix dinner and then you can share more of your memories with me." He pulled on her hand as he stood and led her to the kitchen where he'd already washed the salad ingredients. The potatoes were in the oven and the steaks were marinating. He finished preparing the steaks while Gabriella started in on the salad.

Gabriella enjoyed her surprise dinner and they quickly cleaned up the kitchen so they could move onto the fun part of their evening—decorating the house. He had already sorted the boxes so it made it easier as they began. "I want to save the tree for last," she said as she grabbed the trash bags that contained the reindeer. Let's set these guys up first."

"Since I've never done this before, I'm following your lead." He carried the reindeer to the front yard and positioned them where she wanted them. "May I ask why we're doing this in the dark? Shouldn't we wait until daylight?"

She knew she should, but she was starting to feel closed in. For some reason looking at Jack's bugle ornament really got to her. She didn't know why, but it did. As she hooked up the extension cord for the reindeer, she said a silent prayer for him, hoping that he was well.

She went inside and flipped the switch. She always held her breath the first time she lit her decorations, hoping they still worked. She heard a cheer from Ashton, so she knew the reindeer were bobbing their heads up and down.

Next she hung her wreath on the door and her welcome snowman that lit the front porch.

"I still don't get why you're doing this at night."

She scrunched her face, knowing he was right but kept doing what she was doing. He stood on the sidewalk, watching her work her magic. In no time, the front of her house was lit and inviting. While she hung more wreathes on her windows, she glanced around, looking for Ashton—he'd disappeared. She finished fiddling with the last wreath and straightened.

"Ashton?" she called, craning her head and straining to see in the dark. She heard some bustling in what she thought were bushes when she saw him walk quickly from around the corner of her house.

"Had enough for the day?" Ashton asked quickly.

She narrowed her eyes in suspicion. "What were you doing?"

"What? Oh, nothing. I just thought I saw a… dog."

She lifted her eyebrows. "A dog? I didn't see anything."

"Yeah, I think I chased it away. Anyway," he said, clapping his hands. "I'm beat. What about you?"

"Yeah…" she said, still a little suspicious. "I am a little

tired after working all day. Do you mind if we call it a night and start back tomorrow afternoon? I have a few errands I need to run in the morning."

"Sure thing," he said. "What are your plans for tomorrow?"

"I'm meeting my mom at Coffees & Mocha early and then we're going to a craft fair. After that, I have some grocery shopping I have to do." She picked up the garbage bags that protected the reindeer. As she folded them, she added, "If you still want to help me, why don't you come by around two? We can decorate and then have dinner."

"That'll work for me. Maybe we can go out to dinner then? Oxfords or Pedals sound good to me. I'm itching for some greasy food."

"We can decide tomorrow," she said, trying not to yawn. Ashton grabbed his coat and headed to the front door.

"Thanks for dinner. It was quite the surprise. Oh, by the way, you never told me how your mom's doing."

"She's doing as well as can be expected. They moved her to the rehabilitation center today. I made sure she was settled and then left."

"Oh, I thought you would have stayed through the weekend."

"Why? I'll check in with her doctors on a regular basis. That's all that's needed."

She realized then that he hadn't truly made amends with his mother—there was still a significant distance there. He opened the door, and turning back, he said, "I'll see you at two?"

"Two, it is," she said as she watched him head down the sidewalk towards his car. She waited as he drove down the street and turned at the end of the block, heading in the direction of his home. *He's different somehow. He's searching for whatever's been missing in his life. He's trying to build relationships... Family. What he needs to do is start with his mom and make things right with her.*

She went to bed knowing that somehow she was helping guide him towards a new life. A life that was filled with family and friends.

Chapter Twenty-One

SATURDAY MORNING, ASHTON HAD PARKED at the end of the block, waiting for Gabriella to leave her home. He'd gone to the home improvement store the night before and purchased more than enough lighting to string across the front of her house and through the bushes. His surprise was going to be more than worth the little bit of suspicion he got from her the night before. He didn't think she'd notice the lights on the house as she drove up, especially if she wasn't looking for them.

He easily completed the task and was home by ten o'clock that morning He considered purchasing a Christmas tree for his own home but decided to hold off on it. Maybe he'd get Gabriella to go shopping with him and they could purchase what he needed together.

He spent the remainder of the day getting caught up. He'd been in Branson a little over a week and had laundry to do, mail to go through, and dictations that needed completing. He became so caught up in his tasks that he lost track of time, not looking at his watch until it was a little after two. He abruptly stopped what he was doing, grabbed his coat, and practically ran out the door. As he drove to her house, he hoped that she hadn't discovered his surprise.

He pulled into her driveway and ran to the back door. He chose the back door because he didn't want to draw attention to the bushes that he'd decorated. He was sure when she opened the front door she'd see the extension cords that ran along her front porch. He couldn't wait to see her face when they drove up and the entire front of her house was ablaze in holiday lights. He'd set the lights on timers and knew they needed to head out for dinner well in advance of the timers going off.

As he ran to the door, it opened before he had a chance to knock.

"What's this with using my back door again?"

"I don't know—force of habit, maybe? I never–or should I say rarely use my front door. In fact, you and Joe were probably the last one's that used it when you came over that day and rescued me from my ladder."

"Yeah, I remember that day well. How could I forget your stubbornness?" she threw over her shoulder as she pulled the tea pot from the stove. "I'm brewing a pot of tea. Would you like a cup before we get started?"

"I'd love one," he said, waiting to see if she'd comment on the lights.

"Why are you looking at me like that?"

"Ah, no reason. Just excited about today."

While they sipped their tea, he asked her about her day.

"Mom and I went to one of the largest craft fairs in the area. It was packed to the rafters with people. We had a hard time finding a parking place. On our third time circling the parking lot, we saw a car pulling out. It was touch and go between us and another vehicle, but we were able to take the spot. Who would think of parking lot rage at a craft fair? It was craaazzzy."

"Did you buy anything?"

"I did. I bought another wooden light up display to put on my porch."

Ashton took a deep breath, hoping that she hadn't set it up yet.

"It's still in my car. I was running a little late getting back here and didn't want to miss you. Maybe you can bring it in after we go to dinner?"

"Sure, whenever you want."

"I was thinking—"

"That could be troublesome," he said with a smirk.

She narrowed her eyes at him and ignored his comment, "What I was going to say was that we didn't have our cheesecake last night."

"You're right, we didn't."

"So this is what I was thinking. Let's decorate the mantel and fireplace and all of the other little things I do first and save the tree until after dinner. We can then celebrate its completion with dessert and coffee."

"I like that idea. I didn't have lunch, what about you?"

"No, Mom and I ate a huge breakfast so I wasn't hungry."

"Okay then, let's get what you call the 'simple decorating' done and then head out for dinner. Say around four? That way we can beat the dinner crowd and we can get back here early." *And my lights will definitely be a surprise.*

She agreed to his plan. They put the garland on the mantel and fireplace, covering it with lights. She also added several displays throughout the family room and living room. Some were lighted, others weren't. They had just finished with most of the decorating when Ashton turned with his hands on his hips and perused their progress thus far. Her house was turning into a showpiece. The lights and displays were beautiful.

"Something wrong?" she asked as she grabbed her coat.

"Not a thing. This is beautiful. Come on, let's go get something to eat. I'm starved." He'd left his coat in the kitchen on purpose so they'd have to exit her house by the backdoor. So far, so good. They had ten minutes to get out of there before the lights went on.

Since they were both in the mood for bar food, they ended up at Oxfords where Ox was minding the bar.

"Look who the cat dragged in," Ox called out as the hostess led them through the bar to their table. He came around the front of the bar, pulled her into a bear hug, and shook Ashton's hand. "How are you two?"

"We're good."

"It's been a while since you've both been in here."

Ashton looked at Gabriella and said, "We've both been busy with the Thanksgiving holiday and travel…" Before he said anything further, one of the bartenders called out for Ox.

"Sorry about that, but I need to handle this. I'll try and drop by before you leave." With that, Ox headed off to handle whatever emergency had his name on it.

They had a nice dinner. They both satisfied their cravings for greasy food with burgers and fries. He had a beer while she chose a glass of wine to complement their food. They discussed the changes that Mary was making to Career Day. "I think she's got some good ideas. She's learned what works and what hasn't in the last couple of years. I'm really glad that she's allowing the children to choose the careers they are most interested in. It's going to take work on our part scheduling them into their first and second choices, but in the end this is going to benefit everyone."

"I'd have to agree, Gabby. I also like the idea that she's making everyone attend certain presentations. I agree with her that everyone should be exposed to general business careers and such and then let them choose an area of expertise they're interested in. That way everyone should take something away from the day. And if a child misses out on learning about a career this year, there's always next year when they can be exposed to it. All in all, I'm really excited and can't wait until January."

He looked at his watch. It was well past five and Gabriella's house should be lighting the neighborhood. He hoped she wasn't mad at him—after all, he hadn't checked with her regarding the increased energy expense. In the end, if she didn't like it, he could take it down or just disconnect it. But he was excited to see the expression on her face when he pulled onto her street. "Ready?"

"I am. I can't wait to get my tree up. It's the highlight of my year."

He stood and reached for her hand, helping her from the booth. He didn't release her hand as they walked through the bar, saying their goodbyes to Ox. He'd gotten busy after greeting them and hadn't had the opportunity to drop back by their table.

"Stop in during the holidays, and I'll buy you a round." Ashton raised his hand, thanking him, and she called out a thank-you as they exited the bar. The temperatures had dropped since they went into the bar.

She had thrown on only a light-weight coat, so when a shiver passed through her body, Ashton wrapped his arm around her shoulder, drawing her close to his side.

"Better?" he asked.

"Much," she replied. "Now, hurry up. I can't wait to get started," she exclaimed as he opened her car door for her.

"Okay, okay," he laughed as he closed her door and made his way to the driver's side. As he started the car, his heart began to speed up and his hands began to get clammy. He was nervous—never in his life had he done anything so boldly. He really hoped she liked it. He'd wanted to do something special for her that they both could remember.

He ever so slowly backed his car out of his parking space and pulled out of the parking lot. The closer he got to her house, the slower he drove.

"Is something wrong?" she asked. "Why are you driving so slowly? Are you having car problems?"

"No, there's nothing wrong with the car. I just thought I'd take it slow, that's all."

"And here I thought you were in a hurry to decorate the tree and have that slice of cheesecake."

He made the final turn onto her street. Her house was towards the end of the block, and she wasn't paying attention to her surroundings as he drove. She'd turned on the radio and was humming to one of the tunes.

As he neared her house, she turned her head and said, "Wow, look at those decorations. They're beautiful. I don't remember seeing them before." And then he slowed and started to turn into her driveway. "This isn't my house."

"Are you sure about that?"

And then, she noticed her reindeers on the front lawn, her wreath on the door, and her decorations on the front porch. She gasped and threw her hand over her mouth. "This *is* my house!" she cried as she took in the lights. "This is my house, but it can't be. Who would do this? And when? It's beautiful…" He came to a stop in the middle of her driveway. She threw open the door and jumped out. "Oh my, my winter wonderland… I've always wanted to do this. Ashton, look at the icicles hanging from the eaves. My bushes are all lighted. Look over there. Look at the trees. Who would do this?" Gabriella spun in circles, taking in everything, her mouth agape.

And then she stopped and turned towards him. She ran to his side and threw herself into his arms. "You did this, didn't you?" He didn't say anything at first, a slow smile forming on his face as he watched the sheer happiness spread across her face. He was overcome watching her excitement.

"Ashton, say something. Did you or didn't you do this? You are the only person I told about my dreams of decorating my house this way." She paused, probably remembering him sneaking around yesterday. "I can't believe you did this for me."

"I wanted it to be a surprise, and considering the way you reacted, it was. I was worried all day that you'd notice the extension cords running across your front porch. When you said you bought another display for your porch, I almost had a heart attack. I'm just glad you left it in your car."

She reached up and pressed a kiss to his lips. "Thank you, thank you, thank you! This was the best surprise ever! I mean, *ever*! Oh, wait… It might come second to my surprise thirtieth birthday party. But never mind that…'' She was starting to ramble just like her brother Alec did when he got excited.

"Come on now, let's go decorate that tree," he said as he grabbed her hand and started for the back door.

As they reached the doorway, she again threw her arms around his neck. "I just can't believe you did this for me. I'll always remember this."

"That's why I did it. I wanted to start making memories of Christmases spent with you." She smiled at him giddily as they walked inside.

They spent the rest of the evening decorating the Christmas tree. By the time she had run out to the car to get her display for the front porch, he had pulled her tree from its box and had begun piecing it together.

"Here's the tree stand," she said, handing it to him. "Now make sure it's straight when you set it in there." He set the tree into the stand and tightened the knobs. "It's not straight," she said.

"Sure it is."

"No, it's not. Move it to the left… No that's too far, back to the right. That's good." Ashton tightened the knobs. "No, it's not straight. Come over here and see."

He made his way across the room. "Looks straight to me."

"It's not, and if we decorate it and it's leaning too far one way or the other, the tree will fall over."

"I think it's straight. If you don't think it is, then you straighten it." So that's what she did. She went over to the tree and adjusted its base, straightening it to her liking. When she was done, he started to say that it wasn't straight but decided, what did he know? He'd never decorated a tree in his life.

And so they went about adding the lights, and just

as they were beginning to start on the ornaments, he touched a branch. And then, before he could utter a word of concern, the tree toppled over onto her.

Gabriella gave a short scream, "Hey, what happened? What did you do?"

He pulled the tree off of her, laughing. "I didn't do anything. The tree was leaning and then fell over."

"Why didn't you say something?"

"Well how about the fact that I thought it was straight when I set it up only to have you say it wasn't. What do I know? After all, I am the novice here."

"Really? If you thought it was leaning you should have said something!"

"Okay, fine. Gabriella, watch out the tree is leaning," he said, smirking.

"Too late for that warning. I'm just glad the ornaments weren't on yet. Come on, let's set this baby back up. And I vote that we take a break."

"A break? We just got started. We'll never finish this tree."

"Oh, we will. In time."

He helped her set the tree back up, making sure it was straight in the base. They took the break she deemed necessary and indulged in their slice of cheesecake. It took them another three hours to finish decorating the tree because she had to unwrap each ornament and tell a story of where it had originated. When all was said and done, and the icicles were strategically placed on the branches, they sat and watched their work of art. As the icicles danced back and forth in the breeze caused by the fan on the furnace, the multi-colored lights cast a magical glow throughout the room. They had created her winter wonderland and Ashton was well on his way to creating the memories that, when he thought about it, were the memories he'd always been searching for.

Chapter Twenty-Two

THE DAYS LEADING UP TO the Christmas holidays passed in a blur. Ashton worked non-stop and had happily agreed to take time off during the holidays. Joe had volunteered to be on call for the practice since Alec and Kelly were dealing with last minute preparations for their wedding. Alec and Joe had agreed that Ashton needed time off, which he'd hopefully use to go visit his mother. Jana had been progressing slowly and was expected to leave the rehabilitation center the week of Christmas.

Ashton had seen little of Gabriella since they decorated her house. Mary held the last Career Day meeting of the year right before school let out for the holidays.

"Gabriella, so what are your plans for winter break?" Mary asked as they waited for Ashton.

"I'm going to take it easy. This year's class has been one for the books so far, and I just need time to relax. Maybe I'm getting old, but this class just can't seem to settle. I'm constantly on them, and it's wearing me out."

"It's always tough this time of year. Maybe when they return from break things will be better."

"I certainly hope so. I just found a grey hair the other day and all I wanted to do was cry. All I know is, they're aging me faster than I want to—"

"Merry Christmas," Ashton called as he approached Mary's office door. He stopped and waited for Mary to wave him in. "I'm sorry if I interrupted your conversation."

"You didn't. Gabriella was just telling me about her class from hell."

"I didn't actually use those words, but they are definitely aging me." He sat down and listened while Mary reviewed what they still had to accomplish for Career Day that was scheduled for the end of January.

"While I'm off, I'll organize a schedule, and since we've already had the children indicate their first and second choices for the careers they're interested in, I'll work on putting them into groups for their requested choices."

"Gabriella, that's a lot to do over the holidays. I thought you just said you were going to take it easy, relax."

"I did, but this is different. I won't have a classroom full of students driving me cuckoo."

He looked at Gabriella. "I have some time off during the holidays—I'll help her so she doesn't have to do it herself."

"You're taking time off?"

"I am—at the bequest of your brothers."

"Huh. I didn't know that. I'm glad to hear it."

They spent the remainder of their meeting discussing the agenda for Career Day. Mary set their next meeting for the first week after the holidays. He stood and was just getting ready to wish Mary happy holidays when Mary's phone rang.

"Sorry, I have to take this. It's a parent returning my call."

He waved at her, mouthing happy holidays, and walked out of Mary's office, followed closely by Gabriella. "So, you really have the holidays off? I thought you gave that time up."

"I normally do, but Joe volunteered to take the week. He also conned your dad into service as well."

"Figures," she said as she started down the hallway to her classroom. He followed along. Her students were in art class so she had the last period of the day free. Since it was their last day before break, her desk was filled with gifts that her students had given her. She began sorting her gifts into bags as he looked on.

"Wow, is that all from your students?"

"Yeah, it is," she said as she finished filling the bags. "I was surprised. This has been a challenging class this year, and I definitely didn't expect all of this," she said, gesturing to the overflowing bags.

"Well, it definitely looks like someone likes you." He smiled at her and walked about the room, looking at all of the decorations she'd hung in her classroom. "When do you switch out all of this?"

"I'll come in during the holidays and exchange my holiday decorations for winter scenes. I'm also going to dedicate a section of my classroom for Career Day. I have information on the various careers that will be represented so my students can get up to speed on the careers they are currently interested in, in addition to those they may have never heard about. I've been working on putting this unit together for a while. I'm going to have a writing project and they're also going to have to research an area that interests them and present it to the class. This is the first time I've done it, and I'm excited to see how they take to the unit."

"Sounds like fun. Do you have any other plans over the holidays?"

"Just the usual—Angelina and I try to go out to lunch, but our girl's time has gotten harder to come by since she's had the children. I hope we can work something out, but I'm not banking on it since Alejandro has to work. Kelly usually babysits for her, but she's so involved with her wedding planning that I'm not sure that will happen either. Other than that, my mom has her usual open house and Angelina's mom has a get-together after Midnight Mass. All in all, I hope for a quiet and calm couple of weeks off of school. I feel like lately I've been burning the candle at both ends. I'm really tired."

"I can understand that. Teaching is a hard profession and I know how dedicated you are to your job. Can I take these out to your car for you?" he said, pointing to her gifts.

"Thanks, I appreciate it. I have fifteen more minutes before I have to get my class and I'd like the help."

"Sure thing." He grabbed several bags while she grabbed her backpack full of papers that still needed grading, along with the Career Day information that she was going to organize. It wasn't too cold outside, so she decided to forego putting her coat on. They chatted on her way to her car about the lack of cold weather and snow. She popped her trunk and he eased the bags in. Gabriella had gone shopping and had forgotten to take the packages into her house.

"Oh, I forgot about these," she claimed as she rearranged everything so all of her gifts could fit. "Now I have even more to wrap."

"Don't you like to wrap? Seems like a Christmas-y thing you'd enjoy," he said, smiling.

"I do most of the time but as I said, I've been exhausted and just haven't been in the mood. Usually by now I have all of my gifts wrapped and under the tree."

"Would you like some help?"

"You'd help me wrap?"

"That's what I just said. This holiday season is about making memories. I started with decorating your house, and now I can learn to wrap all of these presents. By the way, how many packages do you have to wrap?"

"You don't want to know." She laughed, rolling her eyes. "Too many is all I can say."

"Well, okay then. When's a good time for you?"

She thought for a moment. "Well Christmas is a week away. I still don't understand why we got two whole weeks off, but I'm not complaining. Christmas is next Friday. Do you want to do it this weekend or sometime next week? My deadline, of course, is Thursday. I have to have everything wrapped before Midnight Mass because I'm toast first thing Christmas morning after spending time at the Samuels'. Angelina's mom sure knows how to throw a party." She paused. "Why don't you come?"

"To the Samuels'? Nah, they don't even know me. I'd be intruding on a family event."

"Come as my plus one, my guest. Jackie always tells me to bring someone with me. So, why not you?"

He looked down at his feet. "I can't."

"Why not? You know everyone that'll be there. It's our family and Angelina's. Her mom started this the year of Colleen's transplant. It's a celebration of sorts—not only for Christmas, but for the gift of life. And if you think my house is decorated, you should see the Samuels'. It's unbelievable. Everyone has a ball, and Jackie's a fabulous cook. I normally don't get home until around four in the morning but it's well worth it. So, will you come? With me? You said you wanted to make memories—why not add this to the album you've already started to create?"

"Let me think about it. I'll get back to you whenever you decide we're going to have this wrapping marathon. That's what it is, right?"

"Yep. I start and I don't stop until it's all done. So be prepared." With that, she glanced at her watch. "I'm late. I've got to get to my class." She started to run back to her classroom calling over her shoulder, "How about tomorrow night? For the wrapping party. Six?"

"I'll be there with bows on my head and tape on my shoes," he laughed as she flew through the door. Ashton chuckled as he made his way to his car. *Who'd have thought I'd be attending a gift-wrapping party? Wow, she's certainly turning my life upside down.*

Ashton came prepared to Gabriella's. He arrived early because he knew it would take them forever to wrap the gifts if those in the trunk were any indication of what she really had to wrap. Not only did he come with extra tape, ribbon, and bows as a joke, he thought they may need a little alcohol to get through the night, so he brought a couple bottles of wine, too.

She answered the door with an elf hat on her head.

"What's this," he asked as he walked through the

door, pulling on her elf's hat, and carried a grocery bag filled with his contributions for their evening.

"My elf's hat. I always wear it when I wrap my gifts. It's a little unusual, I know. But it's a tradition that was started when I was in college and I've kept it up. I'm sure if you called Angelina, she'd tell you she's wearing her hat, too, as she wraps her gifts."

"It's all about traditions and memories, huh?"

"Well, yeah. That's what the holidays are for. Making memories." She grabbed ahold of his jacket, pulling him into her family room. "Another tradition I have is that I wrap in front of the tree with Christmas carols playing in the background. Sometimes, I even turn on an old movie and watch that, too. It just depends what time of day I'm wrapping and what mood I'm in. So, take your coat off and what's that?" she said, pointing to the bag in his hand.

"Wine and a few other things. With the looks of your trunk, I thought we might need it," he said, pulling out the additional tape, bows, and ribbon. "I think this is going to be a long night." He started towards her kitchen while she watched him make himself comfortable. "Oh, and I ordered pizza to be delivered in a half-hour. I'm sure we'll need a break by then."

"You've got to be kidding me. We'll need a break that soon, ha! It's more like we'll need a break in several hours. This is not something I take lightly. I carefully wrap my gifts, applying ribbon and bows. All of my gifts are a work of art when I'm done, so either you're in or you're not."

He waggled his finger at her. "What? Don't you believe that I can do this? I can, and I will show you," he said as he neared her. Popping his index finger on her nose, he added, "Just wait and see what kind of gift wrapper I can be. I may not have experience in decorating a tree or a house, but I have surgery skills, and I'm sure I can cut paper and apply tape and ribbon with the best of them. So watch out, baby," he said as he tweaked her nose again and headed towards the paper and bows.

Their pizza arrived later than he expected. In fact, he had to call Pizzas, Pies & More to find out where it was. According to the order-taker, their pizza had been delivered to the wrong house so they had to remake it. It would be an additional hour until theirs would be delivered, so Ashton grabbed the bottle of wine and poured them each a glass. "To our pizza, that is in the near future," he joked as he grabbed another roll of tape.

By the time their pizza arrived, it was almost eight o'clock. They'd polished off the first bottle of wine and had started in on the second. About half of the gifts were wrapped. There were more bits and pieces of paper strewn around the room from packages being incorrectly measured. "Look at all this wasted paper," Ashton said as he pointed to piece after piece.

"It's not wasted. I'll find a home for it."

"And here I thought you were an expert wrapper. As you can see, I've measured all of my packages accurately. No paper lying next to me."

"Yeah, and how many packages have you wrapped, kind sir? Two, maybe three…"

"Well, it's all about being precise." He walked to her side with a piece of ribbon trailing at his side. He picked up the end and wrapped it around her neck, pulling her towards him.

"Precise? Well, you'll be here all night then, won't you?"

"I'd be happy to be here all night, as long as I can spend it with you." And then he pulled her as close as he could, wrapped his arms around her, and surprised her with a kiss. He cupped her cheek with his hand and then dropped his lips to her neck. Pulling away slightly, he moved back to her lips.

She felt like she was in heaven. She was starting to like these surprise kisses. She felt more and more comfortable the more time she spent with him. She could see a kind, loving man beneath the aura that he portrayed. He had to learn how to love and make memories that he could cherish. And now, she felt they were making these memories together from the decorating of her house, to the wrapping of the gifts— and maybe even Christmas, too.

She pulled away. "What's this for," she said pointing back and forth between them. "That was sure unexpected."

"I just felt like doing it. We're making memories, right?" She nodded and sat down on the couch. "I guess it's a thank-you… I don't know," he said, spinning away from her. He grabbed his glass of wine and took a swallow. "I apologize. I don't know what came over me. It's just when I'm around you, I feel different. More alive than I've ever felt… You're making me think and feel things I've never dreamed of feeling in my entire life. I have to be honest with you, Gabriella. These feelings have come out of left field for me. You're on my mind all the time. All I can say is you've definitely turned my life upside down, and I don't know what to do or how to get it back in balance."

Standing, she made her way to him. She reached for his hand and held it closely against her heart. "Let yourself feel. I know there's a lot about you and your life before I met you that shaped you into who you are today—correction, I mean were. You've changed, Ashton and definitely for the better. Give it time. You can't correct a lifetime in a minute, an hour, a day, or a week. You've got to take your time, embrace the changes that you want to make and live."

This time, she pulled him into a kiss. "I like the man you're becoming. Take the time you need to deal with your past, but at the same time embrace the future and what may be. You're a fabulous doctor. And from what I saw at the Halloween party, a caring one, too. Just live for these changes one day at a time."

He focused on what she was saying to him. She liked the man he was becoming. She believed in him and he had to believe in himself. He needed to realize that his future hadn't been cut in stone when he was a child. He could alter the course of his life and maybe become someone he was proud of.

She pulled away from him. She needed to focus on the task at hand and that was finishing her wrapping. She spun out of his arms, "Okay, now let's get back to what you came here for—wrapping gifts." She finished her last gift and watched as he finished applying tape and ribbon to his last gift.

"Now, you said this one's for whom?"

"I told you, it's for... I forget. What did you just wrap?"

He responded with an exasperated look. He'd already told her three times what he'd wrapped. "Oh yeah, sorry. I guess the wine's getting to me. You said you just wrapped a cookbook, right?"

"Yeah."

"Well, that's for Angelina."

"I thought she didn't cook."

"No, she cooks but it's not always edible. Alejandro's the real cook in that family."

He applied the tag to the package and set it under the tree.

"Is that it?"

"Yep, I think so." It was as far as he was concerned. She'd bought and already wrapped a scarf for him. It was safely hidden in the hall closet.

He grabbed his wine glass, sitting down on the floor in front of the couch. He leaned back, closing his eyes. She sat beside him. "This was fun," he said as he took a sip of his wine.

"It was. Thank you for coming to my aid. Without your help, I'd be here another hour or so." She leaned her head on his shoulder. She was getting tired. And then, all of a sudden, she bolted upright, "Did you decide?"

He looked at her quizzically. "What?"

"I'm talking about coming to the Samuels' after Midnight Mass, and I'm even extending the offer, from my parents, for you to join us at our open house, too."

"Gabriella, I don't know. It's all so much, and I really don't know them all that well."

She raised herself to her knees and reached for his hand. "Ashton, you said you wanted to enjoy the season."

"Well, I am. I'm doing things I've never experienced before. I'm just not sure."

"Please, do it. For me. Let it be your gift to me."

"And you thought I was giving you a gift?"

She scrunched her face. "A girl can hope, can't she?" He laughed as she continued, "Please, this is the last time I'm going to ask. No begging on my part." She didn't speak with her mouth, but she did with her eyes.

Her sad puppy dog expression got the best of him.

"Alright, I'll come."

"To the Samuels' and my parents'?"

"Yes, I'll be there at both."

She smiled and threw her arms around his neck, hugging him tightly.

"Hey, there, don't get too excited."

"I'm just happy that you've seen the light and want to add it to your first-time experiences."

They sat and talked until she couldn't keep her eyes open any longer. He stood and reached for her hand, pulling her up. She lost her balance falling into his arms.

"Gab-ri-ella," he said looked intently at her, pushing a stray hair behind her ear.

"What?"

"I've got to get out of here. I'm sorry, but I have to go," He practically ran out the front door.

What he was feeling at the time was too much. He needed to get out of there before he did something he wouldn't be happy with. He recalled kissing her forehead and grabbing his coat. He'd practically run to her front door. As he drove along he felt the sexual tension that had permeated the air that evening. It had come out of nowhere, but he'd quickly put it in check. Even though his mind was telling him one thing, his heart was telling him another. He wasn't ready to start anything with her right now or maybe not even in the future. He needed to get his life in order, heal, and maybe in time he'd find a place for her.

That weekend, Ashton had his last visit of the year

with Javier. He and his mother were traveling to visit relatives in Dallas, Texas. Javier was a fan of trains, so Ashton decided to take him to the train exhibit at the Botanical Gardens.

On his drive over to Javier's, out of nowhere, the scene of them wrapping presents flew into his mind. He thought about the ribbon and how he wrapped it around her neck. His heartrate increased as he remembered. He picked Javier up at noon and took him to lunch at his favorite fast food restaurant. It was a treat for Javier since he rarely had the chance to eat out. Javier ordered chicken fingers, which seemed to be every child's mainstay, while he ordered a grilled chicken sandwich. He treated Javier to a chocolate milkshake as well. It was a special day for them and he wanted Javier to remember their day.

They arrived at the Botanical Gardens and the parking lot was packed. He drove around and around until he found a spot right up against the fencing that encompassed the parking lot. Javier jumped to the front seat and exited through Ashton's door. Javier immediately reached for his hand, as he was overwhelmed by the crowd.

He made his way to the entrance and paid for their admission. It just so happened to be the holiday walk in the gardens and Santa and his elves were there, too. "What do you want to do first," he asked as Javier took in the hanging glass chandelier that hung above the entrance. He pulled out his phone to capture the look on Javier's face. His eyes were as big as saucers as he took in all of the sights and sounds that surrounded him.

"Let's go see Santa first, okay?"

"Sure thing, it's your day," Ashton said as they headed

up the stairs to the outdoor gardens. Santa was in one of the out buildings in the gardens. Just as they exited the main building to the outdoor gardens, it started snowing. As they walked down the paved walkway, Javier stuck his tongue out.

"What are you doing?" he inquired as they headed towards the pathway that led to Santa's workshop.

"Catching snowflakes."

"I've never done that before."

"Really? I can't believe you didn't do that as a kid," Javier said as he watched Ashton stick out his tongue, mimicking Javier's actions. Javier started laughing.

"What's so funny?"

"You," Javier said, pointing to him. They both laughed and continued on their trek to Santa. They entered the pavilion where Santa was proudly sitting atop his sleigh. They stood in a long line and were greeted by the elves as they approached Santa. As they made their way through the line, Javier was given a candy cane, a stuffed toy, and a package that was wrapped with a tag that read, "Boy, age six."

"What does this mean," Javier said, pointing to the tag.

"That's says it's just for you."

"Oh, boy," Javier said. "I'm not going to open this until Christmas." He had an infectious smile that lit his face as he pointed to his gift. He smiled back at him, realizing again what he'd missed out in his childhood. Javier sat atop Santa's lap and Ashton, along with a photographer, took his picture. When asked what he wanted for Christmas, Javier said, "I want my dad."

Ashton looked at Javier and drew his lips in. He knew that wasn't possible, so he called up to Javier, "What else do you want?" Javier smiled at Ashton and then went through what he hoped Santa would bring him. Finally, after listening to Javier's extensive list, the elves had to draw Javier's attention to a cup of hot chocolate to get him off Santa's lap. He apologized to the elves and Santa and thanked them for the extra time they spent with Javier. He knew this was going to be an exceptionally hard Christmas for Javier since his father had died during the holidays.

When Javier had taken the last sip of his hot chocolate, he reached for Ashton's hand and said, "Can we go see the trains now?"

"Of course, that's why we're here." They retraced their steps back to the main building and took the stairs back down to the main floor where the display was held. As they neared the doors, Javier's excitement grew. He started pulling Ashton's hand.

"Come on, Ashton. Hurry up!" He picked up his pace, and when they entered the room, he grabbed his cell phone and took another photo of Javier. His excitement was written all over his face. As they walked around the exhibit, he took a peak at the last photo he'd taken of Javier. His eyes sparkled with excitement. As he looked at the photo, he realized how much this day meant to Javier. He reflected on his involvement in Javier's life and for the first time truly realized what a difference he was making in his life. He wished he'd had a Big Brother when he was growing up. Maybe he'd have had the chance to see a display like this and maybe he'd also have had the chance to decorate a tree and have memories of the holidays. Instead, Ashton had no real memories of the holidays growing up. He was thankful that he was making a difference in Javier's life now.

Javier watched as the train sped down the track.

"Ashton, hurry up! You've got to see this," he said pointing to a grist mill that revolved around at the side of the track. A little village had been created and there was actual flowing water that turned the mill. Ashton was amazed with what he saw. He'd never seen a display of this magnitude. He'd always wanted a train set and the closet he'd ever come to seeing one was at his father's resort. When he'd visited during the holidays, he'd run and sit underneath the tree and watch it as it circled around the tree. Yearly, his mother would then tell him he was embarrassing her with his behavior. He often wondered what he'd done to upset her because all he'd ever done was sit on the floor and watch the train go round and round.

He and Javier spent over an hour looking at the display. In fact they'd stayed so long that he'd lost track of time. The next thing he knew, he'd received a text message from Jacinta wondering where they were. Instead of replying to the text, Ashton immediately phoned her. "Jacinta, I'm so sorry. I lost track of the time. Javier's been enjoying the train exhibit… Thanks for understanding. I'll have him home in the next forty-five minutes." Javier's expression turned sad. "Sorry, buddy, but your mom needs you home."

"I know," he said, dragging his feet as they left the exhibit. "Thanks for bringing me. I'll always remember today."

"I'm sure you will since I have this picture of you and Santa," He said pointing to the photo he'd received of Javier sitting on Santa's lap. The elves had handed it to him while Javier was enjoying his cup of hot chocolate. When they left the building, it was still snowing. Both he and Javier walked to the car, catching snowflakes. "And I'll always remember learning how to catch snowflakes," Ashton chuckled as Javier got into the car and buckled his car seat.

This day was a memorable day for both of them. And it only got better when he got home and received a message from Alec. He had been chosen to serve as Santa Claus at the hospital's annual children's Christmas party. *How did I get this assignment? And how can I even pretend to do this when I've never sat on Santa's lap?*

He was definitely making memories this holiday season, and they were only going to get better when he'd have to play Santa on Christmas Eve at the hospital.

Chapter Twenty-Three

CHRISTMAS EVE WAS SHAPING INTO a busy day for Gabriella. Not only had she received a reminder call from Matthew about his performance in the children's choir at Midnight Mass, she also received a call from Alejandro. He wanted her to be Mrs. Claus at the annual Christmas Eve party for the children at the hospital.

"You've got to be kidding me. You signed me up for *what*?"

"Mrs. Claus." Alejandro snickered into the phone while Angelina stood by his side, shaking her head. Alejandro had set Gabriella up, and he most assuredly was going to win that bet.

"Alejandro, how could you? I'm not going to know whether I'm coming or going on Christmas Eve. Have you forgotten there's Midnight Mass, and that your son is singing in the children's choir? Then there's the party at Jackie's and the open house at Mom and Dad's. I promised Mom that I would help her. How can I now?"

"I'll have Angelina help her."

Angelina looked at her husband, wide-eyed.

"Alejandro, I can't believe you did this to me. I'm going to be a walking zombie when this is all over with."

"Now, Gabriella, you're going to make a more than believable Mrs. Claus. I'll have your costume waiting for you in my office."

"Are you telling me you're not going to be there?"

He was telling her a fib. "I'm off that day. I'll be spending it with my family," he said, rolling his eyes at Angelina. They would all be at the party. Matthew had vivid memories of spending Christmas in the hospital and he wanted to go and cheer up those children that were stuck spending the holiday there.

"Alejandro, you better show up or I'm withholding your Christmas gift."

Alejandro howled at her comment. "Go right ahead, Mrs. Claus. The clock strikes one o'clock Christmas Eve. Santa will be there with bells on his shoes."

"Oh, you," she groaned into the phone as the line went dead. *I can't believe he's done this to me,* Gabriella thought as she stared at her cell phone.

"I thought Alejandro had to work this week," Gabriella said as she and Angelina enjoyed their lunch. "And then he made that comment to me, when he informed me I was Mrs. Claus and that he was off this week."

"Yeah, he originally was scheduled to work, but one of his colleagues asked if he could switch with him since he isn't married and has no children."

"Wow, that was kind."

"It was since everyone seems to want to be off this

time of year. In fact, Joe stepped up and switched with Ashton. He told me he thought Ashton should go see his mom, and that was the main reason behind him volunteering to take his turn."

"Yeah, I know. He told me the other night that he was off when he helped me wrap my gifts."

"What did you just say?" Angelina said pointing at her. "Did I just hear you say you're spending time with him and that he helped you wrap your gifts? I thought that was taboo for you, as it was one of the things you liked most about the season—wrapping gifts and decorating."

"Well, he also helped me with that, too."

"What?" Angelina asked incredulously.

"Decorating." Gabriella looked down and realigned the silverware in front of her. She was unsure what she should tell her friend. She didn't want to share too much as she wasn't sure what they were. They'd been spending a lot of time together, but had yet to have an official date. She wasn't going to tag them with a label when she wasn't sure what that would be. "Yeah, I have to admit he helped me do both. You know, Angelina, I've learned a little bit about him, and from what I can see, he didn't have much of a childhood like you or I did. I'm not sure what his was truly like, but I do know he never decorated a tree and hasn't really enjoyed a wrapping party like you or I have. Wrapping gifts, decorating your home, and making memories with your family… I think all of that was definitely missing from his childhood." Gabriella's thoughts were interrupted when the waiter brought their lunches to the table. They'd both ordered salads as they were trying to limit their calorie intake before their parties.

Angelina sat and listened to what Gabriella was and wasn't saying. "Gabriella, what aren't you telling me? I heard what you said—heard that you're spending a good deal of time with him. Is there more?"

Gabriella shook her head at her friend. "Nope. That's about it." She smiled at Angelina and dug into her lunch.

Angelina took a few bites of her salad and waited for Gabriella to jump further into their conversation. Instead, she changed the direction all together.

"Changing subjects," Gabriella said pointing her fork at her friend. "I am really mad at your husband."

"My husband or your brother?"

"Both," she said as she forked a tomato and popped it into her mouth. Angelina smiled at her, waiting patiently for her to continue her tirade. Chewing slowly, Gabriella watched her friend. "What's so funny?"

"Funny? I'm not laughing."

"Well no, but you are smiling at me."

"Smiling and laughing are two different things," Angelina said as she mixed her salad around on her plate. She was avoiding making eye contact.

"Angelina, what's going on here? And how in God's name did I end up being chosen as Mrs. Claus? I don't get it." Stabbing a leaf of lettuce, she added, "It should be you and Alejandro as Santa and Mrs. Claus. In fact, I don't even know who Santa is. Do you?"

Angelina definitely couldn't look at her friend now. "I have no idea who Santa is. I'm just glad I don't have to worry about being Mrs. Claus since I've got the kids to worry about. And thanks to your brother, I'm also supposed to be helping Maria with her open house preparations. I don't know how much help I'll be since I'm soooo good in the kitchen," she said, rolling her eyes.

Gabriella snorted and continued to eat. She'd figure out how she was going to deal with Alejandro without Angelina's help.

They finished their lunch and walked to their cars. "Have fun tomorrow, Mrs. Claus," Angelina said, laughing as she pulled her friend into a hug.

"Yeah, yeah. I am so not looking forward to this. And watch out—when I see your husband, he's going to get a piece of my mind," she uttered as she pulled away from Angelina.

⌒

Gabriella rose on Christmas Eve dreading the events of the day. She was looking forward to seeing Matthew perform in the children's choir and attending Midnight Mass, but as she thought about the events leading up to that, the headache she'd woken up with only intensified. Maybe she could send a message to Santa that Mrs. Claus was sick and needed to rest for the evening's activities. She thought about calling Alejandro and begging out of the party, but then she'd only be disappointing the children who were stuck in a sterile setting, looking forward to their special day. She decided to raise herself to the cause, not complain, and go into it with a smile on her face. Isn't that what Mrs. Claus would do?

She pulled into the hospital parking garage at noon. She parked and headed in the direction of Alejandro's office. She knew his office was closed and went directly to his private entrance where she knocked on the door. Her back was to the door when it was surprisingly opened by Matthew. "Aunt Gabriella," he shouted as he threw his arms around her. "My dad said you were going to help out Santa and be Mrs. Claus for the party."

She hugged him back and groaned, "Yeah, I am." Alejandro appeared just as she choked out her words. "You. I am going to kill you," She said as she pointed her finger at her brother. "I can't believe you did this to me. Mrs. Claus? You know I'm busy. It's not fair to Mom."

"Did I hear my name?" Maria showed her face, smiling broadly at her daughter. "Honey, I guess I forgot to tell you. I'm catering the open house this year."

Gabriella felt that there was a conspiracy against her. Was she the only one that didn't know what was going on? Apparently so. Alejandro was off and he, along with the kids, were here for the party. Her mother wasn't cooking...

"And I guess Angelina's hiding somewhere behind this door."

Then Gabriella heard her distinctive laughter.

"I knew it. What's with this? Everyone knows what's going on here except me. Am I being set up for failure here or what? I can't be Mrs. Claus." Gabriella walked through the door as everyone laughed.

"Sure you can. You'll make a perfect Mrs. Claus," Alejandro chimed in as Angelina held up her costume.

"Come on now, I'll help you get into your outfit."

"I don't need your help," she said as she pursed her lips and shook her head at Angelina. "I think I can dress myself." She headed off to Alejandro's private bathroom to change while Angelina, Alejandro, and Maria shook their heads at her.

Ashton dressed in his office at the hospital. He really didn't know what was expected of him other than letting a child sit on his lap and tell him what they wanted from Santa for Christmas. Alec had told him all of the children had filled out a list for Santa. As the children left the party, each would be handed a gift from "Santa" that was on their list. *I can do this.*

When he'd taken Javier to visit Santa at the Botanical Gardens, he hadn't paid attention to what Santa did as the children sat with him. His research told him that he just needed to say "Ho, Ho, Ho," over and over again, so that's what he practiced as he dressed. He stepped into the red pants that were five sizes too big for him and threw on his red coat. What was up with this get-up? It was way too big. Then Ashton realized there were several pillows sitting on the couch ready to be stuffed into his costume.

Ashton pulled up a photo of Santa on his phone so he'd know exactly how to finish off the costume. He had a white beard and mustache, white wig, and wire rimmed spectacles that completed his costume. He put on his spectacles, drawing them close to the tip of his nose. He turned and looked at himself in the mirror. If he didn't know better, he'd think he truly was Santa.

When Ashton researched the part he was supposed to play, he listened to several soundtracks of Santa's voice. He practiced lowering his voice, adding the "Ho, Ho, Ho's" and trying for the special twinkle that Santa always had in his eyes. Now, he just hoped that all of the children believed that he was truly Santa and not Dr. Holder.

Ashton was ready. He was in full character now. He wouldn't break from his role until it was time to take off his costume and resume being Ashton Holder. Ashton heard the rap of knuckles against his office door and Alec walked in.

"Wow, you certainly filled out there, Santa," Alec said as he patted Ashton's belly.

"Ho, Ho, Ho," Ashton said as he pointed at Alec. "What can I bring you from the North Pole?" joked Ashton.

"How about a clear, sunny day…"

He raised an eyebrow at him.

"Santa, how could you forget? I'm getting married in a few short weeks, and I want a beautiful January day."

"Ho, Ho, Ho, there's not much I can do about that," Santa said as Alec laughed at his interpretation of Santa.

"You can't say that. You have to say, 'Have you been a good boy lately? If so, I'll see what I can do,'" chided Alec. "Santa never says things like that."

He shook his head at Alec and prepared to march down the hallway towards the room where the party was being held. "Your Mrs. Claus will meet you there."

"Okay, then let's get this party underway. Alec, I'm in character now, so don't call me by my name again." Ashton declared as Alec led him to the party.

All of the children were happily waiting for Santa's arrival. Just as he reached the closed doors, he was approached by Alejandro.

"Just so you know, your Mrs. Claus doesn't know who you are. She may be upset when she discovers it's you, Ashton." Alejandro joked.

"Who me? Santa? Santa's my name, at least for the next couple of hours."

Ideally, Gabriella would never figure out that Ashton was behind the costume.

"Okay, ready now, Santa?"

Ashton nodded and Alejandro threw open the door. "Look who's coming down the hall... Here's Santa Claus!"

Ashton started to ring the bells that he held in his hand and came barreling through the doorway calling, "Ho, Ho, Ho!" All of the children yelled out his name. Santa was approached by Mrs. Claus. Gabriella was dressed in a long sleeved red velvet dress that came to her knees. It had white fur at the wrists. She wore a red Santa hat with a huge pompom on its end that she draped over her shoulder. She looked him directly in the eyes and he could tell that she had no idea who he was.

"Ho, Ho, Ho," Ashton called out as he made his way amongst the children, shaking their hands and patting them on their heads. He passed Matthew, who had no idea that he was in fact Santa Claus. He made his way to his "sleigh" that was actually a converted couch, and sat down. Gabriella aided each of the children as they sat on Santa's lap. For those that were confined to wheelchairs, she wheeled them as close to him as she could and he took extra care making them feel as special as all of the others that were able to sit on his lap.

Ashton was having an absolute ball listening to the excitement in the children's voices as they shared with Santa their wishes for Christmas. After everyone had visited and had their pictures taken with Santa, they all enjoyed refreshments.

He observed his Mrs. Claus as she relaxed into her part. He could tell she was having a wonderful time. He'd felt the same excitement when she'd played Cinderella to his Prince Charming. He knew she had no idea who Santa was and he couldn't wait until the end of the party for the big reveal. He knew his playing Santa would be a huge surprise, particularly since she knew he'd never really celebrated Christmas.

The two hours passed quickly, and before they knew it, it was time for Santa and Mrs. Claus to fly off to the North Pole, take off their costumes, and reveal their true identities. Alec followed Ashton back to his office while Alejandro led Gabriella back to his office.

"Thank God that's over with," Gabriella said as she joined Alejandro in his office. "Where are Angelina and the kids?"

"They're waiting for us with Mom in the lobby. I don't know how, but Angel fell asleep in all of the commotion and Angelina took her down to the lobby. She thought it might be quieter there. I'm not sure about that, but are you ready?"

"I am. Now, I need a nap. Eleven o'clock will come too soon, and I want to get a good parking spot for mass. I can't wait to hear the children's choir."

"Yeah, I heard them practice and they should be phenomenal."

Gabriella preceded Alejandro out the door. She waited while he locked his office. She couldn't wait to go home and put her feet up. She was exhausted.

When they approached the lobby, Angelina and the kids were waiting with Maria. "Where's Alec? Did he go home already?"

"No, here I am," Alec called as he and Ashton walked up from behind.

Gabriella turned around, catching her brother and Ashton's appearance. "Where did you come from?" She asked, pointing to Ashton. "You should have come to the party. The kids had a blast." Proudly pointing to herself, she said, "And I was Mrs. Claus."

Alejandro shook his head and laughed for what seemed like the hundredth time of the day at her.

"I was there."

"Well, where were you? I didn't see you."

"I was standing right next to you the whole time," he said, smiling.

"Nuh uh. Santa stood next to me the whole—" And then it hit her. Ashton was Santa. "You? You were Santa? I don't believe it. You played the part so well!"

"Ever heard of YouTube?"

Everyone broke out into laughter.

"I can't believe I didn't know it was you! Oh my, you were great."

"As were you, Mrs. Claus." As he smiled at her, his face lit up.

Interrupting them, Angelina said, "Now that you've discovered who Santa was, I need to go home. I've got to get these kids down for a nap." Angelina reached in and kissed Gabriella on the cheek. "I'll save you a seat at church."

"Thanks. I'm sure it'll be crowded when I get there."

In a matter of seconds, Gabriella was left alone standing with Ashton in the hospital lobby. He reached for her hand and led her towards the parking garage. "Come on, let's get out of here. Would you like to grab something to eat?"

Gabriella didn't know what to say as she was still in shock that her Santa was indeed Ashton. "I'm starved after being in that hot costume. Let's run by Ox's and grab a burger. It should tide us over until we go to the Samuels'."

She was apprehensive. She didn't know what she

should do. Yes, they were going to the party together. He *was* her plus one, but she didn't know if she'd regret this. It's not like they hadn't gone out together before. But now things were different. She was starting to have feelings for him, and she already knew he was having feelings for her, too. *Oh, what the hell,* she thought. *You only live once.* "Okay. I'll meet you there."

He told her he'd see her in a few minutes and he sprinted for his car while she took her time walking to hers. She was definitely making holiday memories herself. She hoped that he was, too.

A half hour later, Ashton met up with her at Ox's. It was almost five o'clock and the bar was getting crowded. She'd arrived first and had arranged for a table. Just as the hostess was ready to seat her, he hurried through the doors, practically running to her side. He grabbed her hand and squeezed it lightly, leaning in to kiss her forehead. His eyes were twinkling just as they had when he'd been playing his role of Santa. His blue eyes could bring her to her knees. He squeezed her hand harder and said, "You ready?" he said pointing to the hostess as she'd already started off in the direction of their table.

"Ah, yeah, of course," she replied as he pulled on her hand, leading her to their table. He held her chair for her as she sat. Automatically ordering them both a beer, the hostess headed off to the bar to place their order. He reached for her hand again and looked her in the eyes, "Today was fun, wasn't it?"

She didn't know what to say because it hadn't been fun for her at first. But him playing the role of Santa had actually made it fun. He'd been in his element.

"You were a fantastic Santa Claus. I had no idea it was you. Did you study drama in school?"

"I did, how did you know?"

"Well, you were quite convincing in both of your roles: as Santa Claus and Prince Charming." Ashton laughed, but before he could reply, Ox was delivering their beers.

"I thought I'd bring these over and wish you both happy holidays. I can't stay and chat because we're pretty busy. We're closing early so everyone can spend time with their families. Are you going to Midnight Mass?"

Before she could say anything, Ashton chimed in, "We are. In fact, Gabby's nephew is in the children's choir and we're both going to hear him sing."

Gabriella was shocked. How did he know about Matthew? She'd never mentioned the children's choir to him.

He immediately recognized her shock, and when Ox left their table, he said, "Matthew called and invited me to his concert. Is that okay with you?"

"Of course it is. Why would you think that it wouldn't be?" She realized that he had really started fitting into her family. He was no longer the doctor from hell. In fact, Matthew included him in many of his after-school activities. He'd even invited him to his class's holiday concert, but it had been held during the day and he couldn't attend. She didn't understand why Matthew had grown so close to him. Maybe one day she'd understand it, but it really didn't matter to her anymore.

They enjoyed their meal when Ashton looked at his watch. "It's going on seven." Shaking his head, he said, "Time's certainly flying by today. At least for me, but

I'm not sure it is for all of the good boys and girls." He rolled his eyes and laughed at himself. "So, what time should I pick you up?"

"What do you mean?"

"I thought we'd go together tonight."

She was definitely surprised by his desire to escort her to Matthew's concert and mass. "You don't have to do that."

"Of course I do. Aren't I your plus one? You can't go to the Samuels' without an escort if I'm supposed to be your date."

"Well, if you put it that way. Okay, let's think this through. The concert starts at eleven, and since it's a children's concert, it will be packed. What do you say about ten?"

"Ten? You want to get there that early?"

"How about I compromise with ten-fifteen?"

"You call that a compromise?"

"I do."

"Okay, I'll see you with bells on my shoes."

He grinned at her and she again noticed the sparkle in his eyes. If she didn't know better, she was definitely falling head over heels for him.

She didn't really know how she felt about that. She was worried her heart was moving faster than her head. What she did know was that she wouldn't end up where she did the last time—that about killed her both physically and emotionally. After her break-up, she'd quit eating, lost an inordinate amount of sleep, and became quite ill. She'd contracted the flu and almost ended up in the hospital, missing nearly two weeks of school. No, she needed to slow down and stop moving at warp speed.

Ashton arrived at Gabriella's at nine-thirty. He had his gift in hand and wanted to surprise her. He rang the doorbell and waited. And waited, and then rang it again. He was getting ready to check the back door when she answered. One shoe was on and she was fussing with putting her earring in. "You said ten-fifteen and it's—" She paused, looking at her watch, "Nine-thirty. You're early," she said as she wobbled from the foyer to locate her other shoe. Ashton entered her house, closing the door behind him. He held her present behind his back.

"Will this make up for it?" and drew her package from behind his back. She looked at the present and then at him. "Did you really think I wouldn't get you something?"

She smiled at him. "I have something for you, too, but let's wait and have our Christmas tomorrow, okay?"

"Sure whatever you want... Now get your other shoe on and finish getting dressed. We're going to be late."

She smiled up at him and located her shoe while he made his way into her family room to admire her tree. He watched as the icicles danced back and forth, changing colors as they moved amongst the various colored lights. She reached his side and latched onto his arm. She laid her head on his shoulder and stood there with him for a few moments.

"It's beautiful," he said. "Come on, let's go." He grabbed her coat and helped her on with it. They didn't say a word as he guided her to his car. He opened her door, and as she slid into the passenger seat, he said, "Thank you."

"For what?"

"For this," he said, sweeping his hand out in front of him towards the front of her house. "For allowing me to be a part of your memories." And with that, he closed the door and made his way to the driver's seat.

They arrived at church well in advance of the crowd and even beat Angelina and Matthew. They sat in church, and as the children started to sing, Ashton reached for her hand. He set it atop his thigh, and on occasion, squeezed her fingers as the concert went on. Matthew's enthusiasm as he sang touched him to the core. Another memory he was building that he never experienced in boarding school. And generally, when he did go home, his father was focused on the guests at the resort and his mother was a living hell waiting for his father to come home. They'd had concerts in school, but nothing like this with all of Matthew's family in attendance.

Directly after mass, they headed over to the Samuels' house. Jackie had again outdone herself with the buffet she served. Angel slept through the concert and mass, while Matthew fell asleep as soon as mass was over. Angelina and Alejandro elected to go home after mass, missing out on another post-Christmas Eve party. Their stay was shorter than planned when Ashton noticed her weariness and informed her it was time to go. Gabriella smiled up at him in thanks. Jackie understood, as always, and wished them both a Merry Christmas.

It was almost three in the morning when he pulled up to her house. The house was still ablaze with the lights he'd hung.

"I changed the timers because I wanted to see them when we came home tonight. I love what you did for me. That was a present in and of itself." He opened her door and walked her to the door. "Please come in," she said as she unlocked the door.

"Aren't you tired?"

"I am, but I'd like to sit in front of the tree for a while. Join me," she said, reaching out her hand to him. He grasped her fingertips and walked with her to the couch. They sat down and he wrapped his arms around her. "This is nice. Really nice," she said as she started to drift off to sleep.

He sat with her wrapped in his arms, watching the tree. *I could sit here like this forever*, he thought as he drifted off to sleep.

He woke from a sound sleep at five o'clock when he heard his cell phone ring. He fumbled around in his pocket until his hand landed on his phone. By then he'd not only woken Gabriella, but he'd also missed the call. He checked the caller ID and was unfamiliar with the number. He waited to see if the caller left a voicemail, but they didn't. He pulled her closer to his side. "Sorry I woke you."

"It's okay. What time is it?"

"Just after five…" And then his cell rang again. This time it was sitting beside him on the couch. It was the same number that had called him only moments before. "I'd better get this." Ashton paused and then took the call. "This is Dr. Holder."

"Dr. Holder, this is Harris from Branson Rehabilitation Center."

Ashton knew this wasn't going to be good news. He listened intently as Harris spoke.

He grabbed for her hand, needing to feel her presence. He clenched his jaw tightly as he listened to the caller. "We've taken your mother to the hospital." The pulse at his temple throbbed. He closed his eyes as the caller spoke. "We believe she may have suffered another stroke."

"I see," Ashton said. "It's a four hour drive for me."

"Please hurry," Harris said as he waited for Ashton's reply.

"I understand that time is of the essence," Ashton said as he clenched his hand tightly at his side. "Thank you for the call."

He noticed the worried look on her face as she waited for him to say something.

"It's my mom," he said, "She's been taken to the hospital. They believe she's had another stroke."

She squeezed his hand and leaned her head on his shoulder. "What can I do?"

"Nothing," he said.

She wasn't going to do nothing. She hopped up from the couch. "Give me ten minutes, and I'll be ready."

"Ready, for what?"

"Well, I'm going with you." Ashton stood. "And I won't take no for an answer." She leaned in and kissed his cheek. "Please let me do this for you." She didn't want Ashton's newfound Christmas memories to end in this manner. She wanted to be by his side and she would. She ran to her room and grabbed anything she could put her hands on and threw them into her duffle bag that was sitting just inside her closet.

She returned to her family room finding him standing in the exact same spot she'd left him ten minutes earlier. "Come on. We've got to get on the road. First we'll stop by your house…"

"I don't need to. I've got clothes at the house." She had been surprised when she and Joe visited him in Branson at Thanksgiving. She knew he hadn't stopped at his home to pack before taking off after learning about his mother's stroke. She discovered that when he had left home five years earlier, after his father's funeral, that he'd left a closet full of clothes. When he returned at Thanksgiving, his closet was just as he'd left it—full of his clothes.

"It's too early to call my parents. I'll phone them in a few hours."

"What about their open house?"

"I've been there the last three years. My parents would want—no they'd expect me to be by your side." She turned off the Christmas lights, checked her back door, and threw a few snacks into her bag. She reached out her hand, smiled up at him and pulled him towards the front door. She was where she needed to be—by his side, unfortunately making memories that he'd never expected he'd have to make.

Chapter Twenty-Four

SINCE IT WAS CHRISTMAS DAY, Mochas & Coffee was closed. Ashton needed a coffee badly so he pulled into the gas station, filled up his tank, and when he went inside to pay, returned with not only two cups of hot coffee, but donuts as well. "Merry Christmas," he murmured as he handed her a cup of coffee and the bag of donuts. "I thought we needed something outside of the snacks you grabbed for our long drive."

She looked at the bag and smiled up at him. Upon closer inspection, she noticed the tension on his face, the shadows that were appearing under his eyes, and the fine lines that stood out around his eyes. His light had dimmed—the twinkle that she'd seen the previous day had faded. Darkness had taken over and replaced the joy and happiness that had once shone brightly. Ashton was not the same man that he'd been only a few short minutes ago—that man had faded and was being replaced by the Ashton of old. She could see him withdrawing, shutting down. She wouldn't, couldn't let this happen.

He took a sip of his coffee and pulled out of the

gas station. They drove in silence until she asked if she could turn on the radio. He nodded, never uttering a word. They were half-way to Branson when she pulled out her cell phone. It was going on eight and both of her parents would be up and about preparing for their open house. She pressed the preassigned number on her phone, but the call didn't go through. She glanced at her screen. "No service."

Ashton reached for his phone, handing it to her. "Try mine."

She entered her parents' number into the phone and surprisingly the call went through. Her father answered. "Dad, it's Gabriella."

"Honey, where are you and why are you using Ashton's phone?"

"That's why I'm calling." Gabriella told her father that she and Ashton were on their way to Branson. "They think Ashton's mom may have suffered another stroke, and they've taken her to the hospital. I'm riding with him."

"Honey, tell Ashton how sorry we are and that your mother and I are praying for his mother. Drive safely and please let us know her condition."

"I will, Dad. I'm sorry about the open house."

"Don't worry about that. You being there for Ashton is more important."

"I know. Thanks for understanding and Merry Christmas."

"Honey, Merry Christmas to you and Ashton, too."

She ended the call and set his phone on the console between them. Again, no words were said or needed. She closed her eyes and laid her head against the headrest. Almost immediately, she dozed off.

The next thing she knew, she felt Ashton's hand

brushing her cheek. "Gabby, we're here."

"Huh, what?" She said as she slowly opened her eyes and caught his. *Wow. He looks really tired.* "Where are we?"

"We just pulled into Branson. I thought I'd stop for a minute and gas up the car before heading to the hospital. Do you need to use the restroom?"

"Yeah, I do," She grabbed her purse and opened her car door. She hadn't moved since she'd sat down almost four hours earlier and was slow exiting the car.

She was walking somewhat faster when she returned to the car with two cups of coffee in hand. "I don't know about you, but I need this."

"Thanks, so do I. Are you okay? You looked like you were moving a little slowly."

"I'm fine. I was a little stiff from sitting so long." She took a sip of her coffee. "Are we far from the hospital?"

"Not too far," he said as he put the car in drive and got back onto the highway.

A half-hour later, they pulled into the visitor's parking lot at Branson Memorial Hospital. Ashton pulled into a parking spot and turned off the ignition. He stared out across the lot, his eyes catching the sculpture garden. He brushed his hand across his stubbled jaw, sighed, and opened his door. She felt the distance that had grown between them from his taking the initial phone call only hours ago. He was drifting away, withdrawing into himself. She wanted—no needed to help him, but didn't know how or what she could do. She'd wait to determine his needs until after they checked on his mother. Maybe it was nothing, but yet again, it could be serious.

She jumped from the car and hurried to his side,

grabbing ahold of his hand. She wanted him to know
that he wasn't alone. They checked in at the information desk to discover that his mother was in the same
fifth floor ICU that she'd occupied only weeks ago.
He called for the elevator and when the doors opened
they discovered they'd be the only ones riding to the
fifth floor. He pushed the button for his mother's floor
and stood against the wall of the elevator. She sidled
up next to him and put her arms around him. "Think
positive thoughts," is all she said. And then, the doors
opened and they walked down the brightly lit hallway
to the nurse's station. His mother had indeed suffered
another stroke.

Time stood still as they waited in the waiting room
for the next possible chance to visit his mother. She
listened as he phoned Alistair, informing him that
his mother wouldn't be coming home and that she'd
suffered another stroke. Originally, she had been
scheduled to return home on Christmas Eve, but the
doctors had elected to hold off a day.

"Alistair, I'm not going to lie to you. Things aren't in
her favor… No, I'm not alone. Gabby's with me. I'll
call if anything changes."

Gabriella watched Ashton as he spoke to Alistair.
She saw the tension, as he was once again clenching
his hand as he spoke. Several times he pursed his lips
and closed his eyes as he listened to his friend. He was
hurting and he didn't know how to let his anger flow.
She placed her hand on this leg while he spoke to
Alistair. Never once did he reach out to her. In fact,
as soon as his conversation was over, he jumped from
his chair. "I'll be right back," he said as he fled from
the room.

She sat anxiously awaiting Ashton's return. She

dozed off momentarily and then woke abruptly to someone speaking to her. "Where's Dr. Holder?" the voice asked.

She looked up into the nurse's face. "He'll be right back," she said just as she saw a flash out of the corner of her eye as he returned to the room. She had a sinking feeling. Her stomach dropped as she waited for the nurse to acknowledge his presence.

"Dr. Holder, you need to come now."

Gabriella watched as the color immediately dropped from Ashton's face. She didn't know what she should do, but he reached for her hand and grabbed ahold of it tightly. They quickly followed behind the nurse to Jana's room. She knew it wasn't good news as they approached his mother's bedside. She knew the signs. The monitors had all been turned off. There was no sign of life. His mother had died. "I'm sorry, but she just passed. There was nothing we could do," the attending doctor said as he walked from the room.

She didn't know what to say or do. She watched him as he approached his mother's lifeless body. She lay there so still—almost as if she were just taking a nap. He pulled Gabriella close to his side, resting his head on hers. They stood there for what seemed like an eternity. Neither of them spoke. Then, he pulled away from her and turned from the room, pulling her alongside him as they solemnly walked out of the ICU.

A nurse greeted him outside with all of the information he needed to begin the process for making arrangements for his mother's body.

Ashton drove in a fog to his childhood home, opening the gates and climbing the massive drive to the house on the hill. The view on any given day was breathtaking, but not today. Neither of them took in the view. Today, all he felt was alone. Even though he hadn't grown up in a real family, he'd still had one. But now, he was truly alone without a mother or father. And Ashton, for the first time in his life, truly experienced the feeling of being alone.

He knew he was withdrawing more and more from her. He could feel it and see it in her expressions and actions towards him. Yes, he'd held her hand, but that was it. He hadn't spoken a word since leaving the hospital. He knew she was there to support him, but he felt like she was just an extra appendage, not really needed. He knew she'd stay by his side, and in time, be there when he needed her. Times would be tough for him over the next few days, planning his mother's services, but Gabriella would remain faithful to him, support him, and be the shoulder he needed to lean on.

Gabriella hadn't had the chance to even open her car door when Alistair had opened the front door. He knew by Ashton's presence and his demeanor that something terrible had happened to Jana and that the prayers he'd prayed didn't have the positive outcome that he'd hoped for.

Alistair watched Ashton as he made his way up the stairs. It seemed like he'd forgotten about Gabriella, but he stopped and turned, waiting for her to catch up to him. She hugged Alistair when she met him at the door. Ashton shook his hand as he entered his boyhood home. Ashton led them into the living room where he gravitated to the bar, pouring himself a glass of scotch. Downing it in one gulp, he turned to Alistair who'd been watching him closely. Alistair knew what he was going to say—Jana was dead.

"I'm sorry, Alistair."

"Ashton, I know. Was it peaceful?"

"Yes. She never woke from the time she was admitted. She's in a better place," he added as he poured himself another shot and swallowed it. They sat in the room, discussing what their next steps were. Ashton needed to phone her attorney, contact a funeral home, and... He was overwhelmed all of a sudden. "I'm going to take a walk," he said as he headed towards the back of the house. All the while, he felt her eyes on him as he departed the room.

"Go to him," Alistair said. "He needs you." Gabriella smiled at Alistair, thanking him for his concern. She followed Ashton outside and found him walking towards the back of the property along a tree line. It was winter now and all the leaves had fallen from the trees. You could see for miles. She watched him from a short distance as he stood with his head lowered, looking at the ground, or maybe at nothing at all. She approached as quietly as she could until her foot crunched on a pile of leaves. He lifted his head, acknowledging her presence. She stood next to him, watching him closely as he processed what had transpired only an hour ago. The happy memories that he'd been making, had turned to ones filled with pain and sadness. Instead of remembering this year as a year of hope and change, he'd been forced to face his mother again and all of the sadness that it brought with it.

He reached for her hand and started walking. Then, he began to tell her his story. The story that few people knew—about the childhood he'd never had. About living in a boarding school, rarely coming home, and rarely interacting with the only family he'd had. She learned that his father was wealthy—extremely wealthy. Not that she hadn't already figured that out.

He'd owned the largest resort in Branson and lived the life of a business owner. Never home and someone who never thought of his family. They were always the last rung on the ladder.

She learned about his asthma and the reason why he'd become a pediatrician. He'd been extremely ill as a child. And when his asthma acted up, it was his nanny that made sure he was okay.

She heard the intense pain and sadness in his voice as he spoke. She finally understood why Ashton was the way he was. He'd never had a role model in his life until her father had discovered him in that hospital room. John had taken him under his wing and helped shape him into the man and doctor he was today.

She sighed as she thought about all the loneliness that he'd experienced in his lifetime. She understood why he had no childhood memories. All that she knew was that she was going to stay by his side. He would know that someone cared deeply for him. She would support him and help him through the next several days of darkness. And then she'd be by his side when he needed to deal with his past life.

Ashton wanted to put his mother to rest as quickly as possible, so he arranged a quick wake. Gabriella stood stoically by his side as he greeted his mother's friends and business acquaintances. She stood by his side as he watched her casket being lowered into the grave. Never once did he show one bit of emotion. He appeared frozen in place, like one of the sculptures in the sculpture garden.

Gabriella was worried about him. They were return-ing to St. Louis the following day, New Year's Eve. So much had happened in the last week. He'd turned course and had fallen back into his old ways. He'd lost the life from his eyes, the twinkle that had appeared just a short week ago. He seemed to argue with everyone he interacted with. From the funeral director, to Jana's attorney, to the limo driver who took them to and from the funeral and cemetery. He'd even yelled at Alistair for something trivial. She stood by watching the change.

Ashton barely spoke to her and when he did, he was angry and aloof. She was hurt by his actions but didn't want him to know how much they truly bothered her. She held her head high and waited for the next shoe to fall, which always came when she started to discuss his mother. She should have learned her lesson, but apparently not.

The evening before they left, he had gotten upset with her and had left the house. She wasn't exactly sure what she'd done to set him off. One minute they were sitting in the dining room having an actual conversation—the first since his mother's passing. She'd made a comment about the flowers at the funeral and he exploded at her. She sat while he yelled at her. Whatever he'd said, she blocked out. All she remembered was the tone of his voice and the dark look in his yes. He'd slammed his napkin on the table hard enough to shake the glassware. She grabbed her goblet before it fell over. He took one last look at her and stormed out of the room, never once looking back at her.

She'd watched as he fled the room. On the few occasions he'd had an outburst, she followed him, trying to calm him, but this time she didn't follow. Instead, she went into the library in search of something to read.

She pulled one book after another out of the book-shelves. Nothing held her attention. And then, when she pulled out a book by one of her favorite authors, another came with it, crashing to the floor. She set her book aside as she picked up the one that had fallen.

It appeared to be a leather-bound journal—there was no title or inscription on the cover. She opened the first pages only to discover that it was, in fact, a handwritten journal. She placed her book back onto the bookshelf and sat down in one of the chairs in front of the fireplace. As Gabriella read and got deeper into the journal, she realized it was Jana's journal. A journal about her life, her marriage, her son, and her husband's life of debauchery. Jana had detailed her husband's affairs, one right after the other.

She was shocked by what she read. She began to understand the life his mother had led, her anger towards Ashton's father. She realized that Jana blamed Ashton for his father's ways. He'd changed after Ashton's birth—never having time for her or their son. She didn't know what to do. Should she share this with him? Or put it back amongst the remainder of the books to be found another day?

He had pulled away from her. If she shared the journal with him, would he pull even further away? She toyed with her options, but it turned out she didn't have to choose one. Ashton surprised her when he joined her in the library. She jumped when she heard him and dropped the journal. It fell to the floor.

"What are you reading that has you so engrossed that you didn't even hear me enter the room?"

Startled, she didn't know what to say or do. She could tell he wasn't in a good frame of mind. Before she could reach for the journal, he had picked it up off the floor. As he paged through the journal, he froze. "What is this?" he asked.

"I believe it's your mother's journal. I was looking for something to read when it fell off the bookshelf. I'm sorry that I intruded on her thoughts." Ashton looked at her. "I'm sorry I read it."

She watched as he paged through his mother's journal discovering what she had only moments before. She watched him flinch almost as though he'd hit a brick wall. She could only imagine his thoughts as he discovered the type of marriage his parents actually had. As she sat there, she saw his facial expressions change. He drew in his lips and clenched his free hand. She was sure he'd reached the part of the journal that explained what his mother had endured. She knew he'd read enough when he threw the journal down and walked from the room.

She wasn't sure what she should do. Should she follow him, leave him alone? She hadn't a clue. All she knew was he was in a dark place.

She realized how late it was and decided to head off to bed. She knew Ashton planned on leaving early. He wanted to get home before all of the crazies were on the road.

Gabriella had a fitful night. She tossed and turned, and when she woke, her thoughts immediately drifted to Jana's journal. She believed there were answers written on the pages. She wanted to help him understand his mother and would do anything in her power to make things better for him, if only she could.

Ashton was anxious to get on the road. She'd barely had one cup of coffee when he announced their departure. As he said his goodbye's to Alistair, she returned to the library. The journal sat exactly where he'd left it. She didn't think twice—she picked up the journal and slid it inside her purse. She wanted to find the answers that would help Ashton move on with his life and maybe even allow him to forgive his mother.

It was too late to forgive her face to face, but he could at least put to rest all of the pain and move on with his life. She hoped he wouldn't be upset with her. She had his best interests at heart. Her research could blow up in her face, and if it did, she'd deal with the fallout. Right now, though, she only wanted Ashton to forgive, but never forget. She wanted him to move on, making the happy memories that he'd been making prior to his mother's illness and death.

As soon as Ashton pulled onto the highway, she fell asleep. He knew she hadn't slept the night before— he'd heard her thrashing about in her bed as he walked the halls. He tried to forget about the journal that he'd paged through so quickly, but he couldn't. He knew his parents' marriage wasn't what one would call normal, but he'd never expected that his father had cheated on his mother, and cheated so thoroughly. He wondered if that's what caused his mother's anger, but he decided that he was going to forget about it. He needed to move on and try to live his life as best as he could and maybe, in time, he'd lose all the baggage that he carried.

They were half-way home when he decided to pull over and grab a bite to eat. He hadn't eaten anything since lunch the day before. He'd been upset with her for what he didn't know. He recalled their conversation, their first real one since Christmas Eve. The few words she'd spoken, and not spoken, had thrown him over the edge the night before.

She had been discussing the funeral and all the lovely things that had been said about his mother. He knew it hadn't been those words that affected him as he really hadn't paid attention as her friends and business colleagues eulogized her. It was something else. He remembered her reaching towards the centerpiece that sat in the middle of the table. As she'd ran her fingertips across the petals of the sterling colored roses, she commented on their sweet smell and beauty. She'd smiled up at him and that's when he broke. It was the roses. The way she caressed them like his mother used to stare at her very own roses. The memory, one that had been buried in his subconscious, a moment in time when his mother had been happy—smiling at him laughing at something he'd done. And then the memory faded and that's when he lost it.

After he calmed himself, he returned to the library where he discovered her with his mother's journal, and he really couldn't handle it. He'd had enough with her meddling and had practically run from the house. He drove around Branson, realizing that he absolutely hated it when he visited. The traffic always seemed to be a bear, except there'd been none last night.

He didn't know how or why, but he'd found himself sitting in the parking lot of his father's resort. Or rather his, now that he owned it. Earlier that day, he'd met with his mother's attorney. Surprisingly, he was her sole beneficiary. Ashton was a rich, very rich man, and he had no idea what he'd do with his father's heart and soul, the business that took him from his family. Should he sell it? He didn't know what he'd do. He decided to not make a rash decision and would hold onto everything, including the house, until he was in the right frame of mind to make that decision.

She felt the car slow and woke. "Is something wrong?"

"No, I'm hungry and thought we'd stop and have a bite to eat. Is that alright with you?"

"Sure, of course."

Ashton pulled into a chain restaurant's parking lot. It was crowded, but he found a spot. He grabbed the handle to his car door and pulled. He turned to her to say something, but changed his mind. He stood, slamming his car door behind him.

As he'd been driving, replaying their whole time in Branson, he realized why he was upset with her. She'd made him remember. Remember the happier times of his childhood. He'd long since forgotten his mother's love of her roses. He'd forgotten so much. All of his memories were wrapped up in the anger he carried with him since being forced to leave his home. Forced to attend a boarding school where he had no one except a handful of friends he'd made. Friends were one thing, but family was—

He looked at her through the car windows. She looked lost to him. He watched as she hesitated and then opened her car door. He held out his hand, and surprisingly she intertwined their fingers as they walked into the restaurant. It was crowded, but since it was just the two of them, they were seated immediately.

He watched as she perused the menu. He thought about how she'd held his hand as they walked into the building. And then, he'd felt the closeness disappear. He watched her. Her eyes never focused on the menu. The warmth he'd seen in her eyes had passed. They'd once again grown dark, and she blinked rapidly.

He kept his eyes on her as she did her best to get ahold of herself—he knew she didn't want him to see her cry. He ordered their coffees and watched her as she covered her face with the menu. He'd already decided on a Belgian waffle with blueberries and a side order of bacon. If he didn't know better, he thought he saw tears in her eyes. He reached for her menu and lowered it from her face. Yes, those were tears in her eyes, but she was controlling them. She wasn't going to let them fall.

He pulled the menu from her hand and laid it down on the table. "I think I'll just have coffee. I'm not hungry," she said, doing her best not to make eye contact. He reached across the table, placing his finger under her chin and raised her head so her eyes met his. He could see the hurt in her eyes. He didn't know what to do or say, so he said nothing.

Ashton really looked at her. He watched her draw her lips in. He knew she was doing her best not to openly cry. He knew he'd been awful to her. She'd come to support him. He'd needed a friend he could lean on and what did he do? He treated her horribly. But now as he watched her, he couldn't understand why the tears. They hadn't spoken on their entire drive as she'd slept the whole time.

When the waitress returned to the table, he ordered not only his waffle, but also a stack of pancakes for her.

"I told you I wasn't hungry."

"Well, if you don't eat, we'll take them in the car and I'll snack on them."

She looked all around the restaurant, doing her best not to make eye contact with him.

She stood abruptly. "I have to use the restroom."

Gabriella grabbed her purse and left him. He knew he'd hurt her. She'd gone out of her way to be by his side when she could have stayed at home and celebrated Christmas with her family. But no, she'd jumped at the chance to be with him, only to have her heart broken in the process. He was a dumb ass, he knew it. He didn't know how he could fix this at this point. He'd been downright mean to her. Several times she made suggestions to him on his mother's services and he accused her of meddling. Meddling? She wasn't meddling. She was offering her help when he couldn't think straight. She knew his mother's death affected him more than he let on. He should have embraced her help but instead he cut down everything she said.

He stewed over his coffee, wondering where she'd gone. He was getting worried. The waitress had delivered their breakfasts, and she still hadn't returned. Just as he was ready to ask their waitress to check on her, she reappeared. One look at her told him everything that he needed to know—she'd been crying. She sat down, allowing her hair to cover her face. He motioned to the waitress to bring a fresh cup of coffee to her.

He took a bite of his waffle, watching her closely as she sipped her coffee. Clearing his throat he said, "Gabby."

She didn't respond, only sat there with her head bowed.

"Please look at me." Slowly she raised her eyes. "I'm sorry." She shook her head. "I'm sorry I made you cry."

She looked back down at her plate and brushed a fresh tear from her face.

He was sorry for the pain he'd caused her. He motioned for the waitress to bring them both carryout containers. He slid both of their breakfasts into the containers and reached for the bill, placing it atop the containers. He stood with both carryout containers in one hand, and he reached for her hand with the other. "Come on. Let's go. It's time to go home."

She sniffled and stood, electing not to take his proffered hand. She waited at the door while he paid the bill and then followed him to his car. The happiness she'd felt only a week ago was gone. She was ready to chuck all of the memories they'd made in the last several months aside. The reformed Ashton had been replaced with the unthoughtful, closed-off one she'd first met. She knew he was grieving, but he didn't need to treat her like he'd done over the last several days. She couldn't wait to get home and crawl into her bed where she could forget about the man she had been slowly beginning to care for. One thing she realized was she couldn't lose her heart again to another—she'd been hurt before, and she wouldn't let herself be hurt again.

As they neared St. Louis, they hit a traffic snarl. She sighed when she saw the stream of traffic ahead. She closed her eyes and planned her day. One of the first things she wanted to do was remove all traces of Christmas from her house. And then she'd move forward with a fresh start. A New Year.

He pulled into her driveway, and it was almost three o'clock. Nine hours until the beginning of a new year. She'd thought she'd bring in the New Year in a different, much different way. But instead, she was going to curl up on her couch alone and watch the famous ball drop in Times Square.

He grabbed her duffle bag and walked her to her door. As she unlocked her door, she turned and grabbed her bag from his hand, not once looking at him. "Thanks," she said as she entered her door. "I guess I'll see you around."

"Gabby," he whispered.

"Please, just go." And with that, she closed the door in his face. He stood for a few seconds, looking at her door, and then turned and walked to his car. He took one last look at her house before pulling out of her driveway. He knew he'd messed up, but he couldn't face that now. Time is what he needed to move on from the pain and hopefully, when he was ready, she'd be waiting for him.

Chapter Twenty-Five

GABRIELLA WALKED INSIDE AND SET her duffle bag by the door. Her purse slid off her shoulder, crashing to the floor and spilling all of its contents, including Jana's journal. She picked up the journal, rubbing her hands across the soft cover, wondering what secrets lay inside the pages. She walked into her family room and opened the drawer to her desk, setting it inside. She'd look at it another day.

She reached for the phone, calling her parents and leaving a message on their answering machine, telling them that she was safely home. As she turned towards the kitchen, she noticed the present that he'd left for her on the couch. She shook her head to remove the memories, picked it up, and opened the closet where she set it atop the one she'd purchased for him. She closed the door and leaned up against the doorframe. She burst into tears and slid to the floor.

She didn't know how long she sat huddled on the floor, but it was getting late as the room began to darken. And that's when she realized she needed to get herself together. She pulled herself up off the floor, grabbed her duffle bag, and headed off to her bed-room where she elected to take a hot shower before dressing in her lounge pants and Rivermen sweatshirt. She swept her hair into a high ponytail and headed off to the kitchen where she brewed herself a cup of her favorite tea.

She made her way to the couch where she curled up into the corner with her cup in hand. As she sipped her tea, she rehashed her day and the last week. Today was Thursday, so she had until Monday to get a grasp of herself before heading back to school. She also real-ized she needed to finish grading the papers that she'd brought home and create the schedule she'd prom-ised Mary for Career Day. She knew if she immersed herself in these activities, she'd soon be able to forget about Ashton and all that he'd come to mean to her over the last month. It was time to move on and that's what she decided to do.

Gabriella prepared scrambled eggs and toast for din-ner. Her mother had phoned while she'd been in the shower, inviting her over for New Year's Eve. She tex-ted her back saying she was too tired and wanted to stay home. After finishing her dinner, she sat down on the couch and turned on the TV. All of the various cable channels were starting to carry New Year's Eve festivities, so instead of watching the same reports over and over, she decided to grade her papers. When she completed that, she moved onto creating the schedule for Career Day.

She found it to be more difficult than she first thought, as her mind kept drifting to their last Career Day meeting right before the holidays. They'd been so happy, and then Ashton's mother died and he reverted back to the cold man that she'd hated with a passion.

She took a deep breath and decided to move on. She sorted all of the requests into piles and went about making the various schedules of the careers that were being highlighted. When she came to Ashton's name, she pushed all of her feelings aside until she felt absolutely nothing for him. She was surprised with how many children wanted to sit in on his presentation. By the time she completed the schedules, it was a half-hour until midnight. She grabbed a glass of wine and returned to the TV where she counted down the end of one year and the beginning to the next. Ashton was her past and she had a whole new future ahead.

After he dropped her off, he drove around and ended up at Pedal's Diner. Gus boisterously greeted him when he walked through the door, wishing him a Happy New Year.

"Where's your Gabriella?"

"At home, I guess."

"What do you mean 'you guess'? I thought you were a couple."

Ashton felt his face harden and didn't comment.

"Okay, well I guess I won't go there… What are you having?"

He placed his order and made it a carryout. He decided he wanted to be alone. It seemed like an eternity to Ashton as he sat there waiting for his food, when in all actuality it was less than fifteen minutes. As he sat there, he realized the diner just wasn't the same without her by his side.

"Here you go, doc. Sorry about my earlier assumption… I hope you have a Happy New Year."

"Thanks, Gus," Ashton said as he paid his bill and strolled out of the diner. He was definitely looking through a different lens than he had been just a week ago. His life had dramatically changed and not for the better. He made his way home, grabbed a fork, and sat down at his kitchen table where he enjoyed his dish of pasta.

After eating, he realized how drained he actually was, so he grabbed the remote and sat down to catch some of the New Year's celebrations from across the country. As he thought back over the year, he knew he'd changed and become a better man, but he also realized in the last week that he'd slipped back into his old ways. He'd liked the man he'd become. He'd become a part of the Alvarez family, if only for a short period of time. He hoped that, in time, he'd be able to find his way once again, and he hoped that he could grab onto that feeling that swept over him, that feeling of belonging… That intense feeling of family. He wanted—no needed to feel part of a family unit. He needed to include the people in his life that cared for him and that included Gabriella and her family. Before he knew it, he'd fallen asleep with the hopes to start anew with the New Year. When he woke, he knew he'd have to start looking at life differently.

In the blink of an eye, it was time for Gabriella to return to school. She'd played phone tag with Angelina since New Year's Day, so she wasn't surprised when she heard her name and looked up to see, not only Matthew, but Angelina and Angel standing in her doorway. She'd just come inside from dismissing her students for the day. Her first day back had gone well, but she was tired. It wasn't necessarily a physical tiredness, but more an emotional one.

"Happy New Year," Matthew said as he ran to her, throwing his arms around her waist. Angelina followed, carrying Angel in her arms.

"Merry Christmas, and Happy New Year to you, too, Matthew."

Angelina hugged her friend. Immediately, she knew something was wrong just by looking at Gabriella's eyes. She saw a distance that she hadn't seen in a very long time. The last time she'd seen her, her eyes had been ablaze with happiness. And now... now Angelina didn't know. Gabriella wasn't the same person she'd been just a little over a week ago.

"Matthew, why don't you take your sister over to the table? I've got a few of her toys in my bag."

"Okay, Mom." Matthew grabbed Angelina's bag and guided his sister to the table. Angel had started to walk, but she was still getting her sea legs.

Gabriella watched as her niece made it to the table without collapsing onto the floor. "Angelina, she's really walking now. When did this start?"

"It's been a week or so, but once she started, she hasn't been able to stop. She's fallen a few times, but that's to be expected. But enough about us, what about you? I can tell something's wrong."

"I'm fine, just a little tired today getting back into the swing of things..."

"Gabriella, I know that's not the case. Tell me about Ashton."

"What about him? I haven't seen him since he dropped me off Thursday afternoon."

"What happened? I thought you were getting along

so well. If you weren't, I know you wouldn't have dropped everything, missed Christmas with your family, and gone with him to Branson."

"Yeah, well he's changed. I tried. I really did, but I think he's changed back into man he once was, the one I hated with an absolute passion."

"I don't believe you."

"Well, it's true. And on that note, I've got to get going. I have to be somewhere."

"Okay, well I'm glad we were able to catch you. How about coming over to dinner one night this week? We can celebrate Christmas. We still have your gifts."

Gabriella was busily packing her backpack with papers that needed grading and wasn't paying attention to Angelina.

"Did you hear what I said?"

"Huh? Oh yeah, we still have to celebrate Christmas. Just let me know when you want to, and I'll be there. I can't wait to watch the kids opening their gifts. That's always fun."

"How about I check with Alejandro and see what works with him? I'll call you." Angelina pulled her into a hug. "You know I worry about you."

"I know you do. Just let me know the day and time, and I'll be there."

Angelina gathered Angel's toys while Matthew said goodbye. She needed to speak with Alejandro and Alec to see what they knew about Gabriella and Ashton. Something wasn't right and she needed to find out what it was. She didn't want her best friend hurting, and that's what she was doing right now.

Gabriella waited for Angelina to leave before she hurried out of the building. She'd just closed the door to her classroom and started down the hallway towards the door leading to the parking lot when, out of the corner of her eye, she caught a blur. She turned to look, but she didn't see anything. Her mind was playing tricks on her, she knew it. Why would Ashton be here today of all days?

As she made it to her car, she scanned the parking lot. She didn't see any unusual cars. She threw her backpack into the backseat and decided to go straight home. She didn't feel like fighting the crowds that started this time of day at Schulers—she'd find something to eat at home. Worst case, a bowl of cereal looked pretty good. As she pulled out of the parking lot, her eyes caught a car coming around the corner in her direction. No, it couldn't be him… He was working. She turned her head as the car approached, passing her by. It wasn't him. Her mind was definitely playing tricks on her—she was seeing things. What did she think, that he'd be searching her out? She needed to get him out of her mind. She still had to deal with him in regards to Alec and Kelly's wedding and also Career Day, but that would be over in a few short weeks. She had a meeting scheduled the next three Fridays with Mary and Ashton. The last Friday of the month was Career Day and then she didn't have to see him for a long, long time.

"Mary, I want to apologize up front. I didn't get a chance to assist Gabriella with her scheduling over the break. My mother passed away, and I had to deal with her funeral."

"Oh, Ashton, I am so sorry. Had she been ill for long?"

He proceeded to tell her about Thanksgiving and the call he received Christmas Morning.

"At least she wasn't incapacitated long."

He didn't comment further. Changing the subject back to Career Day, he added, "So I'm not sure what Gabriella was able to accomplish."

"I spoke with her this morning and she completed the scheduling and everything. We just have a few meetings left in order to finalize everything. I feel good about this. Better than I have in past years. I think my pairing of you and Gabriella was a work of genius on my part. Maybe you two can organize it again next year."

"Well, I don't know about that." he cleared his throat. "I'll have to see what Alec and Joe have to say about that. I enjoyed the part I played, but maybe you should think about choosing someone else."

"Why fix something that isn't broken?" Mary said as she walked Ashton to the door.

But it is broken, he thought as he said his goodbyes and started down the sidewalk towards his car. He'd parked in the front of school instead of the teacher's parking lot. Just as he opened his car door, he saw her pulling out onto the street, heading in the direction of her house. His heart sped up as he watched her car disappear in the distance. Ashton felt lost without her in his life. He'd just enjoyed being in her presence. She seemed to always light up the room when she walked in. Her smile was infectious. And her laugh always made him want to smile. He needed to do something to correct his wrong, but he didn't know what.

Alec and Kelly's wedding was the following weekend. Maybe there he'd be able to get her alone and talk to her... apologize for the jerk he'd been. That wasn't who he was today, and he needed to prove that to her.

Ashton didn't get a chance to see Gabriella at their planning meeting that Friday. Mary had to cancel due to the weather. A snowstorm had blown in from the south-west, leaving behind a trail of closed schools and three-foot snow drifts. Kelly and Alec were taking the storm in stride, though. They'd known they ran the risk of bad weather for their wedding, but for them it was a good sign. What had brought them together in the first place was her car sliding off the road into a snowbank and him coming to the rescue. They decided to play it up and had fake deer sitting outside their reception hall, commemorating her attempt to avoid the deer that landed her into the snowbank.

The wedding went off without a hitch, except for the snow that was piled up in the parking lot and along the sidewalks. Kelly was a beautiful bride. While they were waiting for the reception to begin, Gabriella couldn't stop laughing as she recalled the look on Alec's face when he stumbled with his vows. He'd had to correct himself twice before he got them right. The wedding party that included Alejandro, Joe, Angelina, and Colleen had a hard time keeping it together on the altar while they heard snickering from the church full of guests. Indeed he'd been nervous, and when Kelly looked at him kind of stupefied, he burst into laughter.

"Sorry about that," he said. "I really do know your name." Alec was tongue-tied and just couldn't say Kelly Ann.

"Did you see the look on his face? It was priceless," said Angelina. "I thought Alejandro was going to lose it up there. He was trying so hard to contain his laughter that he had to turn away from Alec. You know, this would only happen to Alec, the once confirmed bachelor."

Just as Angelina finished speaking, she noticed Ashton approaching. Gabriella's back was to him and didn't see him coming. Angelina decided she'd watch this play out. She didn't want to see her friend moping around like she had been since her trip to Branson. She knew something had happened, but she also knew she shouldn't step in. When Gabriella wanted her to know, she'd tell her.

Angelina had spoken to both Alejandro and Alec after seeing Gabriella the first day of school after the New Year. Neither of them knew what was up with Ashton. All they could say was that he seemed more quiet than normal, but they attributed it to his mother's death.

Angelina watched as Ashton approached Gabriella, as he tapped his hand on her shoulder. She watched the surprise cross Gabriella's face. Angelina couldn't hear what he said, only that he turned and ushered Gabriella out of the room towards a hallway that led to another room. He placed his hand comfortably on Gabriella's back and guided her through the doorway. At least they were talking…

"Was that Ashton and Gabriella?"

"Yes, it was, and don't you get any more involved than you already are. I'm just about ready to call this bet off."

"I'm not doing a thing," Alejandro said as he shyly smiled at his wife. "I know they've hit a rough patch since Ashton's mom died, but I'm not giving up hope that they'll be the next to get married. We'll see come July. And honey, that's a long time away—anything can happen." Alejandro grabbed ahold of her hand as the wedding party was announced. They entered the ballroom and took their places as they awaited the bride and groom.

⤙

A wave of nerves overcame Gabriella when she felt Ashton's hand touch her back as he guided her from the room. She hadn't seen him in weeks and she had no clue what he wanted with her. As they strode from the room, her hands became clammy and she felt flushed. What was wrong with her? She desperately needed air.

"What's wrong? Are you alright?"

Gasping, she said, "I need to get some air."

He steadied her, then led her to a door that led outside. He quickly took off his suit coat and threw it over her shoulders. He watched her as she took several deep steadying breaths. He reached for her hands, grabbing ahold of her fingertips. She'd closed her eyes as she drew in several quick breaths. "Better?"

"I am. I don't know what came over me." She stood almost paralyzed, not knowing what she should do or say. She hadn't seen him since he'd dropped her off at her home New Year's Eve. She was nervous and definitely unsure of herself. She'd decided she wanted nothing to do with him. Maybe her decision was premature considering he had just lost his mother, but she rationalized that if he could so easily slip back into his old ways because of that, why couldn't he again? She didn't want to associate herself with him if this were the case.

"Are you alright now? Can we can slip back inside?"

She nodded and he pulled her close to his side as he escorted her back through the door into the hallway they'd just come down. He led her towards a conference room at the end of the hall. As they walked towards the conference room, she was reminded that the last time they'd been together hadn't ended well. The way he'd treated her that last evening in Branson was still fresh in her mind. On one hand, she wanted to forget about his treatment of her, but on the other hand, she remembered the pain he'd caused and she still felt hurt by his actions. He led her through the doorway and closed the door behind him.

She was more nervous than she'd ever been in her entire life. Her heart was racing, her hands were clammy, and her stomach felt like it was on a roller coaster—she just knew she was going to get sick. And then when her eyesight started to blur and she got dizzy… She noticed a couch in the back of the room and slowly made her way towards it. She had to sit down and now. The last straw was when her fingers started to tingle—she just knew she was going to faint.

She didn't understand her nervousness. What was there to be nervous about? It wasn't like she didn't know him. She did, and that was the problem. She'd given a part of her heart to him—albeit, a small part, but her feelings for him had been growing every day. She thought she'd put her feelings for him aside, yet when she felt his hand against her back, everything came rushing back at her and that's when she realized she still felt something for him. Something stronger than she realized. She was certain that if they hadn't had their blip after his mother's death, he'd more than likely own her heart completely.

She eased herself down onto the couch. Ashton immediately knew something was still wrong with her. He sat down beside her and made her lie down, placing her legs across his. Her face was pale. He could see droplets of sweat breaking out on her brow, and she was breathing hard. He felt for her pulse and her heart was racing. "Gabby, take it easy. Just lay here, okay?" She closed her eyes and nodded in response.

He brushed her hair out of her eyes and cupped her jaw. She was breathing slower and seemed to be calming down. He reached for her hand and held it between both of his. He watched as she took another deep breath and licked her lips. They sat like this for a few minutes before Ashton spoke again. "Are you any feeling any better?"

Her eyes fluttered open. "Better, yes," she whispered. "I don't know what happened. I felt fine before you asked to speak with me."

"Maybe I'm your problem then." She briefly closed her eyes and reopened them. "Do you feel like sitting up? How about a glass of water?" He eyed several bottles of water sitting on the credenza beside him. He grabbed one and unscrewed the cap. She sat up and swung her legs over the side of the sofa. When she was settled, he handed her the bottle of water.

Slowly, she tipped the bottle to her lips, taking a sip of the lukewarm water. Ashton reached for the bottle when she was done drinking. After she handed the bottle to him, she closed her eyes and put her head back against the sofa.

"Wow, I've never had that happen before. I thought I was going to be sick, and then my vision blurred, the room started to spin… When I broke out into a cold sweat, I thought that was it." She raised her hand to her chest. "At least my heart isn't still racing."

"Do you want to talk about it?"

She shook her head. "What's there to talk about?"

"Okay, how about I start." He was going for broke. He had to make amends with how he'd treated her in Branson. He pulled her hand into his and laced his fingers through hers. She was going to hear him out.

"I just want to say I'm sorry. Sorry for how I treated you after my mom's death... Sorry for not listening to you when you made suggestions for her funeral." Shaking his head, he said, "I'm sorry for everything." He squeezed her hand and went on. "I don't know what came over me. I was back at home, in an environment that had too many memories, of which very few were happy ones. For the most part, I was only home during the Christmas holidays. I came home for maybe a few weeks during the summer, but other than that I lived at my boarding school. Being there during the holidays was just too... Let's just say it brought back too many memories that I'd hoped to forget."

He cupped her cheek, raising her head so she'd look him directly in the eyes. "Gabby, you know I have very few good childhood memories. This year, for once, I was making ones that I knew would stay with me until the day I die. And you were the one behind that. I can still see your eyes when we drove up to your house, and you saw the outside lights for the first time. I clearly remember watching you as you wrapped each present, measuring incorrectly and throwing the paper aside."

"Hey, you saw that?"

He smiled at her. "I did. And I also watched your face light up when you spoke of each and every ornament that your students had given you before hanging it on the tree. Not only did you remember who the ornament was from, without looking at your cheat sheet, you also had a story to tell about that student. Those are the memories I'll remember from this last year. Can you forgive me?" He saw her scrunch her eyes, holding her tears at bay. He watched as she pursed her lips in another attempt to keep from crying. "What I missed most in the last couple of weeks was spending New Year's Eve with you. I wanted to ring in the New Year with you to add to those memories, but I also wanted to begin making new memories, too."

He watched her face closely. A tear leaked out from her closed eyes and then it was followed by a second. She couldn't contain the tears any longer and began to sob. Ashton didn't think twice before pulling her into his arms. A few wisps of hair had come loose from her up-do. He brushed them behind her ear.

"Well, can you forgive me? Will you give me another chance? Because I'm sure, before we had this little talk that I was definitely not on your Christmas card list for this year... Seriously though, I know we've come a long way from the moment I joined the clinic. We hit a rough patch, at least that's what I'd like to call it. Can you forgive me and give me a second chance? What I feel for you, I've never felt before for anyone. For some reason, you seem to get me... the good and the bad. I didn't mean to hurt you. It's just how I had to deal with everything—all of my bad memories."

She opened her eyes and looked at him, swallowing loudly. She wanted to believe him, but could she? She'd been down this road before and had been hurt badly. She didn't know if she wanted to put her heart back out there only to have it crushed again. But she couldn't deny what she felt when he'd touched her minutes before. What if she passed him by, and she never found what she had with Ashton again? The feelings both good and bad, the memories that they'd started making… It was too much for her. She had to think, but she couldn't right now. She was wrapped in his arms, the place she really wanted to be… Should she believe him? Should she take that chance?

"I know this is a lot to take in right now, especially since you're not feeling well. How about we take it one step at a time, one day at a time, and if you're not comfortable with that, I'll step back. I want you in my life, Gabriella."

She threw her arms around his neck, crying harder than she'd cried in a long time. She nodded into his chest.

"Is that a yes?" he asked.

She nodded again. He reached in, placing both hands on either side of her face. Drawing her closely, he placed a soft kiss on her lips. The kiss was a promise of hope, of moving forward. It was his way of apologizing for being the sorry excuse of a man that he'd been. It was his hope for a future.

They sat in the conference room for another fifteen minutes or so until Gabriella got herself under control.

"Now, shall we go join the wedding party and celebrate Kelly and Alec's special day?"

Ashton stood and reached for Gabriella's hand. He smiled at her as she grabbed it, entangling her fingers with his. They made their way back to the ballroom after Gabriella had a chance to stop by the ladies room and fix her makeup. When she rejoined him, she looked beautiful. Definitely happier than she'd been earlier when he'd first approached her.

Yes, anything could happen, but if it were up to Ashton, he hoped and prayed they were over this hurdle. He was still learning—learning how to make friends, learning how to be a part of a family, and learning how to make memories. Gabriella Alvarez had certainly turned his world upside down for the better. He was starting to dream. Dream of a life filled with love, hope, and memories. And he dreamed that she'd be right in the middle of it all as he made these new memories.

Alejandro and Angelina just happened to be walking by the entrance to the ballroom. He quickly noticed his sister as she walked hand-in-hand back into the room. "See, what did I tell you?" he said, pointing to his sister and Ashton. "I bet they worked out whatever was wrong between them."

Shrugging her shoulders, Angelina replied, "We'll have to see. July is a long ways away. Anything can happen."

After their talk, they joined the rest of the family at her parents' table. They had a good time at Alec and Kelly's wedding. They danced and Gabriella did everything in her power to make him feel a part of her family again.

When it came to the bouquet and garter toss, neither of them were lucky enough to win the coveted prize. Angelina made a point of pointing that out to her husband. "At least Gabriella didn't catch the bouquet, and Ashton wasn't even close to snagging the garter. So, if you believed that theory that they'd end up like Kelly and Alec, that didn't materialize."

"Oh honey, I didn't expect either of them to secure the bouquet or garter. That was unique to Kelly and Alec. And, speaking of the happy couple, look at them," Alejandro said as he watched the bride and groom circle the dance floor. "Who'd have thought they'd have ended up here, in the same ballroom where our lives started together? I can still remember watching you come down the aisle. You took my breath away, and you still do." He reached out his hand to his wife. "Dance with me," Alejandro said as he clasped Angelina's hand, raising it to his lips, he added, "I love you more today than I did the day we married."

Alejandro and Angelina danced the night away, along with the happy bride and groom. When it came for Kelly and Alec to leave their reception, at least Kelly knew in advance where she was going. They were leaving the cold north heading to the warm Caribbean where they would enjoy two glorious weeks of sunshine.

Chapter Twenty-Six

A SHTON TOOK IT SLOWLY WITH Gabriella. He didn't want to overstay his welcome with her and often called her in the weeks leading up to Career Day to just check in, making sure she was okay.

Career Day came and went, and just as Mary predicted, was a huge success. Gabriella had been busy with the children and didn't have much time to spend with Ashton, so when the day ended, he surprised her in her classroom. As she dismissed her students for the day, he walked into her classroom, taking in all of the changes she'd made since his last visit. She'd added new bulletin boards and had set up a career center in her classroom. He sat down and started going through the information that she'd put together regarding all of the careers that would be showcased at Career Day.

He was so engrossed in reading the information packets that he didn't hear her as she returned to the room. His back was to the doorway and he felt rather than heard her presence as she neared his side. He looked up and smiled at her. "Wow, I can't believe you went to all of this trouble. You did a lot of research here," he said, pointing to the information packets. "How long did it take you to gather all of this literature and articles? Months? I had no idea that you spent so much time on this."

She sat down beside him, reaching for one of the packets she'd created on the field of education. "I don't consider this time-consuming. I love doing this—gathering information that I can pass along to my students so they can learn and maybe start making decisions on their future. Yes, they are only in fifth grade, but that's when I decided what I wanted to do in life. And I know Alejandro wasn't much older when he decided to become a transplant surgeon after one of his friends died of kidney failure while he was in school. That was a life-changing moment for him." She sighed. "It's my goal in life as I impart values and teach these children about so many things. If I can make that one difference in their lives, I've done my job."

She stood, placing her hand on his shoulder. "You did good today, Ashton. The kids really enjoyed your presentation. You brought everything down to their level, and that's what matters. You also shared a part of your childhood that several of my students can relate to. I know your bouts with asthma led to your pursuit of being a pediatrician. I know how scary it was for you, especially not having your parents there by your side." She walked away from him and started to tidy up her desk.

He watched as she systematically aligned papers on her desk and placed pens back in her pen holder. She was doing busy work. He wondered if he'd made her nervous. Since this was the first time they'd been alone since the wedding, he wanted—no, needed to find a way to make her comfortable again in his presence. He didn't know what to do. He stood, walked to her desk, and reached for her hand. This was his make or break moment. They'd never been on an official date where he'd formally asked her out. And now, he believed enough time had passed since his mother's death and all of the conflict that had caused. Yes, now was the time.

He took a deep breath and raised his hand to her face. Cupping her jaw, he leaned over so he could look her directly in the eyes. This was an important moment for them, and he wasn't going to mess it up. "Gab-ri-ella," he said, catching her attention. He half smiled at her, watching her reaction to her name.

"Yes," she breathed as she watched his face.

He swallowed before continuing. "Come out with me tomorrow."

She looked confused, "Are you asking me on a date? A real date?"

"I think that is what I asked."

"Well, not really," she said as she began to chew on her lip. "It's not exactly clear what you meant by 'come out with me.'"

He screwed his face up, realizing that his question didn't come out exactly as he'd intended, so he decided to try it again. He stroked her jaw as he spoke. "I know we haven't done anything in the right order here. In fact, it's all been half-assed between you helping me with my mom and everything. Yes, we've been out, but not what I'd like to think of as an actual date with dressing up and everything. I think it's time we did that. Have a real date. Dress up, go dancing, and enjoy each other's company. It's time for a redo. Let's forget about the past and start anew. Will you? Will you go on a date with me?"

She smiled broadly. Ashton was speaking from the heart. This was all new to him. He wanted to take that chance with her—see where it went. If it didn't work out, at least, he knew she'd helped him move past the awful memories of his childhood and help him begin making memories he could remember for a lifetime. "Well, when you put it that way…"

"Gab-ri-ella."

"Well…" she said, drawing out the angst that he was suffering waiting for her reply. "Of course I'll go on a date with you."

Ashton sighed loudly. "Way to make me sweat."

"Well, it's definitely a yes! So where and when?"

"I'd say tonight, but I asked for tomorrow. So tomorrow we'll get dressed up, go out, have a nice dinner, and celebrate. Celebrate the new year."

She leaned in and hugged him. Pulling away, she smiled at him. He felt himself lighten again.

Gabriella was excited for her date. She didn't know where he was taking her, only that she needed to get dressed up. She felt like she was going to prom all over again. She phoned her hair dresser late Friday evening when she got home. She had been going to Sheri for years and they'd become good friends. Sheri knew she was excited about their evening, so she squeezed her in for an afternoon appointment. Not only did she schedule a hair appointment, but she also found herself at the mall when the doors opened. She decided to get a special dress for their special occasion: their first date. She wanted a new dress for what she hoped was the true beginning to their relationship.

She walked into her favorite store at the mall and immediately was drawn to the dress that hung on the mannequin in the window. When she looked at the dress, she wondered what Ashton would think of her in it? It was champagne in color and was the perfect color to go with her hair and eyes. An A-line dress with an empire waist with a bateau-styled neckline that plunged in the back. The dress was classic, timeless, elegant, and she knew she'd feel like a million bucks in it. She loved the jeweled neckline. The dress would be mid-thigh on her and was completed with decadent layers of shimmering tulle. She'd look like a princess and that's just how she wanted to feel with him. She couldn't wait to try it on.

She quickly located her size and almost ran to the dressing room with excitement. She couldn't wait to see how it looked on her. She wasn't surprised. She looked just like she imagined, like a princess. She almost couldn't contain herself as she rushed from the fitting room. Thankfully, the store also sold shoes. Almost as quickly as she'd chosen her dress, she located a pair a heels that were simple but elegant, too. They completed the look. She'd never been able to shop this quickly in her entire life. It must be fate.

Gabriella was almost glowing when she got to Sheri's. "What's gotten into you?" Sheri asked as she began styling her hair.

"I have a hot date tonight."

"And who is the lucky gentleman?"

"Do you really want to know?"

"I wouldn't have asked if I wasn't interested."

"Ashton."

"Ashton... you mean Ashton Holder, Matthew's

doctor? The same man that you despised only a few short weeks ago? The same man that you ruled to sweep under the carpet? The same man that broke your heart?"

"Well, he didn't really break my heart."

"It seemed like it to me. After all, I just saw you the day of Alec's wedding. He definitely wasn't on your radar then. What happened?"

"He apologized."

"That's all it took?"

"Yeah, that's all it took." she said with glee.

As Sheri worked, she said, "Please promise me one thing?"

"Sure, what?"

"That you'll take this slowly. I don't want you getting hurt like last time."

"Don't worry. I learned my lesson."

When Sheri had finished, Gabriella hurried out of the salon. She had a little over an hour before Ashton was scheduled to pick her up. She just needed to do her makeup and throw on her dress.

She underestimated her time. She took extra care with her makeup and time got away from her. She'd just finished applying her mascara when the doorbell rang. She glanced at the time. "Oh my gosh," she said frantically. "He's here, and I'm not even dressed."

She didn't know what to do. She threw on her robe and made her way to the front door. She ever so slowly opened her door just a crack. He looked at her quizzically, peeking his head around the door.

"Gab–ri–ella, is there something wrong?" He hesitated, "Is there a reason why you're not letting me in?"

"Ah…"

"Gabby?"

"Okay, okay," she said as she opened the door the remainder of the way. "I'm not dressed yet. Sorry, but I lost track of time." He walked into the foyer, took one glance at her, and started to laugh.

"What's so funny? Do I look that bad?"

"No, you look beautiful… that is, in your robe. Go on and finish dressing. I'll wait here."

She spun around and started running down the hallway. Then she turned and ran back towards him. She surprised him when she threw her arms around him and kissed his cheek. "I'll be right back, promise." And then she was off again, flying down the hallway towards her bedroom.

Ashton made his way into the family room, remembering the last time he'd been there—Christmas Eve. He stood staring at the corner where her Christmas tree once stood. He drifted back to the day they'd decorated it.

"Ashton?" She said as she entered the room. She approached him and placed her hand on his forearm. "Hey, where'd you just go?"

He took one look at her and was speechless. She took his breath away as he breathed in the scent of her perfume. How lucky he was that she'd forgiven him and agreed to go on this long-awaited date. He was hopeful that he could have a future with her. He knew she'd changed him and was shaping him into the man he'd become. He listened more openly and he'd started to open his heart. The icy coldness that once enveloped him warmed with just her smile.

She was looking at him quizzically. "Ready?"

He ignored her comment. For some reason, he wanted to keep those memories close to his heart. He reached for her coat that she left sitting on the chair inside the door. He helped her into it, hugging her from behind. "You look like my fairy princess. Or, better yet, my true Cinderella. Come on, let's go and start making our own memories."

As he escorted her to the car, he turned to her once again and commented on how beautiful she looked in her dress and not her robe.

She laughed at him. By the way their evening was starting, she knew it would be one she'd never forget.

❦

Ashton took her to the restaurant that held so much meaning to her family. The Vineyard on the Hill was where both of her brothers had become engaged.

As soon as Gabriella accepted his dinner date, he'd called The Vineyard to arrange for one of their private dining rooms. From what Alec had told him, these rooms were something you shouldn't pass up. Between the special treatments you received, along with the ambience and the romantic feeling that emanated from the room, it was something Alec told him he'd never forget.

He learned, though, that the private rooms were booked for the evening and he'd have to dine in the regular dining room. Even though he couldn't book one of the rooms, he knew the evening would still be magical and filled with romance. It was a special night for them— their first real date, and he was going to make sure it was an evening to remember.

The Vineyard was about a forty-five minute drive from Gabriella's, and it sat in the rural countryside outside of St. Louis.

"So where are you taking me?"

"You'll have to wait and see." Ashton said as he merged onto the highway and started driving west out of the city. He crossed the mighty Missouri River and kept going. And then he signaled that he was getting off the highway. He speculated that she knew he was taking her to The Vineyard, especially when he'd started towards wine country. They passed vineyard after vineyard until the sign for The Vineyard on the Hill came into sight. He felt her excitement when he signaled that he was pulling into the driveway.

He drove up to the valet and jumped out of the car. By the time he reached her side of the car, the valet had already opened Gabriella's door and was assisting her from the car. Ashton reached for her hand, securing it firmly as they walked into the restaurant. He'd never been there before, but knew from both Alec and Alejandro that it was a one-of-a-kind experience between the views from the restaurant and the historic nature of the building itself. He was awed by the building as they made their way to the hostess. Between the stone on the outside, the turrets, and wood flooring as they walked in, he now understood why Alejandro and Alec had proposed there. Someday, he'd get a look at the private rooms, but what he saw when he was led to their table was enough in and of itself. The room was filled with romance, he thought as he held Gabriella's chair as she sat down.

The waitress showed them to a table towards the back of the restaurant. It was secluded, and he felt like he had his own private room. When he sat down, he reached for her hand. As he watched her closely, he was fully aware of her happiness. Before he could say anything, the sommelier presented their wine choices for the evening. He ordered a bottle of their finest.

They also placed their orders for their dinner. She ordered lamb chops with mashed potatoes and green beans almandine, while he chose their special for the evening, braised short ribs that also came with the same vegetables that Gabriella had chosen.

The sommelier returned with Ashton's wine selection, which he immediately approved. They sipped their wine when they heard the band begin to play. He smiled at her. "May I have this dance," he asked as he stood at her side.

She took his proffered hand and followed him across the room towards the dance floor. He swept her into his arms as they danced to an old classic. He felt at home with her in his arms. He just hoped the feeling continued.

He held her tightly as they danced. He looked deeply into her brown eyes and felt her tense and then relax in his arms.

She seemed happy, and that's what he wanted. As they danced, he recalled his past conversation with Joe about her last meaningful boyfriend and how hurt she'd been when the relationship came to an end. He was having feelings for her but he wanted to take it slow. In fact, he wasn't sure what the ultimate prize would be. His parents' marriage was definitely not the typical one, and they definitely weren't role models for him when it came to raising children.

He didn't know if he had it in him to get married. Maybe he was meant to just date, be a bachelor like Alec had been. He really wasn't sure what the ultimate goal was for him, but one thing was for certain—he didn't want to hurt her. She was unique, so caring of others. He loved how she made time to tutor at the hospital and take time out to be with Matthew. She'd make a fine wife and mother someday, but he wasn't sure if he'd be the one that she fulfilled those dreams with.

They indeed had a magical evening, enjoying the wonderful food, wine, and dancing. But all too soon, their evening came to an end. As they waited for the valet to deliver his car, he pulled her into an embrace. "This was just as Alec said it would be," he said. "It definitely fits the bill when it comes to ambience and romance."

"It certainly does. I never imagined that tonight could be so magical."

When the valet pulled up at the curb, he opened the car door for her and raised his hand to her face. "You're absolutely beautiful, Gabriella. Just beautiful." She smiled at him as only Gabriella could do.

They drove home, each in their own thoughts. When he pulled into her driveway, he turned off the motor and reached for her hand. "I had a really nice time tonight. What about you?"

"It was perfect. I can't believe you took me to The Vineyard. I don't know if you're aware of this, but both Alejandro and Alec got engaged there. Albeit Alejandro was already engaged, he just made it more official there. It's a special place for them, and now it's a special place for me, too. Thank you for this night. I'll never forget it."

He leaned in and kissed her, but he pulled away almost immediately.

"What's wrong?"

"Nothing. But with the way I feel right now, if I kept this up, I won't want to leave."

"Do you have to?"

"I do. Gabriella, I want to take this slow. I don't

want to rush into anything. I hope you're okay with that, but I have to go slowly. What with my childhood and everything… The way my parents were… I have to make sure it's right."

"I understand." She opened her car door. He started to follow her, but she placed her hand on his arm. "I'm fine. You don't have to show me to the door."

"But, I—"

With that she exited the car. As she walked to her door, she turned and threw him a kiss. All was well, he believed as he watched her enter her house. He backed out of her driveway and turned towards his house. He felt good about the evening. Really good. He had to remind himself to take their relationship slowly because, with the way he felt, he wanted to stay the night with her. Time is what he needed. He needed the time to learn about building relationships and also learning what it took to be a true member of a family.

Chapter Twenty-Seven

ASHTON PHONED GABRIELLA THE FOLLOW-ING week. It was the first of February, and he apologized for not following up with her sooner after their romantic evening, but he'd been on call and had been quite busy answering calls about sick children.

"I'm sorry about not phoning you sooner, but I've been pretty busy."

"Don't worry, I understand. I remember what it was like for my dad this time of year. He was hardly home."

"Yeah, we've been dealing with a nasty virus, and strep throat is running rampant through the schools as well."

"I know all about it. A third of my class was out Monday, and I thought Mary might have to close school because so many of the teachers were out, too. Thankfully, that didn't have to happen. I'm just happy I've avoided whatever's going around."

"I'm glad you avoided it so far, too. It's a pretty nasty bug. Switching subjects," he said, "I know I'm a little early asking you this, but do you have plans for Valentine's Day? If you don't, I'd like to take you out. That is, if you want to go out with me again."

"Now, where did you get that idea? Of course I'd like to go out with you."

"Well, I wasn't too sure," he laughed. "But I'm happy to hear that you will. So Valentine's Day is on a Sunday. When would you like to celebrate? I'm not sure if you'd like to go out on a school night."

"That's true, but I'm game for Sunday if you are."

He heard the beep of an incoming call. "Hey Gabby, I've got an incoming call that I've got to take. I'll call you and set up a time. Have a good week."

Gabriella could hardly contain herself after hanging up the phone with Ashton. She had wondered why she hadn't heard from him since their date, but understood what the life of a pediatrician was like.

No sooner had she hung up the phone with him, her phone rang again. This time it was Angelina. They'd hardly seen one another since the beginning of the year and hadn't even had the chance to celebrate Christmas yet.

"So, I think I've finally pinned down Alejandro. Gosh, he's been so busy between the hospital and conferences... I wish he'd slow down. Anyway, how does Saturday sound to celebrate Christmas? Matthew's been after me for days to set something up, so how about it?"

She was still coming down from her high from moments ago that she missed most of what Angelina said.

"Gabriella, are you still there?"

"I'm here. But could you repeat that a little slower? For a moment I thought you were Alec carrying on during one of his rambling sessions," Gabriella laughed.

"Gabriella!"

"Well, I'm sorry. I was distracted with a call that I'd just ended when you rang. What were you asking?"

Angelina slowed down and asked her again if she would be able to come for dinner Saturday.

"Yep, Saturday's fine with me. I'll come early so we can chat and catch up."

"Sounds like a plan," Angelina said.

She heard Angel screaming in the background.

Angelina sighed, "Angel just took a tumble, so I've got to let you go. See you Saturday," she said as she disconnected the call.

She looked at the phone in her hand. *She's gotten too good at hanging up on me.*

The week flew by and before Gabriella knew it, she was sitting in Angelina's family room, chatting about everything and anything. The last time they'd really talked was right after Alec and Kelly's wedding, but they'd spent most of the time rehashing the wedding and Alec's flub-up of his wedding vows. They'd never spoken about her and Ashton's conversation and his apology. She knew Angelina had seen her leave the reception hall with Ashton and knew when they'd returned. Angelina had also witnessed how they'd interacted the remainder of the party, but Angelina had never once asked Gabriella about their conversation.

"So what's new?" asked Angelina after they'd exhausted talking about the kids, Alejandro's schedule, and his recent business trips.

"Nothing much other than I've stayed well during this strep throat outbreak."

"We've been pretty lucky this time, too. I hope it continues. Anything else going on?" Angelina gave her a pointed look.

She knew what her friend was searching for. She decided to just spill the beans as Angelina was a pro at 'asking a generic question' and searching for an answer. She could go on for hours with this line of questioning until she got the answer she was looking for. "Angelina, will you quit asking me the same question. I'll tell you what you're looking for."

Angelina smiled. "You will?"

"When have I ever kept something from you? Yes, Ashton and I worked things out. He apologized for how he treated me after his mom died. Yes, we have gone out on a date, and yes, he just asked me out for Valentine's Day."

"Really? You're not pulling my leg are you? He asked you out already for Valentine's Day?" Angelina looked away. "Oh my, that's not good."

She raised her eyebrows at her friend. "What does that mean?"

Angelina opened her mouth and closed it again, clearly lost. "Ah... nothing. I'm so happy for you." Angelina said as she reached across the couch and hugged her friend. "So where are you going?"

Angelina was acting weird again, but she decided to ignore it. "I don't know. He had another call coming in and had to go. He said he'd call me later in the week."

"That's good. I'm happy for you. And, speaking of Valentine's Day, I just saw where St. Margaret's is hosting a trivia night the week after Valentine's. Are you interested? I'm buying a table of twelve. I've already asked Alec and Kelly, my mom and dad, John and Maria, and Sadie and Lawrence Eberle—you know, nurse Sadie from the clinic."

She rolled her eyes. "Angelina, I know who Sadie is. I've known her my entire life."

"That's right. And, of course, Alejandro and myself. So that leaves you and Ashton to fill out the table."

She bit her lip. "I'm not sure about that."

"Why not? He's like family, and it's not like he doesn't know anyone. He'll know everybody."

"Okay, okay. Count us in. If he can't make it, I'll find someone else."

Gabriella couldn't wait to get home after her dinner with Alejandro and Angelina. Something was going on with the two of them. She couldn't put her finger on it, but she was totally surprised by Alejandro's reaction to her seeing Ashton. She thought Alejandro would go ballistic knowing how she'd felt about him, but instead he was all smiles.

Ashton phoned her that weekend, apologizing for having to end their call so abruptly. "Sorry about not getting back to you sooner, but it's been busy to say the least."

"You don't need to explain. I totally understand."

They spoke for a few minutes and then she asked him about attending trivia night. "So, I had dinner with Alejandro and Angelina the other night. Angelina's buying a table for trivia night at St. Margaret's. Would you like to go with me?"

"Trivia night? What's that exactly?"

She went on to explain, "It's a fundraiser for the school. I can't exactly remember what the proceeds go towards since it's being run by the parish, but it's a lot of fun."

"What do we do exactly?"

"Each table competes against all of the other tables, and the table that answers the most questions correctly wins."

"Huh, is this like Trivial Pursuit?"

"Yeah, something like that."

"Sounds like it may be fun. Sure, count me in. Now, the real reason why I phoned."

She was sitting on the couch. She curled her legs underneath her as he spoke.

"So, about Valentine's Day… I've tried to make reservations at several restaurants, and they're all booked. We can go on a different day, or I could cook for you."

She really didn't care where they went to dinner, just that they spent time together. "It really doesn't matter to me. We could try another night, or if you're sure about it, I'd love for you to cook for me."

"I don't mind cooking in the least, I just wasn't sure if you wanted to experience the ambience of a restaurant."

"Your house is just fine. In fact, it'll be more private. Would you like me to bring something?"

"Just yourself."

"Hey, I have a better idea. Instead of just you cooking, why don't we do it together? It'll be fun, and then we can spend more time together."

"Sure, that works for me." He paused. "How about I come by and pick you up at noon. We can catch a quick bite to eat for lunch and then go shopping for whatever we're in the mood for. Then we can go home and cook." He paused again. "You know, I like that idea. We'll definitely be more relaxed, and we won't have to get all dressed up. I like this idea more and more."

They talked a while longer about their upcoming

week. She groaned when she described the scheduled Valentine's Day party for her class. "That is one thing I hate most about teaching—holiday parties. The kids get all out of sorts, and with it being on a Friday, I'm absolutely dreading the week. I'm just thankful that it's at the end of the day. Not only is it a Friday, but we also have a three-day weekend because of President's Day on Monday. I'm looking forward to that extra day."

"I didn't know you were off. I'm glad to hear Valentine Day's is not a school night for you. That way we can celebrate as long as we want."

Gabriella wasn't sure what he was implying, but she just went along with it. She was looking forward to having a relaxing time with him. She didn't have to get all dressed up, making an impression amongst all of the other restaurant-goers on the special day. She could almost let her hair down and just enjoy the moment.

Gabriella made it through her class's Valentine's Day party, but her good luck caught up with her and she became ill that evening. She'd only been home for a short time when she felt like she'd been hit by a brick wall. She was so tired that she decided to lie down and take a quick nap, but when she woke she had chills, a sore throat, and a fever. Right away she realized she needed to phone Ashton to cancel their Valentine's Day dinner. She'd been so looking forward to their day, but she knew with the way she currently felt, she'd never be able to go out. In fact, she'd be lucky to be well enough to return to school Tuesday morning. In the hopes that she'd feel better, she held off phoning Ashton and fell back to sleep.

She slept fitfully with her fever, awaking several times. She finally fell into a good sleep around six and didn't wake until mid-afternoon. When she woke, she could barely swallow with the soreness in her throat, but she took her temperature and was happy with the results. Her temperature was now normal, but she still felt horrible. She kicked back the covers and swung her legs over the side of her bed. She took her time standing, as she wasn't sure if her legs would support her. She was still exhausted but knew she needed to at least have something to drink, so she made her way to the kitchen.

She fixed herself a cup of hot cocoa and a piece of toast. As she neared the couch in her family room, she started sneezing. She remembered placing a small pack of tissues in her desk and went to retrieve it. She reached her hand into her desk drawer, and as she moved her hand about in the drawer, feeling for the tissues, she felt something soft. She pulled the drawer out further and realized that her hand had come into contact with Jana's journal.

She had completely forgotten about the journal after returning on New Year's Eve. She'd put Ashton out of her mind until he'd apologized at Alec's wedding. She grabbed her package of tissues, along with the journal, and curled up on the couch.

As she sipped her hot cocoa and ate her slice of toast, she paged through the journal. The entire journal was hand-written in what she assumed was Jana's scrawl. As she riffled through the pages, she concluded that the journal had been written over the span of several decades.

She still wasn't feeling well and decided to head back to bed. She laid the journal on her coffee table and headed off to her room. She'd phone Ashton tomorrow and inform him that she had to call off their date. She wanted to be well for Tuesday when school resumed, and she also didn't want to infect him with whatever illness she had.

The next morning she felt a little better, but still had a sore throat. Her temperature was still normal, but she was still lethargic. She got up at eight and fixed herself a cup of coffee. She pondered when the best time to phone him was. She decided to just do it then—no point in waiting.

The phone rang five times before he answered it. She could tell she'd woken him as his voice sounded gravelly.

"Did I wake you?" she barely got out with her sore throat.

"Gabby, is that you?"

"Yeah, it's me."

"What's wrong? You sound horrible."

"I'm sick, that's what's wrong. I'm calling for a rain check on our evening. I've been sick since I came home Friday, and I thought I might get better but I'm not. I need to be well for Tuesday, so I'm sorry but I just can't go tonight."

"Of course you can't go. I'm sorry that you're not feeling well. Can I bring you something?"

"No, I just want to be left alone. Don't take that the wrong way, but I just want to sleep. I really was looking forward to our day, though." She paused, "And evening."

"I was looking forward to it too, but there's always another time. And in fact, don't forget about trivia night Saturday. We'll see one another then."

"That's true, but I really wanted tonight to be something that we'd have, you know, to add to our special times."

"Yeah, me too, but we can always do this another time. You take it easy and get well."

"I'll do my best. Thanks for understanding."

"Gabriella?"

"Yes?"

"Happy Valentine's Day. I forgot to say it when I answered."

"Thank you, Ashton. Same to you, too."

"Go to sleep, Gabby. And feel better soon."

"I will," she whispered as she ended the call.

Ashton was sorry that she wasn't feeling well, but he wasn't surprised in the least that she was sick. The clinic had been inundated with sick children the last few days, and he'd been surprised that she'd been able to stay well this long. That was one of the hazards of being a teacher—they caught everything that circulated the schools.

Ashton decided he'd check in on her later in the day, hoping that she was feeling better. Ashton's plans didn't play out as he intended, though. He ended up having to go into the hospital to take care of one of his sick patients as Alec hadn't been feeling well himself and called asking if Ashton would cover for him. Since his plans for the day had changed, he agreed without thought.

❧

Tuesday morning, Gabriella woke up feeling almost back to normal. She still had a tiny sore throat, but she'd be able to make it through the day. She had lesson plans set aside for substitute teachers that she decided to use. That way, she wouldn't have to tax her throat. Most of the lessons were worksheets which the kids enjoyed doing in small groups. And since she didn't teach her intended lessons, the kids were happy to have no homework.

Just as she was ready to call it a day, there was a knock on her classroom door. Her students were getting ready to pack up for the day. The door opened and the first thing she saw was a huge bouquet of red roses, followed by Mary. "Look what came for you, Ms. Alvarez," she said excitedly as she walked over to her desk. The kids all stopped doing what they were doing. Oohs and ahs could be heard throughout the room.

"These are gorgeous. I didn't know you had a man in your life."

She smiled sheepishly up at Mary and accepted the flowers.

"Here's the card." Mary pointed to the cream-colored envelope.

She was speechless, and she barely uttered a 'thanks' before reaching for the card. She didn't have to reach down to smell the flowers as their scent permeated the room.

"These smell wonderful," Mary said as she smiled at Gabriella and turned to leave the room. "Oh, by the way, I hope you're feeling better, and I'm glad you made it through the day. Go home, put your feet up, and get some rest."

"I will." Gabriella watched Mary walk from the room. And with that, the bell rang.

Mary hadn't gotten far down the hallway, so she returned to Gabriella's room. "You stay here, I'll see them out. Go home and get well."

"Thanks, Mary. I will." Gabriella watched her class exit the room. She quickly packed up her things, grabbed her flowers, and left the building. Carefully, she set her flowers on the floor of her car. She couldn't wait to get home to read the card. He remembered her… and Valentine's Day.

Gabriella made it home and safely got her flowers inside. She changed her clothes, putting on her fluffy lounge pants and a sweatshirt. She returned to her kitchen and removed the vase from its protective packaging. The flowers smelled like heaven—roses were one of her favorite flowers.

She pulled the card out of its envelope. It was a typical card found in a florist, but this one was different. Instead of a typed message, this one was handwritten. She was sure it was Ashton's handwriting because it had the flair of a doctor's scrawl.

> *Gabby,*
> *I hope these make you feel a little better. We'll*
> *have our evening another day.*
> *Take care of yourself,*
> *Ashton*

She ran her finger over his writing and smiled. She couldn't believe he'd taken the time to go into a florist and purchase the flowers, but also took the time to write her a personal message. She set the card down, added some water to the flowers, and carried them into her family room. Since she planned to spend the evening vegetating on the couch, she'd be able to enjoy their beauty there.

She dozed off on the couch and was awakened when she heard her doorbell ring. When she realized what the noise was, she eased off the couch and made her way to the door. Darkness had fallen and thankfully her porch light had come on. She pushed the drapes aside to peer out the window and see who was standing at her door. She wasn't surprised to see Ashton standing at her door. She pulled open the door and smiled up at him. "Hi there," she whispered.

"Hey, how are you feeling?"

"Better, much better." Stepping aside, she invited him into the house. As he crossed the threshold, she noticed a grocery bag in his hand. "What's that?"

"Dinner. I didn't think you'd feel up to cooking, so I decided to pick something up for us and to also check on you. I was worried about you," he said as he made his way through the house. "I see you got my flowers."

"I did, thank you. They were quite a surprise," she breathed as he entered her kitchen. And then she noticed Jana's journal sitting on her coffee table. She quickly scooped it up and returned it to her desk for safe keeping. He had no idea that she'd taken it when they'd left his mother's home, and she wanted to take the time reading it in detail. She'd just finished stowing the journal in her desk when he returned to the room. She made her way to the couch, easing down.

Ashton joined her and looked her carefully in the eyes. He reached out, feeling her forehead. "Do you have a fever?"

"I don't think so. Actually, I'm feeling a lot better. I have a little sore throat left but that's it. I'm hoping that after a good night's sleep, I'll be back to at least 80%."

They sat on the couch, sharing their days. He told her about coming to Alec's aide the day before. He'd brought a roasted chicken, mashed potatoes, and coleslaw for dinner. Double-chocolate brownies were the pièce de résistance for dessert. By the time they'd finished eating, she was tired. She tried to hide her yawns, but Ashton caught on to them pretty quickly. He stood and reached for her hands. "I think it's time for me to go and you to head off to bed. What time do I need to pick you up Saturday?"

"Saturday?"

"For trivia night."

"Oh, I forgot all about that. I think it starts at six, right after five o'clock mass."

"How about we go to mass and go straight over to the gymnasium after mass is over? Four forty-five okay with you?"

"Yep. I'll be waiting." She walked him to the door. He opened the door, leaned in, and kissed her fore-head.

"Feel better," he said before turning around making his way to his car. She watched as he got into his car, backed out of her driveway, and headed down the road towards his home. She still couldn't believe that he'd shown up, brought her dinner, and sent her flowers. If she didn't know better, today was her Valentine's. She felt special and maybe even loved.

Chapter Twenty-Eight

SATURDAY ARRIVED, AS DID TRIVIA night. Angelina phoned her early that morning, reminding her that she needed to bring an appetizer. "I forgot all about that," Gabriella replied. "I also need to bring our beverage, too, right?"

"Yep, we provide all of our food and drink. And don't forget your checkbook as there is a silent auction as well."

"I will. I hope this fundraiser is successful. What did you say they wanted to buy?"

"They want to add this to the fund to purchase smart boards for the classrooms."

"Oh, that would be nice. I've wanted one of those for a long time. I even went to a seminar on the benefits of adding them to the classroom. We're so behind the times. I guess Mary's trying to show the accreditors that we are adding new technology to the classrooms, one room at a time."

"Something like that," Angelia added. "Now, what about you and Ashton?"

"Well I was sick on Valentine's, so we had to postpone our date. But he did send me roses on Tuesday and brought dinner by. He was checking on me to see how I was feeling."

"Well, that was kind of him."

"That it was. We're going to mass tonight, so I guess I'll see you later."

◠

Angelina stared at the phone she held in her hand after ending her call with Gabriella. She decided she wanted to end the bet, or at least not make a big thing out if it. She wanted to see her friend happy, and for once in a long time, Gabriella was happy. Angelina knew about Gabriella's last relationship and how it had ended. She'd been hurt and it still affected her. Angelina wanted her friend happy like she was, and she'd do anything in her power for that to happen.

◠

As promised, Ashton was prompt and right on time. Gabriella prepared two appetizers and had a six-pack of beer on ice, waiting for him to ring her doorbell. They got to the church right on time. Mass was over in a flash—she guessed the priest couldn't wait to make it to the evening's activities. She and Ashton returned to the car, grabbed her cooler, and they met Sadie and Lawrence as they entered the gymnasium.

"Fancy meeting you here," Sadie laughed as Ashton held the door for them. "Are you and Gabriella together?" she said, eyeing Gabriella.

"We are," she said as she reached for his hand, surprising not only herself but Ashton, too. They'd never discussed what their relationship was, but she felt she needed to take charge and put a label on it. As far as she was concerned, they were dating—in a relationship, and she hoped he believed the same, too. When he smiled at her and didn't contradict her claim, she knew she'd made the proper announcement. Sadie was shocked to say the least.

Gabriella had barely made it into the room when she ran into Janet Holmes and her sister Melanie. Janet was the third grade teacher at St. Margaret's. "What are you doing here, Janet?"

"Melanie and I are worker-bees. We're going to go from table to table after each round collecting the answers. Then we'll check them and post the number of correct answers for each table." Melanie was a banker and worked in acquisitions for one of the largest banks in town. Janet kept staring at Ashton. Gabriella knew she knew him from Career Day but probably wasn't aware that they were together.

"Janet, Melanie, I'd like to introduce you to Ashton Holder."

Ashton extended his hand to both women. "It's nice to meet you," He said as he shook each of their hands. He then smiled broadly at her and reclaimed her hand in his. They spoke for a few moments longer when both Janet and Melanie were called over the intercom.

"That's us," Janet said. "It was nice meeting you, Ashton. Oh, and I really enjoyed your presentation at Career Day."

"Thanks," he said as Janet and Melanie moved to the front of the room. "They seem nice."

"Janet is the sweetest. She and I are good friends. Her sister just moved back to town a few months ago after coordinating some huge project for her bank. She was gone for six months and Janet was so happy when she came home." Searching the crowd, she saw Alejandro waving at them. "Come on, there's Alejandro. I guess that's our table." They made their way across the room. They were stopped often by current and former parents as they slowly made their way to the table.

"Wow, you certainly know a lot of people."

"I've taught here ten years and that's a long time."

Alejandro approached her. "What took you so long?" He asked as he leaned in to kiss her cheek.

"Every step we took, Gabriella was greeted by another member of her fan club."

"That's not surprising. My sister's loved here. Now what do you have here?" Alejandro asked as he pointed towards her cooler.

"I made two appetizers and brought a six-pack."

"Beer? I thought you preferred wine."

"Well, I do. But I know Ashton enjoys it, so I just brought beer."

"If you want a glass of wine, I'm sure Angelina brought plenty. Her bag was overflowing with stuff. If I didn't know better, I'd think she was trying to feed the whole room."

"That's Angelina to a tee. She might not be the best of cooks but she likes to make sure there's enough food."

In a matter of minutes everyone had arrived at their table. Jackie and Ben had come with John and Maria, and Lawrence and Sadie were present and accounted for. "I wonder where Alec and Kelly are," Alejandro said. "I spoke with Alec about a half-hour ago and they were just getting ready to walk out the door."

While Gabriella and Ashton talked to Alejandro, Angelina had started decorating the table. She'd spread out a green table cloth and set out a St. Patrick's Day foil centerpiece that was wrapped in green-colored foil. Wire ran up from the base that was also wrapped in green, metallic foil with shamrocks extended upwards with a leprechaun sitting atop the wire. A green satin bow was wrapped around the base. In addition to the centerpiece, Angelina had two pots of gold that sat on either side of the centerpiece, each containing chocolate gold coins. She'd thrown down shamrock confetti all over the table, too.

In addition to the table decorations, Angelina also had green derby hats for the men and "Happy St. Patrick's Day" tiaras for the women. It was a festive table to say the least. Angelina kept fussing with the table.

"Honey, I think that's enough. They're going to start soon."

"Alejandro, we are going to win this."

"Win what?" he asked.

"There's a prize for best-decorated table."

"Hmm, is there?"

Angelina slapped at his arm. "I told you there was. Now, where's your brother?"

"My brother? What about your sister?" Before either could say any more, they heard Kelly's approach.

"Here we are. We finally made it," Kelly called as she made her way to Angelina, pulling her into a hug.

"Where have you been? What took you so long?"

Alec gave his wife a look.

"I'm not going to worry where you were, I'm just glad that you're here now."

"The table looks gorgeous," Kelly said as she added St. Patrick's Day-themed cups, plates, and napkins.

Alec scoffed as Kelly placed her items on the table. Pointing to the tableware, he said, "That's why we're late. Kelly made me stop at the party store to pick all of this stuff up. I just don't understand why we are decorating for St. Patrick's Day. It's weeks away."

"Honey, as I explained in the store, we're going to win the best-table decorations. This is a contest and we will win." She patted the side of his face and turned to Gabriella, changing the subject. "Gabby, how are you? I heard you were pretty ill last week. Alec was sick, too."

Gabriella wondered how she knew about that, then looked at Ashton. He must have told Alec and Joe about it. "Yeah, I was sick. It came out of nowhere. I felt like I'd been hit by a Mack truck." She turned to Alec. "Ashton told me you were sick when he filled in for you."

"I heard you were sick, too. Sorry, bro, for not checking in," said Alejandro.

Angelina passed out the hats and everyone pulled out their food. Angelina also brought several serving platters that everyone could set their food on. Since everyone knew one another, it made for a fun evening. The first round of questions centered on television shows. "We've got this one," Kelly happily said as she read the first question. "What TV cop badgered unwitting suspects with the line, 'Just one more thing…'?"

"I don't know. What about Cannon?" asked Lawrence. "I know it's from the seventies, but I can't remember the show."

"I think it's Perry Mason," said Maria.

"No, it's not Perry Mason. It's Columbo. I just watched a marathon the other day when I was sick. It's Columbo," said Gabriella.

"Okay, I say we go with Gabriella," said Ashton. "I have no idea."

Everyone agreed on Columbo. They made it through the first category on television and their answers were collected.

"I think we have them all correct," Angelina said as she poured herself another glass of wine. "Sadie, can you pass the veggies?"

"Sure thing," Sadie said as she grabbed a celery stick from the platter before passing it.

The next category featured history. Alec read their last question in the round, "What famous document begins:'When in the course of human events…'?"

"I've got this," said Lawrence. Lawrence was a history professor at one of the area high schools. "It's the Declaration of Independence." Everyone agreed with him.

Melanie came around and retrieved their latest answers. "Gabby, I think your team is tied for first place. This next round will be the last."

Gabriella was excited. She leaned over and kissed Ashton's cheek, not thinking twice about where they were or who they were surrounded by. Her mother, who was sitting directly across from Gabriella, noticed her display of affection and kicked John underneath the table.

"Hey, what was that for?" he said, looking at his wife.

Maria leaned over, whispering in his ear, "Your daughter just kissed Ashton."

"Huh, she did? How did I miss that?"

"I guess because your face was practically planted in that slice of cheesecake."

"Well, it is really good. Honey, you always make the best." He said leaning over, and following his daughter's example, kissed Maria's cheek.

"If we don't ace these last set of questions, we have a

real problem," Alec said as he reread the questions.

"And what are they?" asked Ben.

"Our last category is the human body."

They made it through the first nine questions without discussion, but the last question about did them all in. Angelina read the question, "What is the most insect-bitten part of the human body?"

"Piece of cake," called out Alejandro. "I think it's the hand."

"No, it's the forearm," said John.

"Dad, you're wrong. It's the foot," claimed Alec.

"The foot? That can't be," said Kelly.

"I have to agree with Alec," Ashton said.

"Well, you would," said Kelly. "He is your boss after all."

"Okay, let's take a vote on this. Is it the hand, arm, or foot? Who votes for hand?"

Kelly counted two votes.

"What about the arm?"

No one raised their hands.

"What happened to your vote, Dad? Weren't you the one that said forearm?"

"I did, but then I thought about it and have to agree with Alec over there. I remember it's the foot."

"Okay, how many votes for foot?"

Ten hands were raised.

"Okay then, it's the foot."

As they waited for their answers to be tabulated, Gabriella and Ashton perused the silent auction. There were quite a few items that held her interest, among them a spa package and a basket filled with her favorite hand lotions, bath salts, and candles. "I have to bid on this," she said to Ashton as he'd shown no interest and had moved on. She also bid on quite a few restaurant packages.

She caught up to Ashton, who was pondering over several Rivermen offerings. "You know who would love it if I won this?" Ashton asked as he made his bid.

"I do." Gabriella added, "If you win, let it be a surprise."

She heard her name called and stepped away to speak with one of her students' parents while Ashton continued to review the various packages. He bid on three Rivermen baskets and thought he had a good chance to win all three. When he was done looking at the auction, he caught back up with Gabriella, who was talking to Mary. "Mary, hi," he said as he wrapped his arm around Gabriella's waist. Mary said her hello but before he could get involved in the conversation, the moderators were giving them five minutes until the winners were announced.

"I'll see you Monday," Mary said as she turned to return to her table. "It was nice seeing you, Ashton."

He nodded his head before leading Gabriella back to their table.

Angelina sat anxiously awaiting the announcement of the winner. "If we don't win for best-decorated table, I'll—"

"You'll what, honey?" Alejandro said, teasing her.

"I'll claim that it's fixed. Look," she said pointing to all of the tables around them. "Those two aren't even decorated. And see that one over there? They just have a candle as a centerpiece. And that one—"

"I see your point," Alejandro chuckled as he glanced around the room. "Time will tell," he added as they started to make the announcements.

"First, we're going to announce the top three tables," one of the moderators proclaimed.

They all listened closely for their table. The third place table belonged to one of Angelina's former students' family. Second place went to Mary's table.

"And the number one table that missed only one question all evening goes to…"

"My hands are sweating," Angelina said to her husband. "I haven't been this nervous since I married you."

Alejandro laughed and noticed that everyone was looking at their table.

"The number one table belongs to the Alvarezes!"

Their table was all smiles and they were congratulated from everyone around them.

"Next, we have the table for best-decorated, and that goes to the St. Patrick's Day table, also decorated by the Alvarezes."

Angelina jumped up from her seat, shouting for joy and pumping her fists in the air. "We did it! We won!" She shouted. Angelina ran around the table and grabbed Kelly in a hug. "I told you we'd win."

Alejandro just looked up at his wife, laughing while Alec shook his head.

"I guess it was our napkins," Alec quipped as Kelly approached her husband.

"Yes, it was," she said as she hugged him.

"Now for the silent auctions… Since we have so many, we're just going to post the winners at the auction table. If you placed a bid, check it out to see if you're a winner. Thank you all for coming!"

Ashton went up to the auction table while Gabriella helped clean up their table. He knew he'd win the Rivermen packages because he'd drastically overbid for each package. Since she wasn't aware of all of his bids, he decided to keep them to himself. He'd surprise everyone when the time came, especially Matthew and Gabriella. As he paid for his wins, he also paid for Gabriella's. She won her spa package, along with the one that held her favorite body lotions.

He was able to hide his winnings in his pocket since his were contained in envelopes, but when he approached Gabriella with hers, she was surprised. "I won both of those?"

"You did."

"I need to get my checkbook."

"Don't worry about it—I paid."

"You did?"

He nodded.

"I can't believe you did that for me. Thank you." She said as she looped her arms around his neck and hugged him closely.

He felt like all eyes were on them. "Ah, Gabby. Not here, okay? This is a public place." Even though she'd kissed him earlier and they'd shared a closeness, he was still getting used to their relationship and public acts of affection, especially in this setting, were going to take some getting used to.

"Oh, yeah," she said as she pulled away.

Instead of taking her straight home, Ashton suggested they get a bite to eat. "Don't take this the wrong way… I'm not complaining, but I'm starved. Those appetizers or whatever you called them just didn't do it for me."

She laughed, "Would you like to grab a 'real' meal?" She couldn't deny his request. In fact, she was still a little hungry herself. She didn't want their evening to end. She was having a fabulous time and wanted it to keep going, so she agreed. "That's a great idea. I'm a little hungry myself."

"So where should we go? What's still open? I'm really not in the mood for Ox's. It's too noisy there. How about Pedals? I'm sure Gus would love to see us." The last time he'd been in Pedals, Gus had assumed they were a couple and Ashton had put the kibosh on that, but tonight was a different story. He could without a doubt shout from the mountaintops that they were indeed a couple. They'd been on a few dates and in his eyes they were truly beginning to act like a couple, especially after her earlier announcement to Sadie.

She agreed and they headed off to Pedals where they were greeted by Gus. As he showed them to their table, he shook his head and looked back and forth between them. "Am I seeing what I think I'm seeing?" Gus asked.

He chuckled, recalling their last conversation. "Yes, you are," he replied as he handed Gabriella her menu. She had no clue what was going on. There was some untold story she hadn't been included in.

"So, did you both go to trivia night?"

"We did, and we took home the prize," she said, beaming. "And we also won best-decorated table. I thought Angelina was going to go through the roof when she heard we were the winners. I hate to think what would have happened if we'd lost." Turning towards Gus, she added, "She couldn't have cared less that we won the game. Can you believe that?"

"Knowing your sister-in-law like I do, I'd say yes. Well, I'll let you settle in and decide what you want. I'll check back in a few minutes. Glass of white wine and a beer for you, doctor?"

"How well you know us," he replied as Gus walked away, humming loudly.

"I think he's happy about something," Gabriella added. "What's up with him?"

"I haven't a clue." He fully knew what Gus had meant by his comment, he just didn't want Gabriella to know.

As they sat waiting for their meal, Ashton reached across the table and grabbed Gabriella's hand. He felt comfortable at Pedals as they weren't standing in the midst of a gymnasium holding hands. She rested her head on her other hand and smiled at his gesture. "I had fun tonight. What about you?"

"I did. I got to see another side to Angelina."

"Yeah, well when she gets excited over something, everyone is bound to know about it. In fact, I'm sure everyone in the gymnasium knew that her table was the one to win best-decorated. That's what I love about her."

They talked about everything and anything while they ate their meal. She discussed how her class had come back from the holidays more mature and were actually listening to her. He spoke about how busy they'd been with sickness because of all the viruses that had been going around.

It was almost midnight when Gus practically threw them out of the restaurant. In fact, Gabriella was getting tired herself. They strolled to his car arm-in-arm. Gus watched as they left the diner. He was happy to see Gabriella moving on and finally happy with life in general. He'd been around when she'd broken up with her boyfriend all those years ago and she hadn't been in a very good place. He hoped Ashton didn't hurt her. She was a kind and loving person, and he hoped that she'd end up with her happily ever after.

∽

Ashton knew Gabby was tired and still recovering from being ill the week before. As he walked her to her door, he realized that he'd had a really good time. He felt like he was truly a part of her life and her family's. He'd felt it before, but was feeling it even more so tonight. "Thanks for inviting me. I had a blast tonight. Who would have thought I had never participated in a trivia night before tonight. Let's do it again. And be sure to invite Angelina. Maybe we can be the decorators next time."

"I don't know about that. I think she wins that contest hands down." She reached her door and inserted her key. "Would you like to come in?"

"I'd love to, but it's late and I know you're tired." He raised his hand, brushing her hair behind her ear. Cupping her jaw, he leaned in and kissed her. She wrapped her arms around his neck pulling him in as closely as she could. She was just getting into the kiss when Ashton pulled away. She drew her brows together.

"We'll pick this up another time, okay? I don't want to let you go, but I have to. I won't be able to stop, and I'll want to stay all night," he whispered, stroking her face. He smiled down at her, gave her another quick peck on the cheek, and moved away. "I'll call you tomorrow," he added as he stepped away. "I really enjoyed our date."

"I did, too," she called out to him as he started down the sidewalk.

He turned back to her with a huge smile on his face. "Have a good night."

"I will," she said as she entered her house. She watched him pull away from the curb and turn in the direction of his home. She felt really good about their evening. She smiled at herself as she closed the door.

She headed towards her kitchen for a glass of water and was drawn to her desk. She opened the drawer and pulled out Jana's journal. She swiped her hand across the cover, thinking that there were answers inside that she needed to find and share with Ashton. Answers that would help him move on with his life.

She moved to the couch and began to read the journal. She couldn't believe she was reading Ashton's mother's thoughts. She'd written in such detail...

The first few entries in Jana's journal were short, almost cryptic. She sensed the emotions that filled Jana as she read her words. In one entry, Jana wrote about the anger she had towards Ashton. In so many words, she blamed Ashton's birth on the demise of her marriage.

> *It's almost summer—one of my favorite times of the year in the Ozarks. As I sit here, I remember a time when Ian and I enjoyed boating on Table Rock Lake. But now, those days are over. Ashton is always sick. Sick with ear infections, sick with the flu. And that damn asthma of his flares up at the most inopportune time. Just last night at dinner, our first family meal with his father in weeks, he had an attack. Every time I turn around, it's something with that child. I'm tired of the crying and the whining. I've got to do something. I've lost Ian since Ashton was born. I want my marriage back. I'll figure something out.*

Gabriella was shocked. She couldn't believe his mother's anger towards Ashton. He was a little boy, he counted on her to take care of him. But instead he relied on his nanny. Gabriella got more upset as she read Jana's thoughts. Tears began to form in her eyes. She decided she'd read enough for the day.

Gabriella had barely gotten through the first few pages when she drifted off to sleep. She would find the answers she was looking for, and if she needed help to find those answers, she'd get it. Ashton needed to understand why his mother did the things that she did. He needed to forgive her and move forward, and Gabriella promised herself that she'd find the answers that allowed him to do that.

Chapter Twenty-Nine

GABRIELLA HAD FALLEN ASLEEP ON the couch and woke with a crick in her neck. As she stood, Jana's journal slipped off her lap and fell to the floor. She picked it up and placed it on the coffee table. She decided to put all of her errands on hold for the day. She grabbed a quick shower, dried her hair, and pulled it up into her classic weekend ponytail. She hurried to her kitchen and fixed herself a cup of coffee, then she grabbed a notebook—she wanted to take notes as she read Jana's journal. She wasn't going anywhere until she read the entire thing. She returned to her couch, curled her legs up under her, and picked up where she left off the evening before.

She was consumed by what she read and couldn't put it down. She wondered if anyone knew what had happened to Jana over the years, other than Jana and now herself. What Gabriella discovered helped her understand why she was so aloof to her son. Jana had been hurt, too, but she didn't need to treat her son the way she did.

She was so engrossed in reading and taking notes

that she wasn't aware of her phone ringing. When she heard a voice, she recognized that someone was leaving her a message on her answering machine. She jumped off the couch and hurried to the phone before Maria could finish her message. "Mom, Mom, I'm here…"

"Oh honey, I thought you might be out running errands."

"No, I'm here. I just couldn't get to the phone fast enough. What's up? Did you have fun last night?"

"I did and it looked like you were having fun, too," her mother said, referring to her daughter's kiss. "So what are you up to? Would you like to come over for dinner? It's been a few weeks since you had dinner with your family."

"Who all's coming?"

"You really need to know that? Does it matter?"

"Just wondering."

"Who else would be coming? Family, of course. Everyone will be here—even Joe. He said he was on call so I hope he can actually join us."

"Can I come over and help? Do you want me to bring anything?"

"No, honey. I've got it handled, but feel free to come early. Maybe we can chat before everyone gets here."

"I've got a few things to do here, and then I'll be over."

"Take your time, honey. I'll be here." Maria hung up the phone.

She returned the journal to her desk, along with the notes she'd taken. She discovered that his father, Ian, had not only one affair, but he'd had numerous extra-marital affairs during their marriage. She also learned that Jana was extremely unstable right before they'd sent Ashton off to boarding school, and that was about when he'd had the asthma attack that almost took his life. She knew there were more answers to the questions she had in this journal. If she didn't get home too late from her parents, she'd return to her project, finding answers.

By the time Gabriella had tied up a few things around the house, it was almost three o'clock in the afternoon. On her way over to her parents, she stopped by Laketown Bakery where she picked up a coffee cake, danish, and some rolls. If her mother couldn't use the rolls for dinner, her parents could eat them throughout the week.

Maria had been watching for her daughter. She couldn't wait to sit down with her and discover how close she and Ashton truly were. Maria opened the door while Gabriella grabbed the shopping bags from her trunk. She knew what her daughter had as she always brought her something from the bakery and today was no different. Gabriella loved her sweets, and she always enjoyed sharing a coffee and danish with her mother while they talked. Maria always had dinner around seven so this was a perfect treat until dinner was served.

As Gabriella came through the door, she brushed a kiss on her mother's cheek. She raised the bag, showing her mother where the purchases came from and headed towards the kitchen. "I've got a coffee cake for you and Dad for breakfast tomorrow, some danishes for us to share while we talk, and dinner rolls in case you forgot."

"Oh honey, that's perfect. We can serve the rolls tonight. I know Matthew loves those with the cheese sprinkled across the top. I'll save what I have for your father and I." Maria watched her as she grabbed plates for their danishes.

"Mom, sit down, I'll get the coffee."

Maria opened the box that contained the cheese and fruit danishes and grabbed a cheese danish for herself, adding a cherry one to Gabriella's plate. Setting it on the plate in front of her, she looked up and smiled at her daughter. "Gabriella, you seem like you're in a good mood. What's happened to make you so happy? The last time we spoke, your class was driving you crazy. Or is it a *someone* that's putting that smile on your face?"

She turned her back to her mother while she added half-n-half to her coffee. She grabbed their coffees and carried them to the table. She was hiding her face from her mother.

"Gabriella?"

She looked up at her mother. "What?"

"I asked you a question. Is there someone special in your life?"

"Like you don't already know."

"Honey, I saw how you were with Ashton last night. You were getting along—in fact, more than just getting along. What happened? I thought you'd given up on him after you returned at the New Year. Whatever's happened has put a smile on your face that I haven't seen in a long, long time."

She listened to her mother as she picked at her cherry danish. They sat there for a few moments in silence. Gabriella wasn't sure what she should tell her mother. What she knew was that Ashton was never far from her mind, and in her moment of silence, she decided, what the hell? She'd already shared a little with Angelina. Her mother deserved to know the truth, too.

"Gabriella?"

"Okay, Mom you're right. We are getting along right now."

"When did all of this change?"

"At Alec's wedding. He and I had a long talk, and he apologized for his behavior. We've been out a couple of times, but that's about it."

"You sure looked pretty chummy last night."

Gabriella glared at her mom. She knew what she was referring to. She played with the handle of her coffee mug while she pondered her response. "Yes, we had fun last night. It was the first time he's been to a trivia night, and he had a blast. He definitely got a kick out of Angelina and her exuberance over winning the table decorating contest." She paused. "Mom, I've learned that Ashton had a lonely childhood... extremely lonely. And now I think I understand why he acted the way he did when he joined the practice. I know Dad's made a huge difference in his life, as have Alec and Joe. I've seen huge changes in him, and I really like the man he is today."

Her mother smiled at her.

"He's a part of a family now, at least at the clinic. That's something he really never had growing up. The sense of family and being included has changed him. I've seen the changes, and he's admitted that he's changed himself. Where this goes, I haven't a clue. But I promised myself that we have to take this slowly, whatever it is. And I will not get hurt like I did the last time. That about killed me, and I won't go there again."

"Gabriella, there's no hurry. Just take it one day at a time."

"That's what I plan on doing. Now, let's change subjects. What's for dinner?"

She and her mom chatted about what was on the menu for dinner, as well as school and any other topic that came up. Before they knew it, Alejandro had arrived with family in tow, and with it their conversation came to an end. Maria now had to focus on her adorable grandchildren.

While Maria played with Angel, Alejandro and Matthew played a game of ping-pong in the basement, Angelina and Gabriella worked in the kitchen. Maria had prepared a spaghetti casserole that needed to be warmed in the oven. They washed the lettuce for salad and put the casserole in the oven. After they completed putting the salad ingredients together, they sat down at the kitchen table, waiting for the rest of the family to arrive. Angelina knew Kelly and Alec would be there shortly, but they had no idea when Joe would come storming through the door.

"Thanks for arranging the table for trivia night. Ashton had a great time. He got a kick out of your celebration."

"What are you talking about?"

"Do I have to remind you? Winning the table decorations."

"Oh that, yeah that was fun. So, what did you do afterwards? You sure ran out of there."

"We went to Pedals and got something to eat. He was starved." She played with the napkins on the table, aligning them into a neat stack. "You know, Gus said something really strange last night."

"You know Gus. He's always saying something—he just can't keep his mouth closed."

"Well, this was different. It was almost like an inside

joke with him and Ashton, but it wasn't a joke."

"What did he say?"

"He was showing us to our table and said, 'Am I see-ing what I think I'm seeing?' and then Ashton replied, 'Yes, you are.' What do you think that means?"

"Who knows with Gus? Maybe someday you can ask him yourself."

"Yeah, maybe I will." As she finished speaking, the door flew open and Alec and Kelly walked in, along with Joe.

"You made it."

"What are you talking about?" Alec said as he walked into the room.

"Not you—Joe. Mom wasn't sure if you'd make it."

"Well, I'm here for the moment," Joe replied.

Everyone enjoyed their dinner. They hadn't gotten together as just a family since Thanksgiving.

John chimed in at dessert, "I think we need to sched-ule our next dinner before everyone leaves the table. Alejandro, what does your schedule look like?"

Alejandro threw out the dates he was available.

"Okay then, that's settled. Three weeks from today."

"What about me?" asked Alec.

"I'm sure you can find some time. Joe certainly did," John said, looking at Alec. "We'll make it work, I'm sure."

By the time the dishes were done, Angel had fallen asleep in her grandmother's arms. "I think it's time I take my family home," Alejandro said as he reached for his daughter. "Thanks for dinner, Mom. It was won-derful, as always."

Maria and John stood and watched Alejandro and Angelina secure their children in the car. "I think Alejandro's finally back to his old self," John said.

"Angelina has been a God-send for him."

"She has, and so have the children. I haven't seen him this relaxed in I can't say when. I just hope it continues." Maria added. Everyone in the family was aware that the anniversary of Alejandro's first wife and son's death was upon them. They prayed this year would be different and he'd get through it without the sadness that always seemed to overcome him.

Gabriella grabbed her coat right after Alejandro and Angelina left. She wanted to get home and back to her project. She'd made it maybe a third of the way through the journal, and she hoped that between tonight and tomorrow she'd be able to finish reading it and start on her next steps. She wasn't completely sure what they were, but she'd figure it out along the way.

Gabriella said her goodbyes to her parents and brothers and headed on home. She was within a mile of her house when her cell rang. She let the call go to voicemail as she hated answering her phone when she drove and even more so at night. As she neared her house, she saw a car backing out of her driveway. She pulled into the driveway when the driver recognized her and backed up the street. She figured out who had been on the phone—Ashton.

Ashton pulled in right behind her and jumped out of his car. He was at her side, opening her door before she had a chance. "I just called you."

"I know. My cell rang but I don't like answering when I'm driving, especially at night."

"I understand," he said as he reached for her hand, helping her from the car. "I hope you don't mind that I stopped by. I just spent the day with Javier and kind of needed some adult conversation."

She laughed. "I fully understand. Sure, come on in."

He followed her through the kitchen door. "Would you like something to drink? A glass of wine, a beer?"

"You know what sounds really good? That is, if you have the ingredients."

"What's that?"

"Hot cocoa."

"That does sound good," she said as she pulled off her coat and grabbed the milk from the refrigerator. "Whipped cream, too?"

"If you have it."

"I always have it during the winter because what's hot cocoa without whipped cream on top?" She laughed as she poured the milk into a pot and set it on the stove. "So what else brings you here besides adult conversation?"

He walked over to her as she stood by the stove, stirring the milk as it warmed. He reached for her hand. "I hate to admit it, but I missed you."

"I just saw you last night," she smiled.

"I know. It's like I told you the other day, I haven't felt like this with anyone, ever." He dropped her hand and spun around, returning to his seat at the table. "One part of my brain keeps telling me to move slowly, but the other... For some reason, I want to be with you—always. I miss hearing your voice and seeing your smile. You're always on my mind."

She listened as she stirred the milk. She understood what he was feeling because she was thinking and feeling the same thing. But, as she'd just told her mother, she needed to go slowly. She wasn't going to let herself get hurt. As she added the cocoa to the warmed milk, she decided she needed to be up front with Ashton and tell him about her past—why she wasn't going to let him hurt her.

She poured the hot cocoa into the mugs and carried them to the table. "I'll let you put your own whipped cream on. I have to admit I enjoy it, so I'll let you go first since I'm not sure how much is left in the can."

He grabbed the can and pushed the spout. The whipped cream spurted out, shooting over the edge of the cup. "Woah, that sure came out of there." He flicked his finger along the table where the cream had fallen. "This is good stuff," he added as he licked his finger.

She grabbed the can, shaking it vigorously. "I want to make sure it's nice and fluffy." Then she shot out her own whipped cream. It dropped into her cup, splashing the hot liquid over the side. She laughed at herself. "Well I guess I shook it too hard." She grabbed a towel and wiped down the table. When she returned the towel to the sink, she opened a cabinet and pulled out a package of cookies. "A must have," she claimed as she opened the package of shortbread cookies. "I just love to dunk these into my hot cocoa."

"You dunk cookies in your hot cocoa?"

"You mean you've never dunked a cookie into your hot cocoa before? Oh my gosh, you don't know what you're missing."

"Apparently, I don't," he mumbled as he watched her take her cookie and submerge a corner into her drink. She held it there as it absorbed the hot cocoa and lifted it towards her mouth. Of course, she'd left it in her drink too long as the cookie started to crumble as she lifted it towards her mouth. She quickly recognized what was going to happen and placed her hand underneath her cookie as she raised it to her mouth. She closed her eyes and savored the taste. "So good."

He shook his head as he watched her.

"Give it a try," she egged him on.

He dipped his cookie into his hot cocoa and pulled it out. It had barely had the chance to absorb the luscious chocolate.

"No, no, no. You've got to let it go longer." She grabbed his hand and motioned for him to re-dunk it in his cup. When she let go of his hand, he raised the cookie. She could see that it had taken on the milk as it looked like it was going to fall apart. He raised it towards his mouth and ducked his head just in time to catch the cookie as it dropped into his mouth. "That was close," he said as he chewed his cookie. "You're right, this is really good."

"Well, I guess you're glad you came over. I taught you something new—how to dunk a cookie in hot cocoa." She chuckled as she grabbed another cookie.

They sat drinking their hot cocoa and eating cookies for another few minutes when she got serious. She set her cup down on the table and drew in her lips. She wasn't sure where to start. She closed her eyes for a second.

"Gabby, what's wrong?"

She opened her eyes and decided this was the moment to tell him about her boyfriend—the one that had broken her heart. "I need to tell you something. And please listen to what I have to say before you comment, okay?"

"Sure. I hope it's nothing serious and you're not ill."

"No, I'm not ill. But I've kept something from you that I need to share. Come on, let's go into the other room where we can be more comfortable." She grabbed their cups and rinsed them out, placing them in the dishwasher. She reached for his hand and led him to the family room. She reached to turn on the lights and instantly thought of his mother's journal. She breathed a sigh of relief, remembering that she'd stored it safely in her desk before leaving for her parents.

They sat down on the couch with Gabriella grabbing her favorite spot, the corner. She sat at an angle so she could watch Ashton as she told him her story. He sat near her, his leg brushing her foot.

"So, I've been thinking about this a lot lately. And after last night I decided I needed to tell you."

"Tell me what?"

She held up her hand, stopping him. "Just let me get out what I have to say and then you can talk."

"Fine, but may I hold your hand?"

She reached her hand out and he grabbed it, squeezing it tightly, comforting her. "I heard what you said earlier that you haven't felt like this with anyone, ever, and that you want to be with me. I miss you when you're not around, too. I have to admit that you're always on my mind. But then there are days when I tell myself that I can't feel this way. I can't allow myself to throw all the cards down on you.

"Ashton, this has taken me by complete surprise, just as it has you, but I need to be upfront and explain why I feel like I—" She stopped and looked down at their clasped hands. Sighing, she began, "His name was Jeremy Gold. We met my junior year of college, and we were just friends at first. He was an electrical engineering major and we met in a nutrition class. We were paired up on a project. I guess being together all of the time while taking that class put us in the same circle so much that we just began to date. It wasn't serious at first, but after graduation we were inseparable. And maybe that's why I feel the way I do—about us. This has just happened way too fast, these feel-ings…" Gabriella paused. She was now taking shorter breaths and becoming upset. He watched her as she tried to control herself. She squeezed his hand harder with each breath she took. "Jeremy got a job right out of school, as did I. I really thought he was the one. We both expressed our love for one another… and then his company started laying people off. Even though he was the lowest man on the totem pole in senior-ity, he had certain skills that they needed. So, when they finally elected to close his offices, he was offered a job in Seattle…" She froze, remembering too much of their time together.

"He took me out to dinner. I thought he was going to propose. He'd made it through two rounds of lay-offs with his job still intact. I thought everything was going well… and that's when he told me he was being transferred to Seattle. When I heard him speak the words, I was sure he was going to ask me to follow him. But no, what did he do? He basically said it's been fun while it lasted but he was moving on… on to greener pastures."

He reached to pull her into her arms but she pulled away.

"I can't… I need to finish my story."

"Sweetheart, you don't have to. I get the picture."

"No, I must." With a shaking voice, she finished her story, "So he was moving on. Well, I was beside myself and broke down in tears. I told him I would finish out the school year and follow him to Seattle, but he just sat there shaking his head. I can still see his eyes… The way he looked at me, I knew his answer before he told me. Jeremy went on to say that he didn't want me in his life anymore. That he was moving to Seattle, not by himself but with his *girlfriend*. His 'girlfriend' that he'd been having an affair with almost since he'd joined the firm. And to top off his story, this girlfriend ended up being his boss. He'd been sleeping with her to keep his job—that's how he'd bypassed the layoffs. He didn't have a skill that was needed except for his skill in the bedroom."

A tear escaped from her closed eyes. "I remember jumping up from the table and running out of the restaurant. I was humiliated. Here I thought he was going to propose, and what did he do instead? He owned up to an affair. And he didn't think twice about it. He still had a well-paying job that he was proud of. He wasn't ashamed of his behavior at all." The tears started cascading down her face. "I remember walking in a complete daze down the street, unsure of where I was going and then I remembered I had my phone. I called Joe and he rescued me from the street corner."

She wiped the tears from her face. "What I remember most about my brother that evening was he didn't ask me any questions other than making sure I wasn't harmed. All he knew was that Jeremy and I had broken up over dinner. He didn't ask what happened or whose fault it was. I remember him taking me home. I didn't have my house yet and my parents were out of town. Joe held me that night. He let me cry uncontrollably in his arms and didn't pass judgment on me. My brother is a wonderful man, and I will never forget what he did that night. I'm sure he has his own opinions, but to this day no one knows what happened between me and Jeremy except you."

Ashton finally pulled her into his arms. He held her and let her cry out all of the pain she'd been carrying for the last several years. "Gabby, I'd never do that to you, I promise."

"How can I be sure? I didn't think Jeremy would do it either. I loved him with all of my heart and he broke it—just like that." She snapped her fingers. "How could he do that to me? I'll never understand why he kept telling me he loved me while he was carrying on with his boss. I won't feel that way again. I won't."

"Gabby, please listen to me. I'd never hurt you like that—never. It's just not in my makeup. I'm not wired like that. I would never have an affair, even if I were married. I just wouldn't."

"That's what you say today, but what about tomorrow? What about when a beautiful blonde-haired, blue-eyed, big-boobed beauty crosses your path? What then? What I know is I can't go through that again. Jeremy about killed me. I was so lost. That's when I decided to start hiking. I could go out to the bluffs, get lost in my thoughts, and if I wanted to sit down and have a good cry, I could. It was just me and nature." She pulled out of his arms, brushing the tears from her face. "Ashton, I don't have it in me anymore to be hurt like that. I just don't. That's why I've protected my heart for so long. That's why I don't date. That's why I treated you like I did. I just can't…"

Ashton pulled her back into his arms, brushing her brow with a kiss. "Gabby, I'm sorry about what happened to you in the past, but that's what it is—the past. You have to put it behind you and move on. You need to learn to trust again, or you'll never have the family and children that I know you want." She looked up at him, startled. "I see how you are with Angel and Matthew. I see how you are with your students, Gabby. I know that you want those things. You just have to let go and learn to live your life again. No, everything may not go your way. You may get hurt again, but you have to live. And by living you may find what you are looking for in life. It may be me or it may be someone else, but you can't close off your heart because of what Jeremy did. You need to forgive and forget."

"I can't."

"At least try. Please give us a try. I'm not going to sit here begging. I hope that you can see that I am telling you the truth. I want you in my life. I can't promise that I won't hurt you, but I will do my best not to. I'll do my best to make you happy, by putting the smile on your face that I've come to love."

She wrapped her arms around him, crying in earnest now. She heard what Ashton said. He wanted her in his life. He wanted to make her happy. She wanted to believe him—she truly did. He held her until her tears lessened. He placed his finger under her chin raising it slightly. "I want to give us a try. Please? I mean what I say. I hope that you believe me." He gently removed his arms from around her. "Now, I think I'm going to leave you alone and let you think about everything I've had to say. Remember, I'm only a phone call away."

She nodded and watched as he stood.

"Thanks for the hot cocoa and for teaching me how to dunk my cookie. I'll never forget it."

And with that, he spun around and headed towards the kitchen where he'd left his coat. Then she heard the door open and close. She had a lot to think about. Maybe he was right. She should move on, forget about everything that Jeremy did to her. She needed to leave it in her past. She'd come so far and she had a future, a bright one, with Ashton in her life.

She stood and looked out the window just as he

backed out of her driveway.   She placed her hand against the window as he drove away. *He's my future and Jeremy's my past. I'll never know if he's the one if I don't give him a try. Believe in him and believe in us. That's what I'm going to do. Move on with Ashton in my life—and if he breaks my heart, I'll pick up the pieces and start over again. Just like I did all of those years ago. It may take me awhile to forget, but I'll do it because I have to live my life and be happy, not hold a grudge for a lifetime.*

Chapter Thirty

GABRIELLA WAS EXHAUSTED AFTER ASHTON left the night before and she went right to bed. She slept fitfully, waking up more times than she could count. After tossing and turning for the hundredth time, she decided to get up and start her day. It was five in the morning, and she was wasting time trying to get back to sleep. She figured she could take a nap later on in the day if she needed it.

She decided to forgo a shower—she'd take one later on. She slowly made her way down the hallway towards the kitchen. She turned on the light and noticed the package of cookies from the previous night still sitting on the table. She grabbed them and returned them to the cabinet, thinking about everything Ashton had to say the night before. He was right. She should take a chance on him. Nothing was perfect in life. Happily married couples often divorced after years of marriage. Sure, they once had been happy too, but something in their lives had changed and sent them down the road filled with unhappiness. She needed to step out of her protective box and live a life of reality. Some things went your way but often times they didn't. She decided that she wanted to be happy. And the only way she'd be happy right now, right here today, was being with Ashton.

She brewed her coffee and headed back to the couch, grabbing Jana's journal on the way. She opened to the page where she discovered that Ian, Ashton's father, was having an affair with a woman named Eloise. In Jana's own scrawl, Gabriella felt her pain and sadness. She spoke of discovering Ian and Eloise in his office at the resort. Ian had been expecting her as they were having dinner with another resort owner to discuss the upcoming holidays. Jana hadn't knocked on Ian's office door, she'd just entered. And that's when she found Ian lying atop Eloise on the couch, her blouse on the floor and his hair sticking up all over the place. Jana had been speechless. She'd run from the room and out of the resort. Ian hadn't followed her. Jana returned home and discovered Ashton in the throes of an asthma attack. Instead of seeing to her son, she'd run to her bedroom crying hysterically, letting the nanny deal with Ashton's attack.

Jana had known she'd made a mistake in not taking care of her son, but she'd been so upset over finding her husband in another woman's arms that she'd barely been able to take care of herself, let alone her son. Gabriella felt her pain and regret as she read on. And after she was assured that her son was well enough after the asthma attack, she had begun the search for a boarding school. She needed to get him out of the house—out of the reach of his father.

Within two weeks of that awful night, she'd sent her son away. She didn't think she could take care of him—at least not the way a mother should. She'd regretted every minute that Ashton wasn't home, but she also blamed her husband's indiscretions on him. If she hadn't had Ashton, maybe her husband wouldn't have turned away from her. Maybe he wouldn't have had the affairs.

Gabriella kept reading. She discovered that the affair with Eloise lasted many years. In fact, after one entry, Jana mentioned a baby, and then she abruptly stopped writing about Eloise. She just disappeared from the journal like she'd never existed. She didn't understand what Jana had meant about a baby, and she also didn't understand what happened to Eloise. Not once had Jana named Eloise's surname. Maybe Eloise wasn't even her real name. Gabriella made note of that and moved on.

Page after page, Jana wrote about one indiscretion after another. Rarely did she write about Ashton, other than when his birthday passed and she'd remember him. At Christmas time, she wrote of Ashton coming home and catching him sitting in front of the electrical train that circled the Christmas tree at the resort. She'd go on about how mad she was with him for being the kind, gentle boy that he was, but also that he'd caused her so much pain for living and being in her life. She often spoke of her love for her son but then contradicted herself. What was it? Did she or did she not love Ashton?

Jana barely interacted with Ian after Ashton left. She often speculated that he was with Eloise or another of his tramps.

And then towards the end of her journal, she wrote how proud she was of her son. How he'd grown into a wonderful, kind, caring, gentle man who'd become a pediatrician. She wrote how she knew he'd followed in that profession because of his asthma and the time he'd almost died. She knew that he didn't want a child to suffer like he had. He was going to make each child feel special, in his own way.

By the time she read the last sentence in the journal, she knew how much Jana had loved her son. Jana had known she'd been wrong in sending him away. She'd wanted him to know that she regretted her actions.

> *I hope one day you'll read this, dear Ashton. I'm sorry, son, for my ways. I'm sorry I wasn't stronger when you needed me the most. I'm sorry, so sorry that I didn't take you away all those years ago. Away from this life... But the one thing I want you to know is I always loved you. No matter what you say, no matter what your heart told you, I always loved you.*
> *Always,*
> *Your loving mother*

Gabriella was in tears when she read the last lines. She needed to discover who this Eloise was. She needed to know what Jana meant about a baby. And she needed Ashton to know how much his mother loved him.

She sat on her couch for a long time wondering how she could go about finding the answers she needed to provide Ashton so he could move on with his life.

And then the answer popped into her head. She reached for her cell phone and pressed send. When Alec answered, Gabriella asked if she could come over.

"Sure, come on over. Kelly's not here, though. She's at her mom's."

"Perfect, because I am coming to see you, only you.

I'll be there in a half-hour. Is that okay?"

"I'll be waiting."

She hurried to change her clothes. She grabbed the journal, her notebook, and her coat, rushing out of the house in under five minutes. She knew Alec would have the answers she needed and she also knew he'd keep her secret.

She made it to Alec's in record time. He'd been watching for her and opened the door as soon as she started up the sidewalk. "Is something wrong? What's got you so upset?"

"Are you sure we're alone?"

"Chancey's the only one here, so I'd say we're as alone as we can be." Alec led Gabriella back to his office and Chancey followed.

"Oh hi, there Chancey," she said, reaching down to pet his dog. "I haven't seen you in a long time." Chancey looked up at Gabriella, licked her hand, and then walked towards his bed that sat in the corner of Alec's office. He curled up and immediately drifted off to sleep.

"Would you care for something to drink? Coffee, tea?"

"No, I'm fine," Gabriella said as she sat down on the couch in his office. "Alec, you have to promise me."

"Promise you what?"

"Promise me that this conversation stays just between us. No one, including Kelly, can know about this. Not Joe, Alejandro, Dad... No one. Can you do that?"

"Of course I can. Now, what's on your mind?"

She went on to tell Alec everything. "So, I took— no, I guess I stole his mother's journal. In fact, he has no idea that I have it. I remember Ashton taking one look at it and then he threw it down. I couldn't leave it there. I just felt that it had answers that Ashton needed to know about, so I brought it home with me. And then after Ashton and I had our falling out, I completely forgot about it. I'd placed it in my desk. Then when Ashton and I got back together…"

"You're really back together?"

"Yeah, you could call it that," she didn't even pause to take a breath, but continued, "but the other day I decided to tackle reading her journal. I wanted to see if there was anything that would change Ashton's opinion of his mother. And I think I found it. But first I need your help."

"I'm not sure I can really help you. What do you think I can do?"

"I need the name of your private investigator. The one you hired to bring down the guy that sexually harassed Kelly."

"You mean Jonas Sounds?"

"Yeah, him."

"Why do you need to hire him?"

"Because Ashton's father was a first class cheater. He had one affair after another, but there was one that was pretty prominent in his life—one that seemed to last for years. And right before Jana stopped writing about her, she mentioned a baby. And then she stopped. She stopped referring to Eloise—just stopped. I don't know if she had a baby, I don't know if she died. I don't know what happened to her, but what I do know is I need to find out. This Eloise is what changed Jana. After she found them in their affair, she sent Ashton away. She pretty much put him out of her mind. She blamed Ian's indiscretions on Ashton's birth. She felt like if he hadn't been born then Ian wouldn't have turned his back on her. I need to find Eloise. For once and for all, I want to find the answers that will help Ashton move on with his life. I want him to realize that his mother truly loved him. I want him to know that he can forgive her. And lastly, I want him to realize that he can love someone, too."

"I don't know what to say. You just dumped an awful lot on me."

"I don't want you to say anything, just introduce me to Jonas Sounds. I need his help to get the answers I need. Who knows, maybe this Eloise is not really Eloise. Maybe this was just a pseudonym for her. But what if Ashton has a sibling out there? Wouldn't you want to know that you have a brother or sister that you didn't know about? I know I would. So will you help? Will you help me find the answers? If I were him, I'd want to know that my mother in fact truly loved me and did what she thought was best for me at the time. If you could have seen him at the funeral… he was there only because he had to be. I want him to forgive her even though he may not have those same feelings. I want him to know that she loved him all the way to her grave."

"Are you prepared for the fallout?"

"What fallout could there possibly be?"

"Well for one, you stole her journal. You've lied about it, and now you're going to look into his family's background. Maybe those are secrets that need to stay buried. Maybe Ashton doesn't want or need to know to move on. Gabby, you could be opening a can of worms that I'm not sure you're prepared to expose. A lot of people could be hurt by this. I just want you to be sure that you're doing the right thing because, once

I call Jonas, there's no turning back."

"I realize that and I am willing to take the risk. If Ashton and I break up because of this, at least I know in my heart of hearts that I tried to do the right thing. I want Ashton to know that his mother loved him. Right now, he doesn't believe that, and if I can do one thing, that's what I want to do. I want him to realize that he was loved."

"Well, if that's what you want."

She nodded. Alec reached for the phone and dialed Jonas's number. If anyone could find the answers Gabriella was looking for, it was Jonas Sounds. He'd uncovered Ken Jones's past of sexual harassment and helped put him away for many years. It may take Jonas a while to uncover what she was looking for, but he was thorough and would find the answers she needed.

Surprisingly, Jonas answered and agreed to meet with Alec and Gabriella. She was even more surprised that he would meet on a Sunday, so she and Alec jumped into her car and headed over to Jonas's offices.

She shared Jana's journal with Jonas. She didn't want to leave it with him, so he copied the pages that he thought would be the most helpful with locating Eloise. The timeline of dates was the most crucial piece that he needed. He'd backtrack and see if he could discover if, in fact, an Eloise may have been employed by Ashton's father at the resort. He'd start there and see where the path to answers led him.

"I can't promise you anything."

"I know," Gabriella said. "But I need to try and see if I can find her. I need to see if Ashton has a brother or sister out there."

"I understand. Give me some time, and I'll get back to you."

"How much time?"

"I can't say for sure. It may take me a few weeks, a few months. I can't say as I don't have much information to go on. I'll have to go down to Branson and snoop around and see what I can find. I may be lucky, and I may not. We'll just have to see."

"I appreciate anything that you can do."

"But Gabriella, as far as your concerned, he might not want to have these answers," Alec chimed in.

"I know, Alec. I'll deal with it when the time comes."

They shook hands and walked out of Jonas's office. "If anyone can give you the answers you're looking for, it's Jonas. Just give him the time that he needs."

"I will, and thank you, Alec. You know how much I love you."

"I know. I just hope you're not overstepping your bounds here, Gabriella. I don't want you getting hurt."

"I know you don't, but I wouldn't be his friend if I didn't try and find these answers." She wanted to do something special for him. She was in his corner and didn't want to get his hopes up in the event that her search was for naught. She'd keep it her secret for now. She drove Alec home and dropped him off. Thankfully, Kelly hadn't returned and she wasn't the wiser about their meeting with Jonas Sounds.

One Sunday afternoon in early March, Ashton stopped by Gabriella's. It was a beautiful day—the temperatures were in the low sixties. It was a perfect day to take a hike. They hadn't seen much of one another since she'd told him about Jeremy. He'd been on call much of the time, and she'd been busy at school and with her tutoring at the hospital. He'd called her the evening before to see if she were in the mood to go hiking. Since he'd been working pretty much non-stop the last several weeks, and he'd filled in for Joe the previous day, Joe was taking his turn and had given him the day off. This was the perfect day to get back in the swing of hiking—not too cold and definitely not too hot.

She greeted Ashton in a pair of old jeans, a long-sleeved t-shirt, and her hoodie. Her hiking shoes had seen better days. The soles were incredibly worn.

Pointing at her shoes, he said, "Don't you think you need a new pair?"

"Someday, but not today. They're just too comfortable," she said as she jumped into his car.

"Where to?"

"Let's go to Pieres Trail Park. It's close and it's got a fabulous trail. Remember I told you all about it? You can walk along the abandoned railway. It looks over the Meramec River. Today's a gorgeous day, and since the leaves are still off the trees, we should be able to see over into Illinois. Maybe downtown. I can't wait."

"I remember, just show me the way."

Gabriella gave him the instructions. They stopped at the gas station. While he gassed up the car, she ran inside and bought water, a piece of fruit, and some cheese sticks for each of them. She thought it would be the perfect snack as they hiked.

Pieres Trail Park was only twenty minutes from her house. At least, that's all it seemed. She was like a kid in a candy store. She couldn't wait to hop out of the car as soon as he put it into park. It was a beautiful day. She was tired of being cooped up inside during the long winter months. She practically ran to the trail head and then stopped, remembering that she wasn't alone. Ashton caught up with her and reached for her hand. Hand-in-hand, they started down the trail. They walked for at least ten minutes, taking in the sights and sounds before he spoke.

"This is really beautiful out here. I'm glad you suggested coming."

"Wait until we climb that hill over there. It's the tallest point on the trail and you can see for miles. St. Louis County is absolutely beautiful. I love this view."

It took them about fifteen minutes before they made it to the spot that she'd been talking about. She walked to the edge and looked over at the swirling Meramec River. St. Louis had incurred a huge rainstorm during the week and the river was running high.

"Watch it, I don't want you to fall."

"I'm fine. And there's actually a ledge under here. Come on, let's sit down and have our snack." A picnic bench sat off the trail away from the edge. They sat and took in the peace and beauty that surrounded them.

Ashton spoke up. "Isn't your spring break coming up?"

"It is. We have two weeks of school left and then we're off for a whopping ten days. I can't wait."

"Do you have any plans?"

"No, not really. Why?"

"Well, I need to head back down to Branson and handle a few things. Would you like to come? Maybe you could go through some of my mother's things. I'd like to donate them to charity."

She was shocked to say the least. That he wanted

her to go with him, and even more importantly, go through his mother's things. She didn't have to think twice. First of all, this would give them uninterrupted time together, something they hadn't had since Jana's death. And secondly, maybe she'd find some clues that she could pass onto Jonas.

She had spoken to Jonas weekly since their initial meeting two weeks earlier. He'd travelled to Branson and had interviewed countless people at the resort to no avail. No one knew an Eloise. Maybe she'd find some clues while she was in Branson. She could only hope.

"I'd love to go with you. I just want to make sure that's what you really want."

"I asked you, didn't I? Of course I want you to go with me. You've been my guiding light here through all of this. You've kept me centered when she died, making me focus on what I needed to at the time, when what I really wanted to do was hightail it back to St. Louis. So, yes, I want you by my side."

"If that's what you want, you definitely have a travel partner."

They finished up their snack. The light was beginning to wane, so they decided to head back. The days were getting longer, but it still got dark early.

She told Ashton that she needed to finish grading some papers for school and work on progress reports, so he took her straight home.

"Would you like to come in?"

"No, I know you've got a lot to do. I'll call you tomorrow and we can talk about our trip. I had a nice time today. Let's do it again."

"I'd love to," she said as she reached over to kiss him. She pulled away quickly and opened her door. "I look forward to your call."

"Bye," he said as she closed the door. She stood in her doorway as she watched him drive off. Ever since their conversation when she'd told him about Jeremy, she felt like he pulled away, giving her the distance she needed as she came to terms with their relationship. She knew he didn't want to move too fast, and in all honesty, they did need to slow down.

Almost two weeks later, Gabriella was in Ashton's car as they traveled down Highway 44 towards Branson. He had been waiting at her house when she'd gotten home from school. They'd had an early release at school, and she'd practically bolted out the doors with her students. She couldn't wait to spend time with him and hopefully find out more about who Eloise was and maybe also uncover some more of his mother's journals, notes, or whatever else would help with her investigation.

They pulled into Branson just after seven. "I think Alistair is preparing dinner for us."

"Oh, he didn't have to go to all that trouble."

"I think he's lonely since my mother died. He wanted to, even suggested it."

"Well, okay then. Actually, I hope it's ready because I'm starving." They'd stopped right outside of St. Louis and had grabbed a quick snack, but other than that she'd just had a granola bar for breakfast. She'd been too excited as she'd gathered her luggage that morning. She'd wanted to be ready so they could head out the door as soon as he'd arrived.

Ashton pulled through the gates and wound his way up the driveway to the house on the hill. When they were last in Branson, she hadn't had the opportunity to really take in the view. It was spectacular at night. She could see lights so far in the distance, and she wondered how far she was able to see.

"If you're not too tired, we can go for a drive tonight. The town is really a pretty site."

Just as they were getting out of the car, Alistair opened the front door. "Welcome," he called out as they headed up the stairs. She hugged Alistair while Ashton shook his hand. "It's good to see you both. I hope you're both hungry as dinner's just about ready."

"I'm starved," Gabriella practically shouted in excitement.

"Well, okay then," Alistair said as he led them towards the dining room.

"Alistair, you didn't have to go to all of this trouble for us," Ashton said pointing to the flowers and the candles.

"It's a special occasion, and I wanted to. It's so nice having company. This house gets so lonely with just me living here. Would you care for a glass of wine? You know Missouri has some of the best wines in the country."

"I'd love a glass," she said, smiling at Alistair. "Tell me where it is, and I can pour."

"Heavens no, you're the guest."

She looked over at Ashton who was smirking.

"Please do not treat me as a guest. I don't want to be waited on hand and foot. I think I can take care of pouring myself and Ashton a glass of wine."

"Well, alright. Make yourself at home," he called over his shoulder as he went in search of the bottle of wine.

Gabriella started laughing. "What's gotten into

him?"

"I think he's smitten with you, that's what I think."

"Oh, he is not," she claimed as she threw her arms around his neck. "He can't be because he has to know you're the only one that I have my sights set on…"

He looked her in the eyes and smiled. Just as he was ready to kiss her, she heard footsteps. Alistair had returned with the wine but also a bottle of beer.

"I wasn't sure that you really wanted a glass of wine, Ashton, so I brought you a beer just in case."

"I appreciate it, and yes I'd love that beer." He reached for the beer as Alistair poured her wine.

"I have some appetizers, if you don't think it will ruin your dinner—just cheese and crackers."

"That'd be lovely," she said as she smiled over the top of her wine glass. Alistair hurried from the room to gather their snacks while Ashton looked on.

"Lovely? Lovely?"

"Well, it would be. I have to say, I really like him. I'm glad you kept him on."

"Well, he's been working for the family for years, and just because my mother passed away didn't mean he had to go, too. I still have this house and it can't be left unoccupied. This is his home too, and I want it to remain that way until I decide what I'm going to do with it." Ashton grabbed her hand. "Come on, let's join him in the kitchen. Maybe we can convince him that we can eat in there, too. It's just too stuffy in here for me." Ashton led her to the kitchen where he was able to convince Alistair that they wanted to eat in there.

Alistair served chicken brie. When she pierced her chicken and a cheesy mixture spilled out onto her plate, she sighed like she was heaven. "Oh my gosh,

Alistair. This is fabulous. I need the recipe. And this zucchini dish is out of this world, too."

"I'm glad you're enjoying it. It was one of Mrs. Holder's favorite dishes."

She was glad she asked. At least she'd have one of his mother's favorite recipes.

They finished their meal and Ashton pulled her up from her seat. "Let's go take that drive."

"I want to help Alistair clean up."

"That's not necessary, Gabriella. You go on and enjoy yourself," Alistair said, picking up the plates.

She ran over to Alistair and kissed his cheek. She hugged him, too. "Thanks for a delicious dinner. Maybe you'll let me cook you a meal while I'm here."

"Oh, Gabriella, that's not necessary."

"But I want to. I haven't cooked for Ashton, other than hot cocoa, and I'd like to fix a meal for both of you."

"Well, if you put it in those terms…"

"We'll talk about it tomorrow. Have a good night."

Ashton grabbed Gabby's hand and led her out of the house. "Thanks for doing that."

"For what?"

"For doing what you just did. Alistair doesn't have any family, and he's all I have left. I know it meant a lot to him."

"Well, I'm glad I asked." He helped her into the car, and as he joined her, she put her hand on his forearm. "Does he know how to dunk a cookie?"

Ashton laughed, "I don't know. You'll have to ask him."

"I will, and if he doesn't, maybe you can show him how to do it." She laughed as he started the car and headed off down the driveway. They drove down

Main Street and she was surprised with how crowded the strip was.

"That's what I always hated about coming home—the incessant traffic."

It wasn't too long before they pulled into another long circular drive. As he wound the car up the drive, a huge, brightly lit building came into view. The parking lot was packed. He pulled up to the front of the building and pulled into an open spot.

"You can't park here."

"Why not?"

"It says reserved."

"Yeah, and?"

"Well, it's reserved."

"I know what it says." Ashton smiled as he turned off the motor and started to get out.

"Ashton, you'll get a ticket or maybe even have your car towed."

He opened her car door, and she didn't want to get out. He reached for her hand and practically dragged her from the car.

"Well, if you want to take the risk…"

"I do, and I will," he said as he looped her arm through his and headed towards the front of the building.

As soon as they walked through the doors, he was greeted by the concierge. "Dr. Holder, welcome. It's nice to see you."

"Thank you," he said, shaking his outstretched hand.

As he neared the reservation counter, he was greeted by the reservationist. "Dr. Holder, what a surprise. I didn't realize you were in town."

"We just got here."

Gabriella watched everyone with her eyebrows

raised. Every employee that Ashton came in contact with knew him and greeted him by name. He pulled her through a doorway, up a flight of stairs, and through a set of glass doors. He walked down the hallway towards the office in the back. It had a set of frosted doors. He pulled out a key and opened the doors. Gabriella was wide-eyed. She had no idea where they were.

"Where are we?"

"At the resort."

"I can see that, but I don't understand."

"Gabby, this is my resort. I own it."

She was flustered. She started to get a little woozy and made her way to a nearby chair. She sat down and looked up at him. She wasn't sure she'd heard him correctly. This place was huge. It was high-end and full of opulence. One needed to be wealthy to stay there. She knew he came from money, but had no idea he was this wealthy.

"Did I hear you correctly? You own this?"

"I do. This was my father's life. It's why I never saw him. It's why he and my mother had such a horrible marriage. He put the resort over their marriage. When I was growing up, I hated it here. The only thing I liked was coming at Christmas and watching the train circle around and around underneath the Christmas tree. I have way too many bad childhood memories associated with this place."

"But…"

"But now I realize it's a business. A very profitable one to say the least. It's part of my inheritance, along with the house and several other properties around the area."

She was speechless and her mind was spinning.

"Hey, are you okay? How about a glass of water?"

She nodded her head. All of this was overwhelming to her. She looked up at him as he handed her a bottle of water. He was just a normal guy. He didn't flaunt his wealth. He was kind and gentle. Did her father know about this? What about Alec and Joe? She sat there as he made his way around the desk, sitting down behind it. He looked good there, she thought. Really good.

"Ashton, I had no idea. I knew your father owned a resort, but I had no idea it was this lavish. I can't imagine how much it costs to stay here. It can't be cheap."

"It's not. This is the most expensive resort in Branson and we are pretty much filled to capacity ninety-five percent of the time. The five percent that we're not is in the off season, and even then we're still very busy."

All of a sudden she was overcome with a tiredness that consumed her body. All of this revelation, combined with the long drive—she couldn't keep her eyes open. That's when she felt Ashton reach for her hand. "Let's go home. I think you've had enough surprises for the day." *Yes, indeed,* she thought. *I can't imagine what else he can throw at me that would shock me quite as much as I was tonight.*

Chapter Thirty-One

GABRIELLA WENT TO HER BEDROOM as soon as they returned from the resort—she stayed in the same bedroom that she'd stayed in when his mother had died. She changed and went straight to bed, falling asleep as soon as her head hit the pillow.

She awoke and it was still dark outside. She glanced at the bedside clock and it was only five-thirty, but she felt rested and jumped out of bed. She made her way to the bathroom where she took a long, hot shower. By the time she'd finished drying her hair and dressing, it was just after six. She didn't know if anyone was up, so she quietly made her way down the hallway towards the expansive staircase that led down to either the foyer or the kitchen. She chose the kitchen as she needed a cup of coffee.

As her feet hit the kitchen floor, she noticed the sun was just beginning to rise over a hill. As the pinks in the sky brightened, she stood wondering what her day would bring. She didn't know what Ashton had planned. She didn't want to let on to him that she had her own agenda while in Branson, so she'd take the wait-and-see approach.

She turned away from the windows and headed towards the coffee pot. As quietly as possible, she looked for Alistair's hiding place—everyone kept their coffee in different places. She kept her coffee beans in a sealed container in her cabinet, while her mother kept hers in the pantry, practically under lock and key. John drank way to much coffee and her mother was trying to limit his consumption.

She was stretching, looking into a cabinet, when she was surprised from behind by Ashton. She yelped, but he folded her into his arms, pulling her towards him. She felt him kissing her neck from behind. Gabriella was taken aback by Ashton's gestures. It was one thing if they were completely alone, but she didn't know when Alistair would appear.

"Ashton," she cried. "Will you stop that?"

He chuckled in her ear as she tried to duck out from his arms. He held her more securely, resting his head on her shoulder.

"What do you think you're doing?" she chided.

"Saying good morning."

"Well, you can say good morning and not grope me at the same time."

Ashton pulled away grumbling. She couldn't hear what he'd said, but knew he wasn't happy with her. "What are you looking for anyway?"

"The coffee. And, as you can see, I'm not necessarily the nicest person first thing in the morning before I've had my first cup."

"I have no idea where Alistair hides it. He should be coming down shortly and he'll fix us our breakfast."

"Ashton, didn't I make myself clear yesterday that I don't want to be waited on? I can brew a pot of coffee as well as Alistair, and I can fix us breakfast, too. So get out of my way while I try and find the coffee."

"Gabriella, the coffee's in the cabinet next to the refrigerator," Alistair said as he made his way into the kitchen. "I'm sorry I'm late and that I didn't have a pot of coffee waiting for you." Alistair grabbed the container with the coffee beans, threw some into the grinder and then grabbed the purified water from the refrigerator. "Tomorrow, it'll be waiting for you."

"Alistair, I don't want you waiting on me. I can make a pot of coffee as well as you can. I am not your guest."

Drawing his lips in, Alistair nodded.

"I can see the wheels turning in your head, Alistair. Fixing myself a cup of coffee or food is not going to ruin my 'vacation.' I want to be included and not be an outsider here. I enjoy doing it, and I think it's about time you let someone do something for you for a change. So, while I'm here, I will fix our meals."

"Gab-ri-ella," Ashton said.

She raised her hand, stopping him. "Alistair, I want to do this, so please let me. If I don't want to cook, I'll let you know. The meal you made last night was fabulous, but while I'm here, I want you to take some time and relax, too. You need to take care of yourself."

Alistair nodded his head in understanding. "I appreciate your concern, Gabriella. Why don't we do this—while Ashton's out today, you and I can sit down and plan out our meals. Do it together as a team, that way we can both be included. To be honest, Gabriella, Mrs. Holder didn't lift a finger in the kitchen. This has been my—"

"You don't have to go any further, Alistair. I understand where you're coming from. Yes, let's do it together." Alistair grinned as she stood to claim her first cup of coffee of the day. Turning towards Ashton, who'd actually gotten a good laugh out of watching the two of them negotiate who was going to use the kitchen, was sitting at the table. "So what's on your agenda today?" she asked as she handed over a cup of coffee to Ashton.

"Well, I need to run by the resort and check out a few things. Then I have a meeting with my mother's attorney. Will you be okay here with Alistair?"

"Of course I will. In fact, he can show me your mother's things, and I can start sorting them for the various charities you want to donate them to."

Ashton quickly downed his cup of coffee and brushed a kiss across Gabriella's brow. "I'm heading over to the resort. The sooner I get there, the sooner I can come home."

That was the first time he'd referred to his mother's house as home. Maybe they were getting somewhere.

"We'll be waiting," Gabriella shouted as he ran up the stairs to get his things. Turning to Alistair, she said, "Let me finish up here, and then you can point me in the right direction so I can begin going through Jana's things."

Alistair reached for Gabriella's hand. Squeezing it, he smiled at her. "Thank you for being there for him. Ashton is like a son to me. I know he didn't have the best of childhoods, and I know what he can be like, short tempered and all. But since you entered the picture, I can see a softening around the edges. He smiles more, isn't as gruff with me. Not that he was ever really gruff, but Ashton had a way about him. I understood him and tried not to press his buttons. I like seeing the changes in him, and I hope they continue."

She reached over, kissing Alistair's cheek. "I don't

know if it's me or not, but I like the changes in him, too. I have to tell you, I didn't like him at first. In fact, I was a real bitch to him. He did some things to my nephew and brother that made me despise him, but then I don't know what happened. He changed, maybe I changed. I don't know, but I have to admit I like what I see as well."

As soon as Ashton left the house, she grabbed a second cup of coffee and followed Alistair upstairs. He pointed out Jana's bedroom and her office that was at the end of the hall. "You can start in here first," he said, pointing to Jana's bedroom. "I've got some boxes downstairs that I'll bring up later. Do you need some help?"

"No, I'm good right now. You go about your day, and I'll call if I need anything." Alistair left her to her work.

She opened the door to Jana's bedroom. She wasn't surprised by the size of the room—it was huge. It had a formal sitting area with a fireplace, couch, and wing-back chairs. French doors opened from the sitting area into the actual bedroom. A king-sized bed sat in the middle of the room. Sliding glass doors opened onto a balcony that wrapped around the side of the house. She noticed there was even an entrance that led to the sitting room.

She opened a door that she thought may have belonged to the bathroom, but actually led to the walk-in closet of her dreams. It was as large as her family room with built in shelves, cubbies, and drawers that lined both sides of the room. She was flabber-gasted but backed out and turned right, discovering the bathroom that was what every woman dreamed of. A huge walk-in shower with a bench that was large enough to seat three people. It was huge. It also had jets that sprayed out of the walls. And then she turned and saw the tub. She had to walk up steps if she wanted to get into it. It sat against the wall with a skylight above that provided nice natural light to the room. The ledge even contained a cup holder—perfect for a glass of wine.

She returned to the sitting room. She stood in awe as she looked about the room. She sipped her coffee, trying to decide where to begin. The sitting room was just that, a room with a few bookshelves. She could tackle that later. She decided she'd get the most bang for her time by attacking the closet first. She'd sort his mother's clothes into casual and formal, and then go from there.

Gabriella was amazed with the way Jana had organized her clothes. She had been anal to say the least. She had all of her gardening clothes stored in one section of the closet. Next, Gabriella discovered her casual clothes. Jana must have enjoyed yoga because she had quite a few pieces from one of the famous yoga manufacturers.

By the time she made it through half of the closet, she had enough clothes for at least five boxes. She decided to take a break and peruse the books that sat on the bookshelves in the sitting room. Nothing out of the ordinary. Nothing that looked like another journal…

While she looked at the myriad of genres of books that Jana enjoyed, Alistair delivered quite a few broken-down boxes to the room, where he efficiently started to put them together. She decided to get back to work when Alistair left her to get more boxes. She made her way back to the closet and started in on the formal wear. She was taken aback by some of the dresses. Jana had a wonderful flair for fashion and design. She had dresses made with sequins, Australian crystals, fancy beading... long, short, cocktail-length dresses lined the walls. Jana's color palette leaned more towards the bright and pastel colors. She liked yellows, greens, and purples, as these were the prominent colors in her closet, along with quite a few black dresses in various lengths and styles.

Gabriella envied her shoe collection—between flats, pumps, and heels, it was massive and she couldn't fathom the cost of some of them. Next in the closet was Jana's wall of purses. If Jana was anything like herself, Gabriella needed to go through each bag. She was known to keep money, jewelry, and really anything else in a bag, even after she'd cleaned it out. She hoped she'd find something that would provide her with more answers. And what did she find? Just like she expected, a couple hundred dollars in bills, more quarters than she could count in one sitting, and quite a few playbills from various shows that she'd attended throughout Branson.

After sorting through the purses, stacking the playbills into a pile, and laying the money on Jana's dresser, she returned to the closet when she noticed a purse she'd missed. As she walked back into Jana's sitting room, she opened it and noticed another round of what she thought were playbills. As she pulled each booklet out of the leather purse, she was more than surprised by her findings. In fact, what she held in her hands overwhelmed her with emotion. She was right. Jana had loved her son more than she even thought possible.

Gabriella made her way to the couch and eased herself down as she flipped through her discovery. Jana had kept all of Ashton's school programs. She had what appeared to be every school program that she'd attended, all the way from pre-school until when she sent him off to boarding school. And then, she had a copy of his high school graduation program, and what surprised Gabriella even more, a copy of his valedictorian speech. She ran her hand over the embossed crest for Bigsby Hall. *I had no idea he was the valedictorian of his high school class.*

She continued going through the programs. College, med school, every single school that he attended. Did he realize she had even been there? She was overcome with emotion and tears began cascading down her face. Jana loved her son. She grabbed all of the programs and put them back into the purse. She hurried to her bedroom before Alistair could find her and stored the purse and its contents in her suitcase. She'd share this with Ashton in time. She still wanted to learn a little more about Jana and hopefully discover who Eloise was. She was slowly learning more about who Jana was, and she wanted to share what she'd discovered about his mother with him. He needed to know that she'd never forgotten him. She'd been there supporting him in her own way.

Gabriella was tired. After discovering the programs and being overcome with emotion, she decided she needed to take a nap. She walked back to her room. She needed to get her head together. As she drifted off to sleep, she wondered what else she'd uncover.

Gabriella felt a cool breeze and woke up. She opened her eyes and noticed Alistair closing her door.

"Alistair?"

"Oh, Gabriella. I'm sorry I woke you. I came in to tidy up your room and found you asleep. I'll leave you alone so you can go back to sleep."

"No, please don't. Please come in and sit. I'd like to chat with you."

Alistair re-entered the room and sat down in one of the chairs that sat near the bay window. She joined him. "Has Ashton come home?"

"No, not yet. Why?"

"Well, I wanted to ask you a few questions, and I don't want him overhearing us."

"I don't expect Ashton for some time. He has an appointment at three, and he shouldn't get back until at least five. So what do you want to ask me?"

"Ashton doesn't speak much about his mother. What I know of Jana is from Ashton's jaded perspective. What can you tell me about her? Was she as heartless as he makes her out to be?"

Alistair looked down at the floor. He clasped his hands in his lap and looked out the window. "Gabriella," he said. "I don't know what to say… Where to start. It's complicated."

"Just start at the beginning. I want to know what Jana was like. Was she as standoffish as Ashton portrays her? Did she or didn't she love him? He hates her. It disgusts him to talk about her. He may not come right out and say it, but I can tell. Alistair," she pleaded as she stood. "I want Ashton to see his mother in a different light. I want him to know what I've come to believe. I think she loved him with all of her heart, but I believe she treated him like she did so he wouldn't realize what was really going on. Jana didn't want Ashton to know what a womanizer his father was. She didn't want him to know that he had a long-time affair—or rather, affairs. Am I right? Were Jana's actions all in the name of protecting her son from witnessing what his father was truly like? Please, Alistair, help me to know the real Jana. The one I think Ashton needs to learn about."

Alistair became agitated as he sat there, crossing and uncrossing his legs, shifting continually in his chair, and she knew she'd hit the nail on the head. He had a hard time making eye contact with her.

She approached Alistair and knelt down in front of him. She clasped his hands in hers, pleading with him to share with her the real Jana. He sucked in his lips, swallowed loudly, and then grabbed onto Gabriella's hands. He cleared his throat several times before he spoke. "Gabriella, I don't know where you got your information…"

"I'm right, aren't I? She was protecting Ashton. She walked away from her only son to protect him—protect him from their crumbling marriage, protect him from a father that didn't want him. She put the love of her son aside to protect him from a father that—"

Alistair squeezed her hands. "Yes, you're right. She did it all to protect Ashton. To keep him from not seeing the man that his father had become. She loved Ashton with all of her heart. When she sent him away to boarding school, she almost had a nervous breakdown. Not because of what she'd witnessed, but because she wouldn't have her son by her side. She wouldn't see him grow up."

"But she did, didn't she? She saw many of his achievements. She attended Ashton's music programs while he was in school, she saw him in a one-act play, she attended his graduations from high school, college, med school… She was there for everything, wasn't she? Didn't he know she was there? How could he not? She loved him and he never knew it. Why, Alistair, why?"

"It's just like you said. She didn't want him to know what his father was like. She wanted him to think they'd both abandoned him. She had her motives, and I'm not sure what all of them were, but yes she was there. On the sidelines, dressed in wigs… she wanted to remain faceless. She often got to the event either right before it started or right after. She didn't want to draw attention to herself. And she always left right before the program ended. She was there for everything, but how do you know that? I thought I was her only confidant, and I never uttered a word. I generally drove her or accompanied her if we had to travel out of town. We went in the cloak of darkness, getting in and out without anyone recognizing us. How did you find out? When did you discover this?"

Gabriella stood and sat beside Alistair. "I was going through her purses and found program after program from preschool all the way through med-school. They were all neatly kept in a purse in her closet. Some of them were quite worn from being opened and closed. I realized what kind of mother would go to all of this trouble."

"Gabriella, she loved Ashton until the day she died. She would call him and he'd ignore her calls. I remember seeing the look on her face when Ashton took her call on Thanksgiving. After she hung up with him, she had a smile on her face that I hadn't seen in a long, long time. And then, minutes later, I saw the smile fade and crumble as she had her stroke. I'm just thankful that he took her call that day. It meant the world to her."

Alistair reached out to her. "How did you discover all of this? How did you find out about Ian and his indiscretions?"

"I found her journal."

"Journal? What journal?"

"The night before Ashton and I returned to St. Louis after the funeral, I was in the library. I came across a leather bound book that looked interesting. As soon as I opened it, I realized that it was Jana's journal. It was written in her own handwriting and went back many years. I know why she sent him away to boarding school. I know all about Ian's affairs. I know about Eloise."

"Eloise?"

"Yeah, Jana found Ian and her together in his office. That was the night that Ashton almost died from his asthma attack. And that's when she decided to send him away. I still don't know how she did that if she loved him so much. But in defense of Jana, she was protecting her son the only way she knew how to protect him at the time."

Alistair stood abruptly and started for the door. He didn't want to revisit this with Gabriella. He'd known what Jana had done. He didn't necessarily agree with it, but had to follow her wishes since she was his employer. Instead, he stood by her side watching her experience all the events in her child's life from the sidelines. Never once enjoying those special moments by Ashton's side.

"Alistair?"

He turned and looked at Gabriella. He'd had enough for the day revisiting in his mind all the times he'd traveled with Jana to Ashton's events.

"Do you know who Eloise is? Her last name, any-thing?"

He shook his head no and walked from the room. She had to believe he was telling her the truth. She sat staring out the window wondering if she'd ever discover who Eloise was.

⌒

Ashton found Gabriella sitting in her room, staring out the bay window. She appeared not to hear him approach. "Gabby, are you feeling alright?"

She looked up at him and smiled. "Of course I am. Why would you think I wasn't?"

"I don't know. I guess by the look on your face."

She smiled up at him. "Better?"

"Yes." He sat down beside her in a chair. "How was your day?"

"It was good. I went through your mother's closet and packed up her clothes, shoes, and purses. Have you seen her shoe collection? Oh my gosh, I envy every pair. Your mother had a flair for fashion. She had some beautiful dresses. I'm sure someone will be overjoyed with them."

"I'm glad you think so. So what's next?"

"I'm starving. How about dinner?"

"Did you and Alistair work all that out?"

She looked at him questioningly.

"You know? Who's going to cook and all."

"Oh yeah. We actually didn't get a chance to, so I'm going to let him have his way tonight. We'll figure it out tomorrow."

⌒

They sat and discussed their day. Ashton had gone to the resort and then met with his mother's attorney. Gabriella was glad that he was home and able to relax. They enjoyed their evening and Alistair's sumptuous dinner that had Gabriella talking about it even the next morning.

The next day, Ashton took Gabriella to Silver Dollar City. She hadn't been there since she'd been in grade school. She enjoyed seeing the various tradesmen. She became so engrossed in watching the glass blower that she didn't realize Ashton had left her side until he returned with a beautifully blown vase that had been made right there. When he handed it to her, she couldn't find her words. "It's beautiful," she said as her fingers stroked the veins in the vase.

Next, she wanted to visit the bakery and the mill. She wanted to purchase some of the ground corn meal for her mother, as well as some of the apple butter that was made on site. They visited the blacksmith and Gabriella even bought a handcrafted leather belt from the leather shop.

They made their way to the candy shop and watched as the staff expertly pulled taffy. She wanted to select her own taffy, so she reached down and picked up a small, silver bucket.

"What's that for?"

"I'm going to buy some saltwater taffy. I'm choosing my own flavors. Is there something wrong with that?"

"No, I just didn't know what the bucket was for."

She laughed. She couldn't believe how clueless he was about certain things. "Ashton, really now. You didn't know what this is for?" She raised the tin bucket in front of his face.

"No, I really didn't."

She shook her head, not believing him as she threw in samples of flavor after flavor. "Don't you want to try some?" He shrugged. "Just grab a few. Be a kid for once."

He gave her a sideways look and grabbed several different flavors, throwing them into her bucket.

Gabriella wasn't a fan of carnival rides, but Ashton persuaded her to go on the Powder Keg roller coaster. "Open your eyes," he yelled at her as they climbed the track. Ashton knew that the Powder Keg would launch them down the rails, reaching fifty plus miles an hour in under three seconds. He couldn't wait to see the expression on her face as the track fell underneath them. As soon as they crested the top and launched over it, he thought Gabriella was going to pass out. Her eyes about fell out of her head, and she screamed all the way down. She'd been holding onto his hand, and if he didn't know better, she'd broken every one of his fingers with how strongly she held it.

Breathing heavily as their car came to a halt at the exit, she yelled, "I can't believe you made me ride this!"

"Gabby, you had fun. Admit it," he said over his shoulder as they exited the ride.

She huffed. "Okay, I did. But I don't want to go on another roller coaster today. One's more than enough for me."

He grabbed her hand and led her to the ice cream parlor where he bought her a double-scooped cone of apple pie and vanilla ice cream.

"Does this make up for it?"

She licked her cone, nodding.

"I'm glad. Now let's head to one of the shows." They ended up at the Silver Dollar City Saloon where they watched a song and dance revue. After that ended, they headed off to the Lucky Silver Mine restaurant where they enjoyed a luscious buffet filled with many Ozark Mountain favorites. By the time they finished their meal, they decided to just take in the scenery. They strolled throughout the park, making their way through the various shops.

"I can't believe we have only one more day. This has been a fantastic vacation. Thank you for inviting me."

"No, thank you for coming. You've worked wonders. I can't believe you've gone through all of my mother's things."

"I still have a few things I need to go through. I have her jewelry that I want you to look at—I'm not comfortable doing it. I also want to go through the library in her room and the library on the first floor. I think there may be some books that we can donate, too."

"Please go through everything and donate some, or even all, of the books. I don't think there are any that I'm interested in. I have to go back to the resort tomorrow, so why don't you do that while I'm gone. When I get home, I'd like to take you out for dinner. A final celebration before we return home."

"That sounds great. Now, I don't know about you, but my feet are tired from all of this walking. I'm ready to go." They made their way back to the front of the park, stopping at the bakery on the way out. When they'd first arrived, they'd ordered bread and various sweet rolls to take home. She wanted to share their day with Alistair, plus Gabriella could never pass up a sweet roll. "I hope Alistair likes sweet rolls. You know me, I can't pass up a good one."

"I didn't know that about you until just recently. In fact, it's your mother that told me about your love of any and all baked goods."

Slapping at his arm, she scowled at him. "I'm really not that bad. I just like taking my mom a treat when I visit. That's all."

"Whatever you say," he laughed as they paid for their goods and made their way through the final retail shop on their way to the car. He wrapped her arm in the crook of his as they walked to their car, "I had a good time," he said.

"I did, too. I think the fresh air did me in, though. I'm ready for bed," she claimed through a yawn.

Ashton took them straight home.

"Are you sure you're too tired to stay up and have a night cap?"

"I am. Why don't you have one with Alistair? You haven't spent much time with him while we've been here."

"That's a good idea, but I wish I were having it with you," he added as he reached for her hand.

"We can do it anytime. You're rarely here. Spend tonight with him."

Alistair greeted them as they walked through the kitchen door. "I'm off to bed," she told Alistair as she planted a soft kiss on his cheek. "Goodnight."

They watched as Gabriella climbed the stairs to her bedroom. "How about a night cap and a game of pool?" Alistair glanced at Ashton. "We haven't spent much time together since we arrived. Tomorrow's our last day, and I've neglected you since I've been here. This was supposed to be a vacation, but I've turned it into business. Please, I haven't played a round of pool in a long time."

"I'll get the glasses and you find the cue sticks." Alistair poured them each a brandy and met Ashton in the game room. They hadn't relaxed together since before Ashton had left for medical school. Alistair always enjoyed a game of pool with him and he was glad Ashton had suggested it.

They'd played one game of pool, which Ashton lost. Alistair suggested they take a break.

"Afraid you're going to lose the next game?"

"No, but I thought you had a reason for this meeting."

Ashton turned on the gas fireplace and sat down on the couch. He leaned over, holding his brandy snifter between his legs. He sat back and took a sip of his brandy, closing his eyes as he swallowed.

Alistair watched Ashton. He sat in a chair opposite him and also took a drink from his snifter. "Son, what's troubling you?" He waited for him to respond. "I might be sticking my nose in where I shouldn't, but she's good for you."

Ashton eyes flew open.

"She's changed you. You're a better man with her in your life."

"I know. It's just that..."

"What? What's on your mind?"

"Gabby, she's special. So special. You know she once couldn't stand me. At her niece's christening, she basically told me what she thought of me. But now, now..."

"Ashton, I know you don't believe in love and marriage, but I believe you're in love with Gabriella." Ashton had often shared with Alistair his thoughts on love and marriage after witnessing his parents' disastrous marriage.

Sighing, he nodded. "I think I am, too. But I don't know what to do. I've never felt this way about anyone in my entire life. I've never loved anyone."

"You know you loved your mother once."

"Maybe, but that was a long time ago—before I knew better."

"Ashton, there's a lot you don't know. A lot your mother did for you. She was around more than you give her credit for."

Ashton jumped off the couch. "My mother wasn't a part of my life from the time she sent me off to boarding school. And to this day, I still don't understand why she could do that."

"All I can say on the subject is that your mother had her reasons. And I hope, in time, you'll discover what they were and you'll realize you were always close to her heart. She'd have given her life for you. I know you don't believe that, but it's true." Alistair stood as well. He wasn't going to come right out and tell Ashton why Jana had done what she'd done. He'd promised to never divulge to Ashton her secrets. He'd only shared with Gabriella because she'd known her answers before asking him. He just confirmed it, but never added his own opinions. "Take your time, and give Gabriella a chance. I believe she's just as in love with you as you are with her."

Alistair saluted him as he started out the door. He stopped abruptly and turned back. "Ashton, I consider you the son I never had, and I hope that I am a role model to you. I see love in your eyes... Don't let what happened in your childhood influence your future. Find a way to forgive your mother so you can fully open your heart to Gabriella. She's a one-of-a-kind woman, and you'd be crazy to let her slip away. Goodnight, son." And with that, Alistair slipped out of the room.

Ashton sat staring at the fireplace, rehashing Alistair's

words. He knew he needed to forgive his mother, but could he forget what she'd done to him? She'd sent him away from the only home he'd ever known. And when he returned on those rare occasions, his home hadn't felt like home. And he'd never felt the supposed love that his mother had had for him.

Ashton threw down the last of his brandy. He felt the burn as it hit his stomach. Could he forgive his mother? Could he really love Gabriella like she needed and deserved to be loved when he really didn't know how to do that? He needed to answer these questions before he could move on with his life. Ashton stared into the flames. His last thoughts were of Gabriella when sleep overcame him for the night.

Chapter Thirty-Two

GABRIELLA DIDN'T KNOW WHAT HAPPENED, but she overslept for the first time in she couldn't remember when. She showered and made her way down to the kitchen where, as promised, Alistair had a pot of coffee waiting in a thermos on the table. He'd left a note for her.

> *Sorry I missed you. I had to run to the store. Ashton left early this morning for the resort. He'll call you later. The sweet rolls are under the dome on the counter. Thanks for the treat—they were great. I'll be back by noon.*
> *Alistair*

Gabriella poured herself a cup of coffee and headed off to the library. It was almost ten. She wasn't hungry and decided to hold off on eating her sweet roll. She strolled into the library and walked over to the french doors that led out onto the balcony. It looked like a beautiful day. She opened the doors and walked out onto the balcony, taking in the scenery. She'd never been to the estate during the spring or summer months, so she imagined how the gardens looked when green and full of blooming roses and the multitude of flowers that she was sure grew there. She took a deep breath, taking in the fresh air, and returned to the library. It was her last day, and she still needed to discover who Eloise was.

Gabriella ran her fingers along the volumes of books that lined the shelves. It was filled with historical novels, biographies, autobiographies. She decided to rid the shelves of the more current releases, keeping the older volumes of books that may have stemmed back a hundred years or more. Alistair had left her some boxes, so she carefully pulled the books from the shelves. She thumbed through them, making sure there were no notes or money, as she knew her own grandmother had hidden money in her books after being burglarized several times.

She discovered nothing but bookmarks made out of pieces of paper, gum wrappers, and whatever else could be found to mark a page. She packed up ten boxes of books and then returned to Jana's bedroom. There were another twenty shelves that she needed to go through, and then she'd be done.

Gabriella completed going through almost all of the books in Jana's bedroom, and she only had three shelves remaining. That's when her eye caught a book on Branson's Table Rock Lake. She became engrossed with the history behind the lake. She looked at her watch, realizing too much time had passed. She wanted to complete boxing Jana's books before Ashton returned.

She remembered that Alistair had told her that he'd left several boxes in Jana's closet, so she made her way back there. She hadn't been in there since she'd finished cleaning it out several days ago. Since it was pretty much empty now, except for a few boxes and some of the more lavish dresses, she was able to really take in the room.

As she walked to the back of the closet, she noticed a hanger had fallen onto the carpet. As she picked it up, the tip caught on the carpet. She lost her balance and knocked into the wall. And that's when she saw it—in the middle of the solid wall, she noticed a small slit. She hadn't noticed it before because this particular area of the closet had been lined with Jana's formalwear.

Gabriella wasn't sure what she was looking at. She began to run her hand along the wall, hoping to find something, anything that would open what she assumed was a false door that possibly led to a wall safe. She pushed on all parts of the wall, moving above and below what she thought was a door. She'd almost given up, thinking she was imagining it all, when she noticed a small button. It was maybe a quarter of an inch in diameter. *What the hell*, she thought. *I'm going to push it.*

Gabriella pushed the button, and to her amazement, not only was there a hidden door, but the whole wall moved. Behind it stood a small room. It must be a safe room. Gabriella felt along the wall and discovered a wall switch. She flipped the switch and light filled the room.

It was about the size of her guest bedroom at home. The room was ten, maybe twelve, square feet. A large desk sat against the wall. Several filing cabinets stood in one corner. It was an organized and clean room. She approached the desk, unsure of what she would find. She hoped her answers were somewhere hidden in either the desk drawers or the wooden filing cabinets.

Gabriella was immediately drawn to the filing cabinets. As she pulled out each drawer, she discovered the cabinets contained files regarding the resort—the initial purchase of the land, the building plans and specs, upgrades, and anything that had been done structurally over the years. There were files for each and every vendor that the resort had done business with. Gabriella surmised this was a back-up storage facility that Ian may have used to store important information regarding the resort and his various businesses.

She perused each of the cabinets and then sat down at the desk. She was disappointed. She thought she'd find her answers. This had probably been her last hope of discovering who Eloise was.

She opened each of the desk drawers. They were filled with office supplies and various files for the managing of the house. She found a set of keys, and she could only wonder at what they were made for. She found various landscape plans for the gardens and knew exactly what had once been planted, between peonies that would flower in the spring, to roses, lilac trees, and bushes. It was extensive, and as she sat staring at the plans, she could only imagine how beautiful the gardens were during the summer.

Just as Gabriella was ready to give up and call it a day, she pulled out the last desk drawer. The large middle drawer was filled with various papers that surprisingly were not organized and contained in separate files. As the rummaged through the papers, her hand hit something in the back of the drawer. She reached in and pulled out a small locked metal box that was approximately the size of a small notebook and maybe two inches high.

She remembered the key ring that she'd come across earlier, but she couldn't remember which drawer they were in. In her excitement to find the keys, she accidentally pulled out one of the drawers and the contents spilled all over the floor. As she searched through the fallen mess on the floor, she saw the keys. Grabbing them, she tried each and every key. And of course, the last key she tried opened the box.

She opened it and it was filled with photo after photo. As she pulled them out, she realized she was seeing Ashton's childhood. His preschool graduation photo with what she imagined was a self-made mortarboard that he wore precariously atop his head. In the photograph, the mortarboard sat askew on Ashton's head. But what stood out more than the mortarboard was the huge smile that shone on his face. He was happy in this photo. She wondered if he even remembered the day.

Gabriella felt the love that Jana had for her son through each photo. Many were taken at a distance. More than likely he hadn't been aware of her presence, but she had proof that Jana had been at all of the events that she'd discovered the programs for. She needed to share all of this with Ashton. But how? When?

She pulled the last of the photos out of the box and lying in the bottom of the cold, metal box was another journal. She pulled it out, clutching it to her chest. She prayed that she'd found her answers.

Gabriella looked at her watch. It was almost noon and she didn't know if Alistair knew about this room and its contents. She grabbed the box, shoving the photographs and the journal back in. She picked up what had fallen onto the floor and turned off the light.

She wasn't sure how to close the room back up so she returned to the button on the wall and pushed it. Much to her amazement, it worked. She watched the room disappear and the closet wall reappear.

She hurried back to her room. She stored the metal box in her luggage and returned to Jana's bedroom to tackle the boxing of the remaining books. She'd been in there less than five minutes when Ashton appeared. She took a huge breath when she saw him. She was thankful that she'd stopped searching the room when she had.

"Gabby, here you are. I've been searching all over for you. I was in here a few minutes ago and didn't see you. Where were you?"

"I've been here all along. Maybe I was in the closet getting one of the boxes Alistair had left for me." Gabriella pointed to the shelves and quickly contin- ued. "This is the last of it. I've gone through and boxed up the books that I thought you'd want to get rid of in the library. I left the historicals and those that looked like they could be of value."

Ashton approached her, reaching for her hand. He led her to the settee where he urged her to sit down. "I can't believe all that you've accomplished this week. You did all of the hard work while I played."

"I hardly call going into the resort and handling business matters *playing*. Your work was different than mine, I must say, but I also got to know a little bit about your mother. I got a peek into her life. She certainly had a flair for fashion and she loved to read. I think I would have liked her."

Ashton glared at her. "I don't know how you can say that. But I don't want to talk about her. I want to talk about us. I'm giving you ten minutes to get yourself together, and I'm taking you out."

"But I want to finish up in here."

"You can do that when we come back. I want to have a little fun before we have to return home." He leaned in and kissed her, then jumped off the settee. "Ten minutes in the foyer. If you're not there, I'll come looking for you and you won't want to see what I have in mind."

"Get your mind out of the gutter. I'll be there," she said as she hurried off to her room. Gabriella made her way to her room, thanking her lucky stars the entire way that she'd returned to Jana's room when she had. Right now, she didn't want Ashton to discover her findings. She needed to go through the box she'd found and hopefully pass on additional information to Jonas. She was way too deep into this investigation. She wanted to have her answers before sharing her discoveries with Ashton. If she shared her findings right now, she was afraid she'd lose him and that he wouldn't believe her. She hurriedly grabbed her purse, combed her hair, and tore down the hallway towards Ashton. She didn't want to be late because she really wasn't in the mood to discover what he had in store for her.

Gabriella was a few minutes late and caught Ashton on the stairs, making his way towards her bedroom.

"You're late."

"No, I'm not. I'm right here, exactly where I need to be." She laughed as she raced past him on the stairs. Alistair was waiting for them at the bottom of the stairs with a picnic basket in hand. "Alistair, what's this?"

"Your lunch." She reached for the basket but he pulled it away, hiding it behind his back.

"Can't you wait, Gab-ri-ella? It's a surprise."

"Ashton, you know I hate it when you say my name

that way."

"I know you do, and I love your reaction every time I say it—Gab-ri-ella." He reached for the basket that Alistair was protecting and turned to Gabriella. "Ready?" he asked.

"As ready as I'll ever be," she huffed as she reached for his hand. She turned back to Alistair with a smile on her face. "Thanks for lunch, Alistair."

"Have a wonderful time you two," Alistair called out as he closed the front door.

Ashton wouldn't tell her where he was taking her. He termed it as 'an undisclosed location' as he reached for her hand. He squeezed it lightly as he drove down one of the back roads and headed off towards somewhere.

He was driving down roads she had never been on before. He'd turned right out of the driveway and then wound around the outskirts of the city. And then she saw it—Table Rock Lake. The state park bordered the northeast shoreline of beautiful Table Rock Lake. As they pulled through the entrance, she noticed the park offered more amenities than she could read as Ashton passed the signage. She could tell he knew where he was going as he drove down one road and then another. The next thing she knew, they were at a picnic site that overlooked the lake.

"This is beautiful," Gabriella said as she started to get out of the car. She took in the huge oak and hickory trees that surrounded her. "I paged through a couple of Jana's books and learned a little bit about Table Rock Lake. Did you know that the lake covers something like fifty thousand acres and is surrounded by a shoreline that's eight hundred miles? From what I read, the water is 'as smooth as glass,' and it's a prime place for skin divers." She walked to the edge of the overlook.

"I got so engrossed in the book, and I learned so much. I discovered that the Table Rock Dam was built in the 1950s across the White River. It was built to control flooding and generate hydroelectric power. The lake was named Table Rock because of a rock shelf that stands downstream from the dam. The lake winds its way through the Ozark Mountains of Missouri and Arkansas. Can you believe this lake is in two states? That just boggles my mind."

Ashton joined her and listened as she spouted the history of the lake. "No, I had no idea about anything you just said." He chuckled. "I can understand why you're such a great teacher. You sure can tell a good story…"

"I can't believe you're making fun of me."

"I'm not making fun of you. I just enjoyed the history lesson. Come on, let's take a walk and have our picnic." He reached for her hand and led her down a trail that lined the shoreline. He picked up a rock and skipped it across the waters. It was a beautiful day and by the time they made it back to their car, she was starved.

"Let's eat," she called. "I'm starved." Ashton pulled the picnic basket from the car and carried it to one of the tables that overlooked the lake. He opened it, pulling out sandwiches, chips, vegetables, and huge chocolate chip cookies.

"Alistair did a good job with his selections." She pointed to the cookie. "I love these cookies. His are the best."

They sat lakeside, soaking in the breeze. It was a lovely spring day. "I can't believe break is already over. Thanks for asking me to join you."

Ashton took a bite of his chicken salad sandwich.

"I love this area. It's been awhile since I've traveled to the Ozark's outside of when your mom first got sick and all. It's nice to see what Missouri has to offer."

"Yeah, I guess we take it for granted. We should come down more often, explore the lakes, go boating, hiking. We should do it all."

They finished up their lunch and watched the water lap around the edges of the shore. It was peaceful. She got wrapped up in her thoughts—thinking about the metal box that she'd found right before Ashton came home. She couldn't wait to get back to the house and dig into the journal.

"Gabby... Gabby... Gab-ri-ella," Ashton called.

The use of that nickname jarred her out of her head. "Did you say something?"

"I called your name three times. Where were you? You definitely weren't here with me."

"I was just thinking about the week, that's all."

Ashton stood and gathered their trash, throwing it away, then sat beside her at the table. He reached for her hand and clasped the side of her face. "I don't know what I would have done without you this week. Thank you for going through my mother's things. I didn't want Alistair to have to do it."

"Oh, it's not a problem. As I said, I liked looking into her life. I learned quite a deal about her. This wasn't how I originally intended on spending my spring break, but this was definitely more fun than what I had planned. And I got to go back to Silver Dollar City, which was a blast from the past. And today... today was a beautiful way to end our trip."

"Yeah, it's been a gorgeous day. We were lucky with the weather, especially this time of year." He looked away and then adopted a more serious tone. "Gabby, I just want to say… I…"

"Yes?"

"I know I've told you this before, but I need to tell you again. You're extremely important to me. I'm glad you were able to set aside your initial thoughts about me, and I just wanted to say that…"

Ashton became speechless and couldn't formulate what he really wanted to share with her. He believed he loved her but couldn't find the words to actually tell her. Maybe he wasn't ready to say the three words that would change the direction of their relationship.

"Ashton? You just stopped mid-sentence."

"Huh? Oh yeah, sorry about that. I—I just wanted to thank you, that's all."

"Well, you're welcome." She thought there was more going on with him. She decided not to press him. If he wanted her to know what was going on in his mind, she believed he'd eventually tell her. They looked out at the lake until the breeze started to pick up and the air started to chill. "Let's get going."

"Good idea. I'm starting to get a little cold."

Ashton grabbed the picnic basket and Gabriella's hand and led her back to the car. He took his time as they left the park, driving around so she could see the lake from different angles. They made it back to the house in the late afternoon. Gabriella finished going through and packing up the remaining books in Jana's bedroom. They shared a delicious meal that Alistair had prepared. "You know, Alistair, we didn't share the cooking responsibilities. Next time, I'm doing all of the cooking—no arguments. Got it?"

He laughed as she pointed her finger at him.

"I hope Ashton brings me back during the summer when we can enjoy the gardens," she said, smiling at Ashton. He smiled back.

Gabriella helped Alistair clean up, and then she made her way to her bedroom to pack her things. Ashton wanted to leave by mid-morning so they could get back early enough to get ready for the coming week.

She threw her clothes into her suitcase, not caring if they were rumpled or not. Her focus was on reading the journal. She locked her door and sat down on the window bench. She rifled through the journal, speed-reading to see if she could catch Eloise's full name. She'd barely made it halfway through the journal when she found it—not only Eloise's first name, but also her last. Jana wrote:

> *Things have been going better of late. Ian's been paying more attention to me lately. We actually went out for no reason a couple of nights ago. I felt happier than I have in a long time. Yesterday, I even got to go to one of Ashton's school functions. I had to dress incognito, of course. At one point during his performance, he caught my eye and smiled at me. I know he didn't know it was me, but just seeing him smile brought tears to my eyes.*
>
> *And then, I returned home. The happiness and sense of elation I felt was sucked right out of me. Ian wasn't aware I was home and then I heard him on the phone. I hid just outside the doorway listening to his conversation. I wasn't sure who he was talking to. And then, I heard the name that had been absent from my thoughts for ages.*

"Damn it, I told you where she was. Find her."
There was a pause as Ian listened intently to who-
ever was on the other end of the phone. And then
I heard the name. "I told you Eloise is in Okla-
homa City. Can't you get anything straight, or do
I need to hire someone else? Eloise Hightower is
there, now find her!" And then I knew. I finally
knew the last name that had eluded me all these
years. Hightower.

Her name was Eloise Hightower.

Gabriella jumped up from the window seat and ran for her phone. She couldn't call Jonas because she didn't want Ashton or Alistair to overhear her conversation, so she texted him instead.

HIGHTOWER. JONAS, ELOISE'S LAST
NAME IS HIGHTOWER. I'LL PHONE YOU
TOMORROW WHEN I GET BACK IN TOWN.

She had barely finished her message when she got a reply.

GOT IT, the message said. *I'M RIGHT ON IT.*

She breathed a sigh of relief. She now knew Eloise's name. Maybe she could bring this long sordid story to its conclusion. She could only hope.

Ashton dropped Gabriella off at her house by mid-afternoon. The first thing she did was phone Jonas. "I'm home. Did you find anything?"

"Not yet. Gabriella, you just texted me her name

last night. I'm working on it, but it may take me some time. Just be patient."

Gabriella lacked patience, and every day that went by added to her anxiousness. Every time her phone rang, she thought it was Jonas with some news. Days turned into weeks and he still didn't have any news as to who Eloise Hightower was. Every time Jonas thought he was onto something, it turned into a dead end.

Ashton came by late Wednesday evening on the way home from the clinic. It was the middle of April and that weekend was the opening to the Rivermen season. They'd started on the road and hadn't lost a game since opening day. She hadn't expected him, so his visit definitely took her by surprise. Since returning from Branson, they'd seen little of one another. He'd been on call with the clinic and she'd been busy helping Angelina and Kelly. Since marrying Alec, Kelly had been redecorating Alec's home. Between painting and reorganizing furniture, Gabriella hadn't really been home for the last several weekends.

"It feels like forever since I last saw you," Ashton said as he pulled her into his arms, kissing her soundly on the lips. He released her and moved into the family room. "Have you finished up your redecorating project? Alec's been telling me all about it."

"We're close. We're taking the weekend off because Alec and Kelly have tickets to the Rivermen's opening day."

"Speaking of opening day," Ashton said, "So do you and I, along with Alejandro and Matthew."

"What do you mean?"

"Remember the silent auction at Trivia Night?"

She nodded.

"Well, I won four tickets to opening day. I just came from seeing Matthew, and he's more that stoked to go. I've never seen anyone get as excited as he does when it comes to baseball."

"It is his favorite sport. You really want to take me after what happened the last time we went to a Rivermen's game?" Gabriella teased.

Ashton chuckled, "Yeah, I'm sure. Just forget the tote bag and peanuts. And it's definitely not going to be warm enough, so you can forget the fan, too."

"I don't know about forgetting the peanuts. A baseball game isn't the same without freshly shelled peanuts."

"Okay, you can have your peanuts." He toyed with a strand of her hair. "I can't stay now, though. I've got to run by the hospital. I'll pick you up at nine Saturday morning," he said as he leaned in to kiss her goodbye.

"Nine? Why so early?"

"There's a lot going on that day, and Matthew can't miss one minute." She laughed as he made his way down her sidewalk. She was looking forward to the start of baseball season.

Saturday came and Ashton promptly rang her doorbell at nine with a cup of coffee in hand. "Yours is in the car," he said, lifting his hand. "Grab your stuff and let's get going. Matthew and Alejandro are already in the car."

Gabriella joined Matthew in the backseat. Matthew was gushing with excitement. From the moment she got into the car, Matthew talked nonstop. He recited who he thought would be in the starting lineup for both teams. When he was through naming players, he moved on to the various festivities that were being held in honor of opening day.

After that, he about fell off his seat in excitement when he went into explicit details about all of the new food choices available at the ballpark this year. Gabriella was exhausted listening to him. At one point, she told him to stop and take a breath since he was talking so much.

Alejandro laughed. She was sure her brother had been listening to these details nonstop for days. She was overjoyed when they pulled into the parking garage. Now maybe Matthew would settle down since he could partake in the activities.

They were one of the first to enter the stadium and they enjoyed all of the pregame festivities. They located their seats and almost immediately she grabbed her bag of peanuts. Before she had the chance to break open the bag, Ashton grabbed it from her. "Let me open it. I don't want peanuts exploding all over everyone," he said, chuckling.

Ashton pulled the edges of the bag. The harder he pulled the more he scrunched his face. And then, true to form, the bag split open, peanuts flying everywhere.

"And you thought you could do better than me? Ha, see it's not as easy as you think."

"Then you should have opened it before we came."

"You always have a comeback, don't you?" she laughed.

By the time the fifth inning came around, they'd eaten nearly all the peanuts. There was a small break in the game, and Gabriella watched the jumbo screens while they waited. Cameras panned across the stadium, searching for the perfect couples to kiss on camera. At that moment, though, she felt her phone vibrate—it was a text from Jonas.

I found her.

Also at that moment, she heard Matthew yell, "Gabriella, kiss Ashton!"

She looked up at him, but then she caught sight of herself and Ashton on the jumbo screens. She smiled and leaned over, capturing Ashton in a kiss for all to see.

"Wow, that was sure a kiss," Alejandro called over to her.

"Well, I'm happy," she called back. She was happy to be with Ashton, but she was even happier that Jonas had found Eloise Hightower. Gabriella couldn't wait to phone Jonas. She jumped up from her seat, claiming she had to use the restroom. She ran from the stands with phone in hand.

Her phone had barely connected when she was joined by Alejandro. "What's up with you? I thought you had to use the restroom."

"I do, but I have to return a call first."

"Gabby, what's going on here?"

Her brother knew her too well. "Nothing, why?"

"I know you too well, dear sister. I just hope you haven't gone and done something that you'll regret."

"Never," she claimed as she headed off to the restroom. Alejandro could always tell by a certain look she got that she'd said or done something that had repercussions. She couldn't tell him about Jonas. And as far as she knew, Alec hadn't shared her secret with anyone. She decided to hold off phoning Jonas until she got home. She couldn't let her excitement overshadow the fact the she needed extreme privacy when she spoke with him.

The Rivermen handily won the game. Ashton suggested they stop on the way home for a snack, but Alejandro begged off because Angelina was making a special dinner. Ashton glanced in the rearview mirror at Gabriella.

"I'd love to, but I have a lot of papers to grade."

Ashton didn't seem to think anything of her excuse.

Gabriella said her goodbye as Ashton dropped her off first. She couldn't wait to get inside to phone Jonas. She'd barely made it through her entryway when she hit send on her call.

"Sorry it took me so long, but I was at the Rivermen game…"

Jonas went on to explain why it took him so long to locate Eloise. "Gabriella, I've spent so much time focusing my efforts on Oklahoma City when, in fact, she lives in Kansas City. She was in Oklahoma City for a short time, then moved onto Kansas City where she gave birth to a son named Duncan."

"Ashton has a brother," she breathed.

"From what I can tell after Duncan's birth, she married a man named Albert Eberle and then, in time, had a daughter named Sarah."

The fact that Ashton had a brother was all she could focus on. She continued to listen to Jonas. She was in shock and couldn't find her words.

"And you'll never believe who Albert is related to."

"Who?"

"Sadie Eberle."

Gabriella had no idea who Sadie Eberle was. "I don't know who that is."

"Sure you do."

And then it dawned on her. "You mean Sadie Eberle, as in Nurse Sadie from my dad's clinic?" she asked incredulously.

"She's one and the same. Albert and Sadie's husband Lawrence are brothers."

"You've got to be kidding me. Do you know where Duncan is? Is he related to Ashton? Is he his half-brother?"

"I'm not sure. I haven't gotten that far. I believe his last name is Hightower, but I'm still working on that."

"You've got to find him, Jonas. This is big... huge. I can't tell Ashton until you know for sure."

"I know, and I'm working as fast as I can."

Gabriella ended the call and sat down on her couch in utter shock. Ashton had a brother, she was sure of it. How would she tell him about Duncan and everything else she'd uncovered while in Branson?

Gabriella had developed a headache over the call. She couldn't grade papers now. She needed to talk to the only person that knew about her investigation—Alec.

She didn't think about her next moves. She grabbed her car keys and flew out the door. She prayed Alec would be home when she got there. She needed to tell him her news, and if Kelly overheard their conversation, so be it. She needed to put an end to this mystery soon and she couldn't do it without Alec's help.

Chapter Thirty-Three

G ABRIELLA ARRIVED AT ALEC'S AND discovered the he was, in fact, alone. Kelly and Alec had also attended the opener but had left the game early so Kelly could go shopping. "Sis, I thought you were at the game. What's up?"

"He found her."

"What are you talking about?"

"Jonas. He found Eloise, and you'll never believe it."

"Believe what?"

"She's married to Sadie's brother-in-law."

"Sadie? As in Sadie Eberle that works for me?"

"Yep. Can you call that coincidence or what?"

Alec led Gabriella into the kitchen where he grabbed each of them a bottle of water. She sat down at the table and unscrewed her water bottle. Fiddling with the cap, she began, "Alec what are we going to do? Ashton has no idea. When Eloise left Branson, she was pregnant and had a son. A son named Duncan. Jonas is trying to verify if his last name is Hightower or maybe even Eberle. Apparently Eloise also had a child by Albert, too."

"Yeah, her name is Sarah and she wants to go to nursing school. I hope to hire her at the clinic when she graduates, but that's going to be a few years down the road. She's Wyatt's age, I believe."

"Small world, isn't it?"

Kelly walked into the room then, carrying many shopping bags. "Hey, Gabby. What are you talking about? What a small world?"

"Hey honey, when did you get home?" Alec said, glancing quickly at Gabriella.

"Just now. And before you try and cover up your conversation, I heard it all. What's this about Ashton?"

Gabriella had done everything in her power to keep this a secret, but now Kelly knew about it. She couldn't lie to her, so she told her all about Ashton and his childhood.

"Kelly, you've got to promise me that you won't tell anyone." Gabriella pleaded with her.

"Gabby, who would I tell? I don't really run in Ashton's circle. Your secret's safe with me."

Gabriella jumped up, hugging Kelly. "Now, I have to figure out a way to break this to Ashton. I'm not sure how he's going to take the news." The three of them sat around the table, discussing Ashton and how his childhood shaped him into the man he was today. She decided she needed to get her thoughts together and figure out how she was going to share it all with him. She thanked Alec and Kelly for listening to her and then drove straight home.

Gabriella thought non-stop about Ashton, about his mother, possible half-brother, and how she could turn him around and make him understand that his mother had done what she did to protect him. That she loved him until the day she died.

She was obsessed with checking her phone for text messages from Jonas. In fact, one night when she and Ashton were taking a hike at Pieres Park in late April, he addressed his concern with her. "What's up with you and your phone? It seems like every five minutes you're checking it for a text or something. Is there someone else in this picture other than me?"

She drew in her highbrows. "What are you talking about?"

"Every time we've been together since the Rivermen home opener, I feel like you're more concerned with your phone than you are with me. I'll be talking to you and you zone out, grab your phone, and... Gabby, what's going on?"

"Nothing. I'm sorry. I guess it's just become habit. You know how we all are these days. Everyone is consumed by social media. In fact, let's share a selfie of us as we hike. I can post it out to everyone."

"No thanks," he stated as he walked away from her, continuing their hike.

"Ashton, wait up," she called as she ran after him. She grabbed onto his forearm, attempting to stop his advance, but he just continued. "I'm sorry, I'll be better. I promise." She called after him, "See, look! I'm turning off my phone. I want to be with you. Honestly, I do." Gabriella didn't want to share with him her discovery until she had all of the facts. She wanted to be able to answer any and all of his questions. She felt bad about keeping this from him, but decided to take the chance that he wouldn't find out what she was up to until she shared the news with him. He abruptly stopped and waited for her to join him. She ran to him, and as she stopped, her feet slid on the path. "Whoa," she called out, grabbing his sleeve.

"What did I tell you weeks ago? You need a new pair of boots. Look at the condition of them. The stitching is fraying and the soles look like they're worn."

"I know, I just haven't had time. I promise I'll get another pair soon." She grabbed ahold of his hand and they continued on their hike. They decided to take a break and sat at a table that looked out over St. Louis County. It was a breathtaking view.

"So, when does school let out?"

"We've got about three weeks left. We get out the Friday before Memorial Day. I can't wait. This has been such a trying year. This year's gotten better since September, but I still feel like I've aged a hundred years. I'm looking forward to summer and just relaxing—doing nothing to speak of."

"Do you have any vacation plans?"

"No. Angelina and I try and take day trips with the kids, but other than that nothing really. Why?"

"I'd like to go back to Branson. I need to check in on Alistair, and of course, I need to attend at least one of the manager meetings at the resort. I normally skype in for the meetings, but I'd like to attend several in person this summer, if possible. And I'd like you to go with me. That is, if you want to."

"Of course I do. I want to see Alistair, too."

"I'll let you know the dates and we'll schedule it. We're still on half-days on Fridays, so I'm going to schedule a couple of full days off and we can leave on Thursday evenings. We'll get in late, but we'll still have almost three days. How does that sound?"

"Fantastic. Just let me know," she said leaning in and

hugging his side. "Maybe we can go back to the lake and take out a boat. That would be a lot of fun."

"Sure thing. I'll make sure Alistair has the boat tuned up and put in the water this year. I haven't taken it out in I can't remember when."

"You have a boat?"

"I do." He grabbed her hand and started back down the trail. It was getting late and she had school the following day.

As the days passed, Gabriella's anxiousness continued to grow. She was disappointed as Jonas still didn't have the answers she needed. Gabriella had done a lot of thinking. She'd planned a barbeque with Ashton for Memorial Day weekend and that's when she hoped to tell him about Duncan, and also share with him that she'd done this all because she loved him. She hoped Jonas came through with her answers because she wanted this holiday to be a memorable one for them.

Memorial Day weekend was upon them. Alec had invited everyone over for a barbeque. Since he'd become engaged, Alejandro had a Fourth of July party at his house every year. Now that Alec and Kelly were married, Alec wanted to start a tradition of their own, so he decided they'd kick off the summer with an annual Memorial Day party. Everyone was invited to the party that started at noon. Ben and Jackie, Wyatt and Colleen, even James, Kelly and Angelina's brother, would be able to attend since Memorial Day was a bank holiday. The entire Alvarez clan was in attendance, as was everyone from the clinic. Kelly had even invited Melanie and Janet Holmes from trivia night.

When Gabriella and Ashton pulled up to Alec's, she

saw Sadie and Lawrence walking to the door. She gasped. She'd stayed away from Sadie since she'd learned of her relationship with Eloise. She was still waiting for Jonas's confirmation on if Duncan's last name was indeed Hightower or Eberle—not that it mattered what his last name was, but for some reason, it did to her. She didn't understood what was taking him so long, but she learned from Alec that sometimes finding the truth took time and she needed patience. Jonas was the best and he'd discover the truth.

"What's wrong?" Ashton asked.

"Nothing," she said quickly.

"You just seemed—"

"Come on let's get going. I don't want to be the last to arrive," she said, halting any further questions.

He raised his eyebrows and looked at the cars in the driveway. Ashton shook his head. "Hardly anyone's here. I don't think we're the last to arrive. From what Alec told me, Kelly invited a crowd, and from what I see by the number of cars already here, this is not a crowd."

Gabriella gave him one of her looks and opened the car door. "I'm heading on in and you can be the last to arrive." Ashton shook his head again. He opened his door and reached her side just as she was ringing the doorbell.

Angelina opened the door for them. "You should have just come on in—you didn't have to ring the bell. You know how we all are when we have these parties."

"I know, I forgot," she claimed as she walked through the door.

Gabriella heard Ashton talk to Angelina behind her. "I don't know what's up with her. She seems a little upset today."

Ashton made his way into the kitchen where all the ladies seemed to gather. Ben and John were chatting on the patio, babysitting the gas grill while Alejandro and Matthew were tossing the ball in the backyard. Ashton said his hellos as he made his way outside, right to Alec's side while he poured ice into the coolers.

"Need some help there?" he inquired as he held the lid to the cooler.

"Nah, I'm good." Alec peered at Ashton. "What's up with you? Is my sister getting under your skin again?"

Ashton glanced quickly at Alec. "How'd you know?"

"I've gotten to know your facial expressions pretty well. So, what's up?"

"I don't know. She just seems to be... Withdrawn? No, withdrawn's not the word. Maybe preoccupied? Lately every time we go out, she spends more time paying attention to her damn phone than to me. She blames it on keeping up with social media, but I don't buy that excuse. I asked her if there was someone else in the picture, and she adamantly said no. I just don't know what to believe with her. Today, when she saw Sadie and Lawrence walking in, it seemed like she didn't want to see them. Gabby loves seeing Sadie. I haven't a clue what's going on with her, but she won't talk to me."

"She can be that way sometimes. Forget about it for today, and let's have a good time."

Ashton nodded, got involved with grilling, and forgot about Gabriella's earlier behavior. He wanted today to be a memorable one as he'd decided to tell her how he felt about her.

When it came time to eat, he filled his plate and sat beside her. He took one look at her plate and knew something was wrong. She had a few celery sticks and a couple pieces of cheese. "Is that all you're eating?"

She glanced at him but didn't say anything. He was concerned. "Are you feeling alright? You seem a little pale."

"I'm just fine."

He looked at her more closely and noticed that her eyes kept flitting to Lawrence and Sadie.

"Is there something going on with you and Sadie? You seem upset by her presence."

"No, nothing's wrong."

"What's going on then? You seem so distant. Did I do something to upset you?"

"No, it's not you. It's me," and with that, she jumped up from her seat. Ashton watched her as she walked inside. He knew something was going on with her. What, he didn't know—he just hoped he hadn't done something to cause her to turn away.

Alec and Kelly had yard games that everyone seemed to enjoy. In fact, they went all out purchasing a huge Scrabble game. The game board had to measure at least six feet square and had big letter tiles and holders that came with it. They also had giant dominoes and a washer set. Ashton had never seen outdoor games this size. "Where did you find this Scrabble set? It's huge!"

"Oh, I found it online on an outdoor games website. I was amazed at what games are available. There's even a giant Twister and an outdoor chess set where the pieces are like two feet high. I thought everyone would enjoy these, and maybe next year I'll add to what we have. I'm sure Alec will kill me for it, but as long as we take care of them they'll last forever."

Ashton realized he hadn't seen Gabriella since she'd

run into the house after he'd questioned her. Maybe she wasn't feeling well, so he decided to check on her. Ashton meandered through the crowd, making his way inside. She wasn't in the kitchen. He called out her name, but there was no answer. He decided to see if she was possibly resting, so he made his way towards the family room. He heard her voice and decided to turn away. If she was having a conversation, he didn't want to interrupt. And then he heard his name. *Who's she talking to about me?* He froze and listened. And then he wished he hadn't.

"I heard what you said, Jonas. I know I have to tell Ashton."

Who is this Jonas and what does she have to tell me?

"I've got to tell him sooner rather than later. I understand. Yes, I will. Today? No, I can't today. He's not going to understand why I did it."

What aren't I going to understand? What does she need to tell me? He couldn't listen any longer. He rushed out of the house, practically knocking James over in the process.

"Hey there, Ashton. Is everything okay?"

Was everything okay? No it wasn't. He was sure his life was falling apart right before his eyes. The woman whom he was going to tell he loved this weekend wasn't who he thought she was. She was cheating on him. He had to get out of there.

"Ah, James. Something came up. Can you tell Gabriella that I couldn't find her, and I had to leave? Do you think you can take her home for me?"

"Sure thing. I hope everything's alright."

"Yeah, it will be. Thanks."

Ashton jumped into his car and left the party. He didn't know where he was going, but just started to

drive. He knew he should've never gotten in this deep
with her. He knew that he should never have fallen
in love and what did he do—just that. He was jinxed.
His parents' marriage failed and he knew he should've
never contemplated it for himself. He'd learned a lesson from his parents, but he'd hoped things would be
different for him. But they weren't, were they?

Gabriella finished up her conversation with Jonas.
He'd discovered Duncan's last name. It was Hightower
and he lived in St. Louis. Jonas discovered that Eloise and Albert moved to St. Louis when Duncan was
five years old. Sarah, his sister, was ten years younger
than he was. Duncan was now twenty-four and had a
degree in hospitality management. According to Jonas,
he was brilliant and had graduated high school at sixteen. He'd flown through college and already had his
master's degree.   He was working at one of the area
hotels as an assistant manager.

After she ended her call with Jonas, she sat alone in
Alec's family room, pondering her next steps. She was
a little overwhelmed with everything she'd learned.
She was thankful that school was over for the year. She
had to turn in her grades on Tuesday, put a few things
away in her classroom, and then she was done for the
summer. She sat there longer than she thought and
heard her name called.

"Oh Gabby, here you are," Janet said. "I wanted to
say goodbye, and I'll see you on Tuesday. I hope you
enjoy the rest of your weekend."

Janet pulled her out of her fog. "Oh Janet, I'm sorry
I didn't spend more time with you. I hope you had a

good time."

"Don't worry about me—I had a blast. I love your mother. She's so kind. And your nephew Matthew kept me in stitches talking about the Rivermen."

"That's his team for sure. I'll walk you out." Gabriella and Janet caught up with Melanie in the kitchen. They chatted a few more minutes before the sisters left. Gabriella hung out in the kitchen with the girls while all the men were outside having their own conversation.

It was starting to get late and almost everyone was getting ready to leave. James caught up with Gabriella. "Are you ready to go?"

"Ah, I think so. I just need to find Ashton. I haven't seen him in a while."

"Gabby, he left well over an hour ago. I thought you knew. He asked me to take you home."

Gabriella was shocked but said, "Oh, that's right. I thought he might have made it back before I left. He said he was coming back." She laughed off her misunderstanding. She didn't want anyone to know he left her without telling her he was leaving.

"Well, if you're ready, let's go."

She said her goodbyes to everyone and left with James. Gabriella hadn't had the chance to socialize with James in quite some time. In fact, she hadn't seen him since Angel's baptism. "Thanks, James, for taking me home. I really appreciate it. It gives us a chance to catch up."

"It's been awhile, hasn't it?"

"It has. How are things going at the bank?"

"Busy. We've had one acquisition after another. I've been on the road so much lately I don't know whether I'm coming or going."

"I get that. Did you get a chance to talk to Melanie Holmes? She's Janet's sister and also works in banking. I'm not sure what she does, but I know she travels a lot, too."

"Yeah, I saw her. We've crossed paths before."

"Well, that doesn't sound too good. I really like her."

"Let me just say, she's pretty ruthless. And that's all I'll say on the subject. Of course, I've met Janet before when Angelina had one of her parties. She seems pretty easy going…"

Gabriella listened as James spoke about the Holmes sisters. She gathered he didn't have warm feelings about Melanie. She wondered what happened, but didn't want to press the issue.

"Thanks again for the ride, James," she said as they pulled into her driveway.

"Anytime," he said before she got out and ran up her front steps. Her face hurt from smiling the whole way home. What she wanted to do was run inside and cry. She didn't know what she'd done to cause Ashton to just up and leave her at the party without saying anything. She shook her head. It was late, so she decided to head off to bed.

When Gabriella woke Sunday morning, she checked her cell phone. No missed calls, no messages from Ashton. She waited to call him, hoping he'd phone her instead. When she didn't hear from him by noon, she called him. She dialed his phone so many times that her finger grew tired. She decided to walk by his house and see if he was home and just avoiding her, but when she stopped by, he wasn't there. Where was he? Why wasn't he answering? Maybe something happened to Alistair. It was the only explanation she could think of. She grabbed her cell and phoned him on her way home.

Alistair answered almost immediately and he sounded perfectly fine. She didn't want to cause him concern, so she acted like she was calling just to say hi. In their conversation, Alistair indicated that he hadn't spoken to Ashton in several days. "He asked me to get the boat tuned up and in the water. Are you coming down soon? It'll be good to have someone else running through the house besides me. It's been awfully quiet around here since you and Ashton left."

"I look forward to coming down. Ashton mentioned he has some manager meetings that he wants to attend in person. So, I guess I'll see you whenever they're scheduled."

"I'm looking forward to it. Gabriella, you are good for him. You know it?"

"I hope I am."

Alistair paused. "Is something wrong?"

"Oh no, everything's great. Alec had a party yesterday that we attended. My whole family was there. I think he had a good time."

"Did you?"

"Of course I did," Gabriella tried her best to sound convincing, but she wasn't sure how successful she was. Before Alistair could question her further, she made an excuse, "Oh, someone's at my door. I've got to go. I'll call you soon."

"Thanks for calling, Gabriella. Enjoy the holiday."

She hated lying to Alistair. She wasn't even home. The closer she got to her house, the more troubled she became. She didn't know what she had done wrong, or even if she'd done anything to cause Ashton to walk away from her.

When she got home, she pulled out Jana's purse and

journals. She wanted to re-read them and get her own thoughts together. The next time she saw him, she was going to share with him what she'd uncovered. She had to get it off her shoulders, and hopefully at the end of the day they'd still be a couple.

Gabriella lost track of time. She realized it had grown late when the light dimmed in her kitchen. She looked at the clock and it was almost eight o'clock. She'd hardly eaten anything all day. She was starting to become really concerned about Ashton. She'd continued trying his phone, leaving several messages, none of which he returned. She worried that something had happened to him.

Gabriella decided to take a walk out onto her patio. Her flowers needed watering and she wanted to get some fresh air.

She'd just finished watering the last of her hanging buckets when a shadow crossed her path. She turned and Ashton stood before her. She looked up at him and noticed he was in the same clothes he had on the day before. He also hadn't shaved in well over a day—it was the first time she'd seen him with scruff. He looked beaten down. What had happened to him? Had he been in an accident?

"Ashton, are you okay? I've been so worried. I've called you so many times, I've lost count. I've left message after message. Didn't you get them?"

"I did."

"Is everything okay? Is someone sick? Have you been at the hospital?"

"No."

She was baffled. "Then what's going on?"

"Let's go inside. I don't want to have this discussion out here."

She raised her eyebrows. Why did they have to go inside? Had she done something? Questions kept floating through her mind. Ashton preceded her into the kitchen as she finished putting her hose away.

When she walked through the door, she knew then that everything was going to come to a head. Ashton's eyes narrowed on her, his lips pulled in. He raised his hand. He was holding his mother's journal. "Where did you get this?"

She froze. She didn't know what to say. She took one look at him and could see the pain, anger, and sadness in his eyes. She knew she was in serious trouble.

"Gabriella, I asked you a question." He was eerily quiet, but his hand started shaking. "Where did you get this? This is my mother's, isn't it?"

He suddenly threw the journal down with such force that she felt like she'd been smacked. He got close enough that she felt his hot breath cross her face. His hands were gripped into tight fists. Her heart was beating so quickly, but all she could do was look at him with wide eyes. He raised his hands and she flinched. She'd never seen anyone this angry.

He whirled around and walked stiffly towards the sink. He stood motionless, looking out the window. She didn't know whether to approach him or not. She was shaking and unable to find any words to say. She knew then that she'd messed up, and she didn't know how to make it better.

He looked over his shoulder at her. His jaw was clenched and his eyes shot daggers at her. She could see the pulse pounding in his temple. He took a deep breath, trying to control his anger. "I asked you a question and you have yet to answer me. Why do you have my mother's journal?"

Gabriella opened her mouth, but the words continued to stick in her throat. Earlier in the day, she'd planned out exactly how she'd been going to tell Ashton about her findings, but all of those plans had left her. "Ashton... I..."

"Spit it out, Gabriella. You must have an excellent excuse ready for me."

"I—I brought it home with me when we came home after her funeral."

"You've had this since then? What are you doing with it? It needs to be thrown away." He started to grab it, but she finally found her feet and beat him to it. Clutching it against her chest, she said, "I found the answers you've been looking for."

"Answers? I didn't realize I had any questions." He approached her. "Hand it over. It doesn't belong to you."

She eased her way towards the door. She couldn't let him take the journal from her. "Ashton, I found the answers that will prove to you that your mother loved you."

"Loved me? That's rich." He laughed mirthlessly. "She didn't love me." He followed her closer to the door. "She couldn't wait to get rid of me. She regretted having me. She *told* me so. I know it, and so does everyone else."

"Please, Ashton, you have to listen to me."

His face twisted. "Why would I begin to listen to you? I know you're cheating on me. You're just using me—using me to get to my money." He reached out so quickly that he caught her off guard, yanking the journal from her hands. "Consider this relationship over, if that's even what you want to call it. I'm done—through with you. I never want to see you again. Stay out of my life," he hissed.

She felt tears well in her eyes and slide down her face. "I don't know what you're talking about!"

He shook his head and went for the kitchen door. It slammed after him.

"I found her!" she yelled through the door. "I found Eloise. I found Duncan, your half-brother!" But there was no response, only the final vibrations of the door.

Gabriella fell to her knees, choking on her sobs. She bent over, clutching her middle, as she cried and cried. She'd messed up. She'd really, really messed up. She loved him, really loved him. And now he was walking away from her, just like Jeremy had. But this time, he wasn't leaving her for another woman. He was leaving her because of something *she* did, because he thought she was after him for his money. She had no idea what he'd been talking about. Cheating on him? Why would he ever think that?

Gabriella folded herself into a ball on the floor. She cried for so long that her tears put her to sleep.

Gabriella woke the next morning slumped on the floor in the middle of her kitchen. For one second, she forgot about what had happened the night before. Then it all came rushing back.

As she lay on the hard, cold floor, she could feel the puffiness surrounding her eyes. Her eyes hurt to open, and she had a monster headache. It was Memorial Day. This was the day she'd planned on telling Ashton just how she felt about him. He was supposed to come over for a barbeque, just the two of them. To celebrate the start to what she'd hoped would be a wonderful summer.

Gabriella pulled herself up off the floor. She squinted as the sun shone through the kitchen window. Her eyes felt like sandpaper was being rubbed across them. She stumbled to the chair, catching herself as she sat down before falling. She rubbed her hands across her tear-stained face and through her tangled mess of hair. And then, out of the corner of her eye, she saw Jana's purse. At least he hadn't seen the programs. She scanned her eyes about the room and saw the journal lying open on the floor just inside the doorway. He'd left the journal. After all of that, he'd left it. And then the tears started all over again.

She let herself have a couple minutes of crying before sucking in a large breath. She glanced at the clock. It was just after eight. And then she heard her cell. She rushed to grab it off the counter, not even glancing at who was calling. "Hello?"

"Gabriella?" Angelina said. "Are you alright? I tried calling you on and off all last night and you didn't answer."

"I'm fine. What's up?" She tried to sound cheerful.

"Alejandro and I were wondering if you'd like to go to a Rivermen game today. Matthew's chomping at the bit since they've won all of their games so far this season, and they also have some kind of giveaway for children under twelve. I'm not sure what it is, but you know the mind of a child."

"Yeah, I do." She sighed. "I'm not sure that I'm up to it today."

"Ah, come on and go. It's just going to be the four of us. Mom's volunteered to take Angel for the day."

Gabriella bit her lip.

"Okay, now I know something's wrong. Normally you'd jump at the chance to go to a ballgame."

"I don't have any peanuts."

"Well, that's a poor excuse since we can buy them at the stadium. Gabriella? Do I have to put Alejandro on the phone?"

"No, no you don't have to." Dejectedly, she said, "No, I'll go." She could use some cheering up, and it was just the four of them...

"Don't sound so excited."

"Are you picking me up, or do I need to drive myself?"

"We'll come by at around ten. Alejandro's purchased the tickets, and they're waiting for us at will-call. And you know how Matthew is—he'll want to be the first one through the gates."

"If you're coming in two hours, I have a few things I need to do." Namely, get the redness out of her eyes and the puffiness down. "I'll be waiting." Gabriella ended the call.

Groaning, she pulled herself out of the chair and headed off to the shower where she took one of the longest showers of her life. As she toweled herself dry, she felt a lot better. Checking her eyes in the mirror, she noticed that the redness was all gone thanks in part to the eye drops she'd put in right before her shower. And the puffiness around her eyes... Well, it was better but not all gone. If Angelina commented on it, she'd come up with some excuse. Gabriella also needed to come up with a plan on how to get Ashton to listen to her, but she'd worry about that at another time when her head was clearer and her heart was more intact.

The game ended in less than two hours, one of the fastest she'd ever attended. "Would you like to come over for dinner?" Alejandro asked as he dropped her off at her house.

"No, I think I'm going to call it a day. Grades are due tomorrow, and I have to finish writing my comments. Thanks for the offer, and thanks for including me today."

She opened her door and got out of the car. She stood at the door and watched her brother drive off. She was restless and didn't want to go back into her house. She didn't want to think about the previous evening. It was still early and not too warm, so she decided to grab her hiking boots and head off to Pieres Park to lose herself in a nice long walk. She'd clear her head and hopefully everything else would be clearer when she returned.

Chapter Thirty-Four

GABRIELLA QUICKLY EXCHANGED HER RIVERMEN t-shirt and tennis shoes for a long-sleeved shirt and her hiking boots. As she tied them, she recalled the promise she'd made to Ashton. She'd try and replace them this week. Since she was off for the summer, she was going to do her best to hike several times a week before the temperatures became too oppressive, especially now that she seemed to have a lot more time just to herself.

She grabbed a bottle of water on her way out the door. She dropped it in her hurry to get out the door, and she watched as it rolled down the steps. She sighed in exasperation and quickly let go of the door, running after it. She really needed to get out of here.

When Gabriella pulled up to Pieres Park, she was surprised that there were so few cars in the parking lot. She attributed it to the holiday. She reached for her water bottle and tucked her keys and phone into the front pocket of her shorts and started off down the trail. It was almost four in the afternoon. She decided she'd hike for an hour or so and then go home and finish up her report cards. They were due by noon the following day.

As she walked along, she lost herself in her thoughts. She didn't know why Ashton thought she was cheating on him. And then to think she was after his money? She hadn't even known he had money until his mother got sick and she and Joe had traveled to Branson to support him.

She chose a trail she rarely took. It was off the beaten path, but she didn't care. She just wanted to be alone and ponder what had gone wrong. She came upon a clearing and noticed something sparkling at the edge of the trail on a small incline. As she approached to see what it was, her foot caught a rock and she stumbled. She hadn't realized she'd been so close to the edge of the path until she tried to stop herself, her boot sliding on the loose pebbles. She threw out her arms, trying to grab ahold of anything, but there was nothing. She couldn't stop herself, and her boots didn't stop her as she tumbled over the rocky side of the cliff. Then everything went black.

Ashton spent the holiday sulking at home. He regretted everything he'd said and done since Alec's party. He should have never spoken to her in the manner he did the previous day. He had been, and still was, really angry with her, but he should have handled the whole situation better. She'd seemed genuinely upset, like she hadn't known what he'd been talking about. But she still had taken his mother's journal without telling him, and he was still partially convinced there was another man in the picture.

When he'd rushed out of her house, he'd left his mother's journal. Right now, he wished he had it. *Maybe I should read it. Was she right? Did Mom truly love me?* He needed to get out of this funk and do something physical, so he went outside and mowed the lawn and finished up the pergola. He stood back, admiring it and remembered the day he fell off the ladder and looked up into Gabriella's eyes. That day was the beginning for him. The day he'd started to see her for who she truly was—a warm, caring person who once she committed to something, she never gave up. She didn't listen to him that day and she hadn't given up on the notion his mother stopped loving him.

Ashton decided to call it a night. It was his turn to be on call for the week and his day would start off early at the hospital, as one of their patients had been admitted with a broken ankle that required surgery. He'd check on the little girl the next morning prior to her surgery.

Ashton woke Tuesday morning to a light drizzle. According to the weather, it had been raining most of the night, but the skies promised to clear by mid-day. He dressed and hurried off to the hospital before making his way into the clinic.

Alec and Joe had scheduled an early morning meeting before office hours, so Ashton hurried to make the meeting. When he strolled into Alec's office, he heard Joe mention Gabriella's name.

"Yeah, Alejandro said she didn't seem herself at the game yesterday. In fact, he commented on the fact that she didn't even want a bag of peanuts. Joe, I wonder if she's feeling alright—Gabby at a game without peanuts?"

"That doesn't seem possible." Alec noticed Ashton enter the room. "Yeah, Ashton knows a thing or two about Gabby and her peanuts."

"I do," he said as he sipped his cup of coffee.

"Alejandro said she seemed sad. Do you know anything about that, Ashton?"

Ashton opened his mouth and his mind whirled, trying to come up with something to say. He didn't want to go into what had happened—not today. Luckily, at that moment, Joe's phone began to ring, letting him off the hook. He took the call and then they moved onto the business of the day.

Angelina had just looked at her watch. It was approaching the noon hour and she needed to feed the kids. It was tough getting into the swing of things with summer and all. She wasn't used to fixing lunch for Matthew, and he'd started in wanting lunch an hour earlier. She'd just finished making Matthew's sandwich when the phone rang. Angelina was surprised to hear Mary's voice. "Oh hi, Mary. How are you? I guess you're glad school's out for the summer."

"It's been a long year what with the accreditation and all. I'm just glad that's behind us for several years. Way too much work goes into that." Mary cleared her throat. "Hey, I was wondering if you've heard from Gabriella. Grades were due today at noon, and I haven't heard from her."

"That's odd. I saw her yesterday, and I know she was planning on finishing them up last night. Have you tried calling her?"

"I have. Both her cell and house phones, but she didn't answer."

"Well, let me run by and see if she's home. I've got to pack up the kids first. Give me a half hour, and I'll call you back."

Angelina packed the kids into the car and drove over to Gabriella's. Her car wasn't in the driveway, but she ran to the door anyway. She rang the bell, knocked several times, and ran around to the back—but no Gabriella. She phoned Mary to see if she'd arrived.

"Angelina, no, she's not here. I'm getting a little worried. This isn't like her." Gabriella was known for her promptness. She was never late for anything, especially her grades.

"I know. Let me call my brothers and see if they may know where she is."

Angelina called Alejandro.

"Honey, what's up? Is something wrong with one of the kids?"

"No, it's Gabriella. I think she's missing."

"Missing? We just saw her yesterday."

"Yeah, and remember she wasn't herself. Mary called and apparently she didn't show up to turn in her grades. I ran by the house and her car's gone. Mary tried calling her, and so have I, but she hasn't answered. I think something may be wrong."

"No, she certainly wasn't herself." Pausing, she could hear him talking in the background. "Honey, I'm on my way home. I'll be there shortly. Have you tried Alec and Joe?"

"I called you right after speaking with Mary. I'll phone the clinic and your parents. Please get home soon... I'm worried."

Angelina phoned the clinic, and Sadie answered the

phone.

"Sadie, may I speak with either Joe or Alec? It's an emergency."

"Did something happen to John or Maria?"

"No, it's Gabriella. I think she may be missing." In a matter of seconds, Joe was on the line.

"Angelina? Sadie says Gabby's missing. How can that be? You were with her yesterday."

"I know but I'm positive something's wrong. This is just so unlike her. I phoned your parents. Alejandro's on his way home. Joe, I can't find her..."

"Angelina, calm down. Take a deep breath. I'm sure she's fine. I'm going to cancel the remainder of our appointments for the day. Alec and I will be there shortly."

"What about Ashton?"

"I'll let him know."

Ashton had just finished with his last appointment and was standing in the hallway when he saw Joe leave his office. He ran right into Sadie calling out, "Cancel all of our appointments for the remainder of the day." Ashton watched their exchange with furrowed brows.

"I already did. Is there anything that I can do?"

Ashton heard Joe's response, "Just say a prayer."

The next thing Ashton knew, he and Alec were being herded into Joe's office. "I need to see you both," Joe said with urgency to both of them. They glanced quickly at each other before following Joe into his office.

"I just got off the phone with Angelina. It seems like Gabriella may be missing."

"What?" Alec said incredulously. "No, you've got to be mistaken. Alejandro just went to the ballgame with her yesterday."

"That's true, but she didn't show up at school today."

"She probably overslept," said Ashton as he watched Joe raise his eyebrows.

Ashton guessed he'd said the wrong thing as Joe peered at him. "Well, you don't know our sister very well. She's never overslept a day in her life." Joe was looking at him strangely. "We're all meeting at Alejandro's. I had Sadie cancel the rest of our appointments for the day. Come on, let's go."

Ashton stood in shock, watching Alec and Joe run off. His heart had dropped. Was he the reason she was missing? He moved then, rushing off to his office, grabbing his coat and medical bag, and running out the door. She had to be alright, she just had to be. He realized maybe he'd overreacted to Saturday's events, but he was hurt. He'd never felt this way before, and he'd reacted before he had time to think, to listen to her explanation. He loved her. She couldn't be taken away from him, not when he'd just found her. She was the only person that he'd ever loved. He would find her. He had to. He needed to apologize for his behavior and tell her once and for all that he loved her and make things right between them.

When Alejandro arrived home, he found Angelina pacing in the kitchen. She was pale and trembling. "Alejandro, where could she be? We need to call the police. File a missing person's report."

"Let's not get ahead of ourselves. Joe and Alec are

right behind me, and I'm sure Ashton's not far behind.
I spoke with my Mom and Dad. They're going to
check out all of her haunts. Maybe she just lost track
of time. It's possible, especially with how distracted she
seemed yesterday."

"I tried to ask her what was wrong, and she wouldn't
tell me. In fact, she almost didn't come to the game.
I had to practically twist her arm... Alejandro, she
seemed so lost in her thoughts yesterday. She barely
spoke."

Alejandro held her closely, comforting her. "We'll
find her, Angelina. I promise."

Alec and Joe rushed into the room. "Any news?"
Joe asked.

"No. We need to make a plan. If we don't find her
by four, I'm calling the police. That'll be twenty-four
hours since we last saw her." Alejandro made his way
to the white board that Angelina had hanging in the
kitchen. Alejandro wiped it clean and started writing
down the time they dropped her off, when the last
time someone spoke with her. They'd started making
a list of things when the doorbell rang. Angelina ran
to the door, but it was just Ashton.

"Any news?"

"None."

They threw out various scenarios, but Ashton headed
back for the door.

"Where are you going?" Alejandro called. Ashton
didn't say anything as he was already gone.

Ashton was going crazy with fear. The first place
he went was Gabriella's house. Maybe he'd uncover a

clue. He pulled into her driveway. No car. He jumped out of his car and ran around the back. Everything looked in order. He decided to try her kitchen door—he knew that she sometimes neglected to lock it. He walked up to the door, and looked inside. Everything seemed to be in order. He grabbed ahold of the knob and turned—the door opened. He walked into her kitchen. He noticed the Rivermen tote bag thrown on the table. Her Rivermen shirt was lying on top of it. He noticed she'd set his mother's journal on top of her purse. He walked over and stroked his hand across it, knowing he should read it.

He made his way into her family room and his eye caught her boot tray. Normally, her hiking boots sat in the tray, but not today. Her tennis shoes were the only pair of shoes in the room. He pondered what that meant. Did she go buy a new pair, or was she out hiking? He rushed out of her house, closing the door behind him. He jumped into his car and pulled up Alec's number. He threw his car into reverse and backed out of her driveway.

Alec answered on the first ring. "Did you find her?"

"No, but I think I know where she is… Do you know where Pieres Trail Park is? She likes to hike there. I think she may be there. Her hiking boots are missing."

"How do you know that?"

"I went by her house and the kitchen door was unlocked. Nothing was out of place, but when I went into the family room, I saw her boots were missing. She always stores them in her boot tray. Will you meet me?"

"We'll be there as soon as we can."

Ashton made it to the park in record time, and he

immediately saw her car as he pulled into the parking lot. He hadn't had the chance to exit his car when Alejandro came to a halting stop next to him. All three brothers jumped out of Alejandro's car.

"Should we call the police?" Joe said, approaching Ashton.

"Let's first see if we can find her. Maybe she's just lost track of time. I'll take this trail. Joe, Alec, what about you?"

Joe and Alec elected to stick together and followed the path Gabriella normally walked.

Ashton looked over his shoulder. "I'll take this trail. I've never walked it with her. Between the four of us, I know we'll find her." They all ran off in different directions. This behavior was so unusual for Gabriella that they didn't know what to think. They knew she'd never miss a deadline, and not filing her report cards was definitely unusual behavior for her.

She's got to be here. She's got to be alright. Please, don't let her be... Ashton wouldn't let himself finish that thought. As he rushed down the path, he looked for signs of recent travel. With the rain overnight and the damp path, he didn't notice any fresh footprints.

Alec and Joe made their way down the trail Gabriella often travelled. They ran into a couple. They described Gabriella, but they hadn't seen anyone on their walk. Alec and Joe made it to the end of their path and had seen no sign of her. They hurried back to the front of the park and met up with Alejandro. He hadn't seen her either, but Ashton was still out on the trail. All three brothers jogged towards the path Ashton had taken. It was a longer trail and wound back and forth among the trees. Before entering the trail, they decided to phone the police. They believed she was somewhere on the grounds and feared something had happened to her. Alejandro made the call while Alec and Joe started down the path.

Ashton was frantic with fear. The path was much longer and steeper than he first thought. He cursed himself for not forcing her to buy new boots—he'd told her she needed to replace them. He shook his head. He needed to keep forging onward.

Ashton came out of the trees into a small clearing. He noticed a water bottle lying near the edge of the path. He called her name, but there was no answer. He got as close to the edge as he could without falling himself and looked down. That's when he saw her hair.

"Gabriella!" he yelled.

Just as he began calling her name, Alec and Joe came running up. "Alejandro's phoning the police."

"There she is," Ashton pointed. "I think we need an ambulance and fire rescue, too." Ashton paced along the edge of the path, running his hands through his hair. "I've got to get to her." He saw the smallest of paths that ran along the edge of the cliff. He grabbed ahold of a tree branch as he eased himself down onto the narrow path.

"Ashton, be careful," Joe yelled as he and Alec watched.

The path was so narrow that he held onto the wall of the cliff to aid him in keeping his balance. Each step he took sent pebbles falling over the edge. Ashton took frequent pauses to get his balance under control, taking deep breaths.

"Ashton?"

"I'm alright. I'm almost to her. Joe, I can see a gash on her forehead." As he neared her, he watched to see if she was breathing. Stuttering, he called out, "She's b-breathing. I can see her chest moving. Ten more feet," Ashton called.

"You're almost there, Ashton."

And then, he was at her side.

He immediately took her pulse. It was fast. Her skin was pale and clammy. "I think she's in shock." Ashton wished he had something to cover her with, but he didn't. He looked around, wondering if he could carry her out, but the path was far too narrow. He hoped Alejandro thought to call for fire rescue. He leaned over and brushed a kiss to her forehead.

"Gab-ri-ella," he called. She didn't move. "Gab-ri-ella?" He was afraid to move her—he didn't know if she had a spinal or neck injury. He needed to warm her. Her clothes were soaking wet. "I think she's been here overnight," he called. "Her clothes are wet." Easing his body down, he covered her, doing his best to keep his weight off her while allowing some of his body heat to pass to her. He brushed her hair out of her face. He kissed her brow. "You've got to be alright," he whispered. "You've got to be. I love you, Gabby. I love you so much."

Within minutes, Alejandro came running with a fire rescue team behind him. A fireman appeared at his side carrying medical equipment—he'd rappelled down the side of the cliff. While they secured her neck, another pair of firemen lowered a basket for Gabriella. Carefully, they transferred her to the basket and she was lifted upwards. Joe, Alec, and Alejandro surrounded her. Alejandro took the lead examining her. The rescue crews pulled him back as they set to stabilize her. Luckily, the path they'd chosen was wide enough for an ambulance to drive back to where she had been injured. She was loaded into the ambulance and Alejandro jumped in with the paramedics. Neither Joe nor Alec questioned his decision. He was the most qualified to deal with her injuries. Alejandro tossed his keys to Joe. Before any of them could catch their breaths, the ambulance was speeding off down the trail going as fast as it could.

Alec whipped out his cell, first phoning his parents and then Angelina. "I don't know her condition. I just know she was breathing. Alejandro rode in the ambulance with her."

Ashton was hauled to the top by the firemen. As he listened to Alec, he leaned over at the waist, trying to catch his breath. The harder he tried to take in air, the more difficult it became.

"I've got to get to her," he called out, beginning to run down the path to his car. Alec stopped him.

"Ashton, take a minute and slow down. Catch your breath. We can't do anything for Gabriella right now. She's in good hands."

"I need to get to her," he gasped. He didn't have his inhaler on him—he hadn't had an asthma attack in years. Both Joe and Alec knew the signs.

"Ashton, take it easy. Take deep breaths." Joe looked at Alec. "Is your medical bag in the car?" Ashton nodded as he continued gasping for breath. "Do you have an inhaler in there?"

Ashton nodded again. "I do. I always carry one in the car, too."

"Come on, let's go." Alec said. "We'll get that inhaler of yours, and then you're going to get checked out, too."

"I'm fine. I just need to use my inhaler."

They made it to Ashton's car and he took a quick couple of puffs from his inhaler. Almost instantaneously, he felt the relief from the medicine. His breathing slowed and almost returned to normal.

"Come on, I'll drive," Joe said they made their way to Alejandro's car. They piled into the car. Ashton threw his head back against the seat as Joe drove towards the hospital. "How're you doing back there?"

"Better, thanks."

"I still think you should be checked out, Ashton."

"I'm fine. Nothing that I haven't experienced before."

As they drove to the hospital, Alec's cell rang. Ashton listened as he spoke to Kelly on speakerphone. "I just heard. I'm going over to Angelina's to watch the kids so she can join you at the hospital. How is she?"

"I really don't know. I know she had a gash on her forehead and appeared to be in shock. We think she's been there since yesterday because her clothes were wet. Alejandro rode with her in the ambulance. We're just now on our way. Ashton had an asthma attack that slowed us, but we should be at the hospital in fifteen minutes or so."

"Call me when you know something."

"I will. Kelly, I love you."

"I love you, too. Now go take care of your sister."

Ashton couldn't help but listen to the exchange between the married couple. He silently prayed that he'd have the opportunity to tell Gabriella that he loved her.

Within minutes, Joe pulled up at the ER. They made their way into the waiting room and were greeted by John and Maria. Since all three brothers had privileges at the hospital, Alejandro was allowed back in the ER.

Joe and Alec waited with their parents while Ashton went off into a corner. He sat down and leaned over in his chair, placing his head in his hands. He ran his hands through his hair, silently praying that she would survive and not be seriously injured.

It seemed as though hours passed before Alejandro came out to see everyone. Angelina had arrived shortly after Alec, Joe, and Ashton. They all rushed Alejandro. Maria grasped his hand as he told her what he knew about her condition. "She's dehydrated, and she has a nice gash on her forehead that the plastic surgeon is stitching right now. She has a concussion. Her most serious injury appears to be a broken wrist. She's going to need surgery to stabilize it. There appear to be no internal injuries and no brain bleeds. She was lucky. She fell a good ten, fifteen feet."

"Every bit of that and maybe more." Alec said as his mother hugged her son.

"It's going to be a little while before they take her up to a room. The orthopedic surgeon won't operate until tomorrow. Now we just need her to wake up."

Ashton heard everything Alejandro had told his family. Her family, not his. He couldn't sit there any longer. He jumped up from the chair and walked out of the ER. Ashton made his way across the street to a small park where he sat down on a bench facing the flower beds. He closed his eyes. He was thankful that she would be okay. Her injuries weren't serious in nature except for the fact that she was in a coma and needed to wake.

He wasn't aware that he'd been followed until he felt a hand on his shoulder. He opened his eyes to see Alec standing before him.

"She's going to be okay."

"I know. I heard."

"We weren't excluding you."

"I know that."

"Then why did you run? You know you're a part of the family."

"I have no family," he replied. Alec sat down next to him. "And I don't even know if I still have Gabriella in my life."

"Why wouldn't you? She loves you."

Ashton ignored him. She hadn't expressed her love for him. And if she had, he was sure she'd have withdrawn it at this point. "We had an argument the other night. I said some really awful things to her. I accused her of so many things. I accused her of cheating on me."

"Cheating on you? Gabriella? Never in a million years. Not after what Jeremy did to her. She'd end the relationship before she'd cheat on you."

"Okay, then tell me who Jonas is. I overheard her conversation with him. She said over and over again, 'I know I have to tell Ashton. I've got to tell him sooner rather than later. He's not going to understand why I did it.'" He turned and looked Alec directly in the eyes. "What wouldn't I understand, other than she was having an affair? What was she keeping from me?"

Alec sighed deeply. "I'm not the one to tell you. This is Gabriella's story. What I can tell you is that Jonas is a private investigator. She hired him to look into some things. That's all I'm going to say. I guess she found the answers she was looking for, but just didn't have the opportunity to tell you. Give her a chance to share her findings, then you can decide what you want to do. I believe my sister's just as in love with you, but she's too scared to tell you. She was hurt badly by Jeremy, and I'm not sure she's over it yet."

They sat for a few minutes more. Alec turned to him, "Come on, let's check on our girl." Alec stood and Ashton followed.

"Do you need your inhaler?"

Ashton shook his head. "No, I don't."

"At least you're in the right place if you pass out," Alec said lightly.

"I don't think that'll happen," Ashton said, not laughing.

Both men returned to the ER. Maria pulled Ashton into a tight hug. "She's going to be just fine, Ashton. Have the faith."

"I do."

They all waited in the ER until Gabriella was moved to a private room. Ashton stayed back while her family started down the hallway towards the elevators that would take them to Gabriella.

"Aren't you coming?" called Angelina. She made her way to his side and reached for his hand. "You're family. Come with us."

Ashton gave Angelina a half-smile and squeezed her hand. "Thanks."

Everyone sat down in the waiting room as they waited for Gabriella to be settled into her room. Her parents went in to see her first, then her brothers and Angelina. Ashton stayed back. He was uncomfortable. He wasn't a family member, and in all honesty, he wasn't sure where he stood in Gabriella's life any longer.

The evening wore on, Alejandro and Angelina returned home, John and Maria went to the chapel to say a few prayers, and Joe and Alec went to the deli across the street from the hospital and got everyone something to eat.

Ashton was alone. He hadn't taken the step to see her. After everyone left the floor, he made his way into her room. He greeted the nurse as she was leaving after checking her vital signs. "Dr. Holder, she's stable." Ashton nodded and entered the room.

The lights were turned down. She had a bandage across her forehead, covering the cut. Her arm was stabilized by an ace bandage awaiting surgery. Her face was pale, so pale. He pulled a chair over to her bedside and eased down next to her. He ran his fingers over the back of her good hand, watching her face for any signs of her waking. Nothing. He rested his chin on the bedrail and closed his eyes. He had to make amends with her. He needed to know what she had to tell him. He also knew that he needed to read his mother's journal, learn the truths that Gabriella kept trying to convince him of. He'd make his own decision, but if she were right... he'd lost his mother without acknowledging the fact that he'd loved her. Yes, he had to admit it to himself. He loved his mother.

Ashton felt his chest start to constrict. He didn't know if it was the onset of another asthma attack or just the shear upset from the day. His heart started beating faster and faster. What was wrong with him? And then, he felt it. A soft touch. He opened his eyes. Gabriella was looking at him. "Ashton," she whispered.

"Gabriella," he choked out. "You've come back to me." He reached over, stroking her jawline. "You're awake." He reached for her hand, holding it in his. He stared at her beautiful brown eyes. "Gabriella, I'm sorry, so sorry."

She struggled to reach out to him when she noticed her arm wrapped in a bandage. She looked at her arm.

"You've got a broken wrist. You need to have surgery tomorrow and have pins put in to stabilize it. You have a cut on your forehead, and you have a mild concussion. Other than that, you were lucky. So lucky. We could have lost you."

She was having a hard time speaking. He reached for her glass of water, helping her with the straw as she took a few sips of water. "What happened?"

"You were hiking at Pieres Park and somehow fell over the edge."

She scrunched up her face. "I remember. I saw something sparkling on the ground. I thought it was someone's ring. I stumbled, and when I tried to stop myself, my feet slid out from under me. That's all I remember."

"You fell because of those damn boots of yours. See, I told you to get a new pair." He attempted a rough chuckle.

"Well, now I will."

Her parents came through the doors and realized that she'd awakened.

"She just woke up. I'll leave you alone."

"Ashton, don't go," Gabriella called to him as he neared the door. He ignored her request and walked out of the room.

Chapter Thirty-Five

Two weeks later...

GABRIELLA RETURNED TO THE HOSPITAL for a follow-up visit with her orthopedic surgeon. She'd had surgery the day after being rescued and had four pins inserted to stabilize her wrist. She'd been extremely sore and had several deep bruises on her hips and legs, so when she was released from the hospital, she went directly to her parents' home to recuperate.

The orthopedic surgeon's office was located in a wing off the hospital, so her mother dropped her off at the lobby and headed off to park. Maria planned on meeting her in the doctor's office.

She had almost a half-hour until her scheduled appointment. As she made her way through the hospital, she ran into several of her father's friends. They offered their get-wells and told her how happy they were that she'd hadn't been more seriously injured. She made her way to the elevators and pressed the up button. She was the only person waiting, which surprised her, but she turned her head slightly and noticed the blond hair and the strong jaw line and knew she was in trouble. Ashton was standing beside her.

Ashton leaned in, placing his arm midway down her back and spoke her name. "Gab-ri-ella."

She looked up at him, unsure what she should do. "Dr. Holder," she replied.

"Are you here for a doctor's visit?"

"I am. My mother's right behind me."

"I'd like to speak with you. Do you mind if I drop by this evening? I've stopped by your place several times and you didn't answer the door."

"I've been staying with my parents. Depending on my appointment today, I may go home tonight." The doors opened to the elevator and he ushered her in.

"Gabriella, please. I need to see you."

"You haven't tried very hard. Alec and Joe both knew where to find me."

She could see how much this affected him. He seemed despondent. When she really looked at his face, she noticed that the fine lines that had appeared after his mother's death had reappeared. He looked tired—dark shadows surrounded his eyes. *All he wants to do is talk. I can't deny him that.* She was still hurt by his absence up until now, but she also realized that she should listen to him—give him a chance. "Stop by tonight after seven. I should be home." She saw a glint of hope in his eyes and even a smile touch his lips, and then the elevator doors opened at her floor.

As she exited the elevator, he spoke one word to her: "Thanks." And then the elevator doors closed again and she was alone. His presence had affected her. After seeing him for just those few minutes, she felt more alone now than ever. She hadn't had that feeling for a number of months. In fact, she hadn't felt alone since before working with him on Career Day. The feeling had been erased once Mary had pitted them together that day in her office right before school started. She stood in the hallway, lost in her own thoughts. And then she heard her mother.

"Gabriella, is something wrong?"

She acknowledged her mother's presence and then turned to her doctor's office. Ashton had gotten under her skin again. She'd do her best to listen to him, to understand why he'd walked away from her that night right after waking from her fall.

Promptly at seven o'clock, Gabriella heard a knock on her door. She'd gotten approval from her doctor to live on her own and had returned home that afternoon. Gabriella opened the door. Ashton stood there with a bouquet of flowers. "Welcome home," he said softly as she led him into the kitchen where she pulled out a vase. While she added water to the vase, she waited for him to speak. As she arranged the flowers, he didn't say a word, just stood watching her.

And then, he approached her. He reached in, running a hand down her hair. "Gabriella." She stood motionless. "Please, please look at me."

Gabriella stopped what she was doing, turned, and looked at him. She swore he'd aged ten years in the last two weeks. *What's happened to him?*

"Gabriella, I'm sorry. So sorry." He turned away from her. "I never should have said the awful things that I did to you that night. Can you forgive me?" Her earlier comment regarding his lack of interest had stung. He hadn't spoken to her brothers about her wellbeing since she'd been released from the hospital.

He'd confirmed her release and that was the last time he'd asked about her because he'd needed to keep his distance.

In the last several days, he realized enough time had passed. He came to the conclusion that he missed her more than he ever thought possible and he needed to tell her that. But he also had to discover who Jonas was. Yes, Alec had told him, but he needed to uncover what he was doing for Gabriella.

"I'm trying now. Please?"

She walked over to the table and sat down, motioning for him to join her. Ashton eased down onto the chair and reached for her hand. She surprised herself when she grabbed onto it. Clutching her hand, he seemed afraid to let go. She didn't want him to.

"When I saw you lying there on that ledge, I thought I'd lost you. Can you ever forgive me?"

"What are you talking about?"

"I know you would have never gone hiking that day if it weren't for me. I should have never accused you of cheating on me." Sighing, he continued, "I can't believe I thought you were after my money. That was a low blow, and I didn't mean one word of it. I was upset. Upset because I thought you were seeing someone named Jonas." He paused as he closed his eyes and ran his other hand through his hair. "I thought you were…"

"Why? Why would you think that?"

"I guess my insecurity. I've never loved anyone in my life and then you came bursting into it. I'd been unloved, unwanted, and then suddenly I felt loved and wanted. Gabriella, what I'm trying to say and not doing a very good job at it is—I've fallen in love with you." He squeezed her hand. "I love you… You,

Gabriella Alvarez. You are my life and when you went missing I thought I'd lost you and that's one thing I could never live with."

Gabriella heard what he was saying and was somewhat surprised by his declaration. She also realized at that moment that he needed to discover the answers that he was looking for on his own—the answers that he wasn't even aware that he was looking for. She pulled her hand from his and stood, walking from the room. Moments later, she returned with Jana's purse.

She sat down and set the purse on the table. She slid it towards him. "Before we go any further, you need to go through what's inside this purse. And then, after you absorb everything, we can talk again. Yes, I believe you love me, but you also need to love yourself. You need to know that there was always someone in your court, you just didn't know it. Now, you need to go Ashton."

She stood and opened her kitchen door. "You also need to speak with Jonas Sounds. He's the man I was talking to that day. He has the answers that you're looking for. I'll call him and let him know that it's alright to speak with you. You can find his number in there." She motioned to the purse. "Now, if you don't mind, I'm really tired and would like to go to bed." Ashton followed her lead and made his way to her porch.

"I love you, Gabby. I truly do." And then Ashton turned and walked out of her life again. This time it was her doing. He needed to find himself.

❧

Ashton went home that night. He carried the

purse into his office and set it down on his desk. He could only imagine what was inside, but right now he couldn't face it. He felt like his heart was breaking. She'd all but rejected him. Rejected his love. *She didn't even react when I told her I loved her. She sent me away.* He grabbed the purse and threw it inside one of his desk drawers. He couldn't look at it because right now it reminded him of Gabriella's rejection.

Ashton went about his daily routine getting up at dawn and going to bed late at night. The long hours were starting to wear on him. One evening, as he was finishing up his dictations, he heard a knock on his office door and then Joe walked in and closed the door behind him.

"I'd like to speak with you for a minute."

Ashton nodded and motioned to the chair that sat opposite his desk. Joe sat down, crossed his leg over his knee, and looked at him. "I'm going to be completely honest here, Ashton. You look like hell. Haven't you and my sister made up yet?"

Sighing, Ashton ran his hand across his cheek. Raising his eyes to Joe, he took a deep breath. "Not really. I went by to see her when she returned to her house, and she basically said I need to get my head together— find the answers that I am looking for, even though I'm not looking for any answers. Then she handed me this purse and told me we'd talk after I reviewed what was inside."

"Well, have you?"

"No, I haven't. I took it home and threw it inside a desk drawer." He paused, thought for a moment, and then asked, "Do you know this Jonas Sounds character?"

"I do. He's a PI that helped out Alec when Kelly was having her issues. He's also investigated a few things for the practice. He's well-known and does a hell of a good job. Why?"

"Your sister told me I needed to speak with him."

"Then I guess you do." And with that, Joe rose and walked out of Ashton's office. Ashton stared at the seat Joe had just vacated. *What just happened here? Did I just receive a take down?* Ashton grabbed his bag and left the office. He drove home in a fog, thinking about everything Joe had said to him. *Maybe I should look at that damn purse. And maybe I should seek out this Jonas Sounds.*

Ashton didn't have an appetite after speaking with Joe. He changed his clothes and went outside to weed his flowerbeds, but he couldn't focus on pulling weeds. He left more roots in the ground, and he realized he wasn't into it, so he went back inside and walked directly to his desk. He pulled open the desk drawer and yanked out the purse. He threw it down onto his desk so hard that the clasp flew open and the contents spilled out and fell onto the floor. "Damn," he yelled, hoping someone would hear him but knew otherwise. He reached down and grabbed the papers that had fallen to the floor. And then a motif caught his eye. He grabbed ahold of the program. As he raised it into the light, he knew what was in his hands—it was the emblem from Bigsby Hall, his high school, the boarding school where he'd lived more years than at his own childhood home. What was Gabriella doing with this? Where did she get it?

Ashton plopped down into his desk chair, rummaging through what he'd retrieved from the floor—school program after school program and programs from music concerts, one-act plays. And then he came across a copy of his valedictorian speech. Where the hell had she gotten these?

He reached inside the purse and pulled out a small book—it was his mother's journal. Taking a deep breath, unsure of what he'd find, he cracked open the cover and started reading his mother's words.

It was nearly two in the morning when he finally closed the back cover. Ashton gave in, tears falling from his eyes. She was right. *My mother had loved me. She'd done everything to protect me.* But there had to be more.

Ashton couldn't sleep, so he read and reread his mother's words. He discovered that she'd always been by his side, whether he'd known it or not. She was the one who'd attended his concerts, plays, and his graduations. She'd documented it in her own hand. *How could I have been so wrong? I can't tell her I forgive her. I can't tell her that I always loved her.*

Ashton phoned Alec in the wee hours of the morning after reading his mother's words—he needed a day off. Surprisingly, Alec was awake. Ashton told him he needed to resolve a few things. Alec didn't ask any questions. "Take the time you need to find yourself. And then I hope you can come to terms with my sister, because I know she misses you as much as you miss her."

Ashton couldn't wait. At seven that morning he phoned Jonas Sounds—Gabriella had left his card inside his mother's purse. Jonas answered, and when he discovered it was Ashton on the other end said, "I've been waiting for your call."

They met later that morning. Not only did Ashton discover that he had a half-brother, but he also discovered that Eloise was married to Sadie's brother-in-law. Jonas provided Ashton with Duncan's address and telephone number. When Ashton left Jonas's office, he didn't know where to go, who to turn to. He drove around for hours when he found himself pulling up in front of the Rodgers Hotel. It was a privately-owned, high-end hotel nestled on a quiet street in Clayton.

Ashton was met by the valet when he pulled into the circular drive. The valet handed him his claim ticket and drove off with his car. In a daze, he walked into the hotel, making his way to the front desk. He was greeted by a polite clerk.

"Is Duncan Hightower available?"

"I believe he's in. I'll check."

Ashton was unsure of himself. He was having second thoughts on coming to the Rodgers without calling in advance. *Maybe I should leave. I didn't leave my name...* Ashton had turned away from the front desk and was about to leave when he heard a voice.

"May I help you?"

Ashton knew he couldn't turn and walk away then. He had to face reality head-on. He had a brother—a half-brother, and he was no longer alone in the world.

Ashton turned around. He looked at Duncan straight on. One look at Duncan and he knew they were brothers. Duncan was the spitting image of his father. He extended his hand. Duncan raised his own hand, grabbing ahold of his brother's for the first time.

"Ashton Holder," he said, shaking Duncan's hand.

"It's about time," Duncan responded. "I was wondering when you'd finally come and see me."

Ashton shook his head, unsure he was understanding correctly.

"We met five years ago."

"Five years ago? Where?" And then the memory struck Ashton with a force. He ran his hand through his hair. "My father's funeral."

"Our father."

"Yes, our father."

Duncan motioned to the bar. "Let me buy you a drink."

He followed Duncan. As they passed the bartender, he ordered two scotches on the rocks. Duncan led him to a secluded table near the back of the bar where they sat in silence waiting for the bartender to deliver their drinks. Almost as soon as the bartender walked away from the table, Duncan took a quick drink from his glass while Ashton stared into his.

Ashton picked up his glass, swirling the contents as the ice clanked along the sides of the glass. "I didn't know I had a brother until this morning. How did you know? Why didn't you come to me?"

"My mother told me all about our father. She told me how he'd played her for years. She thought he was going to divorce your mother and marry her. And then, when she popped up pregnant with me, he turned his back on her and walked away. My mom eventually fled to Kansas City, with a few stops in between, where she met the man I now consider my father. They hadn't met yet when I was born, so my mother gave me her maiden name, Hightower. Albert wanted to adopt me and give me his name, but I decided to keep my mom's name. That was my heritage, and I didn't want to give it up." Duncan took another drink from his glass and then reached for the peanuts that sat on the table.

"Mom told me when our father died. I traveled to Branson to say goodbye to the man that was my father in blood only. I needed to put closure on that part of my life. I'd never met him, but I did meet you."

"I remember now... At the cemetery." Ashton gazed off into the distance. "You stood off to the side. And then when the services were over and they were just ready to lower my father's casket into his grave, you approached the grave and stood there. I remember asking my mother if she knew you, and she acted like she didn't. I often wondered who you were but never dreamed that you were my brother."

Duncan reached for some more peanuts, popping one into his mouth. He seemed like he was pondering his next thoughts. He took another sip from his drink. Ashton stared into his, watching the ice swirl around the glass.

"I met your girlfriend."

He raised his eyes to Duncan, surprised.

"She came by a few weeks ago, out of the blue actually. What's her name? Gabby?"

"Gabriella."

"Yeah, well she's beautiful. You're one lucky man."

I'm not so sure about that anymore.

"She called me up one day and asked to meet with me. She said she had something she wanted to talk to me about. You know she really loves you. There aren't many girlfriends out there that would put their relationships on the line like she did. She told me you had no inkling that she was searching for me and that you weren't even aware of my existence. The entire time we met, she was worried how you would react to the news that she was investigating me."

"Well, I was shocked. Gabriella discovered my mother's journal after her death and learned about your mother. All she had was the name Eloise. She hired the best if she was able to locate you on just your mother's first name."

"I hear that my Uncle Lawrence's wife works at your office."

"She does and has for many years. It's a small world, isn't it?"

They talked for well over two hours about everything and anything that came to mind when Duncan was interrupted by the desk clerk that had first greeted Ashton.

"Sorry about that, but I need to take care of this." Duncan whipped out a business card, handing it to Ashton. He reached for his own, but Duncan stopped him. "I know where to find you, and Gabriella gave me one when we met anyway. She'd hoped I'd seek you out." Duncan shook Ashton's hand and hurried from the bar.

Ashton took his time finishing his drink, pondering his next steps. It was nearing the dinner hour, and with rush hour traffic upon them, he decided to go home and pack for a few days away. He was returning to Branson where he could seek the remaining answers he now knew he was searching for.

Ashton was on the road before dawn as he hoped to arrive in Branson by nine o'clock. He drove directly to the resort where he'd arranged a meeting with one of his father's cronies. Heath Silverstone was the owner of the resort that sat adjacent to his father's. Heath met him in Ashton's office, the one that had previously belonged to his father.

"I'm sorry, Ashton, but what your mother wrote is true. I knew both of your parents well, and I often saw your father out and about with a different woman on his arm. Your mother and I once spoke about his indiscretions. She was well aware of his behavior, but she took her marriage vows seriously and basically looked the other way. She knew what she was doing when she sent you away to Bigsby Hall. She wanted you out of sight so you'd never learn about your father's behaviors. She loved you Ashton, and she suffered every day you were away from her. I know you don't believe that, but it's true."

Ashton's worst fears were confirmed. *How did I not know about his reputation?* While he'd always blamed his mother for sending him away, his father was the one who was truly responsible. He thanked Heath for his honesty, and he went home after their meeting. Alistair was taken aback when Ashton walked through the door.

"Where's Gabby?" he inquired.

Ashton led Alistair into the library and shared with him everything that had happened.

"Ashton, you need to fix this. She loves you, and you love her."

"I do love her. She's the first person that I've ever loved, and I think I've finally gotten my head on straight. I just met with Heath Silverstone, and he confirmed everything that my mother wrote. I wish she'd have told me. I didn't think she loved me and now I know otherwise. I know that if Gabriella hadn't found the journal, I'd never have known about my father. And can you believe this? I have a brother, too. A half-brother."

Alistair listened as Ashton recounted everything that had happened to him in the last twenty-four hours. "Gabriella hired a private investigator, and he located Duncan Hightower, my brother. If it weren't for her…" Ashton paused, his mind drifting to Gabriella. "Alistair, when I discovered she had my mother's journal, I was outraged. I accused her of cheating on me with the man that she'd hired to find Duncan. And then… then, I went right for her jugular. I accused her of wanting me only for my money."

Alistair sighed and shook his head. "Ashton, I can't believe you did that. I'm going to give you one piece of advice. You can take it with a grain of salt or embrace what I am about to say… Gabriella is genuine. Did she know that you are as wealthy as you are before she came here to Branson when your mother first became ill?"

"No."

"If you'd have thought with your brain, you'd have had your answer. She is a loving, caring soul. I certainly hope that you can right your wrong because she's someone you can't lose. She's been by your side. You've got to fix this."

"I plan on it. Do you know where my mother's jewelry box is?"

Alistair retrieved the box and handed it to Ashton.

"I hope you follow through on your plans." Alistair walked away and headed towards the kitchen. "Dinner will be ready in the hour. And then I hope you decide to retrace your steps back to St. Louis and do something about all of this. Son, you're not alone anymore. You've found a brother and you have Gabriella."

It was late when Ashton got back to St. Louis, near ten o'clock. He intentionally drove by Gabriella's on his way home. He noticed the light was burning in her foyer, and as he turned into her driveway, he noticed her kitchen light was still on. He didn't think twice as he jumped out of the car and started for her kitchen. He took the stairs two at a time, anxious to see her. He knocked softly on her door, trying not to startle her. She looked up at him through her kitchen door and smiled.

Alistair had phoned her just as Ashton had left Branson. He'd told her that Ashton had visited for the day and was returning home. He didn't know if he'd be stopping by, but he wanted her to be prepared in case he did. "Gabriella, I know what happened. I want you to know I'm in your corner. You're the best thing that's ever happened to him. When you crossed his path, you started a process that has set him free. Free from a childhood that was filled with loneliness, free from a life that was filled with lies, untruths. Ashton was confused by so much. His whole childhood was filled with mixed signals. He's finally getting his head on straight where it concerns his childhood and his parents. Do one thing for me. Listen to what he says— have patience and give him the room to forgive. He's going to continue to make mistakes along the way as he finds himself, but know that whatever he says or does, he means well. He knows he was wrong with the way he treated you, but he has to be the one to show you how regretful he is for his actions. I know you have a heart bigger than all of us put together. Wrap him up in it so he knows he has a home with you. That's one thing Ashton always believed—even though he had a physical residence here in Branson, it wasn't a home to him. Home is where the heart is, and from what I've seen, you're his home.'

Gabriella had hung up the phone with Alistair and walked among her garden. She believed what he'd told her—that she was Ashton's home. She'd have the patience and give him the time he needed to realize what she'd done was all in the face of love.

She wasn't surprised when she heard the soft knock on her door. When she opened it, she saw a man that had once been broken but was now renewed. He looked like the weight that he'd been carrying on his shoulders for more years than he could count had been lifted.

Ashton took one look at her and pulled her into his arms. He rested his head on her shoulder and held on for dear life. She was his life. He pulled back and brushed a soft kiss on her lips, walking past her into her kitchen. He reached for her hand and led her into the family room where he pulled her down onto the couch and into his arms. He brushed her brow with another kiss, not saying a word.

"Thank you. Thank you for everything. Gabriella, I'm so sorry for doubting you. I still can't fathom what you did for me. You gave me a family. I have a brother that I never would have known existed, but through your perseverance, you were able to track him down. And no matter what happens between the two of us, I will always be grateful for that act of kindness. You put everything on the line and did that for me."

A smile broke out on her lips. He stopped and looked at her.

"You're welcome."

"That's all you have to say?"

She nodded.

"Well, I'm not done. I told you this the other day, and I need to say it again. I love you, Gabriella Alvarez. I love you with all of my heart. Never in a million years would I have thought I'd be saying these words to you, especially after the way you treated me."

"Treated *you*? What about—"

Laughing, he pulled her closer. "It doesn't matter how I treated you or you treated me. What matters is today. I love you."

The winsome smile that he loved crossed Gabriella's lips. She stroked the side of his face, cupping her hand around his chin. "I love you too, Ashton."

A huge smile crossed his face. He turned his head and kissed her palm.

"To think I couldn't stand the sight of you," she said, laughing. "But it's true. I love you, too. I'm glad that you were able to see that what I did was for you—because I love you. And now look what you've found. You've found a brother."

"I went to see him yesterday. He told me about you."

She looked down. He reached his forefinger out, turning her head so she'd look him directly in the eyes. "I'm still in shock that you were able to locate him. I saw him five years ago at my father's funeral. We never spoke and my mother had no idea who he was. I'm still stunned that he even exists. I have a brother. Someone I can actually call family. I owe it all to you, and I thank you from the bottom of my heart." Gabriella looked down at her hand where he'd just kissed her palm.

"I need to thank you, too."

"Thank me? For what?"

"For teaching me how to trust again. I never thought I'd be able to trust a man and actually fall in love again. But, you showed me that I could and I'm eternally grateful for that."

She smiled at him, but he also noticed that she was having a hard time keeping her eyes open, and Ashton wasn't too far behind her. He pulled away from her and rose from the couch. "Do you have plans for tomorrow?"

"No. What do you have in mind?"

"I don't know. All I know is I want to spend every possible minute that I have with you. I know I can't make up for lost time, but I'm going to do my best."

She walked him to the door and kissed him soundly on the lips. He got in his car and drove off down the street towards his home. After their conversation, he felt like they were in a good place, travelling down the same path headed toward what he wasn't sure. He just knew she was happy once again.

Chapter Thirty-Six

OVER THE NEXT TWO WEEKS, they spent as much time together as they possibly could. The Fourth of July was nearly upon them and Angelina had asked Gabriella to help her prepare for their annual party. "I can't believe the Fourth is almost here. It just seems like yesterday that Alec announced their engagement and now they've been married six months. I just wish time would stand still. Matthew and Angel are growing like weeds. I'm afraid they're going to be out of the house before I know it and I will have missed something."

"Now, Angelina."

"Well, that's how I feel. And I have to say, it seems like you and Ashton are getting along well." Sheepishly, Gabriella turned away from her best friend. "Gabriella, what are you trying to hide from me?"

"Nothing."

"Gabriella, out with it!" Angelina gave her a stern eye. "Gabby."

"Okay, okay. I told Ashton I loved him."

Angelina screamed and jumped up from the chair

she was sitting in, spinning around in circles and clapping her hands.

Matthew ran into the room. "Mom, is everything okay?"

"It couldn't be better. Now you go back and play." He returned to whatever he'd been doing before his mother had gone crazy with excitement. "I heard you right, didn't I?"

"Angelina, you're crazy. I can't believe how excited you are."

"Gabriella, I'm just so happy for you. I know what you went through when Jeremy left. And how you and Ashton started out. This is epic—" She stopped. "What was Ashton's reaction? I bet he wasn't happy with it. Isn't he pretty messed up with family and all. I thought you told me he'd never loved anyone."

"He did, but he actually told me he loved me days before I told him."

"What?" Angelina's mouth fell open.

"It's true. It's a long story, but in the end he discovered that he was loved all along by his mother. He just needed to uncover it and obtain some answers that he hadn't even realized he was looking for. And the best part of it is, he's discovered a half-brother whose name is Duncan Hightower. His uncle is Lawrence Eberle, Sadie's husband."

Angelina sat wide-eyed, unable to say anything.

"In the end, Ashton realized what I did was for him. I had no ulterior motives behind it. I wasn't cheating on him, and I wasn't after his money. He had to make those discoveries on his own before he could rationalize his feelings for me." Gabby clapped her hands. "Now, let's finish up here. I've got a ballgame to go to this evening."

Angelina was beside herself with excitement. The year was almost up on the bet she and Alejandro had made at Angel's christening. She didn't care if she won or lost. She was elated that her best friend had found the love that she'd been looking for since Jeremy had left her side.

∼

Ashton was taking Gabriella to a Rivermen's game. He'd been putting his plan into motion for several days now. He'd driven home to Branson the previous weekend while Gabriella had attended a girl's weekend with some of her teacher friends—they'd driven down to the Lake of the Ozarks for a weekend of fun in the sun.

Ashton had taken advantage of her time away. He'd had a managers meeting at the resort and used his time to finalize his plans. Gabriella had been fully aware of his trip home and was glad that he wanted to return without her. He was becoming more and more comfortable with staying at the house.

In the days since his initial meeting with Duncan, Gabriella and Ashton had met with him once again at the Rodgers. He seemed to work non-stop on his quest to become hotel manager. Ashton informed Duncan that he'd like to meet his parents at some point. He wanted to apologize for his father's behavior and try to make amends with the past. Ashton believed once he did this, he could let go of everything and move on with making a life for himself that he was proud of. He was an accomplished pediatrician, and now he wanted to start his own family with the one woman he knew he'd always love.

Ashton felt energized after his managers meeting. It was a beautiful day in Branson and he decided to take a drive. He rode through the Ozarks returning to Table Rock Lake. He made his way to the picnic area he and Gabriella had visited and watched the calm waters of the lake. It was early afternoon and families were milling about. He heard children's voices as they played on the nearby playground. He listened to their laughter, discovering for the first time that he enjoyed listening to a child's quirky giggle. He'd never let his mind go there before, imagining that he couldn't possibly have that in his life.

Ashton walked along the shoreline, once again skipping rocks across the lake. He sat down on a large rock that rested along the water's edge and let his mind wander. He relived the last year. He'd gone from being the hated cynical man that Gabriella disliked with a passion to a man that she knew and loved. They'd come a long way and he hoped that what he was about to do would tie them together for a lifetime.

Dark, heavy clouds started rolling in. Ashton hadn't checked the weather report and he wasn't sure if rain was on the horizon, so he decided to pack it in and leave the park.

On the way out of the park, he decided to make one last stop before returning home. Ashton drove down a winding road and through the gates of the beautifully manicured lawn of a site that he once thought he'd never visit again. He wound his way through the confusing roads until he pulled to the side of the road and placed his car in park. He glanced around his surroundings, remembering the last time he'd been here. It had been a bitter cold December day. The winds had whipped around them and snow flurries had danced in the air.

Ashton sat in his car for a few moments and then made his way across the uneven lawn. A recent burial had left clumps of mud in the grass after sealing a graveside. He wound through the markers until his parents' oversized granite monument came into view. Of course, being the burial place of a Holder brought money with it. His parents' monument was the largest in sight. The beautifully inscribed piece of granite loomed over the graves surrounding it.

Ashton approached his parents' graves, still not believing he was standing here in this cemetery. He ran his hand across the Holder name. Images of his parents from his childhood popped into his mind... The happier times, before his life changed in just a minute and he was whisked off to Bigsby Hall. So much time had passed since those memories had been burnished into his mind. And then, there were no more. Only times of loneliness and sadness. That is, until he let Gabriella into his heart and discovered Duncan Hightower. So much had happened during the course of the last year. He'd experienced a lot of pain, but also so many moments of joy. He was happier than he'd ever been and he owed it all to Gabriella.

He ran his fingers across his mother's name. "Mom," he whispered. "I'm sorry. Sorry that you felt you couldn't expose Dad for what he was. I'm sorry we didn't have a better relationship. I want to thank you for keeping that journal. You opened my eyes and made me realize that what you did was the best thing you could have done for me. You kept a secret that you carried to your grave. You honored your marriage vows when you should have walked away. I respect you more today than I—" Ashton stopped as he noticed a parting in the clouds. Rays of sunshine broke through, illuminating the area where he was standing.

"Mom, I want you to know that I love you. I regret not telling you, but in your own way you shared with me your love by writing that journal and allowing Gabriella to find it. I now know what love is all about, and I've finally found it for myself. I wish you were here today but…" Ashton paused, looking towards the sky. "In fact, I know you are here looking down on me. I want you to know that I've forgiven you, and I'm ready to move on. I've found my happiness. Gabriella has definitely turned my life upside down. I never dreamed that I'd be as happy as I am today. I just wish you could meet her and see how she's changed my life. I'm going to do something I may regret, but now's the time. It feels right."

The sun was again consumed by the dark clouds. He knew his mother was listening to his confession. It was too late to share his feelings with her in person, but he knew that she was listening to him as he spilled his thoughts.

As Ashton left the cemetery, the skies opened with a torrential rain. It was like his mother's love was pouring down on him. He was glad that he'd taken that step and visited her grave.

After leaving the cemetery, he stopped by the grocery store and purchased a huge bag of peanuts. The peanuts would play an important role in his plan that would unfold in the coming week.

He had a lot to do before he returned to St. Louis. He knew Alistair would be more than happy to assist him with his plan. In fact, he knew Alistair would get a kick out of what he was intending to do.

Ashton finished going over the last week as he pulled up outside Gabriella's home. Today was make or break for them. She greeted him at the door with the same oversized tote bag that she'd taken to the Transplant Awareness game the previous year. He assumed she had her fan inside, along with a bag of peanuts and whatever else she brought to a game.

He reached for her bag. "I guess you've got peanuts and your fan inside."

Reaching to close the door, she replied, "Nope. With the way you reacted to my peanuts the last time, I chose popcorn today—less messy." She looked at his shoes. "I didn't want you worried that I'd ruin your shoes like I did last year." She laughed and added, "But I do have my fan. It's hot today, and I'm not sure if we're sitting in the sun or not."

He grabbed her hand and escorted her to the car. "Well, I've got your peanuts," he chuckled, pointing to his shoes. "I don't care what happens to these shoes. They're old, but last year's pair was brand new and it took me forever to pick the peanut skins out of the lining."

They made it to the park with plenty of time to spare. "Come on," he grabbed her hand and led her to a special entrance.

"Where are we going?"

"Remember trivia night?" She nodded. "I won this package and it includes a trip onto the field." She scrunched her face up. "What's wrong? Don't you want to go on the field?"

"Of course I do, but you should have brought Matthew instead of me. He would have loved it."

"Hey, this is going to be a special game. I just know

it. I wanted to share it with you. Matthew was on the field last year, and I would speculate he'll be on it again in a couple of weeks. Let's you and I enjoy it, okay?" He smiled at her and pulled her through the entrance.

Not only were they treated to a trip onto the field during batting practice, they also had a tour of the clubhouse and press box. Right before the game began, they were escorted to their seats that were right behind home plate.

"Ashton, I can't believe these seats. We can hear everything that's being said by the players. You really should've brought Matthew."

"Yeah, maybe, but I wanted to share this day with you—only you."

The game started and everyone stood for the National Anthem. The Rivermen were having a fantastic year. They were in first place and the nearest team was almost ten games behind in the standings.

The first couple of innings passed in the blink of an eye. The Rivermen had just scored three unanswered runs and the opposing team decided to change pitchers. While the new pitcher was warming up to face his first batter, Ashton asked if she'd like some peanuts.

"Peanuts? Did you say peanuts? Where have you been hiding these? I didn't believe you earlier when you said you had some."

When Ashton had slipped her bag into the backseat of his car earlier, he'd added his bag of peanuts to her tote bag. He'd then carried the bag into the stadium and had been the one to dole out the popcorn and her fan when she'd needed it.

"Yep, I bought you a bag. Here, would you like to open it?"

She grabbed the bag from his hands and dropped a

quick kiss on his cheek in thanks.

"I can't believe you've been hiding these from me all day. You know how much I love peanuts."

Ashton had prepared for this moment. He'd imagined how she would react and hoped that everything came together like he'd planned. Between Alistair and himself, they'd expertly opened and resealed the bag of peanuts. No one would be the wiser that the bag had been previously opened.

He watched her as she opened the bag. A huge smile swept across her lips. As she started to pull open the sides of the bag, his heart began to beat just a little faster. His hands became clammy. It was now or never.

She tried pulling the bag open, but it wouldn't budge. She balled her face up and gave it one hard tug and the bag burst open, peanuts flew everywhere. He held his breath. He hoped his surprise hadn't flown out. He hadn't seen it. "I'll get these," he leaned down and started picking up the peanuts that had scattered all over the ground at their feet. He held his breath and waited. Nothing.

When she didn't react, he perused the ground again, and he didn't see his surprise anywhere, so he assumed it had to still be in the bag. So he waited. And waited. And then he heard her shriek. He looked over, and she held what he'd hoped she would have discovered minutes before. Ashton dropped to his knee beside her.

"Oh my. No, this can't be happening."

It was between innings and the teams were warming up. Everyone around them turned to watch as Ashton reached for her hand. As he looked into her eyes, he noticed the tears starting to form. He squeezed her hand and smiled up at her. "Gab-ri-ella…"

Smiling broadly, she choked out, "You know I hate it when you say my name that way."

"Okay then, Gabby. You are the best thing that's ever happened to me. You've taught me so much about myself, you discovered a brother I didn't know existed, and you proved to me that my mother loved me. And most of all, you taught me how to love someone. Gabriella, I love you more than I ever thought possible. I want to share my life with you. I want to have that family that you want so badly with you. A year ago, I'd never have imagined this day. Remember our first Rivermen game?" She burst out laughing. "Well, after that game and everything that happened here, if I was a betting man, I'd have lost because you definitely won my heart. So, Gabriella, will you marry me? I know I have a lot of baggage that I'm still working through, but with you by my side, I know I'll make it and be a better man."

She threw her arms around his neck. Tears cascaded down her face.

The catcher from the Rivermen stood at the backstop. "Hey man, did she say yes or no?"

Ashton looked up and laughed at him. "I'm not sure. Gabby, is that a yes?"

She nodded her head into his shoulder. Pulling away, he reached over and wiped the tears from her face. "Gabriella, will you marry me?"

"Yes, I'll marry you, Ashton. I love you."

The catcher from the Rivermen dropped his catcher's mitt and everyone around them stood applauding. Ashton pointed up to the score board. Flashing across the screen were the words, "She said yes." Gabriella covered her mouth with her hand, crying even harder. Ashton reached over, kissing her softly on the lips. "I love you, too."

The catcher called out "Congratulations," as he returned to the catcher's box. Ashton returned to his seat as the next batter stepped into the batter's box. He glanced at the box she still held in her hands. "Don't you want to look at your ring?"

"I forgot about it," she claimed handing it to him. "Open it for me, please?"

"Of course." Ashton popped open the lid to the box. He reached in and pulled the ring from the velvet. She raised a quivering hand to her mouth.

He reached for her trembling hand. "You're shaking." She smiled at him through her fresh tears. "Gabby, I love you so much. Will you marry me?" he asked as he slid the ring upon her finger. Words seemed to be too much for her. Nodding her head yes, she hugged him closely.

"I love you," she whispered. "Yes, I'll marry you." After she'd recovered from her second bout of tears, she glanced at the ring that sat proudly on her hand. She had no idea how many carats were contained in her ring. The center diamond was the largest stone she'd ever seen. It was flawless and sparkled brilliantly in the bright sunlight. Additional smaller diamonds ran down the side of the band. She couldn't take her eyes off of it.

Ashton let her savor the moment. He leaned in and added, "It was my mother's. She would have wanted you to have it." Gabriella was shocked. She knew he'd put all of his anger aside, that he'd come to love his mother in the wake of her death. She'd be with them always as long as Gabriella wore her ring.

"Now, how about some of those peanuts?"

Gabriella looked up with the largest smile he'd ever

seen. He laughed. Peanuts would always have a special place in their lives. They'd brought him full circle from a life filled with loneliness and pain to one filled with laughter and happiness.

Epilogue

ANGELINA LOOKED AT ALEJANDRO AS they finished setting up the patio for their annual Fourth of July celebration. She wrapped him in her arms, looking out over their expansive backyard. "I can't believe we're setting up again for the Fourth. It seems just like yesterday when we had our first party right here and announced our engagement."

Alejandro looked down at his beautiful wife. "A lot has happened in the last three years. We have two beautiful children and our siblings found one another and married." He looked down into her eyes. "What will this year hold?" he asked as he slid his hand across her lower abdomen. Smiling, he added, "Won't everyone be surprised." She looked in Alejandro's eyes. "For some reason, this celebration is made for surprises. We can't let everyone down now, can we?" She chuckled at his words.

Before Alejandro and Angelina knew it, their guests were arriving. Angelina's entire family was present. Jackie and Ben had arrived with Wyatt and Colleen in tow an hour earlier than expected, as per usual.

Jackie was known for arriving early and Alejandro and Angelina were well prepared for her antics. Now she blamed her earliness on the chance to visit with her grandchildren. Angelina knew James would appear at some point, she just didn't know when.

John and Maria walked through the doors right behind Ashton and Gabriella. Joe had run in an annual race and would appear at some point. Angelina missed her friends from school and had begun to invite them to the party as well. Mary, along with Janet Holmes and her sister Melanie, arrived at the same time Sadie and Lawrence pulled up. Alejandro had included several of his colleagues, but they were all on call and would appear at some point during the day.

Maria stood and looked at everyone that had arrived. "Where's Kelly and Alec? Shouldn't they be here by now?"

Angelina scoured the grounds, thinking she'd missed her sister but Maria had been right—she and Alec hadn't arrived. "I was just thinking the same thing. I talked to Kelly earlier and she said she was practically ready to walk out the door."

Alejandro fired up the grill, and true to form, Wyatt was by his side watching everything he did. Angelina stood back and watched her guests. Everyone seemed to be mingling, enjoying themselves. She saw her brother James. She noticed an immediate change in his behavior as he laid eyes on Melanie Holmes. She knew they'd worked in the same circles, but his reaction to her presence took her by surprise. She knew James had issues with her, but she hoped there were no surprises like there'd been at Angel's christening when Gabriella and Ashton had gotten into not one, but two verbal altercations. Angelina was almost certain that she'd lost her bet with her husband, but she didn't care. She was just ecstatic that Gabriella was in love with someone.

Kelly and Alec joined the crowd. Alec was his normal jovial self but Kelly seemed distracted, almost as though she didn't want to be there. "Kel, are you feeling alright? You don't seem yourself."

"Oh hi, Angelina. I'm fine. We just got held up. Sorry we're late."

"You're not late, you're right on time."

Angelina looked up and spotted someone she didn't know. She thought she knew everyone that had been invited, but then thought maybe Alejandro had invited another of his colleagues. A new set of fellows had come on board the first of the month at the hospital so it could be one of them.

Alejandro looked at her, also unsure of who the man was that engaged with Sadie and Lawrence, and then she realized who it was. Duncan Hightower, Ashton's half-brother. Ashton and Gabriella both greeted him then led him over to Angelina and Alejandro where they introduced him.

"Angelina, Alejandro, I'm sure you're wondering who this is. I'd like to introduce my brother, Duncan Hightower. Duncan this is Angelina and Alejandro Alvarez, our hosts."

"Angelina's my best friend." Gabriella added.

"It's a pleasure to meet you." He nodded at them.

Angelina liked Duncan. He made a good first impression. He seemed bright and had a killer sense of humor. They stood around talking when Wyatt called out to Alejandro, needing help with the grilling.

Everyone seemed to enjoy the food and conversation. Alejandro looked at this wife—it was time to make his annual speech. Alejandro reached for her hand, drawing her near his side as he stood in front of their guests. "Angelina and I would like to thank everyone for coming to our annual Fourth of July celebration. For those of you that have been here every year since our first party, there always seems to be some sort of excitement on this patio. At our first barbeque, we announced our engagement." Alejandro paused and smiled at his wife.

Angelina was getting excited waiting for Alejandro's announcement.

"Last year at Angel's christening, Alec and Kelly announced their engagement. I have to say that took us somewhat by surprise, but I called their union at our wedding. I just knew Alec would be the next to be married in the family when he caught the garter at our wedding. I predicted it that day, and true to form, they were married earlier this year."

Alejandro paused and squeezed his wife's hand. "This year I have another announcement to make." He had caught everyone's attention. "I'd have to say this came as a complete surprise to Angelina and me," Alejandro paused and then, and with exuberance in voice, said. "Angelina and I are expecting another child."

His announcement caught everyone by surprise, but no one more than her mother. Ben grabbed ahold of Jackie, fearing that she was going to faint from excitement.

"Oh my," Jackie cried out and ran to her daughter, pulling her into a tight embrace. "You're really pregnant?"

Angelina couldn't stop laughing at her mother. "Yes, I am. It came as a complete surprise to Alejandro and I, especially after what we went through. But yes, I'm pregnant and this time, so far, I'm not experiencing the morning sickness like I did with Angel."

Alec looked at Kelly before saying, "Can I get everyone's attention?" All of the guests stopped what they were doing. He held out his hand and Kelly joined him. "I was waiting for Alejandro to make his annual speech before I made my own announcement." He looked out over the crowd, catching his mother's eye. Maria had a look on her face like she already knew what Alec was going to say.

"Alejandro, you sure know how to excite this crowd. Well, Kelly and I have our own excitement to share. We're pregnant, too."

Cheers rang out. Maria ran to Kelly's side and Jackie... well, the news was more than she could take. Ben slid a chair underneath her to prevent her collapse from the excitement. Jackie had tears of joy flowing down her face. Both of her daughters were pregnant at the same time—a mother's dream. Angelina was thrilled with the news. She and her sister would have children close in age. She knew they'd be the best of friends.

Gabriella and Ashton were stunned by both announcements. They'd planned on using the party to make their own announcement. All of their friends and family were in attendance, and he was only going to do this once. Ashton shrugged his shoulders. "Let's do it," he whispered to Gabriella as they took the stage.

Ashton tried to get everyone's attention, but with the excitement of two pregnancies, no one was listening. Gabriella took over. Placing her fingers in her mouth, she let out a whistle that someone in the following county could hear. Startling everyone, she started laughing. "Well that sure got everyone's attention." She chuckled at Ashton. Placing his arm around her waist, he drew her close to his side.

Angelina stood wide-eyed, looking at her best friend. This couldn't be what she thought it was, was it? She reached for her husband's hand. He pulled her in front of him, wrapping his arms around her waist. Leaning down, he whispered into her ear, "Is this what I think it is?"

"I don't know. She hasn't said a word to me."

Ashton continued, "Well I guess everyone is wondering what Gabriella and I are doing standing up here after witnessing two of the best announcements ever. Congratulations to Kelly and Alec and Angelina and Alejandro. Gabriella and I are thrilled with your news." He stopped and looked down at Gabby. He looked across the crowd, catching her parent's eyes. They knew what was coming, albeit Gabriella didn't know that he'd spoken with them when she'd been out of town. She was their only daughter and he wanted to do right by her.

He'd gone to John and Maria the evening Gabriella had left for her girls-only weekend. He'd started off their evening thanking John for taking a chance on him and for recommending him to fill his spot in the practice. He'd been introduced to their family and had never looked back. "I want to thank you for everything, John. You changed my life the day you pulled me aside for my bedside manner. You've been the role model I needed in my life and I appreciate it more than you know." Neither John nor Maria had understood the reason behind his comments. And then he'd asked the question that had been on his mind for weeks.

"John, Maria, I'd like to ask you a question. I want you to know what a caring and truly genuine daughter you have. I know we didn't start out on the right foot, but she's changed me, and I'm definitely a better man since she's entered my life. She's been in my corner for longer than I realized. I'd like to ask you for her hand in marriage. I love her more than words can say."

John had smiled at Ashton and they'd both expressed their approval. Ashton filled them in on his plans, and if all went according to plan, he'd intended to announce their engagement at the Fourth of July party.

So as Ashton looked at her parents, he nodded at them and continued his announcement. "I knew this party was known for its surprises, but wow, two pregnancies. That's so exciting. So, I'm sure everyone's wondering what Gabriella and I are doing standing up here." And then the biggest of smiles crept across his face. "I'm here to announce…" And then he motioned to Duncan to join them. "First of all, I need to introduce everyone to my brother Duncan Hightower. I just discovered that I had a brother and I owe it all to this woman standing right here by my side. See, Gabriella came across a journal that belonged to my mother. And after a long search, that I knew nothing about, she located Duncan. I was surprised to learn about my brother, but it's the best thing that's happened to me outside of having Gabriella by my side. She gave me the family that I've been looking for, but more than that, she taught me how to love.

So, why am I standing up here you ask? Well, as for my announcement, I asked Gabriella to be my wife and she's accepted."

Everyone broke out in loud cheers. Ashton continued, "I hope she knows what she's getting into—" Everybody laughed. "But honestly, I think she already knows. We've had our ups and downs as we got to this day, but I'm happy to be standing here in front of my friends and now family. Yes, family."

Before he could say another word, everyone had erupted into more cheers and well-wishes. In an instant, they were flanked by Gabriella's entire family. And then, Gabriella heard her brother's voice.

"See, I told you I'd win the bet," Alejandro said.

"Bet? What bet?" she asked.

"Oh you know, I bet Angelina at Angel's christening that you two would be engaged by..." turning to his wife, he said, "What was that date?"

Angelina swatted him. "Does it really matter now? They're engaged and that's the best news ever. I gave up on the bet a long time ago, especially when I saw how she'd turned Ashton's life upside down. He didn't know what hit him then, and I certainly hope he knows that he's in store for now."

Ashton stood listening to the conversation around him. He finally felt like he truly belonged in this family. They'd welcomed him with open arms, and now he was ready to start his own family with the one woman who never gave up on him and led him to believe in the power of love. Gabriella was his life now, and he hoped someday to be standing back up on this stage announcing to his family that he was beginning a family of his own. He now understood what a wife and children meant. Alejandro and Alec were beaming with excitement over the news of their impending births. He hoped that someday he'd follow in their footsteps with the same feelings they had.

His life had been turned upside down in the last year. He'd lost his mother but discovered her never-ending love for him in her passing, and that he wasn't broken and could find the love of a woman. Gabriella was his, and he'd never forget what she'd done for him in teaching him about falling in love and making memories that would last a lifetime.

Author's Note

THANK YOU SO MUCH FOR reading Life's Turned Upside Down, the third book in The Show Me Series. If you would like to be notified about new releases, please sign up for my newsletter. You'll be treated to sneak peeks, giveaways, and bonus material just for signing up.

If you enjoyed reading Life's Turned Upside Down, please consider leaving a review. Reviews are always appreciated!

Anne

About the Author

ANNE STONE WAS BORN AND raised in St. Louis, Missouri but now lives in the cold state of Wisconsin with her faithful Cavalier King Charles Spaniel. She writes heartfelt sweet contemporary romance and is the author of the Show Me and Williams & Company series. She loves to tell a story and that's what you'll definitely get in an Anne Stone novel.

Anne's degree is in education but she has worked in the corporate sector managing a large number of staff. Now, she works from home where part of her day is still spent in the corporate world and the other part is dreaming of her heroes and heroines.

Anne loves to share giveaways and free books through her newsletters. Sign-up to learn more about her new releases.

Learn more about Anne by visiting www.Anne-StoneAuthor.com.

Connect with Anne online:
Visit Anne's website: Annestoneauthor.com
Follow Anne on Facebook at: Anne Stone Author
Join Anne's Facebook Street Team
Follow Anne on Twitter at: @AuthorAnneStone
Sign up for Anne's newsletter
Email Anne at: Anne@Annestoneauthor.com

Also by Anne Stone

The Show Me Series:
Life's Second Chances
Life's Gateway to Happiness
Life's Turned Upside Down
Life's Second Journey (Coming soon)

Williams & Company:
Never Lose Hope